TORRENTS OF FIRE

Author of *A Savage Culture* and *Reap the Forgotten Harvest*, published by Quartet Books, Remi Kapo has contributed to the *New Statesman* and *New Society*; was a researcher for Yorkshire Television and Thames Television's *TV Eye* programme; the director of the Roundhouse Arts Centre; and produced *Moon on a Rainbow Shawl* at the Almeida Theatre, directed by Maya Angelou. He lives in London and Oxford.

TORRENTS OF FIRE

AN ABOLITIONIST'S TALE

REMI KAPO

ACACIA TREE
BOOKS

First published in 2017 by Acacia Tree Publishing Limited,
10 Knights Park, Kingston-upon-Thames,
Surrey, KT1 2QN

A catalogue record for this book
is available from the British Library

ISBN 978 0 9955844 0 2

Typeset by Josh Bryson
Printed and bound in Great Britain by
TJ International Ltd, Padstow, Cornwall

Dedicated to
African Sanctus
RK

…and 'een the shimmering
twilight and icy dawns in that
land of tinted pastures,
laundered cliffs and rolling downs,
where they were thought to be
gods, it came to be natural in the
order of things, that Pertigua's
peoples saw that land as
the kingdom of the gods…

Pilgrims

The Highway
Deptford, London
24 August 1760
10.00 hrs

It all began in the wilting dog days of a dusty August.

Set back off the potholed Highway hard by Deptford Creek was Pilgrims. Under the bright morning sun, the elevated Georgian residence shimmered in the leafy shade of plane trees.

Inside the panelled ground floor office, Alice Beecham pursed her lips. She was pondering an iconoclastic notion she intended to put to the afternoon's meeting of the League Against the Importation of Negroes from the Coast of Guinea. In preparation for an occasion of such consequence, she had donned an elegant salmon silk gown, its elbow-length sleeves finished with cuffs and lace frills.

Sitting with her back to the bay window, she absently perused a set of accounts laid out on a mahogany kneehole desk. Occasionally she looked fondly across the chamber at Jonas, hunched over the partner's table updating the order books. Their quietude was shattered by jarring shouts from the Highway.

'Stop that runaway!'

'Seize that nigger!'

'Good God, Jonas!' she cried. 'Do my ears deceive me?'

Peering out of the window, Jonas turned back, visibly incensed.

'Nay,' he said, breathing heavily. 'It sounds like hue and cry has been raised for a runaway. Methinks I hear the Bow Street Runners, but I see none as yet.'

Rising swiftly, she joined him at the window. Above the clatter of horses and carriages, tumbrils and pedestrians on the Highway, they heard shouts from the adjacent Bottom Lane.

'There 'e goes!'

'Where away?!'

'Up Bottom Lane!'

'Nab him 'fore 'e gets to the Highway!'

'I see 'im!'

'Where?!'

'Outside Pilgrims!'

Pointing down at a raggedy black man panting against the left corner of Pilgrims, Jonas exclaimed:

'There is their quarry!'

'Great Heavens, Jonas. That man's a slave!'

The sweat-streaked bare-footed character was plainly terrified. He had a spiked iron collar fixed around his neck. Clad in grimy fragments of a jerkin, his tattered breeches exposed a testicle. His eyes rolled in terror and drool dangled from his thick convulsing lips. Throwing wild looks left and right, he looked unexpectedly upwards and met her gaze.

His crazed eyes screamed an invective of terrors beyond her imagination. The bodily consequence of man's inhumanity to man stood right outside her home on the cobbles of a busy London street.

Trembling with horror, she turned helplessly to Jonas.

Before she could utter a word, the runaway sprinted off up the Highway. Frantically looking this way and that, he was clearly seeking a route across the thoroughfare between the hurtling carriages.

Four mastiffs on long leashes materialised at the corner of Pilgrims. Restraining their canine charges were four musketed men. Stomping close on their heels was a tubby character clad in a brown Garrick coat with a gold-crowned tipstaff.

''Tis Farthingale the parish constable with the Bow Street Runners,' she said.

'Free them dogs!' yelled the constable. 'Don't let nigger get too far up the Highway. We'll lose 'im. No musket fire!'

Freed salivating molossers hurtled off after the runaway. Setting off in hot pursuit, the Bow Street Runners fanned out to outflank their prey.

Seeing Jonas close his eyes and shudder with fury brought a lump to her throat. Gently grasping his arm, she sought to reassure him.

'Fret not, Jonas, the constable has no lawful cause to lay hands on thee.'

'The wrath you see is not for me,' he replied hotly. 'Times like these remind me how powerless I am to help others of my skin. The lowly status of the black citizen devalues the response of another black. A slave therefore stands no chance. For now, let us at the very least bear witness.'

Poking their heads out of the window, they watched events develop on the Highway.

Backing away from the snarling mastiffs, the runaway lost his footing and disappeared under the hooves of four horses and a heavy carriage. Horses whinnied and reared amid screams and shouts as colliding carriages ricocheted. Traffic screeched to a deafening standstill. A groan from bystanders wrenched the air around the trampled man. Blood streaked the cobbles of the Highway.

'Nigger's dead!' yelled a Bow Street Runner.

'Shame on the Runners,' someone shouted.

Several women swooned and onlookers rushed to their aid.

'Clear the blackguard off the road,' yelled the constable. 'Throw plenty of sawdust on 'is sap. Dump 'im in barge fer Gravesend. I'll inform 'is master.'

As if not anything had occurred, carriages and flatbeds were soon rumbling back and forth along the Highway.

'This man alone justifies the existence of our League,' she said angrily.

She glanced at Jonas. Shuddering with rage, he was riled as she had never seen him before. Sweat trickled down his brow and his trembling jaw was clenched.

Stroking his back gently, she soothed, 'That some English men can be so depraved galls me. But 'twill not always be so, Jonas. That is what we of the League and likeminded citizens strive for.'

'Thank God that runaway is dead,' he said. 'His mortal troubles have ended. The Bow Street Runners handed him to God.'

'That spiked collar around his neck, Jonas. That I will never forget.'

'Aye, I have seen it before in Pertigua,' he said. ''Tis akin to the mark of Cain. The wearer is separated from others through that contraption of humiliation and, as well, he cannot rest or sleep without the greatest effort.'

Grimacing at the degrading device, she retorted, ''Tis settled then.'

'What is settled?' he enquired, his attention still focused on the Highway.

'I have a matter I wish to discuss with you, Jonas. But after such a fright, let us firstly fortify ourselves with an uplifting tipple. Come.'

In the withdrawing room, she poured brandy into two goblets.

'Methinks I need a nip,' she muttered.

'Likewise,' he said, taking a large swig.

'For some time now, I have been intending to offer you joint proprietorship of Thomas Beecham, Chandlers.'

Dropping down with surprise onto a wing chair, he was dazed and excited. He spluttered, 'Flabbergasted am I by your kind offer and—'

'Allow me to finish, Jonas,' she said, smiling and taking a sip of brandy. 'This afternoon we entertain members of the League, some of whom are also shareholders of the chandlery. I intend to gain their agreement. And before you thrust your judicious counsel forth, I will brook no opposition from you or from them.'

'Indeed, this appointment may not be to everyone's taste.'

'I grant you that it may not be to the liking of one or two members, Jonas. But 'tis high time the shareholders recognise that there is dire need for change. Given our beliefs and the abolition we so keenly support, I suggest we of the League embrace change. 'Tis fortunate then that I am the majority shareholder and can make an appointment that warrants no discussion. Nonetheless, they are among my closest friends and I desire their willing concurrence.'

'May I ask if the death of that runaway provoked this appointment?'

'Do not be absurd, Jonas. I do so because it is just.'

'May I then make a suggestion?'

'You may indeed. I have confidence in your counsel.'

'Lest some members think you recommend my appointment in a moment of weakness, let not a word of the runaway pass into their ears beforehand.'

'Given the odds of a jaundiced mindset, 'tis shrewd counsel.'

'We both know that given a preference,' he said, 'one or two members might baulk at a black man managing an English company.'

Enthused by his diplomacy, she continued, 'Do they not claim to be broad-minded? I shall give them opportunity to prove it. What we suspect about one or two members may or may not be true. Now is a chance to prove loyalty to the cause. Do you recall your proposal for liberating runaways?'

'Aye,' he replied, frowning.

'Of late, I have been giving that proposal some hard consideration.'

'And you have come to a decision?'

'I have. We should do it.'

'Because it is just?'

'Nay, Jonas. Because it is the class of action the League ought to be undertaking.'

He nodded his agreement.

'Raise your glass, Jonas,' she said, tapping her goblet against his. 'I give thee a toast to a consequential meeting and furthermore a change of tack for our League.'

'You have me on tenterhooks,' he said with narrowed eyes.

Furnishing a warm smile, she sipped her brandy thoughtfully.

Lone clouds drifted above a glorious afternoon. A flight of starlings winged across the pale blue sky. Whisked by a sudden gust across the cobbles, dust and fallen leaves soared into eddies. A number of carriages rattled to a halt. It was three o'clock. Pilgrims had visitors.

Soon, chatter flowed from the Prussian blue panelled dining room. It was a high-ceilinged chamber with four open box-sash windows. Perched around the mahogany Chippendale table were a Deptford cleric, a shipowner and his wife from Greenwich, and a banker and his lawyer son from the village of Rotherhithe.

Discreetly casting a look around the members of the League, Alice Beecham prepared to speak. In her late sixties, she topped the table like a matriarch, a bronze table bell by her hand. Fanning herself with a lacquered Chinese fan, she smiled benignly.

'Members of the League,' she announced. 'Right glad am I to welcome thee again to Pilgrims. Before we begin our discourse, we should partake of some refreshments.'

Happily returning her greetings, the well-heeled company tucked into gooseberry hops, pippin knots, preserved apricots and cherry syllabub from cut-glass bowls surrounding a pierced silver cake basket bearing a pyramid of candied fruits.

'Given the abundance of tea I daresay supper will be served late,' she said. 'I therefore ask you to make our preprandial chatter engrossing enough so none will demur.'

Laughter filled the chamber.

Befitting the Methodist campaigners, they began a discussion on Doctor Johnson, who they had all met a few days previously at his home in Gough Square.

'I garnered much from the exchange regarding the Royal African Company,' said the banker, Elijah Drinkwater. 'It was as well on that occasion John Wesley informed me of one Granville Sharp, a young scholar who has visionary notions on slave emancipation. For instance, he promulgates that slavery is in itself evil. He even proposes resettling freed slaves on the coast of Guinea. I trust before long he will join our League.'

'Approbation from John Wesley is indeed a great tribute, Elijah,' said Reverend Whitehouse. 'I as well have heard first-rate opinion of this Granville Sharp. We should most certainly invite such a progressive thinker into our League.'

Toddling quietly into the chamber bearing trays, two maidservants then served tea.

Soon, the floral nose of Darjeeling unleashed the effusive words of Grace Puddlewick.

'I have to say,' she said imperiously, as if her judgment was the only one that mattered, 'that as a man of God and as an anti-slavery advocate, John Wesley is second to none.'

Garbed in a pale yellow sack-back gown of hand-embroidered Chinese silk with a precipitously low neckline, she looked the prima donna she was. Set against her pallid complexion, pale eyebrows and powdered wig, her red beauty spot quite lit up the chamber.

Turning to Mistress Beecham, she gushed, 'My compliments on a most delectable table, Mistress Beecham. Such divine gooseberry hops I have not beheld or eaten for many a season. And might I inquire when Jonas will be joining us?'

Irritated by Grace Puddlewick's unwarranted familiarity, she was nevertheless diplomatic.

'You are too kind, Mistress Puddlewick. As for Mister Guinea,' she said, emphasising the Mister, 'he is at his desk attending to company matters. He shall be with us shortly.'

'Cannot be soon enough,' said Mistress Puddlewick snootily. 'It behoves me to say that he behaves not anything like a Negro. Owning such a tropical charisma, he is more diligent than his kind. I have to say—'

Turning the colour of his powdered ashen wig at his spouse's injudicious words, a discomfited Jeremiah Puddlewick changed the subject.

'I did note the effrontery of the beggars hereabouts, Mistress Beecham,' he said contritely, smoothing the wrinkles of his coat. 'Are you not troubled by them?'

'I trust you were not accosted en route from your carriage?'

'Nay, Mistress Beecham, we were not,' he replied, 'though we did see one or two shamelessly confronting respectable citizens.'

Clearing his throat, Reverend Whitehouse coughed himself hoarse. Bewigged, with side curls, cravat, clerical bands and fitted black coat, he looked quite the portly asthmatic English clergyman. Inhaling pinches of what he said was 'medicinal' snuff, he set down his Bilston Battersea Truth enamel snuff box on the table. Inscribed around the quaint lid were the words: *This and my Hand are at thy Command.*

I see Whitehouse is now dabbling with snuff, thought Alice Beecham with a quizzical frown. And by his technique he looks fairly experienced. What next? Typically, the inscription on the lid speaks to the zealous piety of the man.

'Only the day last past,' Reverend Whitehouse wheezed, 'I did see a body slumped quite insensibly against a buttress of the parish church. I thought he was merely intoxicated by the devil's liquor, but on close examination it transpired that the poor fellow was in fact quite dead.'

'On occasion, London Town resembles a cemetery,' said Jeremiah Puddlewick. 'Did you know that a barge laden with dead citizens, like empty bottles, departs daily from Wapping Wall for Gravesend? I daresay your body will turn up there.'

Tittering behind her hand at her husband's comment, Mistress Puddlewick added, 'Not by himself, he won't!'

Furrowing her brow, Alice Beecham was gripped by the suspicion that unless she intervened her guests would rabbit on about trifle. Setting aside her qualms while composing herself, she produced a radiant smile.

Despite their apparent equanimity, she thought, some seem a little apprehensive. I've heard queries of my stewardship of my late husband's business and its fleeting differences with the League. 'Tis providential then, that I am the Principal Shareholder. They cannot but concur with my request. Having solicited their presence on the pretext of a social gathering, I will not have it drift into a discourse on the shenanigans of the streets hereabouts. Methinks 'tis time to shed some light.

Fingering the lettering on a glass bearing *God Save King George* on the stem, she enquired, 'Punch or cherry bounce anyone?'

After satisfying requests, she sat down and addressed them.

'You all know that I have for some time been struggling with a notion of my late husband. And you all knew Thomas Beecham to be a plain-spoken man of his word.'

'Indisputably,' said Reverend Whitehouse.

'I am certain you will believe me,' she continued, 'when I tell you that had he lived, the venture I am about to propose was one he intended bringing to fruition. Mister Beecham discussed the scheme with Reverend Whitehouse and Mister Guinea, who were as well of like mind.'

Jeremiah Puddlewick belched.

Smirking rippled around the table.

'Begging your pardon, Mistress Beecham,' said the shipowner bashfully. 'Might we share the fundamentals of this project?'

'I will come to that in a little while, Mister Puddlewick. But first I have an announcement. One that I am sure will gladden you all. In the years since the passing of Mister Beecham, Jonas Guinea has, with my counsel, functioned in his stead. I judge you will all agree that for nigh on six years, he has performed his duties confidently and conscientiously. He has sustained a good set of books, and orders for our chandlery continue to increase.'

'Indeed,' agreed Elijah Drinkwater readily, 'the books do show goodly profit.'

'However, a pertinent fact is, as we are all well aware and much to my chagrin,' she added, 'that it is deemed quite improper for a woman to be engaged in the conduct of business. Good society frowns on such. It would seem that business is considered far too grubby for the delicate sensibilities and sensitivities of women. 'Tis presently deemed fit only for the God-given talents of men.'

Putting down his glass, Elijah Drinkwater protested, 'That is a bit steep, Mistress Beecham—'

'However, Mister Drinkwater,' she said, pointedly interrupting, 'we should note that good society says not anything about a silent partner, which I have been and shall continue to be. I have decided therefore that hereafter, Jonas Guinea's pro tem stewardship of the chandlery is at an end. He is this day appointed joint proprietor of Thomas Beecham, Chandlers. Without hesitation, I commend his appointment to you. I ask you, the shareholders of the company, to endorse my decision.'

At once she felt the unease of the allegedly open-minded waft around the chamber.

Frowning at first, a thoughtful smile crept onto Mistress Puddlewick's lips. After taking a sip of cherry bounce, she spoke.

'An innovative appointment I have to say, Mistress Beecham,' she said, patting her lips with a napkin. 'Although I must confess that I do have some concern for Mister Guinea. And I shall tell you why. Given his hue, you are doubtless aware of the fact that in some quarters his appointment will not be met with your munificent outlook. Nonetheless, I certainly support your judgment.'

'Why thank you, Mistress Puddlewick,' she replied with a taut smile.

'You well know my position on this matter, Mistress Beecham,' said Reverend Whitehouse, 'on which you have always had my backing. A right commendable Christian act, I have to say. On the issue of Negro rights, Mistress Puddlewick, methinks that it behoves an English company to take a stand. Why not we? You have seized the moral initiative, Mistress Beecham. If we are to bring change, I believe we must indeed espouse your judgment. I reckon Mister Guinea's appointment to be an indispensable part of that process.'

Taking a sip of punch with a banker's reserve, Elijah Drinkwater flourished a watery smile and dryly added:

'You might think Mister Guinea's appointment is a good investment, Mistress Beecham. But is it a wise one? Acting for the company in a temporary role is one thing. Parading his equality in the guise of proprietor may present a predicament for the ignorant and bigoted, of which I suspect there are a fair few about. That said, I'll have you know that I of course endorse your judgment.'

A circuitous endorsement if ever I heard one, thought Mistress Beecham.

'There are others like Mister Guinea,' she said, casually averting discomfited faces. 'Did we not meet Doctor Johnson's Negro butler, one Francis Barber?'

'Aye, that we did,' said Mistress Puddlewick.

'A fine upright man he was too,' said Mistress Beecham. 'Let me be candid. The practice of engaging Negro secretaries and servants is growing. While we were in the good Doctor's company, Mister Guinea struck up a lengthy conversation on the trade with his butler. They are set to renew their acquaintance in Gough Square shortly. I digress. Let me return to the matter in hand. I judge Mister Guinea's thirty-three years have bequeathed him an assurance that will be greatly needed for his proprietorial responsibilities. Most significantly, I have heard not anyone deny his ability. And I would ask you to keep in mind that profits have increased throughout his six-year stewardship of this company, despite the colour of his skin.'

'Pray do not take an erroneous impression from what I have said, Mistress Beecham,' said Elijah Drinkwater hastily. 'Indeed I deem Mister Guinea to be worthy of the management of the company. Nonetheless I appreciate Mistress Puddlewick's observation. Lawfully emancipated he may be, but given the conduct of the Royal African Company, the Flemings and them of like attitude towards those from the coast of Guinea, I as well harbour concern for Mister Guinea.'

Examining each face in turn, she beamed and then said, 'Let me be frank, dear friends. Reservations may well be founded on what good society might say or how friends might react. I should point out that as members of the League, each one of you is already out on a societal limb. And we all recognise that good society progresses at snail's pace. It will be a great many years before this unspeakable trade in slaves is ended. But given your long association with Jonas, do you fret *for* him or *about* him? I cannot be certain which. Of good opinion I am of all of you and I trust your counsel. God knows I sorely need your support and advice at this time.'

Fastidiously selecting a candied apricot, Mistress Puddlewick broke the hush.

'Are you of firm opinion, Mistress Beecham?'

Nodding her resolve, she smiled.

'Has Mister Guinea not kept our dividends ever increasing for the past six years?' she asked quietly, looking intently at each face. 'Does anyone doubt that he has established an evident grasp of the business better than any other we know of?'

Biting into the apricot, Mistress Puddlewick said nothing.

A flurry of starlings unsettled the awkward silence in the dining room. Carts and carriages thundered along the Highway. Averse to contesting her question, they all sat like puppets nodding their heads.

'That's settled then,' she said crisply. I have them, she thought.

Smiling to herself, she sat further back in her chair. Even so, she felt that of all those present, Aaron Drinkwater remained somewhat taut inside.

Sipping punch with a pippin knot in hand, he spoke querulously, 'I grant you Mister Guinea well-comprehends shipping and the chandlery trade. And undoubtedly he is an asset to the Company. But have you considered your neighbours?'

A taint of dogmatism affects his person, she thought.

Glancing awkwardly at his father, Aaron Drinkwater shrank back in his chair.

'Notwithstanding your neighbours, Mistress Beecham,' said Elijah Drinkwater, 'what of your kinfolk?'

'I am glad you raised that topic, Mister Drinkwater. As you all know Mister Beecham and I were, much the pity, without issue,' she said, pausing to dab her eyes, 'and consequently no heirs of the blood. His passing has thrown a cloud over my skies. Lawfully adopted, Jonas is our own recognised son. And though he keeps the name Guinea, he is an heir beyond hue. Anywise my neighbours keep to their own affairs. And my kinfolk have paraded no interest whatsoever in the chandlery. Mister Guinea was well taught by the late Master. He has a comprehensive understanding of shipping. As well as being able to tell the difference between a caulking iron and a marlinspike, he is conscientious and solicitous and knows the market better than they. And my kin all know it. I have nurtured him for more than twenty of his thirty-three years. For him I can vouchsafe. I cannot say as much for them.'

Wiping her eyes with a monogrammed handkerchief, she continued, ''Tis six long years year since Mister Beecham went to meet his Maker. God rest his dear soul,' she said, heaving a heavy sigh. 'Since that distressing occasion, Mister Guinea has been a font of comfort and counsel to me. What is more, he has grown acquainted with the merchants, the agents, the supercargoes and master mariners. By driving hard bargains, he has increased our revenues. What else is there to know or to consider?'

Unable or unwilling to counter the thrust of her contention, the shareholders smiled at one another and then unanimously nodded their agreement.

A little after five o'clock, smiles and greetings heralded Jonas Guinea's entrance into the dining chamber. Dressed in a blue frock coat with matching breeches, he flourished a graceful bow to all.

'Heartily glad am I to see thee all,' he said cheerfully, examining the appetising fare.

This is a sugary affair, he thought. I cannot in all conscience easily swallow slave produce. Sugar is not to my taste. I will wait for supper.

Taking the chair between Mistress Beecham and Reverend Whitehouse, he began a surreptitious appraisal.

Judging by some flushed expressions, he thought, I would say that my appointment has been the subject of a revelatory discourse. Mistress Puddlewick appears a little off-colour and Aaron Drinkwater ill at ease. I suspect their agreement with my appointment was not entirely unqualified.

Extending his hand, Reverend Whitehouse was hearty.

'My hand on your appointment, Mister Proprietor Guinea,' he said, smiling affectionately. 'Thoroughly deserved, I might add.'

'Many congratulations, Mister Guinea,' said Elijah Drinkwater, bestowing a rare grin followed with a sip of cherry bounce. 'In these bewildering times, Mistress Beecham, methinks you have made a spirited choice.'

'Aye,' said Mistress Puddlewick, chortling.

'I thank you all kindly,' said Jonas, looking around the table. 'As I have always sought to conduct myself, I shall be industrious in my labours to justify your continued confidence in me, which you shall no doubt see reflected in the accounts.'

Nodding her approval at his response, Mistress Beecham rapped the table.

'My dear friends,' she said boldly, 'I invited you here to address what I deem to be the gravest issue of our times. Regarding the question of what next for our League, I am tabling a project of my late husband. I judge that our age requires an exploit. Nay, it warrants decisive action.'

Out of the corner of his eye, Jonas caught the shipowner's brow creasing with curiosity.

'Did I just hear the words decisive action?' asked Jeremiah Puddlewick.

'My husband's plan was not incomprehensible,' said Mistress Beecham jauntily. 'Even I understood it. Without decisive political action, this trade in slaves proves too profitable to be ended. The gentry will have none of it. And neither can we of the League continue sitting on our hands while such a crime against humanity persists.'

'What do you advocate, Mistress Beecham?' asked Jeremiah Puddlewick.

Pausing long enough to marshal the attention of her guests, she lowered her voice.

'I am certain you will all agree that, despite the challenging conditions, we have a duty to further the cause of our League with, shall we say, an unanticipated exploit. The League has not the resources or finance to put an end to the slave trade. But we can in a very small way hinder it. We can return a small number of runaways from whence they were abducted. I propose the League commission a barque for a trading mission with a legitimate Bill of Lading. After engaging—'

Incapable of restraining himself an instant longer, Jeremiah Puddlewick exploded: 'Good God, Mistress Beecham! Do you comprehend the perils in the project you propose?'

Impervious to the shipowner's outburst, she fluttered her fan and ploughed on unabated.

'We shall engage a Captain and officers sworn to secrecy,' she said, glancing at the shipowner, 'and dispatch them to Pertigua to fetch a lawful consignment of rum and sugar. On clearing the capital, Jamestown, our barque will lay off the coast at an agreed location, where she shall embark runaways. From there she shall sail to the coast of Guinea, where our passengers shall be freed. 'Tis not possible to return them to their homes and families. We know not from whence they came. But we can at the very least restore them to the coast of their motherland. On our vessel they shall not be fed the ghastly slave-fare of horse beans boiled in lard, with occasional lumps of salt pork or shark thrown in. Instead, we shall serve them excellent victuals. Without further ado, I ask you, the members, to endorse Mister Beecham's project.'

Glasses hit the table. Gooseberry hops and pippin knots were gulped down.

Sitting upright, Jonas's breathing shallowed. At last we have action, he thought. Mistress Beecham's logic is practical. She owns a plain-speaking approach this day.

'Methinks that took our minds off our bellies,' said Mistress Beecham, smiling. 'Now we have something more venturesome to gnaw upon. 'Twas concocted by Jonas, who brought the project to the attention of Mister Beecham, who fancied it, as did Reverend Whitehouse and I. We believed the plan to be plausible, bold and just. Most significantly, it could be executed with little risk. Such an act ought to help assuage the restiveness and guilt we all feel.

'In case it has slipped your minds, I would remind you that we never consented to this barbaric trade in slaves, yet we still feel implicated by our whiteness and our Englishness. 'Tis a foisted strain of shared liability. Yet even in the company of you principled members, as broad-minded as we proclaim, a man of colour could not dare to propose this scheme, for there are those who would not ever accept it. I truly understand. However, we will need the services of trusted others outside this company. Safe to say that people are the primary flaws in this enterprise, on our side and on the other.'

Glancing at the shipowner, Jonas caught a visage alive with dismay.

Tall and pale with quirky features and wide full lips, Jeremiah Puddlewick stayed with his eyes fixed on Mistress Beecham. Apprehension stuttered out of his mouth.

'M-might our barque not come into c-contact with His Majesty's Navy? What if she was apprehended, m-might the Captain not be open to a charge of larceny and the vessel seized as a prize? Is not the enterprise you advocate merely an idealistic gesture, Mistress Beecham?'

Taking a pinch of snuff and calmly raising his hand, Reverend Whitehouse replied, 'Idealism is an offence we should all be glad to commit, sir. Fortunately idealism is not a felony in the eyes of God. You would undoubtedly agree. He would take issue with a person being regarded as property. Besides, to be charged with anything, our barque must first be apprehended. In possession of an authentic Bill of Lading, His Majesty's Navy will be given no cause to board our vessel, which for all intents and purposes will be plying a lawful voyage. Humour me awhile, Mister Puddlewick.'

Sitting back in his seat slightly mollified, the shipowner nodded and began his third glass of punch.

This enterprise is fraught with betrayal, thought Jonas. Yet the unflustered disposition of a man of the cloth appears to be appeasing our shipowner.

'Believe me, Mister Puddlewick, I of course appreciate your fright,' said Reverend Whitehouse in quiet untroubled tones. 'Consider this, if you will. You would confess that to harbour a profound conviction and be powerless to bring it to fruition, to say the least, vexatious?'

'That much I would admit,' agreed Jeremiah Puddlewick, frowning.

'For that reason,' continued Reverend Whitehouse, 'should we not hold out more than mere hope that by some means, somehow, some day or by someone else, this trade in slaves will cease? I say we should. Perforce I say we are duty-bound to act. Have we not for years held meetings, attended gatherings and preached against Negro importation for the slave trade, to no avail whatsoever?'

'That we have,' he agreed, emphatically downing another mouthful of punch.

'By taking action, will we not be striking at the very heart of this trade in slaves?'

'Aye, that we would!'

'Feast your ears on what has become of our beloved England,' said Reverend Whitehouse, picking up his snuffbox. 'We own the glossary of a racially obsessed society. We use specialised words for people with dissimilar origins. Do you know that on our slave islands, a mulatto has one white and one black parent? A quadroon has three white grandparents. A mustee has one white parent and one parent who has one black grandparent. An octoroon has one black great-grandparent and no other black ancestors, and a sambo, on the other hand, has three black and one white grandparent. I ask you all, is that not a glossary of a racially obsessed society?'

By the dazed expressions around this table, thought Jonas, I can see that the clergyman's disclosure has wrought a moral levy.

Pensively lifting his glass to his lips, the shipowner sat preoccupied.

'Greed and opportunity instigated England's slave trade,' said Reverend Whitehouse. 'The traffic was set in motion in 1663 when Charles II founded the Royal Adventurers in Africa Company and granted it a monopoly for slaving for one thousand years. In 1672, it was renamed the Royal Africa Company. 'Tis little wonder then that the company deemed that Royal Warrant gave them *carte blanche* to subjugate those specifically from Africa. Once the Royal Africa Company's monopoly was broken by the Bristol merchants in 1698, the contagion rapidly spread. It opened the trade up to anyone who wanted to make their fortune with a ship, irrespective of her condition. I say 'tis time our League changes that state of affairs.'

Pausing to take pinches of snuff and sip punch, Reverend White-house continued:

'Our endeavour ought to go unnoticed. I should point out that 'tis to our distinct advantage that we shall not be expected. 'Tis my judgment, sir, that a successful venture will substantiate to the likeminded the efficacy of our League Against the Importation of Negroes from the Coast of Guinea. By our actions we shall embody the sinews of change. Is that an idealistic gesture? To the likes of the Flemings and the Royal African Company, idealism is a starry-eyed notion to be held in contempt. Whereas I believe bouts of idealism are the harbingers of change.'

Carefully putting down his glass, the shipowner appraised his companions.

'Given such a cogent précis of our Christian duty in the prevailing state of England's affairs, Reverend Whitehouse,' said Jeremiah Puddlewick with compunction, 'you can count me in. But given the sheer scale of the trade, you should all know that this venture will have but a paltry effect.'

Despite the shipowner's last comment, the members concurred. An agreement of sorts had been tacitly endorsed.

'To bring this venture to fruition, Mistress Beecham,' said Jeremiah Puddlewick, 'from where do you suggest we acquire a seaworthy vessel?'

Taking his face out of his glass of punch, Elijah Drinkwater spoke, almost as an aside:

'Do you not possess several barques, Mister Puddlewick?'

'I do indeed, sir.'

'Are any in dock?'

'Alas as we speak my three vessels are all at sea.'

'With your connections in shipping, might you be acquainted with someone whom we could strike up such a covert and fiscally reasonable agreement?'

'I could make discreet enquiries with my agent.'

'I thank you, sir,' said Elijah Drinkwater.

A genteel cough from Mistress Puddlewick drew Jonas's attention. The woman was biting her lower lip, clearly anxious to speak.

'May I remind you, sir,' she said quietly to her husband, 'that your agent is not a member of our League.'

'Nay, madam. Does that matter?'

'Would confiding in him not jeopardise the members by acquainting an outsider with our, might I say, unlawful intentions?'

'Ayes,' were muttered around the table.

Smiling affectionately at his wife, the shipowner's voice held sincerity. 'I concede to your reasoning, madam,' he said softly.

Clearly heartened by her husband's affable acquiescence, she took the initiative. 'I am taken by the audaciousness of this project, sir,' said Mistress Puddlewick. 'Will it not deliver one of the principal objectives of our League, which is to impair this obnoxious trade in any way we can?'

'Aye, that it does, madam,' said Mister Puddlewick.

'Two days last past I took tea with Mistress Battersby,' she said. 'She conveyed to me that her husband, Captain Rowland Battersby, fresh from the Netherlands, has berthed your barque the *Redemption* at Gravesend. As we speak, the vessel is discharging her cargo hard by Fort Gardens. The Captain is presently resting at his home. In my haste to attend the gathering at Doctor Johnson's and as well preparing to be here this day, I forgot to share with you the intelligence she imparted in my conversation with her.'

'You should have informed me, madam,' said Mister Puddlewick, smiling.

'No matter, dear husband,' she said softly, 'the Captain will attend you at our house on the morrow. Bear in mind that the old seadog has no liking for slaving merchantmen and will have not anything to do with their kind. He has conviction, is upright, a Methodist and a long time member of our League. An honourable man so much so, he would not die with a lie in his mouth. Dispatch him on this mission, sir. I venture he is your man!'

Throughout her plainly heartfelt account, Jonas glimpsed in the eyes and expression of the shipowner the affection and regard he held for his wife. Stifling his euphoria, he looked down at his glass. Then raising his eyes, he assessed the man upon whom they all appeared to be eagerly waiting. It felt an age before he spoke.

Downing a sturdy swig of punch and a pinch of snuff, Mister Puddlewick looked around and beamed.

'Finally a proposal that raises my blood, madam,' he said. 'All the more that it has so garnered your support. Coupled with your persuasive analysis, Reverend Whitehouse, it would be uncharitable of me to rebuff such a Christian obligation. You have clearly evaluated and cogitated over Mister Beecham's project before tabling it this day. I see it like this: if this project proceeds along intended lines, there should be little danger for our crew or our League. I agree 'tis a simple scheme. Therein lies its appeal. I look forward to acquainting Captain Battersby of this enterprise on the morrow. I am certain he will agree with his orders.'

Her eyes sparkling, Mistress Puddlewick clapped her hands and cooed, 'Good gracious, Mister Puddlewick! Indeed, I find your perspicacity positively inspirational.'

Reverend Whitehouse raised his glass.

'Fretful times lay before us, sir,' he said. 'Provided we disguise our preparations, I am certain we can go unnoticed and even succeed. On behalf of the Church, clerics give benedictions over slave-laden vessels leaving the coast of Guinea. Likewise, we will arrange a dockside benediction of the *Redemption* that will imply ecclesiastical endorsement of her expedition. That should soothe a few ruffled feathers. It might even bamboozle the eyes and ken of dockside agents. I shall offer prayers at the church in Aldersgate for the returnee runaways. I am certain Our Lord would approve.'

'Capital!' cried Mister Puddlewick.

'I shall invest in this audacious project, Mistress Beecham,' said Aaron Drinkwater suddenly. 'And I shall as well, on this matter, tender my legal services to the League without charge.'

'Why thank you, Mister Drinkwater,' cried Mistress Beecham, raising her glass. 'A toast with punch and cherry bounce to the first venture of the League outside England's sceptred shores.'

Clinking glasses all round, the members fell into jollity.

Above the chatter and laughter, Jonas heard a persistent rapping. His eyes descended on Elijah Drinkwater.

Poker-faced, the banker sat rapping his fingers loudly on the table until the chamber fell silent.

'Thus far I see expenditure for a worthy cause,' he said. 'But we have yet to hear about the breakdown of profits from this project.'

'Profit, Mister Drinkwater?' reiterated Mistress Beecham. 'Why, sir, we can expect goodly profit from the *Redemption*'s cargo. Outward bound, Captain Battersby shall carry hogsheads of brandy, brass pans and casks of pewter and firkins of tallow for barter. And with his trusty contacts homeward bound, he will return with rum and sugar from Pertigua, as well as gold, sandalwood and ivory from the coast of Guinea. As to the breakdown of profits — I propose that they be divided equally between Elijah and Aaron Drinkwater, Mister Puddlewick, Thomas Beecham, Chandlers, Captain Battersby and our two supper guests, should they choose to participate.'

Suitably placated and beaming around the table, Elijah Drinkwater said enthusiastically, 'I shall seek out intermediaries and ask them to hatch a way for making contact with the runaway stronghold of Freetown. I am told they hide out somewhere in the mountainous swamps of northern Pertigua.'

'We shall certainly need their services,' said Mistress Beecham, fanning her face.

Narrowing his eyes, Jonas glanced around the table.

An outsider, he thought, could be forgiven for believing they had stumbled on an 'only investors can speak' guild.

Shafts of dust-laden sunlight suddenly bathed the Chippendale table in a discordant glow, heightening the tension in the chamber.

Turning to him, Elijah Drinkwater asked, 'What say you, Mister Guinea?'

Caught by surprise, he responded with an awkward smile.

'Pray think me not uncouth for what I am about to say, sir,' he said, after a moment's pause. 'Since my arrival on England's shores I have received your kind and generous charity. Yet, I must confess I have not the funds to invest in this most principled venture. Those who can fiscally participate are justly in a strong position to vote on this project. Given my circumstances, I must remain in the shadows. And I am certain you are aware that in the withdrawing rooms of England, one of my hue walks on thin ice.'

'What do you mean by thin ice, Mister Guinea?' asked Aaron Drinkwater indignantly.

'Allow me to enlighten you, Mister Drinkwater,' he said, with unruffled civility. 'Take my friend, Henry Jackson. He served his master as valet and secretary for over twenty years. Through an unsolicited remark, he offended his master in the presence of the house guests. It was said that it warranted a simple ticking off. Instead, his master had him hurled from the house for being impudent. Effrontery was his crime and eviction was his sentence. Yet he was fortunate.'

'Fortunate?' exclaimed Aaron Drinkwater.

'Aye indeed fortunate, sir,' he reiterated, smiling. 'On occasion, Mister Drinkwater, the hapless black servant is discarded and sold to the captain of a slave ship. Present company excepted of course, but from my observations, life in London Town, even for a tutored black, is oftimes akin to threading an obliged soul through chilly streets. Vigilance was my watchword from my first secretarial days when visiting anchored vessels. Guided by prudence, I avoided being labelled 'cocky' by their master mariners. A slight indiscretion would have seen me bound and gagged and dumped on a 'tween deck bound for the plantations. Thus, survival guided my actions and my words. Notwithstanding the warm-natured invitation to speak, I nevertheless do so with caution. I am asked what say I. Well, I say that Mister Beecham would be unequivocally content with these proceedings.'

Visibly perplexed, Elijah Drinkwater pressed his point. 'I appreciate your diplomacy in your depiction of London society, Mister Guinea. We Jews have had our share. But what say *you* — the man in you? Speak up, sir. We sail to Pertigua to liberate your people. Surely then, sir, like we, you must feel somewhat delighted?'

'Indeed, sir, I do. Heartily I thank thee all. On their behalf, Mister Drinkwater, I am decidedly grateful. As well, I am obliged to say this: my heart bellows with gladness for the runaways we liberate. Perchance they will be shocked by their comprehensive turnabout in fortune. But once freed, they will take with them a grander impression of English men and of England. God does indeed work in mysterious ways. So much so, I have yet to understand why He truncated their liberty in the first place.'

Restraining a smile, Mistress Beecham laid down her fan, raised her eyes to the ceiling and mused aloud, 'I have oft cogitated on that most baffling question.'

Suddenly, a hawker yelled, 'Wood, three bundles a penny!'

Startling the company, the street cry served as a diversion from Mistress Beecham's contentious aside. A flock of starlings rustling past the gaping windows provided a further distraction.

'Indeed, Mistress Beecham,' said Aaron Drinkwater. 'I am myself well versed in matters of jurisprudence and such like. Oftimes I find the hypothetical quite confounds my reason. Nonetheless, I steadfastly believe in God. Though occasionally I find even that condition somewhat challenging.'

'Faith, Mister Drinkwater!' snapped Reverend Whitehouse. 'We must own heaps of faith. 'Tis not for mere mortals to reason why or to dispute the words or works of Our Lord. Faith supplies the succour that soothes the soul. At times like these we could all do with a good splodge of that.'

Sounds like a hackneyed priestly notion to me, thought Jonas.

A deferential breather followed the cleric's God-fearing utterance, during which time the roar from the cobblestoned Highway echoed throughout the chamber. Momentarily, they seemed besieged by clattering hooves and stage-coaches, flying wagons and tumbrils, entirely eclipsed by the cries of the hawkers.

'Wood — three bundles a penny!'

'Sallop for climbing boys!'

'Matches! Matches! Wan' any matches?'

'Diddle, diddle, dumplings, ho!'

Quaffing punch to settle his nerves as the street cries faded, Jonas began, 'It is at such times like this that a man must be prepared to take a stand. Not having the resources compels me to propose otherwise to you, the members of the League. In the stead of hard cash, I shall make an investment in this project with my labour, on the vessel and in Pertigua, as a liaison with the runaways. Besides, I hope my presence will help assuage the suspicions of the runaways and assist communications with them. For these reasons, Mistress Beecham, I seek your agreement for me to sail with the *Redemption*.'

Shooting a horrified look at Reverend Whitehouse, who chuckled and nodded, Mistress Beecham then scanned her guests. Her hurried enquiry complete, she collected herself with a winning smile.

'All these years, Jonas Guinea,' she said affectionately, 'you have served our family and Thomas Beecham, Chandlers loyally. You have asked for not more than is due to you. How then can I deny you the chance to fulfil your mission to aid your own? What is more, I commend your pluck. Though I would have you remember you are my son. And I shall bide with bated breath until I see your safe return.'

Beaming bashfully at Mistress Beecham, Jonas sat back contentedly in his chair.

'Your altruism is commendable, Mistress Beecham,' said Mistress Puddlewick. 'And what you propose is decidedly audacious, Mister Guinea. Aboard the *Redemption*, I am certain Captain Battersby and his crew of Methodists will keep you safe.'

Bowing courteously, Jonas smiled. Screeching chair-legs turned his head.

Aaron Drinkwater had shifted his chair to lean ominously over the table.

'Your choice, Mister Guinea,' he said darkly, 'may well prove to be an injudicious option.'

Shocked by the retort, Jonas froze.

Calculatedly folding her fan, Mistress Beecham flung a sharp look across the table.

'Pray why, Mister Drinkwater?' she asked apprehensively, 'I beseech thee do tell.'

Drawing a consequential breath, Aaron Drinkwater leaned forwards.

'Were this enterprise to go awry, Mistress Beecham,' he said gravely, 'Mister Guinea could well find himself arrested and enslaved in Pertigua. And we know plantation owners dispense astonishing brutality on their slaves. Given the legal complexities we would encounter in his extraction and defence, which I might add are set undeniably against his person, extracting him may prove to be well nigh impossible. Mister Guinea would consequently remain a slave, in perpetuity. Not only would he be lost to himself — he would be lost to us all.'

Envisioning himself slaving in a cane field, Jonas shivered.

Bouncing in her seat at his dark caveat, Mistress Beecham was adamant. 'Mister Guinea shall carry documents attesting to his manumission, Mister Drinkwater! Why then would he need extracting?'

Startled by the vigour of her riposte, Aaron Drinkwater's face clouded.

'M-Mistress Beecham,' he said contritely, with a nervous glance at his stony-faced father. 'I-I was simply drawing your attention to a potential obstacle for this most worthy project.'

'Mister Guinea shall benefit from the protection of Captain Battersby,' said Jeremiah Puddlewick matter-of-factly, 'whom I shall carefully instruct. I can see no compelling reason why Mister Guinea should not sail with the *Redemption*.'

'To forestall Mister Guinea being kidnapped or arrested,' placated Mistress Puddlewick, 'I counsel that on no account shall he set foot on that diabolical island.'

'Methinks your counsel is a tad presumptuous, my beloved,' said Mister Puddlewick affectionately. ''Tis the law of the sea that conduct on or off a vessel remains the domain of the Captain, particularly away from home shores.'

Gracefully acquiescing, Mistress Puddlewick nodded and smiled at her husband.

Glancing at the mantelpiece clock, Jonas noted the time. It was twenty minutes to seven.

Mistress Beecham waggled the table bell and three parlour maids entered the chamber. Smiling at them, she turned back to her guests.

'Dear friends,' she said, 'while we await our supper guests, we can continue our discourse in the withdrawing room.'

The light was waning. Carts and carriages rumbled along the Highway. Twilight crept into the room. Maidservants scurried around lighting the candles and oil lamps, shutting the windows, drawing the curtains and lighting a fire in the hearth. A homely feeling soon pervaded the chamber. Jonas was heartened by the smell of wood smoke. Effluvium from the sewers of Bottom Lane made his nostrils twitch.

The bells of St George in the East struck seven.

He heard the barely audible greetings at the front door above the mirth and chatter in the room. Leaning towards Mistress Beecham, he whispered, 'Methinks Mistress Bradshaw and the Parson Merriweather have arrived.'

The door opened.

Broadening her smile, Mistress Beecham turned around.

Waddling in slightly inebriated, Tuppence Honeypenny, the absent-minded housekeeper, scratched her head.

'Now let me see,' she mused to herself. 'Ah yes, I remember now. Mistress Bradshaw and Parson Merriweather have come to grace Pilgrims with their charming company.'

Winking at the housekeeper for her unconventional introduction, Jonas stood up to greet the visitors.

Having previously been captivated by Faith Bradshaw, his heart was softly pounding as he eyed her entrance. Her jet-black bun garnished with tiny wax flowers readily complemented her pale soft features. Though there seemed a quiet ache in her mien, she looked fetching in her delicately embroidered silk gown. Once more, he found himself beguiled by her. He smiled at the crapulous figure beside her. Recalling Parson Merriweather's penchant for liquor, his bloodshot eyes confirmed his present condition. Probably from yesternight's bacchic revelry in some seedy tavern. Abolitionist activism and clerical bands they have in common, otherwise no two men of the cloth could be more dissimilar. Whitehouse is a portly well-fed Methodist accustomed to a cosy living visiting withdrawing rooms. In striking contrast, the polished beads of Merriweather's rosary would not ever be believed if they divulged what they had witnessed on the coast of Guinea. Our gangling companion is a remorseful Catholic swashbuckler.

''Tis a joy to meet up with you both again,' clucked Mistress Beecham. 'Methinks you would benefit from a tonic after your tiresome journey?'

Extending his hand towards the Parson, Reverend Whitehouse chortled.

'One must drink as one brews, sir,' he said. ''Tis not surprising that you, my Catholic brother, seasoned in the mosquitoed swamps of Guinea, owns the stamina to effect an expedition from Kent in this sapping August heat. A stimulant will no doubt reward your noble efforts and cool your weary brow.'

'Those who drink water will think water,' replied Parson Merriweather, chuckling and shaking his hand. 'A bodied tonic would certainly mollify the ache in these old bones, particularly in such delightful Methodist company.'

Everyone laughed.

'Your welcome is indeed heartening, Mistress Beecham,' said Faith Bradshaw, shyly squinning at Jonas.

Smiling nervously, he gave her a courteous bow.

Six years had passed since they had first met, soon after she had landed in England fresh from the slave uprising on Pertigua. Seemingly oblivious to her wounds on her first visit to Pilgrims, she had bounded from the carriage with the Parson, set on joining the League Against the Importation of Negroes from the Coast of Guinea. Angry she was, spitting a horrific account of multiple murders on English slave plantations. In the presence of her mother, her estranged stepfather had narrowly escaped with his life during the uprising. However, she gained financial independence in her family's post-uprising legalities. Her parents would remain permanently on Tamarind Trees, the slave plantation in Pertigua. She inherited Greensleeves, the family's mansion house and its surrounding green acres near Tunbridge Wells, Kent.

Over the port late one memorable evening, while recounting a litany of gruesome incidents that had transpired in the uprising, she broached the name Randolph Fleming. His hackles rose recalling Fleming's visit to Pilgrims when the planter had voiced his belief in the inferiority of the African because of 'a comprehensive lack of any civilisation'.

'Fleming is one treacherous tyrant,' she had seethed.

Describing the Machiavellian tactics employed by the planters to suppress the uprising, she vented a sneering belligerence. By her account, the island had been 'awash with blood' on both sides. Having witnessed the effect of the plantation owners' duplicity, spurring the slave uprising and, in addition, the heartbreaking death of the man she loved, she was surely a riven woman. None at Pilgrims had ever learned the identity of her lover or how she herself escaped death. During those first aching months in England, weighed down by a farraginous clutter of ghastly memories of that final battle, she spoke only of the uprising. In her wintry melancholy, she seldom smiled.

Now, six years on and striding into Pilgrims with an inborn grace, he saw a spirited yet demurely pleasing woman with not a trace of yesteryear about her person. Mistress Beecham's voice broke his reverie.

'Following supper,' he heard her say, 'Tuppence will show you to your bedchambers.'

'I am gratified by your hospitality, ma'am,' said Parson Merriweather.

Nodding her appreciation to the cleric and then beaming around the chamber, Mistress Beecham raised her dulcet voice, 'Cherry bounce or punch for anyone? We were about to chirp-merry with a celebratory beverage.'

'So that one may partake, Mistress Beecham,' said Faith Bradshaw, accepting a glass of the cherry liqueur, 'may one know the cause for your celebration?'

'Our League is set to sally forth from these isles, Mistress Brad-shaw,' she said quietly. 'And if what I have to impart engages your interest, we would most welcome your contribution.'

Gulping down a mouthful of punch, Parson Merriweather addressed his host. 'What venture bestirs you so, Mistress Beecham?'

Smiling to himself, Jonas leaned back in his chair.

Pointing at the Chippendale sofa with high scrolled arms, Mistress Beecham sat beside Faith Bradshaw. Sinking into a wing chair close-by, Parson Merriweather was by now halfway through his second glass of punch. Leaning conspiratorially forwards, Mistress Beecham began enlightening her listeners about the League's Pertiguan project.

Before long, Jonas's attention was drawn across the chamber by gasps from Mistress Beecham's coterie.

Falling back into his seat, the Parson drained his glass.

'Good heavens,' he said aloud. ''Tis high time such a blooded endeavour was made.'

Beaming thoughtfully, Faith Bradshaw set down her glass.

'I am sensible to the honour of your proposal, Mistress Beecham,' she said. 'Heartily glad am I to hear of such a bold action. Set against this gallant venture, I have of late been rusticating and frittering time on inessentials in Kent. Oftimes during my day, in my mind's eye, I can still see the hideous mutilations meted out on the slaves by heart-less overseers. My senses seethe at night. For six long years I have been quietly desperate to act. I have many reasons. Methinks, save an ele-mental change of tack by the politicians towards this criminal trade, conspiracies such as that you propose must be encouraged. Suffice to say it comes not a moment too soon. Truthfully, it bestirs me with joy. Count me in, Mistress Beecham. I will gladly invest.'

Gladdened by Faith Bradshaw's participation in the League's pro-ject, Jonas caught her eyes above the candle flame. Holding his gaze fleetingly, she lowered her eyes, smiling.

Raising his third glass of punch with a shaky hand, Parson Merri-weather wheeled unsteadily around spewing praise.

'A toast to you, diamonds of the first water!' he cried, with his eyes sparkling wildly. 'Count me as an investor. I say 'tis time to scold the piper!'

Goaded by the sheer effrontery of the enterprise, Jonas raised his glass.

'We are set to liberate runaways,' he said. 'Lest we believe our enterprise will bring an end to slavery, 'twould be wise to accept that our efforts will reduce the magnitude of the trade not a jot. That is as well the strength of our project. We shall not be expected. Thus, we should go unchallenged. It should be remembered that a solitary vessel cannot end this cold-blooded trade, but in all Christian conscience we cannot turn back.'

Applause followed his statement.

Glancing furtively around the chamber, he caught sight of Faith Bradshaw. A beguiling look danced in her eyes. Nodding at her, he turned shyly away.

The door opened. Mistress Honeypenny wobbled into the chamber.

'Supper is served, Mistress Beecham,' she happily announced. 'It pleasures me to say that cook has a fine rabbit for you and your guests.'

Strolling into the candlelit dining room, Mistress Puddlewick brushed against Tiger, the family grimalkin. Disturbed by the invasion, the tabby snootily made for the open door, tail in the air.

'We seem to have vexed the sentinel of the house,' said Mistress Puddlewick.

'Not as quick as she used to be,' said Mistress Beecham, taking the chair at the head of the table, 'but she is still good at catching mice.'

'I have two cats,' said Faith Bradshaw. 'One is an excellent mouser — seizes them from thin air. But the other could not so much as identify the species *rodentia*.'

'And why might that be?' asked Mistress Puddlewick, smothering her giggles behind her hand.

'Daylight is unfamiliar and wearisome to her — as is night,' replied Faith Bradshaw. 'Indeed, one might say the condition of being vigilant is quite alien to her.'

Clapping her hands at the comment, Mistress Puddlewick's cackling turned hoarse. Then she added, 'You could as well postulate that it slipped her wits the reason for which she was procured.'

Sniggering and laughter followed her comment.

From a shouldered decanter, Mistress Honeypenny shakily poured Madeira into a row of glinting glasses.

Wine soon loosened inhibitions and tongues. Hence the roast rabbit, boiled potatoes and gravy was consumed in a mood of animated camaraderie.

Over the steamed pudding, Faith Bradshaw began a barely audible inquisition.

'It has come to my ears 'tis your intention to sail with the *Redemption*, Mister Guinea,' she said unemotionally.

Her manner makes her words seem more like an accusation than a question to me, he thought. Her inquiry has caught me unawares.

Sweat trickled down the nape of his neck. Looking awkwardly around the quietened chamber, he answered:

'Indeed, Mistress Bradshaw. 'Tis my intention to assist Captain Battersby — and 'tis as well my investment in this project. You would doubtless support such a contribution?'

Noticing the scowl that darted across her forehead, he knew support would not be forthcoming from her quarter.

Shaking her head robustly, her eyes glistened as words spilled from her lips.

'You may not be a slave sir,' she said in a prickly voice, looking directly at him. 'You may indeed have manumission. Among the whites of Pertigua, who could tell you were a freeman by the hue of your hide? Who would believe that one the colour of a slave could submit authentic papers on a slave island? I cannot agree with you, Mister Guinea. Not so much as I would wish you to plunge your hand into the fires of Hell!'

Gasps and shocked looks followed her unambiguous depiction.

Regaining her composure with casual sips of Madeira, Faith Bradshaw appeared impervious to the consternation she had provoked.

Assurances breezed around the table.

'Mister Guinea shall have the protection of Captain Battersby, Mistress Bradshaw!'

'Aye. And he shall carry his papers of manumission on his person!'

'There are many free blackamoors aboard English merchantmen as well as serving in His Majesty's Navy. Signed on, Mister Guinea shall merely be a member of the crew aboard an English vessel visiting an English colony.'

The fervour of her opposition has pitched misgiving on my participation, thought Jonas. Glancing around the members, he then looked more closely at her. Coursing from her is a tale borne from heartbreak. She appears sincere about the threat she feels to my person. But is it just possible that she does not want me to ever sail from these shores?

Sighing and looking from face to face, Faith Bradshaw spoke almost in a whisper. 'Do any of you know what befalls black men on that island?' she asked.

Startled and intrigued by her question, her listeners leaned towards her.

'If the authorities on Pertigua detain Mister Guinea,' she said vehemently, 'he will be stripped of the fine garments that presently attire his person for coarse jerkin and breeches. He will always be hungry. He will want for rest from cutting cane all hours God sends. And he will thirst for freedom, for he will rightfully, in my view, be viscerally affronted by the unilateral proscription of his liberty by others. Thanks to the slaves' unremitting struggle for freedom, many a tear have I wept at the maelstrom I witnessed every day on that island, which sadly continues to this day.'

'Aboard the *Redemption*, Mister Guinea shall be well protected,' said Mistress Puddlewick reassuringly.

'I am confident you will all try, Mistress Puddlewick,' she replied tersely. 'I believe Mister Drinkwater has advised that the risks are not only considerable, they are far too great. I believe his summation to be entirely accurate. No matter. For I see you are all set on this imprudent course of action by approving, nay indeed encouraging, Mister Guinea to sail with the *Redemption*. Facing such odds, I am obliged to yield to, if I might say, an injudicious decision. Against my better judgement, I give way. May my prayers stay in your counsels. For your part in this wild enterprise, Mister Guinea, my prayers and good wishes sail with thee and as well, I bid thee a safe and speedy return to us.'

'You are most generous, Mistress Bradshaw,' said Jonas. 'Your concern for my wellbeing is indeed heartening. Although I might add that I had hoped for your hearty support and—'

Raising her hand, Faith Bradshaw interrupted him.

'Lest you deem me insensitive, sir,' she said jovially, 'I could not have you carry away such a mistaken notion. Before the *Redemption* sails, I bid you pay a visit to Greensleeves. Parson Merriweather and I would be charmed with your company. The tranquillity in the house and gardens would suit you so well. And the song of the woods would surely agree with thee. Amble 'twixt the cornflowers and yellow rattles in the wild flower meadows. What with the lichens, grasses and flowers, the battalions of cherry trees and the fragrance of fruit, the orchards of Kent hold such a breathtaking splendour at this time of year. To convey my delight, I shall show you myself.'

'Aye, Mister Guinea,' said Parson Merriweather. 'Come visit us, sir. I shall conduct you around Kent's hop gardens. After that, we can imbibe the fine beers of Samuel Shepherd. We shall take a carriage to Winchelsea, where beer was introduced from the Low Countries around 1400. We might even down a fine Madeira or two at a table in The Prodigal Son. 'Tis a well known watering hole for smugglers and—'

Sniggering stopped the Parson, who puckered his brow.

Squinting around, Jonas alighted on the culprits.

Shaking with mirth was Mistress Puddlewick. Likewise, Reverend Whitehouse was chuckling quietly to himself. As was Aaron Drinkwater, shaking his head and rolling his eyes in mock despair.

Glancing around the chamber, the Parson smiled boyishly.

Gracefully setting down her glass of Madeira, Faith Bradshaw spoke with a quiet sincerity:

'Set against the Parson's manifest acquaintance with the devil's brew are the other varied diversions of Kent, Mister Guinea. Why every autumn, we hie down to the county fair for a day of good fare; to laugh at the clowns and jugglers and to watch or partake in games and farming contests. We could, for instance, walk the heath land of the High Weald and the forest of the Low Weald. Only the day last past I did hear that an ancient artefact from St Augustine, the first Archbishop of Canterbury, has been found in the Cathedral. We shall go there. I shall take you.'

'Given such an agreeable set of pursuits in this invitation, Jonas,' said Mistress Beecham, ''twould be churlish not to accept Mistress Bradshaw's kind offer to visit Greensleeves. Before a protracted sea voyage which at times will no doubt be tempestuous, you would benefit from the airs and pastoral climes of the garden of England. Fret not. In your absence I shall manage the chandlery with our workforce.'

'Health-wise you would gain much from the respite,' said Mistress Puddlewick. 'A bout of country air will put you in fine fettle for the fight. I believe the *Redemption* will not sail for a number of weeks. There are a great deal of victuals and apparel to be ordered and stowed for our runaways.'

'Aye,' said Elijah Drinkwater, with a roguish glint in his eye. 'I did hear that the womenfolk are somewhat fetching in Kent. Weeks with your nose in her rambling acres will whet your appetite for adventure. Then I daresay you might, if you find the time, even try your hand at a pheasant shoot. I suspect familiarity with firearms could prove useful during your expedition.'

Rattled by the mention of firearms, Jonas simply smiled.

'Heartily I accept your kind invitation, Mistress Bradshaw,' he said, 'and yours too, Parson. I very much look forward to visiting you both at Greensleeves.'

''Tis settled then, Mister Guinea.' said Jeremiah Puddlewick quietly. 'To summarise then, on your return from Tunbridge Wells you shall be ready to sail with the *Redemption*. Furthermore, provided your safety is not in jeopardy, you are happy to assist Captain Battersby to establish the connections required for implementing the League's strategy.'

Happily nodding his agreement, Jonas pressed his lips together.

'A toast to the *Redemption*,' cried a chorus of voices, followed by clinking glasses.

Perusing the faces around the table, he saw a buoyant Faith Bradshaw raising her glass.

He smiled.

By the evening's end his visit to Greensleeves had been set for two weeks hence. Thereafter, Honeypenny showed the visitors to their bedchambers.

Early next morning, he stood on the carriage drive with Mistress Beecham waving away the carriage bearing Faith Bradshaw and the Parson on their return to Kent.

The Lone African

'A good day for a hack along country lanes, Mister Guinea,' said the driver.

'Aye, that it is, Mister Spice.'

'You be keeping Mistress Bradshaw's company then, Mister Guinea,' said the driver, giving him a knowing wink.

'Aye, Mister Spice,' he replied with a broad grin, 'and I will be keeping Parson Merriweather's company as well.'

'The Parson's company not be snug as hers, Mister Guinea.'

Staring straight ahead with a preoccupied smile, he said, 'I daresay you are right, Mister Spice.'

Bathed by the warm September sun, the carriage rumbled into the county of Kent. Intent on giving a good impression, he had donned a freshly-tailored collarless camel frock coat with matching breeches. Mistress Beecham had insisted he take the chandlery's carriage and driver. For fear of highwaymen, her man was armed with a blunderbuss and 'to provide companionship and protection for a travelling person of colour'. Rattling along in the carriage and four, he sat in animated humour with the driver. They were making for the hamlet of Langton Green, two miles west of Tunbridge Wells, a town he had been told was founded around a chalybeate spring.

'Methinks we be close, Mister Guinea,' said the driver.

Catching sight of his destination over the hedgerows, his spirits soared at the thought of his attractive host. In the distance stood the tower of St Mary's, the fifteenth century church prevailing over the adjacent village of Speldhurst. It was a landmark the Parson had described most precisely.

Crossing Old Pack-Horse Lane, the coach lurched to the right. Shortly afterwards, they were jolting along a wide track through oak woodland.

''Tis the ancient track from Newhaven to London, Mister Guinea,' said the driver.

Nodding his gratitude, Jonas sighed with contentment.

Enthralled by the unaccustomed song of woodland, he was as well rapt in the abundance of spreading trees. Half a mile trotted by through the woods. Soon, they were clattering between wrought-iron gates onto a gravelled carriage drive at the end of which stood three figures.

Faith Bradshaw was arresting in a fetching amethyst gown. Beside her stood a jolly Parson Merriweather, cutting a sexagenarian dash in a white cravat and clerical band with straggling wisps of white hair dancing about his shoulders. Waiting next to him was a plump middle-aged woman. Well-groomed in a frilled mobcap, she was noticeably deferential.

His carriage shuddered to a halt.

As his feet touched the gravel, Faith Bradshaw stepped forward with outstretched hands.

'Greetings on the first of your many visits to Greensleeves, Mister Guinea,' she said, with a beatific smile. 'We have planned outings for your visit. Indeed, we have spoken of not anything else. Come, sir, we shall take good care of you and your driver.'

'By what I have delightfully observed, Mistress Bradshaw,' he said, 'your estate more than surpasses your description. Since your last visit to Pilgrims, I have very much looked forward to returning the compliment by visiting you and Parson Merriweather.'

A laddish smile dissolved the cleric's dissolute features.

Disreputable old goat, thought Jonas, beaming.

Turning to the unknown woman, the Parson chuckled amiably.

'May I present Mistress Bracegirdle,' he said warmly, 'the indefatigable housekeeper of Greensleeves.'

'A good day to you, Mistress Bracegirdle,' said Jonas cordially. 'I trust my presence will not prove an imposition on you and your staff.'

The housekeeper curtsied politely. 'Pleased ter make your 'quaint-ance, Mister Guinea. I trust you will find our servants 'ave an obliging disposition. I might add that word of your good character for one of your colour precedes you, sir.'

Bestowing a strained smile, Jonas turned to his host.

Closing her eyes at Bracegirdle's *faux pas*, Faith Bradshaw steered him into a stroll along the carriage drive.

'Come,' she said crisply, smiling broadly. 'Allow me to take you on a tour of my grounds. There are about twelve hundred acres of grassland, pasture and woodland, much of which is leased to tenant farmers. The house was built by my maternal grandfather around 1700, with later additions by my stepfather. He changed the name from Manderston to Tamarind Trees. In memory of my blood father, Nathan Greensleeves, who lost his life in Pertigua's uprising, I renamed her Greensleeves.'

Surrounded by sheep-shorn lawns, the mansion house was bordered by tiered flowerbeds. Mellow brick and sandstone ground floors supported two tile-hung upper floors, culminating in a pitched clay tile roof. One of four tall chimney stacks was dated 1702 in turquoise mosaic. Abutting a copse of apple trees was a six-horse brick and wood stable block and timbered barns. Encircled by oak woodland and off the beaten track, Greensleeves' residents enjoyed commanding views over the gardens and orchards. From the rear of the property, the landscape dropped gently down a huge escarpment onto a bucolic panorama.

Thankful to have been shown around the house and grounds by the owner, he nevertheless felt uncomfortable.

All this from the proceeds of slavery, he thought. God help us.

Smiling at her, he was tactful:

'A charming estate, Mistress Bradshaw,' he said. 'Many thanks for showing me around.'

'We shall make your abide with us an agreeable one, Mister Guinea,' she said, pushing open the front door. 'Tea?'

Following her down a passageway and into a large withdrawing room, he smiled. Sunlight streamed through half a dozen stone mullion windows set into three walls. An inglenook fireplace claimed the middle of the opposite wall. In the far corner, an old brass cuspidor had been converted into a planter for a flowering aspidistra. Porcelain cups and saucers with a jasmine flower motif had been marshalled on a round beech table, already occupied by the seated Parson. Sighting the polished oak floors, silk embroidered walls and cherished ornaments, his mouth dried. Momentarily, he was unsettled by the sight and proximity of the exquisite fineries set against the plangent cry of slavery in his head.

Between the architects of this venture, presumption can play no part, he told himself.

Shaking off his doubts, he looked at her.

Taking the lid off a hand-painted blue and white Chinese porcelain teapot, she began her tea-making ritual. Gently stirring the hot fragrant jasmine flowers, she replaced the lid and lifted the pot.

'Given the League's imminent action, Mister Guinea,' she said quietly, 'it behoves me to share a somewhat delicate intelligence with you.'

'Delicate, Mistress Bradshaw?'

Pouring the aromatic beverage into a cup, she said, 'Aye, Mister Guinea, delicate.'

'I am your guest, Mistress Bradshaw,' he said, 'and as such I am happily obliged to listen to whatever you wish to say.'

Passing him a cup of tea, she looked directly at him.

'You see before you an independent woman, Mister Guinea,' she said forthrightly. 'Greensleeves was built before my birth from the proceeds of slavery. I had no hand in her finance or construction. I regret that it was ever so. Having inherited this manor, I am the mistress of Greensleeves. As such, I could not in all conscience live off slave labour. Thus I receive no allowance for the upkeep of this estate from the family plantation in Pertigua. I am self-sufficient. I recount all this to you for good reason. Owing to potentially alienating obstacles ahead of you, Mister Guinea, I want you to understand my position to prevent you from faltering in your task. In this emancipation business hesitation can be dangerous. As I see it we are indisputably after the same end. Indubitably then methinks the liberation of runaways sets us at the same table.'

Her petition is worthy of note, thought Jonas.

'Considering your plainspoken declaration we are indeed co-conspirators, Mistress Bradshaw,' he said. 'Your frank account of your circumstance is, I find, an excellent basis for trust.'

'I can vouch for Mistress Bradshaw's remarkable account, Mister Guinea,' said the Parson. 'I was well-acquainted with Nathan Greensleeves. A steadfast figure of a man he was too. Prior to and all through the uprising he gave his support to the rebels — as did she. Unfortunately, Nathan paid with his life. Sickened by the sight of tortured slaves and the horrors of the uprising, we quit Pertigua for England on the *Gold Coast*, a barque of the Royal African Company. Forever etched in my mind is that tempestuously memorable voyage through which my esteem for her grew. During that voyage we took a solemn oath to join the League. There you have it in a nutshell, Mister Guinea. We both will have no truck with slavers, particularly in the guise of men like Randolph Fleming. That man's swagger needs curbing.'

Casting his eyes casually over her, Jonas was encouraged by her manner towards him. Further heartened by the fact that she had sided with the rebels, he scowled at the thought of Randolph Fleming.

''Tis not my business to gainsay yours, Mistress Bradshaw,' he said. 'What you have disclosed cheers me, for it precludes doubt. Now that I have your enthusiastic connivance I undertake this mission with a greater fervour. But while we abhor the activities of the slave traders, I do not ever forget that I may be the lone African.'

Wearing a perplexed expression she turned to the Parson, whose brow puckered.

'The lone African?' he reiterated.

'The one who is free,' said Jonas, grinning.

Slapping the table, the Parson suddenly guffawed.

'I take your meaning, Mister Guinea,' she said, laughing. 'Nonetheless, having reflected on your part in this hazardous mission, I desired that you were aware of the truth of my circumstances prior to your sailing.'

'I thank you, Mistress Bradshaw. Methinks—'

'While we are about it, Mister Guinea, I would have you call me Faith. Mistress Bradshaw harbours far too much formality for such a delightful occasion as your visit.'

He bowed courteously.

'Faith it shall be,' he said, with a smile that narrowed his eyes, 'provided the name Jonas graces your lips.'

Throwing back her head, she laughed. 'I am partial to your name, Jonas.'

In her exuberance, she laid her hand on his. Her eyes glistened and her skin felt silky and cool. A flame flickered deep inside him. He heard himself say, 'And I am taken with your name, Faith.'

A growl from the Parson terminated their nascent union.

'And ye can both call me Parson.'

Jonas laughed.

Giggling like a spirited girl who had attained the height of felicity, she sashayed out of the chamber and returned with a decanter of Madeira. Erupting with chatter upon the sight of his favourite companion, the Parson proceeded to guzzle goblets of the fortified Portuguese wine. Listening to his remorse-filled epiphany in the punitive post-uprising action across the island of Pertigua, they stared aghast at the copious amounts the cleric was downing.

'Before these very eyes,' continued the Parson mournfully, 'captured runaways were trussed-up and spit-roasted by my countrymen.'

Mercifully, after his fifth goblet and owing to his predilection for a nap following his afternoon tipple, he rendered garbled excuses and retired.

Catholic footsteps faded up the stairs. In the clergyman's wake, Jonas was alone with her for the first time. His eyes skipped coyly about the withdrawing room until at last they locked on hers. A captivating smile parted her lips. Traces of eau de cologne entered his nostrils. A flurry of passionate scenarios tumbled through his head.

Not once has she alluded to our difference. She appears not to perceive colour. Can it be she sees only a man? Silent and spoken bigotry quivers in elements of the populace. In much of those quarters black with white is frowned upon. That matters not, for she arouses me.

Without taking his eyes off her, he smoothed the pocket flaps of his frock coat, picked up a crystal glass from the table and took a long swig of Madeira. Throughout his wordless performance, her glistening eyes held his gaze.

He befuddles me, she thought. I have bodily desires when he nears me — an ache I had long forgotten. To contribute to this Pertiguan project, he eagerly takes on a dangerous assignment, back to an island where he was once a slave. I have strived but cannot persuade him otherwise. The fellow is a risk-taker, an adventurer — a thoroughly unwholesome attribute. Yet his physique and his confounding appeal flout my defences. I am drawn to him.

Grasping his hand, her fingers broke his woolgathering.

Without a word, she led him to a Chippendale sofa swathed in needlepoint tapestry. Sinking down beside her, he was close enough to feel her bodily tremors. Throughout the afternoon, enveloped in her company, he listened to the minutiae of Pertigua's plantation regime and specifics of the island's topography. Progressing to his mission, he noted the angst in her voice when fleshing out the hazards he would face 'day and night' on the island.

At length the crickets were chirping in the gloaming.

Halting her descriptions of the island's grisly procedures, she raised her eyes.

'Should harm come to you during this mission,' she said with watery eyes, 'I cannot but foresee that I shall have you on my conscience for the rest of my days.'

'Conscience will exact a far higher price on us both if we do not try,' he said quietly.

Lowering her eyes at his rejoinder, she pushed a folded piece of paper into his hand.

'Take this,' she said softly. 'I trust these men to help you establish your credentials.'

Scent wafted from the paper on which was inscribed, in her copperplate hand, two names.

Alexander Fairfax.

A white man, he thought.

The other was a solitary Christian name — Zachariah.

Perchance a slave, he thought.

Irked by the thought of a fettered man, he nevertheless smiled his gratitude at her.

'These men have my utmost confidence, Jonas,' she said. 'During the uprising they saved my life a number of times. I will give you letters of introduction. Zachariah can read. Alexander Fairfax is a shipping agent — except he deals in contraband on the side. The man is a rascal but he has the ear of the influential, who unsurprisingly are his clients. But 'tis to our advantage that the man despises overseers. Because he was repeatedly flogged by his father and his tutors for his Latin verbs, he is instinctually revolted by brutality. Injustice turned him rebellious and he fell in with the runaways some years before the uprising. In his last letter, he said Zachariah had been sold to the Jamestown port authorities to work on the waterfront as a warehouse watchman. Unbeknown to his new owner, Zachariah was the scourge of that very waterfront during the uprising with the Shadows of Night Gang, through whom I made his acquaintance. Put your trust in these men and none other. I want you to return home safely.'

''Tis expected of your ilk to mix in like society with Fairfax,' he said. 'Zachariah? I ask myself, how did a white woman befriend a member of a notorious gang during a slave uprising? Methinks 'tis not the season to inquire. You are packed with surprises.'

Laughing out loud, she made no response.

'Your participation is encouraging,' he continued. 'Having trustworthy contacts will improve the odds. Methinks Zachariah can help me find a way to meet Freetown's runaways. Fairfax can attest to my Letters of Manumission. And both can help me evade the harbour watch and the powers that be.'

'My friends are dependable,' she said reassuringly. 'They will make certain you get all you need.' Raising her head, she whispered, 'I am heartened by your pluck, Jonas, for you return to the island that enslaved you.'

'Methinks 'tis merely audacity.'

Looking tenderly at him, she placed her hand softly on his knee.

His heart pounded.

From the neighbouring village of Speldhurst, the bells of St Mary's struck seven. A vespertine veil slipped across the windows, darkening the orchard and stranding the house. Twilight turned to night.

Chattering into the withdrawing room, maidservants put flame to the logs in the grate, the girandoles and the candle branches of a tripod perfume-burner. Soon traces of lavender and woodsmoke redolent with wellbeing drifted through the chamber.

Wreathed in smiles, the claret-cheeked housekeeper shuffled into the sallow-lit chamber.

'Supper is ready, Mistress Bradshaw,' said Mistress Bracegirdle. Giggling behind her hand, she added, 'Due to the devil's brew, the Parson is worse for wear. The poor man sends his regrets and remains in his cot. He hopes to join you for a beverage afterwards. Where will you take supper?'

'Why here in the withdrawing room, Mistress Bracegirdle,' Faith said, making for the table. 'Mister Guinea and I shall take supper in here.'

Still enveloped in the glow of the afternoon's unspoken affections, he was enchanted by her conversation during the repast.

At evening's end, he gazed at her with a heartfelt look.

'I am in your debt for your assistance,' he said.

'The gratitude is mine, Jonas,' she said, 'for you stimulate my wits and senses and have brought laughter back into my life.'

'Live well each day, Faith,' he said softly. 'The past becomes good memory and the morrow inherits hope.'

Taking his hands in hers, she squeezed and smiled.

His first day at Greensleeves had ended with undeclared feelings and high spirits. Bidding her good night, he retired buoyantly to his bedchamber.

Under azure skies they roamed the meadows and pastures of the Weald and picnicked with poetry in flaxen fields. Halcyon days slipped into weeks. Deptford's street cries faded away. His rustic respite was developing into more than he had expected.

In the early mornings they would meet for a constitutional to respire in the fragrance of the rose gardens. Disturbing ground-nesting corncrakes, they crossed the whispering meadows. Amid birdsong in a small wood, they strolled along dusty trails looking for flaws in his mission to Pertigua. Exercise paved the way for a hearty breakfast of tea, coffee or chocolate with wheat cakes and mutton cutlets, chased by biscuits and sherry. Freed briefly of responsibility for the chandlery, he felt at peace — so much so it seemed that nothing could mar his serenity.

On a warm sunny day while they were on a walk outside her estate, his composure clouded. In the low meadows he had been hearing news about the County and discussing John Locke's theories on liberalism. At the top of a hill near a copse of sloe berry trees, they encountered the cleric out on a stroll.

'A good day, Parson,' she said happily. 'I was just regaling Jonas about the fire in Chatham Dockyard.'

'I believe it was arson,' said the Parson, frowning, 'but they have not as yet apprehended the culprits.' Turning around, he pointed across the valley and asked, 'Did you know that Jeffrey Amherst hails from Sevenoaks over by that wood yonder?'

'And who might he be, Parson?' she asked.

'Commander-in-Chief of British forces in Canada,' said the Parson, sniffily puffing out his chest. 'He threatens Montreal as we speak and is expected to take it for England. It will end French rule in North America. Our local man is a great hero.'

'Is that not just wonderful, Jonas?' she asked breathlessly.

Closing his eyes in despair, Jonas sighed.

Deeming the admiration of a white invader to be virtually idolatrous, he felt his good humour draining away.

'Is this commander not just taking the land of another by force?' he asked tartly. 'When will the taking stop? The French take this. The Spanish take that. The English take it back. How many will have to die before the dying ends?'

Momentarily, his companions fell into an awkward silence.

'We are remiss, Jonas,' she said contritely. 'For the fact of your being here in England is the consequence of such action. I appreciate your indignation.'

'As do I,' said the Parson ruefully.

True to the Parson's promise, in the morning they boarded a carriage for the ancient cinque port of Winchelsea. Rumbling through the quaint villages of Peasmarsh, Rye Foreign, Playden and Rye, they arrived late in the afternoon at the bottom of a long steep hill. At the crest, the brackish odour of the sea breezed through the carriage. Jonas's nostrils twitched. Trundling along a cobbled street, he heard chatter.

'Jesus!' exclaimed a voice. 'Yer see 'im, Jasper?'

'See 'oo, Ned?'

'Black 'un in that swanky carriage,' said Ned. 'An' clad like a gentleman 'e were too.'

'I sees a nigger once on a stinkin' ship in Gravesend,' replied Jasper gloomily. 'An' 'e were in rags an' chains. Looked right sickly 'e did too.'

Squirming in his seat, the Parson remained tight-lipped.

Giving the cleric a wry smile and turning to the passing streets, Jonas was sarcastic.

'We journey into undeveloped climes, Parson,' he said.

Laughing out loud, the Parson clapped his hands.

Passing through Strand Gate, a medieval portal of the town, the carriage swung to the right and trundled past hawkers plying goods from barrows and doorways. Children playing a noisy game of stickball in the road scattered to let the carriage pass by. Headscarfed women chattered by shop fronts. Tottering out of taverns, fishermen lurched along the cobbled streets. Near a vintner's gate, porters were peeling wine casks from stockpiles and rolling them into the yard. Song, laughter and the spry notes of fiddles spilled from fleeting hostelries.

''Tis an engaging town, Parson,' he said heartily, 'situated in an uncommonly favourable position.'

'Old Winchelsea Town was destroyed by the sea, Mister Guinea,' said the Parson, impatient to flaunt his acquaintance with the locality. 'King Edward I personally provided land for a new site. On a shelf of land flanking the River Brede and below the northern side of Iham Hill, the town this day is founded on a gigantic shingle bank. 'Twas originally the principal port of Sussex.' Lowering his voice as if imparting a confidence, he added, 'In truth, 'tis a smuggler's sanctuary and a parish to my taste. 'Tis as well famed for beers from the Low Countries and an import of fine wines, which by the way are stacked under the streets in vaulted stone cellars. I am told there are above fifty of them. An average vault holds an unbelievable one hundred and twenty hogsheads.'

Shaking his head drolly at the cleric, he then rolled his eyes at the notion of such vast quantities of alcohol. Trust thou to be acquainted with the intoxicating locations hereabouts, he thought.

Soon, the carriage halted and was paid off. After visiting the market's merchants, at twilight they stopped on a narrow cobbled street outside a tavern sign-boarded The Prodigal Son.

Following the cleric into the tallow-lit timbered tavern, he saw a host of weathered white faces.

'From what I see, Parson, these men and women are more than knee-deep in smuggling,' he whispered. 'Piracy, slavery and other nefarious activities come to mind. Prodigal is an apt designation for this place.'

Before the Parson could respond, a voice cried out:

'Why kiss me blind-cheeks!'

'Not 'fore I kiss me woman's soft 'uns,' roared a gravelly voice.

Laughter bubbled around the hostelry.

Backed against the bespattered oak bar, old tars were fiddle-faddling with young salts and clod-hoppers. Shipowners sipped Bristol Milk and intrigue at the bench-tables with masters, merchants and lawyers.

Chatter died on his black appearance. Eyes examined every inch of his person. But, for a few ogling him with suspicion, he received affable nods from the majority. Hesitantly nodding back, he returned an uncertain smile. Then, as if a barrier had fallen, raucous laughter and rowdy banter resurged in the tavern.

Eyeballing a pretty brightly-dressed bosomy woman sporting a large red pimginnit on her cheek, the Parson raised his voice above the hubbub:

'You certainly turned heads, Mister Guinea, but mercifully none of concern. Come let us indulge in a firkin of the foul stuff.'

Jonas smirked.

Downing beers and Madeira throughout a jolly evening, he chattered with the tavern's dullards, babblers and boon-companions. Eventually, having gleaned much about Winchelsea he lurched groggily up the stairs for his cot, leaving the Parson and the innkeeper sitting on a bench propped back-to-back, leaning against the table.

Church bells pealed across the meadows. Rather than attending church with Faith and her household, Jonas stepped out into a glorious morning graced with a cloudless blue sky. Striding into the gardens with a copy of Thomas Gray's poetry, he began his fifth week at Greensleeves.

Wallowing in the fragrance of the rose gardens awaiting her return, he sat on a stone bench to read *Elegy Written in a Country Churchyard*. Catching sight of her through the tall red apothecary roses, he closed his volume. Blithely strolling up the path, she gave him a coy smile.

'Walk with me, Jonas.'

'My pleasure, Faith.'

Wading giddily through wildflower meadows, they laughed all the way to the grassy top of Stoneywish Hill. Far below them stretched a patchwork of green and yellow fields dotted with hay meadows, fallow land, wet grasslands, forests, roads, tracks, towns and villages. Following a dusty track speckled by fragrant agrimonies, white, blue and red columbines, bitter candytufts and wild basil, they wandered into a dark wood dappled with specks of lambent sunlight stabbing through the leafy branches.

'The silence is uncanny,' he said, gazing into the canopy of the wizened trees. 'Old world shadows hang heavy among these ancient oaks.'

Some distance along the track, they stopped on the edge of a glade and lay on their backs among grassy tussocks, gazing at the skies.

Sitting upright, he surveyed the wooded setting. Blackberries were on the turn. Plucking two ripened berries, he gave them to her. Placing one between her lips, she pushed the other gently into his mouth.

Pheasants scuttled across the track to stand rustling in the thickets. Thrush, wren and wood pigeon darted constantly from bough to bush. Through the cover of sagging branches, he glimpsed a herd of four-legged animals with offspring basking in sunshine.

'Fallow deer and fawns,' she said, peeking through the foliage. Rolling onto her back, she sighed, 'I do find these woods vitalising in your company, Jonas.'

Pointing at pale silvery-blue winged insects fluttering about the sunlit shafts, he whispered, 'Butterflies?'

'Chalkhill Blues,' she said.

'Such enchanting creatures.'

'Those delicate insects would not endure long in the florid grime and smoke of Deptford,' she said, giggling. Turning solemn, she lowered her voice:

'For a while I have wanted to be with you away from all others. To be in a setting perfect for what I have to say. This glade is ideal and rarely visited.'

'I have as well longed to be alone with you,' he said, gently taking her hand. 'Never before have I had such feelings. Was there something particular you wished to tell me?'

Sitting upright and staring fixedly at the woods, tears welled into her eyes.

'I want to share a confidence I have shared with none other than the Parson,' she said in a low voice. 'Promise not to say anything 'til I am done.'

'I will do as you ask.'

'I lost my heart to a slave in Pertigua,' she said, blinking back tears. 'He hailed from the village of Ake on the coast of Guinea. His name was Kayode. Long before he arrived on the plantation, I had already grown inured to the suffering of slaves. His bedraggled appearance was alarming at first sight, but I was somewhat captivated by his seething appeal. On my orders, on favourable nights I would send for him to come secretly to my summer-house. Over many months I fell in love with him. When first I set eyes on his bleeding wounds after a flogging, I was besieged by guilt and fury. So much so I confessed what had bled through my life since childhood —

the methodical enslavement of men, women and children by the rich of my countrymen. Sheer hate propelled me against Frederick Bradshaw's Tamarind Trees plantation. Remorse made me perpetrate my greatest act of vengeance — helping the escape of Kayode and his woman, Asabi, and two others—'

'What—'

'Let me finish, Jonas,' she chided.

'Pray continue.'

'Safe in the mountains with his woman,' she said, 'Kayode fomented and led the uprising you have heard about. Leading his runaway militia into winning encounters against the Redcoats, he virtually occupied the entire island. Defeated in a decisive battle with the Redcoats in the Bay of Thanksgiving, he was apprehended. In prison awaiting execution, following the charade of a trial, he took his own life. Thank God! We had a child — a fine-looking boy who did not once lay eyes on his father. In the dead of night my stepfather stole him from his cot. I had held my beloved newborn once only in my arms. Early next morning, in a secret auction, my stepfather sold him into slavery and robbed me of life itself. I shall never forgive him. Had I had strength enough to bury the hatchet in his head, I would have done mankind an act of kindness. He lives with my mother in Pertigua. I reside here, which suits me perfectly. But not a moment passes when I do not churn with grief for my stolen son. I have nursed grief from the instant he was taken.'

'Good heavens!' he exclaimed. 'You have shown not a trace that you have been so deeply hurt.'

Burying her face in her hands, she wept gut-wrenching sobs.

Putting his arm around her shoulders, he dabbed her eyes with his handkerchief.

'Now I understand why you keep your own counsel,' he said softly. 'Now I too yearn to learn the whereabouts of your son. Let us seek him out together.'

'I would like that,' she whispered.

'We need a strategy,' he said.

He knew his words were hollow — it was all he could think to say. He suspected it would be nigh impossible to locate her son through the fog of slave transactions that were intended to confuse or leave no trace. Unvarying grief had been her constant companion. Hostility surged through him.

'Your stepfather must be wormed with corruption to sell your son,' he fumed, and then he softened. ''Tis now I see why at times you appear somewhat elsewhere. As God is my witness, I swear to bring joy and laughter into your life.'

Caressing his cheek, her heart beat hard.

'I believe you will,' she said quietly.

Seven days later they shared a candlelit supper in the withdrawing room. Following a meal of drunken cider chicken with honey, steamed greens, mashed potatoes and trifle, they retired to the sofa with filled glasses.

A pony-tailed Parson shuffled into the chamber.

'Brandy, Parson — fresh from Augier Freres,' she said, pointing at a stoppered cruciform decanter amid the supper debris on the table. 'I trust you feel somewhat improved?'

'Indeed I do, Mistress Faith,' he said, tossing brandy down his throat. 'So much so that while I lay petitioning for Our Lord's absolution, I was struck by a pertinent thought.'

Jonas gave him a quizzical look. 'May we share your reflections, Parson?'

Taking a swig of brandy, the Parson replied, 'Can ye stomach the ramblings of an erstwhile priest of the slave trade?'

Knowing the clergyman to be a savant of the trade, Jonas smiled. 'To be sure we can, Parson,' he said. 'You have the undivided interest of two pupils.'

'Beseeching Parliament on the abolition of slavery has proved fruitless,' said the Parson. 'Many Whigs, Tories and gentry alike make handsome profits from their slave holdings. Without compunction, they will eliminate anyone interfering with their trafficking.'

'Parliament must support our cause,' she said adamantly. 'But until the Commons declares to the contrary, slavery will remain lawful.'

'In my ponderings,' said the Parson, 'I thought that before we sally into Pertigua's waters, we should reflect on the works of John Wesley.'

Frowning at Jonas and turning to the cleric, she asked, 'What made you think of Wesley?'

''Tis not just hearsay that great men often get forgotten,' the Parson said. 'Consequently, Wesley's activities must be recorded lest an opportunist purloin the acclaim that is his due.'

'John Wesley has my admiration, Parson,' said Jonas. 'My friend, Francis Barber, gave me a volume of his works. I daresay Faith feels likewise.'

Nodding her concurrence at him, a titillating smile played on her lips.

A burning sensation assailed him. Smiling bashfully at her, he turned back to the clergyman.

'I am certain we shall not forget the great man, Parson,' he said solemnly.

'Wesley disregards ridicule and lambasts the hard of hearing,' said the Parson, ignoring the overt chemistry in the chamber that clearly excluded him. 'Since his visit to England's plantations in our colony of Georgia in the Americas, he has waged war against the slave trade. In inclement conditions, the man has carried on horseback his anti-slavery message to ports in the kingdom.'

Downing a swig of brandy, Jonas raised his hand. 'What difference has Wesley's intervention made to the abolition of slavery, Parson?'

'Thanks to the spate of slave rebellions on the plantations and Wesley's rousing speeches to the citizenry of several ports,' replied the Parson, 'slavery teeters on the brink of the political agenda. But igniting an outcry against the slave trade cannot be accomplished by one man alone. 'Twill take countless shoulders to turn Abolition into an Act of Parliament. Come the day when England's slave trafficking is abolished, it will be largely due to the efforts of the slaves themselves and men like John Wesley. I wonder if England will remember that?'

'I as well believe that slavery will be abolished,' said Jonas matter-of-factly. 'Time is against the trade. Ultimately, the slaves will regain their freedom. And we will play our part.'

'But how could England forget John Wesley?' she asked.

Snorting, the Parson replied:

''Tis a habit of these troubled isles, Mistress Faith, that when a moral issue rears its head, the champion who hoists the standard heralds the change. And as a rule, he gets elbowed aside by the opportunist who snatches the acclaim. Is our Parliament not infested with opportunists? Barring a moral change of heart by slave-owners, abolition of slavery demands a political solution. Ergo, the credit for abolition will eventually be cabbaged by a politician.'

Breaking into a broad smile, Jonas asked, 'Has it not been said that slavery is the bedfellow of the rich?'

'On the issue of slavery, Parson,' she warned, 'Parliament plays with fire.'

'Sniff the prevailing wind, Mistress Faith,' said the Parson. 'The Commons is replete with men who profit from torching the hopes of others. Principally, the Members hold proxies for those with sizeable property or wealth — they who are entitled to vote.'

'Great heavens, Parson, I did not know any of this!' she cried.

Masking his surprise at the cleric's revelation with a puckered brow, Jonas asked, 'Exactly how many are entitled to vote, Parson?'

'About two hundred thousand men. Women, of course, have no vote.'

Stunned by the Parson's reply, Jonas was aghast.

'Mother of God!' she exclaimed. 'Two hundred thousand is but a fragment of our population of about seven million souls.'

'Aye, Mistress Faith, that is so,' the Parson chuckled. 'In effect that fragment, as you put it, decides England's trade, its wars, its politics and its fate. And it is those same men who have been racking up profits from African enslavement on the plantations. Why! The lure of profit for the Members of the Commons has spawned an aversion to even hearing about abolition.'

'The effrontery of the gentry, Members of the Commons and the shipping owners,' she said acidly. 'It is they who took it upon themselves to sail to the shores of Guinea, furnish the inhabitants with bibles and then enslave them. What next? Give them more bibles and take their land?'

'In time,' said the Parson flippantly.

'The longest road...' muttered Jonas.

The bells of St Mary's struck midnight.

Entering the chamber, the housekeeper said, 'If you not be needing me, Mistress Bradshaw, I bid thee all a very good night.'

'That will be all, Mistress Bracegirdle. I thank you muchly for a truly appetising supper. I bid thee a decidedly good night.'

'Good night, Mistress Bracegirdle,' the gentlemen chorused.

Rising to his feet and raising his goblet, the Parson rendered a garbled address to them and his 'beloved' cot. Bidding them goodnight, his pony-tail unravelled. In his black frock coat and wisps of shoulder-length silvery hair, he cut a biblical figure lurching towards his bedchamber.

Shortly afterwards, Jonas also took his leave and stepped into the candlelit hallway. Faith quickly followed, brushing past him and mounting the stairs. Outside her bedchamber, she pressed her lips lightly on his cheeks, mouthed 'goodnight' before closing the door teasingly behind her.

In thrall to her bodily odours, he waited, momentarily nursing the ache in his loins. About to enter his bedchamber, he heard her door latch rattle. Turning around, her door was now slightly ajar. His breathing grew shallow. Crossing the passageway, he stepped inside and fastened the door quietly behind him.

Moonlight streamed through the casement windows, illuminating a carved four-poster with drapes tied back and her contours silhouetted beneath the bedclothes.

A whisper danced from the shadows. 'Come, Jonas.'

Speedily disrobing, he slid beneath the covers. Her soft skin was torrid.

'I am hungered,' she whispered, sliding her hand across his back. Suddenly her fingers found a long raised weal scoring his shoulders blades. Stiffening abruptly, she fingered the wound and drew him closer. He said nothing.

Rolling onto her back, she cupped his face in her hands.

'My famine is ended,' she breathed.

'And mine,' he whispered, tenderly kissing her.

Her lips yielded. Her tongue urged him against her. He touched her silken mound. Her breathing quickened. Through downy hair he stroked her until her back arched and she slipped lovingly beneath him. In amorous throes for an age, they lingered on the edge of a mesmeric haze, 'til at last the heat had risen. Stifling her cries with her hand, she shuddered intensely. Groans burst spontaneously from his lips and he quaked. Sweating and breathless, they collapsed in waning, heady spasms. The marrow in his bones melted. With her head over his heart, giddy waves of love flowed through them.

A Cheated Life Crafts Nightmares

New Freetown
12 December 1760
05.00 hrs

In the early morning sun, a cerulean sky yawned over a clear wide horizon. Standing inside a cave within the rugged cliffs of the northern peninsula, Asabi eyed the slow sporadic wing-beats of frigate birds. In the fresh north-easterly, gulls, guillemots and shearwaters were plucking sprats from transparent waters. On an ebbing tide thirty feet below her feet, Atlantic rollers crashed relentlessly against rocky protrusions and the lichened cliffs of Freetown, the fortified cave of the runaway stronghold. Mists gathered where the sun was vaporising the moisture of first light. Shimmering heat was rising.

Sighing and wiping her brow, she sat on the rim of the cliff-face entrance to the grotto, dangling her feet above the waters, her jerkin and breeches rippling in the breeze. Behind her in the towering cavern, the runaways were emerging from their shacks. Dolefully dropping her head, she stared fiercely into the waves.

'Since you gone, Kayode, runaways make me Captain of Freetown,' she muttered. 'Not been easy alone. I now got chance to go back to Ake. Ship cannot take all. What them do I leave behind? Runaways trust me. My heart say I mus' go. The burden hangs heavy. Runaways' mus' find a new Captain. I want to go home. I mus' see Ake. Just now I pray them twelve slaves died quick…'

An arm settled around her shoulders. Abisogun, her eight-year-old son, squatted beside her.

'You fretting, Ma?'

Giving him a watery smile, she cupped his face lovingly.

'You know me, Abi,' she said. 'Sad 'cos I get news 'bout them slaves caught plotting in Sidford.'

'What happen to them?'

'They dead,' she said quietly, choking back her fury.

'Dead?' he cried. 'How them get catched?'

'They bin betrayed,' she said bitterly, 'an' they get caught with muskets. What you think, son?'

'Them dead, Ma.'

Suddenly, Truelove slumped down beside them.

'Dead?' he asked. 'Who dead?'

'Slaves from Sidford caught with muskets. You know how they die?'

'Them pared,' he said tersely, angrily shaking his head. 'Them took two long days bleeding to death. Whitey now got big problems.'

'Huh! Then you not hear what Redcoats done,' she said scornfully.

'What? Whitey got no problem?'

'Slave called Jacky get angry 'bout what happen to his friends in Sidford,' she said. 'He take field slaves from dead men's plantation on a hunt for revenge. They ransacked the Great House on the next plantation, chop up the owner an' his wife an' kill his overseers. They set fire to a storekeeper in Jamestown, steal muskets, gunpowder an' food from Great Houses on two more plantations an' killed them in their cots. Redcoats mash up the gang, grab Jacky an' butcher his up-rising. Slaves were forced to watch them give him a big licking in the barracoon. Then they hack him up with cutlasses. Striped with cuts, they hanged him right away for leading Jacky's Revolt. 'Cept for that small slip-up, Jacky do well.'

'Jacky get hanged, Ma? How he do well?'

Reminded of her son's immaturity by his question, she just smiled.

'Your papa in you, boy,' she said, putting her arm affectionately around his shoulders. 'That what he would have said. If he be here, he would tell you what I tell you now. Forget not my words, Abi. To stay free, we fight or we hide. Fight only your enemies my son. Forgive them if they will let you. White man too frightened to let we forgive him. We too pained an' angry to forgive. So we fight to stay free. 'Fore he die, Jacky give the white man grief on the plantations. He mash up his mills, set fire to his cane fields an' burn down two 'o his Great Houses. An' 'fore he get cut up an' hanged, he take many white men down. That is why he done so well.'

'I not forget what you say, Ma,' he said admiringly.

Piercing shrieks echoed above her head.

Raising her eyes into the cavern's lofty ceiling, she scowled at the bats.

'Flying rats!' she hissed. 'Filthy things come back to hang about. Your papa smoke them out long long ago. We smoke them out again.'

Putting a fatherly arm around her son's shoulders, Truelove spoke softly.

'Let me tell you story 'bout whitey, Abi,' he said. 'Redcoats got big reason to catch Jacky quick. Them afraid Jacky's runaways start big rebellion like what happened hereabouts when you still a baby. It start when your pa an' ma lead a runaway army an' make uprising. Fighting put slave 'gainst whitey. We take the island. Then we fall out with each other an' lose it. Redcoats take back the island. I tell you this, Abi, our fight be so bloody it shock Redcoats so bad they now very scared. Cutting up Jacky bad 'fore they string him up was to teach slaves not to do like him. Slaves will never give up fight to be free.'

Nodding he understood, her son lowered his head with an approving smile.

My boy a quick learner like his father, she thought.

'Set eyes in Bamboo Bay to watch for Jacky's runaways,' she said abruptly.

'I set eyes,' said Truelove.

'Three with muskets go with me to Lake Disappointment,' she said, 'to keep lookout for Jacky's runaways an' the Mongoose Gang.'

'I get Tomba,' said Truelove, rising to his feet.

Raising her hand sharply, she snapped, 'Wait man! I got message for Tomba.'

Flopping back down, Truelove and Abi leaned eagerly towards her.

'Zachariah send word from Jamestown,' she said quietly.

Slapping his thigh, Truelove smiled. 'What 'im say?'

Casually looking out to the horizon, she turned back to him.

'Zachariah hear from Fairfax the shipping agent,' she said, changing the subject. 'I heard they been stretching the necks of Jacky's runaways along the waterfront. Bloody chaos on Promenade Road.'

Scowling deeply, Truelove groaned, 'Slaves live fighting to live.
Them bleed from time them born into living white hell. What Zachariah say 'bout we?'

'Fairfax talk 'bout a bold plan.'

'Bold plan?'

'Plan so stupid it can work.'

Turning away, her son giggled into his hand.

'Fairfax said men been plotting in London to send a ship called
Redemption to Pertigua. When she leaves Jamestown, she sail to bay
east of Freetown to anchor. We board her and sail to coast of Guinea.
What you say to that man? Now is that not stupid?'

Looking directly at her, Truelove's eyes glazed with apathy.

Scowling, she leaned towards him.

'You been here forty years an' you not want to go home, Truelove?'
she asked. 'Since you sold at Auction House when you child, you
been cutting cane all your born days. It been six years since you break
out of plantation. It be so you have all you know and all you need
here in Freetown. Now you act like that land called Guinea find no
welcome in the heart of her stolen son.'

Closely eyeing her, Truelove held suspicion in his voice. 'Them
send ship? Who send ship? Who them be?'

Somebody think the man be forced to eat shit, she thought.

'Them,' she said forcefully, 'be white men who say they had it with
slave-owners. Slavery offend their God. So they plan to ship slaves
back to the coast of Guinea. They start with we.'

'Why them tek so long to know slavery offend them God? Where
we meet this ship?'

'Ship anchor soon in Deception Bay,' she replied. 'We row out
from Heddon's Mouth. It out of sight and got quiet waters. Good for
small boats. I send word 'bout Deception Bay to Zachariah.'

'How many this ship take?'

'Twelve!'

Pressing his lips together, Truelove stayed mute.

Turning a motherly eye on her son, she smiled.

Rapt in the unbelievable exchange and awaiting his reply, the boy was straining on hands and knees towards Truelove. In his tensed cat-like posture, she could see his father, Kayode, 'cat of the forest' as he was called by the villagers of Ake.

'You so like your papa, Abi,' she said. 'You quick like he. You read like he. You got nerve like he. An' you free like he.'

Smiling bashfully, Abi kept his eyes on Truelove.

Grunting brusquely, Truelove turned to the horizon.

Yanking him around to face her, she shook him.

'Listen man,' she pleaded. 'Pull your years from the grave of this land! Eat yam from the soil of Guinea with the Yoruba. Eat meat wi' your own people.'

'I eat meat an' yam an' den do what?' he snarled. 'What more me backside do on that coast?'

Scowling at him, she snapped, 'What your backside do roun' here?'

'Not 'member where me from on that coast. Me spen' so more years slavin' in cane fields than all the time me spen' in motherland.'

Her mouth crashed open. His defiance vexed her. Bending forwards, she narrowed her eyes.

'You born in Guinea, Truelove,' she said irately. 'Not like you, them born on this island not know their blood tongue or blood family. An' they would not know the motherland, even if they saw her. In time to come, children of these very white men may reap an angry harvest from children o' them who 'ave never seen their blood land.'

'Me stay here.'

Irritated by his quarrelsome attitude, she retorted, 'You not from roun' here, Truelove!'

'Me not know a soul on the coast of Guinea!'

'Huh! You not free to choose roun' here,' she countered. 'Quit this wicked island. Come wi' Abi an' me. Wade in waters on the free shores of Guinea. Is you he?'

Doggedly shaking his head, he wailed, 'Me too old to go back to that place! Got nuff freedom 'ere in Freetown!'

'You stay here — you die here!'

'Me die wi' friends,' he said brusquely. 'Me live in Freetown! Me got friends in Freetown. Me die in Freetown!'

A galling awareness rattled her wits. Even her son's disbelief was evident. Consumed by vexation at the threatened loss of a precious companion, she lowered her eyes.

'Bidding you farewell will hurt me, Truelove,' she said softly. 'Since Kayode gone I let no man lay a hand on me. Six years I sleep alone. In the last month you touch me deep. We grow close. I want you with us on shores of Guinea for fresh start. We build a house together and—'

'You believe them bring ship call *Redemption*?'

'I believe it 'cos I want to. Some call it hope.'

It was a blind leap of faith and she knew it. Only her pride had ensured her survival on the plantations. In the wake of her kidnapped years on the plantation, faith in her senses was all she had left.

'Come man!'

Leaning darkly towards her, Truelove lowered his voice, 'When runaways hear Zachariah's plan, them will stampede gangplank. Many get cut or killed. An' it tek only one who don't make it onto ship, Asabi, to get so vexed he run an' tell whitey. We mus' tell only twelve. Tomba mus' be told. The man 'as never stopped aching for the motherland. He frantic to go home an' can keep a secret.'

Truelove was resolute. So was she.

'I hear what you say man,' she said, rising to her feet. 'I go to set watch at Lake Disappointment for Jacky's runaways. I pick out three from here, an' take Abi. We pick six more.'

'Six,' he repeated. 'I make list an' tell Tomba. He meet you at Lake Disappointment.'

Walking glumly away to the back of the tapering cavern, Truelove climbed through the roof into sunlight. He set off across the scrub plateau above.

Looking down, she saw the tide was out. Ambling further into the cave near the huddle of shacks, she sought out three friends for her scouting party — two men and a woman with muskets. Trailed by her son, she led the way from the cavern's edge down the sisal ladder onto the apron of sand. Traversing the driftwood and boulder-strewn shore in an easterly direction, she arrived at her marker and headed inland.

Crossing the swamp in the heat of the early afternoon, she trudged into the abandoned island encampment of Lake Disappointment. Dispersing the three lookouts and her son around the camp, she made for her deserted shack alone.

Swiping away the cobwebs of the long-legged spider lacing the entrance of the makeshift dwelling, she entered its musty confines and dropped to her haunches. Tears blurred her vision. Images of Kayode swirled before her eyes.

'We destroyed a nightmare an' break free,' she intoned softly. 'You make rebellion an' your spirit lives in our memories. *Olorun* take you to Him too early. Your son an' me He leave alone an' fatherless. I miss you so, Kayode.'

Through flimsy walls she heard brushwood crackling under heavy feet. Wiping her eyes and stepping outside, she was joined by her son and the lookouts.

Sporting a broad smile, a bare-chested Tomba came from behind his old shack. Years had fallen from his face, as if his soul had been reborn. Recalling his wretched condition in the dungeons of Cape Coast Castle, she smiled at the rejuvenated man she saw before her.

Turning to the lookouts, she said, 'Tomba been listening to Truelove.'

'He glowing like the sun, Ma.'

'Big man look fresh,' sniggered a lookout.

'Stay here an' keep your eyes open,' she said, walking towards Tomba. 'I have words for the big man.'

'*E'kasan*, Asabi! - Good afternoon Asabi,' shouted Tomba. 'Home to Guinea! Home! Home! Home to Guinea!'

'*E'kasan*, Tomba,' she shouted. 'We go as one!'

E'kasan is the first Yoruba word I have heard him utter in a very long time, she thought. Yoruba too feels strange on my lips.

Tears had fashioned tracks down Tomba's dry, weather-beaten cheeks. Through all the painful years she had known him, she had not once seen him shed a tear. Gone from his face was the runaway marque, that haunted and hunted look that springs from constant anxiety, continuously on his toes through six challenging years in Freetown. Flaunting rebirth from ear to ear, he was clearly wracked with joy. If he could find his way back to his village, to his blood family from the shores of Guinea, his property would still belong to him according to Yoruba law, despite his ten year absence.

'A cheated life crafts nightmares,' said Tomba.

'Live your dreams 'fore you turn to rage,' she warmed.

'White men take my years, Asabi. An' them twist an' twist a dagger through my soul. Chop off these arms if ever again you catch me trading with slavers. These past years I cut cane from can-see-light to can-see-dark to pay for selling my people to slave traders. *Olorun* give me second chance. I go back to tell the Yoruba that their rulers sell them to slavers who also kidnap them when they want. Guinea's kings an' rich white men 'ave turned the coast of Guinea into a slaver's paradise. To sit in the bosom of my family will ease my pain. By the end of my days, it will ease my hate. Now we talk, my sister.'

Taking his face gently between her hands, she looked affectionately into his eyes.

'Hear me Tomba,' she urged gently. 'When we leave this wicked island, long dark nights will draw to a close behind us. Wide horizons, a full belly and laughter lie ahead. When we set foot on the red soil of our motherland, life begins for a second chance. I will be at your side on the shores of Guinea.'

Glancing down at Abi, Tomba smiled and pulled his cheek caringly.

'Night get dark just 'fore dawn, Asabi,' he said. 'Come sunrise we be in Guinea an' we go—'

'We got sixty in Freetown,' she said, stopping him mid-sentence. 'The *Redemption* take twelve. If we tell our people 'bout ship to Guinea, we won't get talk 'bout what we do next, we get a stampede. Them who don't make it aboard the *Redemption* can turn informer. Truelove set to stay in Freetown. As well as we six here, we tell six we know well — six who can keep their mouths shut.'

Given their familiarity with the inhabitants of Freetown, with their factional and sometimes fractious friendships, a list of six names was speedily agreed.

'We now wait to hear from Zachariah where *Redemption* be,' she said, raising her head. 'I pray it be not too long.'

Love and Hate

Beaumaris Great House
Turtle Island
16 December 1760

The day was hot, dry and glorious under a deep blue sky. Hummingbirds darted in and out of red trumpet flowers along the dusty rutted track.

Appraising the lush landscape over the lacquered sides of the yellow landau, Matthew Fleming sighed with smug satisfaction.

'Wood smoke and fresh cane reeks of profit, Mary,' he said.

'Particularly when one does not have to exert oneself, Matthew,' she replied, giggling.

Owned entirely by his family since the late 1620s, Turtle Island was the smallest of the three-island Pertiguan archipelago. Nearing the Great House in the bright afternoon, everything seemed just as it should be. Primped in fitted coat and breeches the shade of sliced pomegranates and finished by a white muslin cravat, he felt at ease. Smiling at his sister, arresting in her rose silk gown, he turned idly to watching slaves in the fields.

Flicking his whip over glistening torsos, a horse-backed overseer yelled, 'Get them lazy backs into some grind!'

Sweating buckets in Grace Fields, the grunts, groans and disagreeable stench of the First Gang made him reel away. Preferring to wallow in the top notes of her eau de cologne, he ran his eyes affectionately over her. His twenty-two-year-old younger sibling was a red-lipped, flaxen-haired damsel who had many a moneyed rake vying for her favours. Smiling at her mildly sozzled condition, he shook a brotherly head.

The carriage halted before the frescoed portico of Beaumaris Great House. Assisted by house slaves, they descended from the carriage onto the drive. Flushed from a planters' muster in the creaky Pilgrim's Rest on the southernmost peninsula of Little Pertigua, they linked arms and wobbled through the house into the jade withdrawing room. The Huygens long-pendulum clock struck three.

'A distinguished gathering, Mary,' he said with a skewed smile, reaching for the brandy in the mahogany cellaret. 'The ladies were particularly charming, don't you think? Madeira?'

'Charming, did I hear you say? Madeira? Aye. That woman was a brazen hussy!'

'Harriet Beaufort? Pray why?'

'The coquettish little madam flaunts cornucopias of suggestion.'

'Suggestion? I know not what you mean.'

Tossing back a swig to avoid divulging his interest, he then frowned at her. 'Harriet is couth is she not?'

'She is couth, the instant she has identified her prey.'

'I find her engaging. Methinks—'

A grunt from the daybed turned their heads.

His eyes fell on their pater's tricorn hat; the one lovingly braided along the edge by their mother. Clad in his favoured burgundy knee-length fitted coat and black velvet breeches, the sexagenarian Randolph Fleming was sprawled asleep on the elongated daybed clutching a letter.

Rolling his eyes in feigned despair, Matthew put his hands on hips and shook his head.

Walking forwards to her wakening father with a deep frown, Mary said, 'You are here, sir? You were to take tea with Squire Hathaway. By your haste I believed it was important.'

Sinking onto the daybed, she clasped her father's hand. He smiled.

'Aye, lass,' said her father softly. His brow furrowed. 'I was about to leave when a messenger delivered a shocking intelligence. At once, I dispatched a man to Squire Hathaway with my apologies. I sent another with a letter to Governor Curzon on Pertigua, alerting him of a treasonable state of affairs. Pondering on the options for an apposite response, I dropped off. Did you know that Curzon will receive my dispatch by this night? Twenty years past, that letter would have taken a week.'

Disturbed by her father's uncharacteristic anxiety, she let go his hand and stroked her temples.

'Where is Mother?' she asked.

'Visiting the Hendersons in Jamestown,' he replied. 'She returns on the morrow. Fret not lass, Mother shall hear it all from me.'

Mistaken for a coxcomb, Matthew's clear brown eyes, round head and manicured sideburns belied his fervour and ruthlessness. A tall, slim, unremarkable-looking twenty-five-year-old, he had for all practical purposes been given the management of the Augustfields estates. Aided in the day-to-day running of the estate by his beloved sister, he held much confidence in her counsel.

Provoked by her unease, he asked, 'May I enquire the nature of the intelligence that has you indisputably troubled, sir?'

Sitting bolt upright, waving his letter angrily, the old man blurted out, 'That blasted secretary seeks to outwit us!'

Slumping into a chair, Matthew exclaimed, 'Jonas Guinea?'

'Aye, Matthew. That insolent secretary, Jonas Guinea, looms large. You will remember that I first crossed swords with him in Deptford, London a few years back in the home of that virulent evangelist, Thomas Beecham. At present, Guinea is a principal member of that irksome League Against the Importation of Negroes from the Coast of Guinea.'

Grimacing at the name, Matthew said, 'After what you have so painfully related of that meeting, sir, 'twould be difficult to forget that cocksure nigger and that do-gooding League of Christian evangelists.'

Quietly, Mary interjected, 'Is Jonas Guinea not a freeman and a partner of Thomas Beecham, Chandlers?'

Matthew smiled at the precision of his sister's intelligence — her trademark.

'You are typically right, Mary,' chuckled the old man. 'The nigger is indeed a partner of Thomas Beecham, Chandlers. I hearsay he was appointed soon after Mister Beecham had passed away. In all my life I have never heard the outrageous like of it — a nigger dressed like an English gentleman, pretending to be the equal of white men and heading the board of a respectable English company.'

Furtively raising his eyebrows in jest at his sister, Matthew smiled.

'Hatched no doubt by that League,' vented the old man splenetically. 'I believe Jonas Guinea to be one of the prime movers of this duplicitous scheme. The blackguards' plan to dispatch a vessel to Pertigua to embark runaways from some anonymous cove and then spirit them from under our very noses back to the coast of Guinea. 'Tis that not bald-faced treachery! What should we do about this false-hearted little plot? I say we catch them red-handed with the goods. At the same time, we shall lay hands on some principals of this little League. And I have it on good authority that Mister Guinea himself will be aboard the vessel!'

'Great heavens!' Matthew exclaimed. 'Are there no depths to which that nigger and this League will sink? Methinks Thomas Beecham bequeathed a goodly number of his shares to Guinea as a parting shot at us. Simultaneously, he bolstered the membership of the League. That being the case, they surely intend to dislocate our trade? Is that not their stated aim? I see no other interpretation. Demand an urgent meeting of the West Indies Sugar Cartel, sir. May I know how you came by this compendium of treachery?'

'A dispatch from Harry Blake,' replied the old man. 'The man is still proprietor of Blake's Coffeehouse in Eastcheap, an uncommonly leaky part of London. Despite a life of high jinks and mercantile skulduggery in cahoots with the politicians and insurance brokers, my dear old friend repudiates retirement. His intelligence on the intrigues between shipping agents continues to be above reproach. A member of Bootles, Harry is well placed to eavesdrop on market intelligence and all manner of scurrilous secrets among the indiscreet of both establishments.'

'How are we to trounce this League, sir?' asked Mary.

'To defeat the likes of the League, Mary, we ought to do like-wise. Send out men to flush out information. Someone in James-town must know something. Find out who is in the know. As for putting an end to the Atlantic slave trade, the efforts of the League will not alter the present state of affairs. That would necessitate thousands of vessels sailing constantly back and forth for years. As well, the acquiescence and connivance of the plantation owners in England and all her colonies would be required. Trust me, my children, the government and the cartels will not ever sanction that!'

'Blake has served you well, sir,' said Matthew. 'To elicit the name of the League's vessel and its estimated time of arrival, we need men with persuasive talents in Jamestown's taverns. And in the boarding houses to press the harlots for loose pillow talk. What with the slubberdegullions loafing around the Careenage, finding out shouldn't prove impossible. Find the name of the vessel and we find the runaways. When she is set to sail with the runaways embarked, we will seize the evangelists. Catch them in the act of helping slaves fleeing from their lawful owners. Hmmm. 'Tis fortunate free rum tends to loosen the tongues of Jack Tars.'

'In for the jugular, aye brother?' jested Mary.

''Tis indeed advantageous, Matthew,' said the old man, rubbing his hands gleefully. 'And 'tis undeniably to our advantage. Nevertheless, whoever else you snatch, make certain you take Jonas Guinea. That nigger must pay for the way he cast his black eyes over me. Servitude exacted with the lash should amend his pretentious manner. Regrettably, the nigger has venom in his tail. He will be carrying Letters of Manumission.'

Snorting, Matthew thumped the arms of his chair.

'Easily burned and rubbished!' he said. 'Without his letters, who will know him to be a free man by the blackness of his hide on a slave island? To our citizens he will just be another anonymous nigger!'

Shooting a pretended scowl at him, Mary then giggled into her hand.

Exploding into hoarse laughter, the old man degenerated into a coughing fit. Crimson-faced and chortling, he pulled himself together to further hearken to his son.

'A lone vessel once over the horizon, sir,' said Matthew conspiratorially, 'will be difficult and costly to keep track of in the immensity of the Atlantic. Giving chase is a chancy option. Methinks the instant the League's vessel is sighted, we block her escape from these shores — even if we have to blow her out of the water. We need to muster eyes to keep watch for her. On the other hand, even if the said vessel evades the Protective Squadron's naval patrols and reaches the coast of Guinea, the endeavour can never reverse England's trade in slaves. Weighed against the countless transactions of England's trade, the League's mission will be but a drop in the ocean. Would you not agree, dear sister?'

'Matthew's summing up is sound, sir,' said Mary. Following a pause, clearly contrived to register the consequence of her counsel, she was forthright:

'Forego your difference with Jonas Guinea, sir. Apprehending the perpetrators of this plot is our primary objective. 'Twould be folly to lose sight of what must be accomplished, which is to thwart the League's efforts to make off with our property. Methinks Guinea may well prove to be more trouble than he is worth.'

'You were not in Deptford, Mary!' snapped the old man. 'You did not witness the insolence with which he addressed me. His kind give me great cause for concern. As God is my witness that nigger portends the morrow. Just one like Guinea among our subversive cane-cutters could prove disastrous. Nay! His skin and astute employ of the English language has thrust him into a key position in this League; thus he must remain a primary target. On this subject, I am adamant. I intend to end his gilded steps through refined withdrawing rooms and stick his black snout in cane and molasses. Aye. I hear what you both say as regards the League's pathetic efforts. Not as much as a veritable plank shall sail from these shores laden with a single runaway. You hear me. Not one plank!'

'Vex not, sir,' said Matthew, winking at his sister. 'Not a plank shall leave these shores.'

To mollify and avert a clash with the old goat, he thought, I'd best reiterate his stipulation that the nigger will be a prime target.

'And while we are about it, Mary, we shall make certain Jonas Guinea is apprehended. Brandy, sir?'

Concurring with her brother, she nodded at him with a furtive smirk dimpling her cheeks.

Contented by what entered his ears, the old man sighed and leaned back with a cold look.

The Die is Cast

A haloed crescent was darting through slate-grey clouds. Frost, snow, ice and freezing temperatures welcomed Jonas Guinea into the drab river-port of Gravesend. Rattling over snow-covered cobblestoned streets, the draughty carriage was making for the adjoining Fort Gardens Dockyard. He had shared the long-winded company of Mister Puddlewick's shipping agent, Berry Pridmore, a Bridgewater man, rotund and rubicund with blue eyes and mousey hair. The man had been tasked by the Captain of the *Redemption* to fetch him.

From the entrance of Fort Gardens, he spotted the *Redemption* lying in between the barques *Annabella* and *Good Hope*. By the light of the moon and the dockyard oil-lamps, the carriage drew up alongside the vessel. Alighting from the lukewarm carriage onto frozen cobbles, he was muffed up to the eyes. Snowflakes soon began settling on his cloaked shoulders.

''Tis a wretched setting, Mister Pridmore.'

'You'll soon be in sunny climes, Mister Guinea.'

'Difficult to envisage such heat by what I feel hereabouts.'

He scanned the waterfront restively.

Like jagged teeth, icicles hung in battalions from eaves and door-ways, derricks and mooring cables. Frozen fishing nets draped be-tween posts. Due to the gagging stench and gases of rotting fish and seaweed, his eyes began to water. Gazing up at the men bent over the lofty silhouetted yards of the *Redemption*, he was awed. He had arrived at the point of no return. Lowering his eyes and scanning her snow-streaked ratlines, her capstan, deck gear and pitch-black hull, he felt his legs briefly buckle.

'All hands on deck,' a gruff voice shouted. 'Haul in them forrard an' after breast ropes.'

His ocean-going abode had been well-described by her owner, Mister Puddlewick. Of one hundred and ten feet in length, twenty-two feet wide and fifteen feet draft, she was a quirky three-masted wooden barque with fore-and-aft sails on the aftermost mast and square sails on all other masts. In the early morning light her crew were preparing for sea. He gulped. It had been agreed that he would help work the vessel only if the need arose. Thank God, he had thought. It only now dawned on him that that 'need' would most likely arise in gale force winds when the ship was imperilled.

An icy gust sent the falling snow into a squall, momentarily reducing visibility. He shifted uneasily. He was calmed by the West Country brogue in his ear.

'Right, Mister Guinea,' said the shipping agent. 'Let me help you with your gear. I figure you be wanting to report to the old man right away.'

Frowning at the agent, he asked, 'Who is the old man, Mister Pridmore?'

'That be the Captain, Mister Guinea,' replied the shipping agent, grinning. 'I will take you to the sea-god.'

With the letter from Faith Bradshaw tucked in his pocket and his mahogany box firmly under one arm, he picked up his gear. I gave her my word, he thought. I would open her letter only when the *Redemption* stands well out to sea.

Lifting one anxious foot after another, he fell in step with the agent.

Given her eleventh-hour counsel, bidding farewell to Mistress Beecham had been distressing.

'Keep these close, Jonas,' she had finally said, pushing into his hands a shallow box of varnished mahogany.

Glistening within on a claret-velvet cushion lay a pair of brass-barrelled flintlock pistols. Prising them out, he inspected the finely crafted firearms. On the top of each barrel was the inscription 'Heylin

Cornhill London'. Engraved under the powder pan was the signature of the famed Joseph Heylin, gunmaker of London.

Startled by her lethal gift, he was however grateful for the security they would give him on his mission. Though having not ever killed a man, he felt in no doubt that he would use them if the need arose. Bolstered by the caring instincts that lay behind her present, he beamed at her.

'I thank you,' he said quietly. 'I trust I shall not have to use them.'

Placing his right hand over his heart, he said, 'I swear to keep these deadly companions close to my person at all times.'

Smiling her approval of his oath, she lowered her watery eyes.

Not once had he ever doubted the love she felt for him. Much had happened between them since Mister Beecham had passed away. For many months his death had thrown a shroud of emptiness over her life. Thus, along with the League, he had made certain they had spent the following years in jolly camaraderie in the well-appointed Pilgrims. Heightening their respect and amity were the increasingly profitable decisions they had made at the chandlery. Upon the moment of his departure she had succumbed to cherished memories and wept openly. Reverend Whitehouse had been on hand to help assuage her grief.

'You are my son. May God keep thee from harm, Jonas,' were her final sobbing sentiments.

Sorely affected by her parting embrace, he had turned forlornly away from Pilgrims. Mounting the snow-streaked carriage alongside the shipping agent, he tried to focus on the task ahead. When the vehicle, driven by a reputed flashman, began the twenty-mile journey from Deptford, he trembled with unease.

Over and above the dangers of highway robbery that he had been forewarned about, the moonlit passage to Gravesend had been potholed, jarring and debilitating. On the lookout for Isaac Darkin, the popinjay of highwaymen, the shipping agent had counselled him to load and tuck his new pistols inside the top of his boots. Arriving at the forebodingly exposed rolling pastures of Blackheath, the highwayman's hunting grounds, he grew apprehensive.

A ribbon of moonlight snaked over the contours of the snowy topography. Flanked by hoary gorse bushes and snowdrifts, the carriage had slowed to a crawl along a furrowed icy track. Visibility had shrunk to yards. Sweat had trickled down his neck.

'Surely, Darkin wouldn't attempt a robbery in these conditions, Mister Pridmore?' he had whispered anxiously.

'I wouldn't put any money on that, Mister Guinea.'

Pistol in hand, he had peered out of the window into the gusting snow. The onrushing flurry had blinded him. From the shadows of a spreading oak, the dreaded words exploded in his ears.

'Stand and deliver!'

Skewing crazily from side to side, the carriage slowed.

Raising and cocking his pistol, his finger had frozen on the trigger.

A pistol shot rang through the night. Cramming his podgy self out of the opposite window, the shipping agent had discharged his weapon in the direction of the tree. Screened by the lower branches of the oak, a horse stamped and whinnied frantically. Hooves thudded the frozen turf backwards and forwards in consternation. Seconds later he had heard hooves gallop away to the west.

'Lay it on there!' the driver had screamed at his three startled horses.

The carriage jolted forward. Flicking his driving whip over the snorting steeds, the flashman had the carriage rumbling southwards for Wricklemarsh Manor and the lights from the village of Blackheath.

Shaken by the report from the agent's pistol, Jonas asked, 'Has he gone? Was it Darkin?'

'Highwayman didn't give me his name as he galloped away, Mister Guinea,' said the shipping agent, grinning and cockily blowing smoke from the end of his pistol. 'I didn't even lay eyes on the villain. I just fired in the direction of the tree. For all I know it could have been Beelzebub himself!'

The episode had left him feeling abashed and impotent. Worse still, he owed his life to the speedy reflexes of a fat shipping agent. Had he been truly faint-hearted? Or had he been taken by surprise. Nevertheless, he now held a profound conviction that it required a great deal more than tenacity and braggadocio to bring down a man with a pistol shot.

''Twould be folly for you to falter likewise in Pertigua, Mister Guinea,' said the shipping agent kindly. 'Be on your guard. You may not get a second chance.'

'I shall not forget your advice, Mister Pridmore,' he had replied, gritting his teeth.

Daylight was filtering across Gravesend's lacklustre skies. Gulls wheeled above the docks. Like jaded sentinels, the timbered warehouses, capstans and dockyard tackle peered drearily from under a mantle of snow and icicles. Snow was steadily falling. Gusts of sleet stung his face.

A woebegone locality, he thought.

'I will take my leave of thee, Mister Guinea,' said the shipping agent, dropping his gear at the foot of the gangway. 'The *Redemption* sails with the tide.'

'Your speedy response most likely saved the day, Mister Pridmore,' he said, shaking his hand. 'I go on breathing because of your actions.'

Boarding the carriage for his return to Deptford, the shipping agent stuffed his portly frame through the window and shook his hand warmly.

'I have to say 'twas a right surprise and pleasure to greet one of your colour, Mister Guinea. First of your kind you are. And right glad am I to meet you. I bid you a safe voyage and a speedy return.'

Winking at him, the shipping agent added, 'As for the likes of Isaac Darkin, Mister Guinea, I have no doubt that next time you will pull the trigger. A body remains alive that way.'

Pursing his lips uncomfortably at the comment, Jonas waved farewell.

Lugging his frame and gear across the icy gangway, he stepped into the turmoil of the *Redemption*'s main deck. He was abruptly accosted by a stockily-built, lantern-jawed, cropped-headed character clad in a faded boat cloak of coarse green wool. Sizing him up with a weather eye, the man supplied a windswept smile and stuck out a thick hand.

'Thaddeus Hopkins, the Mate,' he said affably in a Kentish brogue. 'Mister Guinea, is it not?'

'Jonas Guinea, at your service, Mister Hopkins,' he smiled, warming to the officer.

'I have been expecting you, Mister Guinea. It gladdens me to meet a body with your mettle, and one who embarks on such a risky assignment. Captain Battersby sends his compliments and will send for you in a while. Let me help you to your quarters with your gear. We sail with the tide.'

'I am heartened by your welcome, Mister Hopkins,' he replied, giving a firm handshake. 'And I shall do my best to meet the standards of your crew. Methinks 'tis an apt moment to quit this bitter climate. I shall wait in my quarters for the Captain's summons.'

'A good place for a landlubber, Mister Guinea,' said the Mate with a gruff chuckle.

Through falling snow a fresh westerly rattled the halyards. The tide was on the ebb.

Suddenly cocking an eye at the yards, the Mate grunted.

Instinctively, Jonas stepped against the gunwales out of the way.

Dropping his eyes over the gunwales, the Mate roared, 'Hoist them staysails! Haul in that there gangway!'

Severing the final link with land in the bleak morning light, the gangway was lashed against the ship's side. The *Redemption* was underway.

When he saw the dock falling away, his heart pounded. His raised anxiety, brooding for the past few days, suddenly surfaced into panic. He shuddered. Clenching his teeth and fists, he reassured himself.

'I know I am capable of this mission,' he told himself beneath his breath.

While the *Redemption* eased into the tide, he gazed mournfully at the disappearing shore. On the dockhead, a caped, Moses-like figure unexpectedly materialised out of the swirling snow to make the sign of the cross. The voice of Parson Merriweather burst into a benediction and then cried out, 'Godspeed the *Redemption*! Godspeed, Jonas Guinea! Come back safe from the gates of Sodom!'

With watery eyes and the Parson's words echoing in his head, Jonas waved at the fading figure. The cleric's raised arms were soon lost in the falling snow. Behind the Mate, he dropped below to be shown into a gloomy spartan cabin beneath the poop deck.

In the cold comfort of his tiny berth, clutching on to the fleeting frosty image of the Parson, his nostrils were besieged by the stench of seasoned oak. Dropping his gear and the mahogany box, he slumped down on his bunk and fell asleep.

Hours later the *Redemption* was off North Foreland in the English Channel, running before following seas. He was awakened by his rumbling belly and the queasy sway of the ship. Glacial draughts whistled beneath the door. His biliousness reminded him of his stormy voyage to England as a twelve-year-old. Curling up on his bunk with rebelling innards, he prayed for the end. But slowly and surely he had a respite in his condition. Sitting up shakily, he opened her letter with trembling fingers. A trace of eau de cologne wafted from the unfolded missive. Smiling at his memories, his eyes lingered over every word of her neat script.

Greensleeves
Nr Speldhurst
Kent
10 January 1761

Promises

Dearest Jonas,

I want my words to be of some comfort when a bare horizon means the *Redemption* is standing well out to sea and where earthly fetters fain into nothingness. Only two days past Mister Puddlewick did say that Captain Battersby is his finest master mariner and the *Redemption* a most trusty vessel. Bless your heart, how cleverly you managed to chatter and charm all at Greensleeves, now this one, now that. Everyone was delighted. Indeed, we all agreed that we had met a soul of the first degree sure enough. And that we had not ever seen such fine dance steps before.

Joy and laughter have rent the impediments in my being. I yearned for you the moment your carriage departed for Deptford.

Lord knows how I ached at the thought of your absence. My only consolation is the notion of your homecoming and the glad times we shall have. What with the tragedies in my life and the imminent difficulties in yours, we richly deserve our time. What an occasion that shall be. Carry these feelings on your voyage — I love thee. There I have said it. I love thee. I love thee. Hold my words close to your heart my dearest, like I clasp to my bosom the deep affection you have expressed for me. It behoves me to say that I trust and pray that our union prospers. Good-naturedly then my love, I await your return. Be safe and come home to me sweet Jonas. I love thee.

With loving promises,
Faith

In receipt of such a blooded admission, her bodily qualities reared into his mind's eye. A strong urge beset his groin. Over and over, he reread her letter. Unsettled by the roll of the ship, the incessant shouts and the screeching pulleys above his head, sleep was not possible. Sitting up with a prolonged groan, he stowed his pistols under the bunk with his gear. There was a sharp knock at the door.

'Aye?'

'Och, Mister Guinea,' said a Scottish voice. 'Captain wants ye.'

Smartening himself up, he opened the door and lurched after the red-haired seaman. Weaving woozily through the stern of the vessel under the poop deck, he was shown into the Captain's well-appointed airy cabin. In comparison with the miniscule dimensions of his quarters, the orderly berth was positively spacious. A large fitted polished bunk spanned the starboard side. Of polished panelled oak, the cabin curtailed at the square ports across the gleaming transom. In an old seadog's effort to transform it into a home from home, familial keepsakes, antique quadrants and astrolabes were fastened along the bulkheads, jostling with exotic curios from foreign lands.

His belly gurgled noisily. Prickly sweat burst down his temples.

Squeezed onto an oak banquette, the Mate sat at a gimballed table in a dripping boat cloak polishing the lens of his telescope. Hunched over a worktop in a deck-length, coarse-woollen boat cloak, the Captain put his dividers down on the chart and shook his hand.

'I shan't offer you a beverage in your sickly condition, Mister Guinea,' he said, giving a kindly smile. 'Given your impending escapade, I was eager to make your acquaintance. I have to say you have my admiration for a somewhat thorny project. Be certain, I will render you all assistance. You have of course met Mister Hopkins?'

'Pleasantly so, Captain,' Jonas replied, dipping his head at the Mate.

'First things first; I trust you are content with your quarters?'

'Thank you kindly, Captain Battersby,' he replied, swaying. 'Though a little draughty, I have a well-found berth. As for my innards they unhappily have not.'

Winking at the Mate, the Captain was candid. 'Pitch a tankard of seawater down your gullet, Mister Guinea. 'Twill all come up or all stay down. Either way you'll not ever suffer seasickness again. I swear by it.'

He indicated a chair and Jonas gratefully, if unsteadily, settled himself.

'I want Mister Hopkins in on our little chat. First let me say this, Mister Guinea. Many merchant captains are affronted by the sight of a slave ship and will have not anything to do with them. All my officers are members of the League and have as well signed up to this project. Thus they fully recognise that they must aid you to bring it to fruition.

''Tis high time such an action to challenge this trade in slaves were attempted,' he said, pausing for effect, 'lest it might, in the course of time, be accepted that all Englishmen were implicated in the trade by their skin.'

'You are right, Captain,' he said.

Dropping his eyes to the deck, the Captain guffawed.

'Fitted coats, fancy heels and black leather shoes with silver coach-harness buckles are excellent for the elegant carpets of withdrawing rooms, Mister Guinea,' he said. 'But they are treacherous companions on the wet rolling decks of a ship at sea.'

A little embarrassed by the gentle challenge, he said, 'With your acquaintance of my business in ship's chandlery, I understand your dismay at my attire. I thought it best to dress like a gentleman to present myself to my Captain.'

'Your fashionable efforts are appreciated, Mister Guinea,' said the Captain.

'Engrossed in your cultured self, Mister Guinea,' said the Mate, shaking his head, 'I sighted not your unbefitting shoes.'

'A cordwainer delivered a batch of turnshoes in Fort Gardens, Mister Hopkins. Tell the boatswain to fit our shipmate with turnshoes and a boat cloak from the ship's stores.'

'Aye, Captain,' said the Mate.

'Many thanks, Captain.'

'Aye, Mister Guinea,' said the Mate, chuckling at his footwear. 'Fancy heels won't grip wet decks and ratlines like turnshoes.'

Sitting down and plonking the open logbook onto the table, the Captain was light-hearted.

'Now we wouldn't want you to go breaking your corporate neck, Mister Guinea,' he said, with a placating smile, 'at least not before our business is concluded. Pray be seated, sir. We have much to go through. I agreed with my owner, Mister Puddlewick, that we shall review our strategy at the earliest occasion. Methinks this an opportune moment to pull together what we know. I would like to concentrate on three aspects: our primary contact, coastal rendezvous and an undetected departure. At which juncture we must assume that with the runaways embarked, privateers bearing adjusted letters of marque will start combing the coastline for us. With regard to making contact with the runaways, when we reach Jamestown you shall accompany Mister Hopkins ashore to reconnoitre the taverns on the waterfront. Drinking with indigent ale-soaked rogues, you should find an amenable go-between who could be—'

Unable to restrain himself a moment longer, Jonas said, 'Alexander Fairfax!'

After a tentative pause, the Captain asked, 'Who might he be, Mister Guinea?'

'A shipping agent with an office on Jamestown's waterfront and who, as well, has covertly befriended a slave,' he replied. 'Fairfax is the confidante of my good friend, Mistress Faith Bradshaw. You may have heard of her involvement with the League. She dwelled in Pertigua before the uprising. After that she settled with the gentry of Kent. She is an investor in our project and a good friend of your owner, Mister Puddlewick. To aid us, Captain, Mistress Bradshaw wrote to Mister Fairfax some time past, on which occasion she furnished me with letters of introduction. To be concise, Captain, this very shipping agent awaits our arrival in Jamestown.'

Nodding approvingly and smiling, the Captain heaved an inflated sigh.

'Great heavens, Mister Guinea,' he exclaimed heartily, 'my regard for your gumption grows. Your tidings may well resolve a principal predicament.'

'With a tad of luck, Mister Guinea's intelligence could well hasten our contact with the runaways, Captain,' said the Mate.

Scribbling in the logbook, the Captain said, 'Pray God Fairfax makes the speedy connection we need.'

'You be a useful shipmate, Mister Guinea,' said the Mate genially. 'Mistress Bradshaw's letters of introduction may well expedite a brief stay in Jamestown.'

'Nonetheless, Mister Hopkins,' said the Captain, 'given the informers infesting the taverns of Gravesend and Fort Gardens, 'tis prudent to presume that by now, the powers that be on Pertigua have been informed of our intentions before we had Fort Gardens in our wake. Once ashore you shall proceed with extreme vigilance.'

Catching the unease that flickered across the Mate's brow, Jonas pressed his lips together. His belly rumbled and hot bilious contents entered his throat. He swallowed and swayed. Suddenly seizing the table, he croaked, 'Permission to pitch a tankard of seawater down my gullet right away, Captain?'

'Permission granted, sir. Oh, and if a purler crashes over the stern, Mister Guinea, leap for the rigging and hang on tight.'

Nodding woozily, he groaned.

'You look a tad grey in the gills, Mister Guinea,' said the Mate. 'Follow me.'

Where Lies the Grazing Herd

Beaumaris Great House
Turtle Island
15 February 1761
12.00 hrs

Scarcely a breath of wind was evident under the pallid blue sky. The chant of the First Gang echoed down rows of cane as they trudged to Grace Fields in weary voice. On bended knee in the parterre beds of the gardens around the Great House, the Second Gang toiled in whispers. Hatted horse-backed overseers trotted about waving whips and muskets, harassing eighty-four slaves.

In linen shirtsleeves, a sweating Matthew Fleming paid no heed to the slave gardeners kneeling in the flowerbeds. Bent on catching the noon breezes along the shoreline, he hurried with Samuel Davenport, a thirty-six-year-old Member of Parliament for Aylesburn and a thorn in the side of England's government. Alleged to be the ugliest man in the realm, Davenport had an unsightly squint, a protruding jaw and a charm that carried all before it. Given his conceit, Matthew reckoned it took the politician mere moments to talk away his face.

Powdery sands scrunched beneath his soles on the water's edge. A cooling wind dried his face and neck. As expected, the noontime Turtle Airs had arrived. Surveying the fine white sands and aquamarine waters, he beamed.

'On this your last day, Samuel, Turtle Island's clement breezes may well be prophesy for the forthcoming general election.'

Stretching out his stubby arms, Davenport twirled around with childlike glee.

'You have an unrivalled seat, Matthew,' he said. 'This island estate is known to make goodly profit. No trouble with your slaves then?'

'Nay, Samuel. On a speck of land like Turtle Island, maintaining order is a simple matter. 'Tis not so on Pertigua. She suffers from incessant sabotage and revolts. Wytham Woods, my head overseer, keeps our slaves in line. The man brooks no slacking or insolence.'

'Turtle Island has furnished you with robust revenues then?'

'Aye, that she has!'

'One you would no doubt be loathe to lose?'

'Aye. Why would we suffer such loss?'

'If slavery was abolished?'

'Have you taken leave of your senses man? We would lose the best part of our profits. Land and assets would have to be sold to stave it off. We may not possess a sufficient amount. Insolvency would be upon us. Who would compensate us for the loss of our slaves? Which parliamentary nincompoops would be sufficiently dim-witted enough to abolish slavery? Such an Act would imperil England's economy, ruin the gentry and the merchants, and afflict the working classes.'

'That it would,' said Davenport vehemently. He pondered aloud, 'methinks we should do something about it before someone cries abolition.'

Slumping down pensively on the dried-out shell of an upturned boat, Matthew did not respond. Taking off his shoes and wading into the crystalline shallows, he laughed and asked, 'A hand of quadrille before supper, Samuel?'

'Splendid, Matthew. I shall partner your sister and you her fetching companion, Hermione Pickwicke.'

'Somehow I already scent victory, Samuel.'

Davenport paused. 'Apropos your sister, Matthew.'

'What about my sister?'

'The damsel dazzles. May one enquire if she is spoken for?'

'Stow your gaff, man! Mary has eyes for someone known only to her,' he said, tapping his nose. 'Island life and plantation culture has made her headstrong, independent and fearless. 'Twould be exceedingly imprudent to meddle in the affairs of her heart, as I have learned to my chagrin.'

Looking briefly at the brigantines on the horizon, Davenport relented with a gracious bow.

Suddenly guffawing, he slapped Davenport on the back. 'Aside from your unvarying ache for my delightful sibling, Samuel,' he said, 'I have a great regard for your doggedness.'

'How so?'

'As the Member for Aylesburn,' he replied, 'you have argued for the rights of voters to determine their representatives rather than the House of Commons. You have been sorely castigated for doing so. They appear to make not a jot of difference to you, for you are nonetheless set on radicalising England's political philosophies. I have to say that your most recent essay is a compelling *vade mecum* for politicians.'

'The dogged mind is the captain of change, Matthew,' said Davenport. As though there were unseen listeners, he lowered his voice. 'I expect to hold Aylesburn at the next election. After four decades in government the Whigs scrap among themselves. The Duke of Newcastle leads them for a fresh mandate. But we cannot count on Newcastle and his poltroons to do what's right for the slave trade. The lily-livered dastards will act too late. Certain Members of the House have prevailed on me to approach you, Matthew. We could do with your services.'

'Who is 'we'? How could I possibly be of service? Why would I relinquish my halcyon bask on this sundrenched isle for the bleak freezing fog of mud-slinging London?'

'We, my dear friend, are plantation owners and shareholders. Some of us as well are Members of Parliament, many with whom you are acquainted. Abolition begins to rear its monstrous head across England. Presently, it whispers into the ears of the undecided. Without anticipatory counteractive action, its prose may escalate and eventually howl from the lips of the resolved. Prominent among the troublemakers is the League Against the Importation of Negroes from the Coast of Guinea. I believe these agitators are known to you and your family. Now they skulk in the meadows. Soon they'll be on the streets. We want you to help stifle a spawning disease, lest abolition be contagious and breaks into an epidemic.'

'Why me?'

'Naturally, we cannot petition your bedridden pater, Matthew. Given his connections in London, finer than any I know, you would be his accepted proxy. Help us pool the resources of a coalition of like-minded men of influence who believe that, in the service of an infinitely superior civilisation, plantation slavery is justified.'

'Father would favour a curative exploit. Were he in good health he would indeed participate. I am certain he would give me his imprimatur. I will partake in his stead. Where do you want me, Samuel?'

'In London, Matthew, where lies the grazing herd. The abolitionists are growing in numbers around the table. They must not be allowed to devour too much.'

Accompanied by his sister, Matthew took tea with Hermione Pickwicke and Samuel Davenport in the withdrawing room. No sooner had the beverage been dispensed than the raconteur and braggart in the politician leapt to the fore.

'I recall one prospective candidate in the last general election, who shall be nameless,' Davenport chortled. 'The rascal bragged about how he had spent at least seven thousand pounds sterling on bribes to voters. Subsequently, he bribed a ship's captain to disembark a shipload of opposition supporters from London in Norway instead of Berwick. Even with his unconstitutional tactics, the voters holed his efforts below the waterline. And as one might expect, the fellow was less prospective after the election.'

Squeals and guffaws erupted in the chamber.

The clock stuck the hour.

Following a garrulous hand of quadrille, deftly won by the politician's side, Matthew excused himself. Percival Sedgwick, a rich planter from Troublesome Creek on the neighbouring island of Little Pertigua, had arrived.

Poker-faced, of middle years and desirous of height, Sedgwick strutted bumptiously into the chamber with a younger, taller escort, the immodestly buxom spinster, Harriet Beaufort. Flaunting cleavage like a mating Delilah, she wore a pale mulberry silk gown with a vertiginously low neckline.

Smilingly avoiding her eyes, Matthew said, 'Felicitations, my dear Sedgwick.'

''Tis a pleasure, Matthew,' replied Percival Sedgwick, turning to his companion. 'You are of course acquainted with Mistress Beaufort of Nonsuch Hall.'

'I am indeed,' he said, giving her a crisp bow. 'Welcome to the Beaumaris Great House, Mistress Beaufort. I am heartened you could attend our little gathering.'

'Delighted, Matthew,' she purred.

Pained by the sight of her manicured hand perched atop Sedgwick's veined paw, his temples grew feverish. Jealousy hovered.

Turning away to check on his guests, he muttered to himself, 'Of all the fillies on these islands, I harbour feelings for this chancy one. Chafing at the bit to be wed, she taunts me with this rich midget.'

Turning back, he looked directly at his tormenter, Harriet Beaufort.

Hand on hip, mischief was writ large in her posture. A bewitching half-smile played on her painted lips. His sister flung a censorious look in his direction. While smiling at both, he was distracted by the entrance of his last four guests: two members of the West Indies Sugar Cartel with their fashionable wives. All his guests were assembled for the night. The chamber shifted into frivolity and scurrilous gossip.

The kettle gong heralded supper. Chortling into the summery dining room, his guests fanned around the polished mahogany table. Matthew sat at the head with his sister perched gracefully beside him. Sniffing affectedly, he looked at Harriet Beaufort sitting opposite. Catching his eye, she threw him a come-hither look. Just then, Percival Sedgwick's eyeballs were rammed down Hermione Pickwicke's bragging cleavage. His sister giggled.

Bearing tureens, groomed house slaves traipsed into the dining chamber with roast lamb, boiled potatoes, dripping pudding, broccoli and green beans. Terrantez Madeira wine was decanted into a sparkling set of Georgian Jacobite wine glasses. The libation sent tongues wagging about the bodily indiscretions of the archipelago. Conversation sped into the sabotaged cane yields and the horseracing fixtures on the Savannah. Diverting into the Seven Years War, they then argued over the imminent signing of the Treaty of Paris by England, France and Spain.

Interrupting the discourse by raising his voice, Percival Sedgwick flaunted the strangled accent of his class.

'Think me not incurious regarding another tedious War,' he said, stifling a pretentious yawn. 'On the contrary, I want it understood I am a patriot, first and foremost. But it is my belief that our sugar plantations, not England's wars, are England's lifeblood and salvation. Need I remind you all that the *raison d'être* for this gathering is critical? The War is but a triviality while we have before us the imminent thievery of our property by, unbelievably, English men of a scandalous League aboard an English vessel! Anglo-Saxon they may be, but they are nevertheless Anglo-Saxon traitors!'

Without demur, his guests turned to talk of the League.

Putting a hand over her mouth, Harriet Beaufort yawned.

Thankful that Sedgwick had broached the question of the League in his characteristic tactless manner, Matthew smiled at Harriet Beaufort, who wrinkled her nose at him.

Turning aside from the table talk, his sister lowered her voice. 'You plan an expedition to London, Matthew?'

'Who told you?'

'Davenport.'

'The wily rogue seeks to ingratiate himself into your favours. Nevertheless, he has put to me a scheme worthy of serious consideration. I shall recount all to you after supper, and then we will notify Father. Did you know Davenport was a member of Francis Dashwood's Hell Fire Club? He was reputed to be quite a hell-raiser. I witnessed as much when I last visited his lodgings in Piccadilly. Though he said it in not so many words, the poor devil is quite taken with you. Fret not, Mary, I left him in no doubt of your disinterest.'

'Fiddlesticks to his wants,' she said frostily. 'You well know politicians oftimes hallucinate. I find Davenport somewhat sycophantic, truly ugly with an extremely hideous squint. Charming he may be, but let us not forget that he is as well beset by an exceedingly limited set of talents.'

'Gather you're impressed. You'll have no problem with him then. On the morrow, he sails with the *Swift* for England to fight for his Aylesburn seat in the general election. I will go to London, Mary, but only after we have apprehended the League's vessel.'

'Pray forgive my intruding your guarded conference with Mistress Fleming, Matthew,' said Percival Sedgwick. 'In the course of the erudite discourse on the subject of piracy, methinks I heard you mention the League Against the Importation of Negroes. May one ask what intelligence you have received concerning the League's contemptible activities? Have your agents, for instance, discovered the name of the barque they have dispatched to commandeer our slaves?'

Smirking furtively behind her hand, Harriet Beaufort rolled her eyes.

Seeing her mocking expression, Matthew smiled and looked away.

'How English men could set about freeing slaves by policy beggars belief,' exclaimed Samuel Davenport. 'Do your plantations not give them food, shelter, work and, I am reliably informed, impart even the scriptures? Besides, they cannot care for themselves, so who would care for them if not you? By my reckoning, plantation slavery is compassionate compared with slavery at the time of Christ, which I believe, He did not condemn. And while we're about it—'

Matthew interrupted, to forestall another airing of Davenport's litany of disputed sanctimonious justifications.

'As it happens we suspect several barques,' he said confidently. 'But three are of particular interest: the *Oriel*, the *Phoenix* and the *Redemption*. As well, we are informed they have by now sailed from the Pool of London. That being the case, we can expect them in Jamestown in two to three months. I have agents stationed along the waterfront keeping a close watch on all vessels arriving from England.'

'Scant intelligence if I might say,' said Percival Sedgwick tersely.

Lowering his voice for effect, Matthew continued, 'This is what we have learned. The *Oriel* and the *Phoenix* are owned by Mathesons & Company, a limp snivelling family concern out of Canvey Island. Moses Wilkes, who was previously trafficking slaves from the coast of Guinea, is the proprietor. According to our agents, the man seems to have, of late, suffered a curiously spectacular change of heart. Spurred on by a do-gooding conversion, he has been heard expressing muscular opinions against his erstwhile occupation. And you all well know how the convert oftimes aches with fanaticism. Little else is known about him.'

Pausing to sip Madeira, he then added, 'The *Redemption*, on the other hand, is owned by Jeremiah Puddlewick of Greenwich, who for some years has been up to his armpits in suspect transactions with the League. He owns three vessels, attends Methodist church regularly, pays his dues punctiliously and is a member of Bootle's. Apart from his unwholesome connections with the League, he is by all accounts a pillar of society. But methinks Puddlewick is too good to be true.'

Downing a mouthful of Madeira, Samuel Davenport asked, 'Which barque would you put money on?'

'The *Oriel* or mayhaps the *Redemption*. In truth, Samuel, I know not which. But I am certain we shall furnish whoever with a blunderbuss up the backside for a hellish reception.'

Titters and chortles followed his avowal.

'Better a veritable roasting,' said Percival Sedgwick acerbically. 'I say we terminate that League's vile project at this first instance. Who will come next? A vessel crewed by ostlers? In next to no time, while we're shipping slaves out of Guinea, the likes of the League will be shipping back the same slaves again. They will surely become giddy?'

Cackles, guffaws and squeals resounded in the chamber.

Smiling furtively at Harriet Beaufort over the quaking pudding, Matthew was scornful.

'Lest you forget the distasteful nature of our project, my dear Sedgwick,' he said, 'methinks I had better mention the dark aspect of our proposed action. If indeed the vessel we await turns out to be any of the three suspects, then let me be perfectly clear: while foiling the seditious scheme by recapturing the slaves, we shall at the same time apprehend any members of this League, some of whom we believe will be aboard the said vessel. I tell you this and on this we must all speak with one voice. No matter what their colour, arrested members from whichever vessel shall not ever again set eyes on England's shores!'

As he hoped, his decree struck Sedgwick with the ferocity of an axe. Apprehension quailed on the visage of the would-be suitor. A prickly hush grew palpable. Encouraged by the apprehensive anticipation of his listeners, he delivered his chilling masterstroke:

'Sentencing white men to death or exile is a grim affair,' he continued. 'But we have arrived at a critical stage in this matter. We must be confident we carry all with us. In jeopardy is the survival of our plantations, the bedrock of our capital. Consensus on captured members of the League is mandatory. We cannot ever let them return to England.'

Calmly examining each face in turn, he posed his portentous question quietly. 'Are we all agreed?'

Like marionettes, his listeners nodded unanimously.

Glancing at Percival Sedgwick and then smiling around the table, he asked, 'Champagne?'

'Aye,' chirruped a chorus of voices.

Raising his glass, he cried, 'A blight on the likes of the League!'

'Aye!' they shouted.

Following his toast, the clink of glasses and convivial chatter told him the deathly contract had not tainted their *joie de vivre*. Indeed, with youthful jollity, they carried their drinks into the withdrawing room.

Accosting Harriet Beaufort beside the walnut writing cabinet, he lowered his voice.

''Tis excellent you tarry the night at Beaumaris, Harriet,' he said. 'Methinks in the morning you might favour me with a ride along the shore?'

'I shall expect thee at the crack of dawn, Matthew,' she said coquettishly. 'I ride like a man and fancy a feisty mount.'

''Tis fortunate then that I have such a stallion.'

'Does he buck?'

'Nay, Harriet. He is spirited but of doggedly good temper. Did I hear you say the crack of dawn?'

Glancing at Percival Sedgwick who, engrossed in Hermione Pickwicke, was oblivious to all, she turned back with an inviting look in her eyes.

'Were you expecting sooner, Matthew?'
He winked.
Beaming at him, she winked back.

Dispossessed Blood

Village of Ake
Coast of Guinea
20 March 1761

On the sweltering coast of Guinea, the sun had surged past noon. Coast eagles and vultures were circling in a cloudless sky and rose-ringed parakeets screeched in the rainforest's primordial green canopy. Tumbling from bough to bough, mandrill monkeys chattered noisily. Buffaloes and elephants threshed tracks through the forest undergrowth. Forest cats slumbered in the trees. The chilling cries of spotted hyenas screamed through the labyrinth of hardwoods. On the lush eastern bank of the River Ogun, the mud-brick houses of the Yoruba village of Ake stood quiescent on a large deforested tract of red loam.

It was the weekly market day. Children shrieked around the village playing the snake game. Under shady trees in the heat, youths sat cross-legged playing *ayo*, counting grey nickernuts on a dimpled board. Women haggled at trading stalls. Engulfed in peppery odours, others proffered cowry shells for goat meat, croaker fish, guinea fowl, vegetables, herbs and spices.

Wearing only cotton *sokoto* – trousers – a motley group of gruff bare-chested men ambled brashly around the marketplace. Prepared against surprise attack, the men of the guard-patrol were taking no chances. Equipped with heavy black palm bows and poisoned arrows, they also carried the *jomo* – short sword – and the *ogbo* – heavy cutlass.

Casting weary eyes over the marketplace from the grassy border of the market, Taiwo Sodeke smiled. He was a tall, stocky, round-faced farmer, clad in a worn cotton *buba* – shirt – and *sokoto*. Insensitive to the optimism of a sunny day, he was pondering on what to say to the village blacksmith.

'Ake breathes again,' he said to himself.

Heartened by the harmony in his village, he leaned against a stall selling *fufu* – mashed yam.

'Shamed by English men who buy and kidnap our kith and kin,' he muttered, 'Ake grows with confidence and echoes with laughter again.'

Just then, the chiselled-faced bald-headed blacksmith arrived.

'*E'kasan* – good afternoon – Taiwo.'

'*E'kasan* Babarimisa,' he replied, smiling broadly. 'Your face lifts my spirits at this sad time. *Adupe* – thank you. Your *buba* glows this day.'

'You sell a lame smile, brother Taiwo,' said Babarimisa affectionately. 'I am not fooled. Your heart is heavy. Inside me too the wound still bleeds. We all learned much that day of the brutal ways of English men.'

'When they kidnapped Kayode, Babarimisa,' he said, 'they made hostages of the memories left behind. No matter the passing of time, the pain never weakens. It sticks like shit. I still feel ashamed.'

Plodding heavy-heartedly away from the market, he was trailed by the blacksmith. After wading through an expanse of tufted *koriko* grasses, he turned onto a rutted track snaking towards the rainforest. Here and there in the distance, towering above all, stood the tallest tree in the forest, the giant silk cottonwood — mighty, mystifying and majestic. Narrowing his eyes at the black howler monkeys scrambling along branches at dizzying heights, he smiled. Near the edge of the forest, he stopped by a solitary *abura* tree. Sinking to his knees in the cooling breeze, he clasped his hands in prayer.

'Here?' asked the blacksmith, sweating profusely.

'*Bee ni* – yes. On this very spot, I say my last words to Kayode.'

'What words did you use?'

Pausing momentarily, tears welled in Taiwo's eyes. With quiet brevity, he said, 'Be not too long, Kayode.'

Tight-lipped, he averted the blacksmith's gaze. His eyes watered as they scanned the bushes where he had last seen his younger brother.

Settling back on his haunches, he dropped his head despondently.

'I, your brother, was not there to save you, Kayode. I am forty years on this earth now. Gone eleven years since you were taken. Grief vexes my day and hell my night.'

Rage churned in his head. The helplessness crowding his being was expelled in a long, drawn-out groan. Raising his arms and beseeching the heavens, he shouted, 'Where did they take you, Kayode? Family sick and blind since you taken. What you eat? Where you lay your head? Am I yet an *arakunrin* – uncle? I feel you breathing somewhere out there. I grieve for you, my beloved brother. I grieve for Asabi. Until you all come back, no matter how many years you are gone, we will be forever scarred by the loss of our dispossessed blood. *Olorun* – God – watch over you, Kayode.'

Stepping from the shade of the *abura* into sunlight, the blacksmith raised his head.

'Kayode,' shouted Babarimisa. 'We still talk of the great journey you made with Taiwo and Asabi. We will never forget you. We will not ever give up hope. I pray *Olorun* watch over you and Asabi.'

Staggering to his feet, the last words to his brother pealed loudly in his head, 'Be not too long, Kayode.'

Putting a reassuring arm around his shoulders, the blacksmith gently squeezed.

'Until the enslaved Yoruba return to the mother country, Babarimisa,' he fumed, 'the Yoruba will linger in darkness. We know that with the profits from slave sweat, England develops her people, her country and her possessions. The trafficking of thousands and thousands of men, women and children for the past *ogoorun odun* – hundred years – will live with us and cripple the Yoruba for generations. And this traffic deprives us of the company, the strength and abilities of the sold. This evil trade weakens us. We fight back and suffer great losses. England has powerful weapons we cannot match. Forever mourning the dead and the disappeared and then burying our heads in more and more meaningless rituals, we foolishly forgot to develop weapons to fight back — so we stay powerless against England's *opas* – muskets.'

'Englishmen take us by surprise, Taiwo,' said Babarimisa defensively.

'Surprise?' he asked in amazement. 'What weapons do you say we use against rulers who sell their own people? This tragedy begins by first being powerless against our chiefs and kings, who are no surprise. We the people shrink in fear of them. And they like it. Is it not time to strike back at England, at the *Alafin* and his fawning courtiers?'

'Rebellion is in your eyes this day, Taiwo,' said Babarimisa, stepping back and scrutinising him quizzically. 'You got fire in them balls an' devil in your gut. This night I will dwell on what you have said. I witness the nightmare wreaked by the English men with their attack on Ake. Only idiots not hear what you say now. You know the Yoruba, Taiwo — dripping with tradition and deaf to change. And change is what they will get if we make them listen. Tread softly, my brother. Between we and the palace, the *Alafin* got eyes and ears in every kola nut and palm tree. If our words meet his ears, he will say we plot rebellion. Come Taiwo, your family await us.'

Gazing thoughtfully at the blacksmith for a moment, he turned back towards the village.

'Why did *Olorun* give us these years?' he asked petulantly. 'Soon we gather for the Vigil for the Taken. Why we do it? After white men's attack with *opas*, seven children, twenty men and women and the *Bale* – Mayor – were killed. Torching our huts and houses, they turned our village into a scorched wilderness and torched our morrows. Fifty-two men, women and children were marched away before they had time to say goodbye. Our weapons could not stop them, Babarimisa. Why *Olorun* give us this life?'

'England sail them far away in *eru okos* – slave ships – across the Ocean Sea to a wicked place, Taiwo,' said Babarimisa gloomily. 'I even heard that some of our people get eaten.'

'Rubbish,' he scowled.

'Has one ever come back?' asked Babarimisa sharply. 'Eleven years they have gone. Every year on the twelfth new moon, we grieve over our missing on the banks of River Ogun. With palm torches and eyes of tear-river, the village gathers for the Vigil for the Taken. We are lucky for we were not among the kidnapped or the sold. We remember those we lost and how we lost them so that we never again suffer a surprise attack. That, Taiwo, is what we now live for.'

'From that day, Babarimisa, hunger twist in our bellies,' he said sourly. 'I had to beg to help feed the family. Father take out a big cowry loan from our neighbour, Salako. To repay the interest on that loan, I became an *iwofa* on Salako's farm.'

Disturbed by painful memories, he drifted into his mind's eye to an uncomfortable conversation he had had with an old family friend, Chidike, the Igbo storyteller...

Whilst picking bush beans in the family compound in the early morning, Chidike had sidled up to him.

'They say you are an *iwofa*, Taiwo,' he had said. 'What is an *iwofa*?'

'Among we Yoruba, my friend,' he had replied tetchily, 'an *iwofa* is a man, woman, boy or girl who works for another in place of the interest on cowries borrowed. He stay free; his rank and rights stay unchanged. He is ruled by his master only for working off the interest.'

'Sound like a slave to me,' the storyteller had said flippantly, picking his teeth.

'An *iwofa* is not a slave, Chidike!' he had snapped irritably. 'A slave is bought and must live with his master. His master owns his life. He can be forced to work all the hours his master wants and can be punished with a beating. An *iwofa* enters a contract to work for six days out of seven. He live where he want, come and go as he please and cannot be punished. A man has one big reason for giving up life, Chidike. My family is my reason.'

'You right, Taiwo, you not a slave,' the storyteller had said apologetically. 'Will you be an *iwofa* forever?'

'When Baba repays his cowry loan to Salako, I will be freed from being his *iwofa*. For now I pay off the interest on my father's loan with my sweat.'

Deep in conversation with the blacksmith, he retraced his steps through the village. Greeting his friends and neighbours on their way to market, he arrived at the tall acacia tree opposite his home. Smiling at the yellow bush daisies festooning the foot of the house, he gazed awhile on the mud-brick bedrock of his family. Enlarged during re-building from its fire-gutted shell, the laterite-red house now held six sleeping rooms and three family rooms topped by a low conical roof of plaited banana leaves. Surrounded by a well-laid mud-walled compound, it held a large vegetable garden at the far end.

At the rear of the house on a levelled piece of land beneath a spreading mango tree, Chidike sat beside Taiwo's wife, Sade. Attended by brightly dressed, crestfallen relatives, his elderly parents sat listening to the ceremonial order of the Vigil for the Taken. They were drinking palm wine and eating *fufu* with chicken and peanut soup. All eyes turned to him when he appeared.

'*E'kasan, Taiwo. E'kasan, Babarimisa,*' his relations chorused.

'*E'kasan, Baba. E'kasan, Iya* – mother,' he said respectfully, prostrating before his parents. 'Have you chosen what we do for the Vigil, Baba?'

'I will need your courage, Taiwo. When you go to work?'

'At cock-crow, Baba.'

Shaking her head with vexation, his mother asked, 'Your *oluwa* – master – let you go to the Vigil?'

'*Bee ni* – yes, *Iya*. Salako let me go. The tyrant will be at the Vigil. His father and sister were also kidnapped.'

'Salako treat you good?'

'*Bee ko* – no, *Iya*. The English assault on Ake turned him into a monster. He hurls abuse at me when he passes me with his friends. He got five more *iwofa* on his farm. He treat them like slaves. His riches has turned him into a power-hungry brute.'

'How can Salako abuse the *iwofa* system?' retorted his father indignantly. 'That *eba*-headed idiot defies the laws of the *iwofa* agreement.'

'Who can stop him?'

'Who can stop him? What you mean?'

'Who can force him to honour the *iwofa* agreement?'

'*Onigbowo* – the witnesses!' snapped his father. 'They can force Salako to honour the agreement.'

'Only if the *onigbowo* are told.'

'I tell them!'

'That would be unwise, Baba. The *iwofa* will receive a merciless beating. The witnesses for his other five *iwofa* are all close friends of his. Who dare tell his bogus witnesses? Parents of these *iwofa* were kidnapped. So they have no one to speak for them. Only the last day one *iwofa* was bleeding from a flogging and—'

'Your witnesses are no friends of Salako,' said his mother.

'Baba select reliable friends as witnesses for my contract,' he said. 'Salako may throw surly looks and veiled abuse at me, but he will honour my contract. He takes out his bad temper on his other *iwofa* and beats them hard. He sweats their backsides in the fields 'til they drop. His *iwofa* have time only for little sleep. It will take only—'

Suddenly from inside the house, his ailing grandmother cried out.

'*Lowo! Lowo!* – Help! Help!'

Rising to her feet, his mother shuffled off.

Beckoning Taiwo to sit beside him, his father spoke quietly. 'We must make the *Bale* speak to Salako's *iwofas*.'

'Not possible, Baba. This *Bale* face back and front and talk from both sides of his mouth at the same time. So hungry for cowries, his gluttony decides his leaning. First Salako swamp him with cowries to turn deaf to all. Now this *Bale* won't even hear you call his name — even if you shouting in his ear.'

'Salako must be stopped, Taiwo. His wicked ways must be exposed.'

'Whatever we do and however we do it, Baba,' he said softly, 'must be done this very night beside the River Ogun — before the eyes of the *Bale*, the elders and the villagers. This one night Ake grieves as one. All will be there and wide awake. So awake they will even hear a cricket visiting his aunt. Only then before all can Salako be shamed.'

'Ah-ah,' his father cried crossly. 'Salako get rich by turning *iwofa* into slaves?'

'Turning *iwofa* into slaves is not new, Baba,' he replied impassively. 'Rich Yoruba men have been turning *iwofa* into slaves for a long long time. Who can stop them?'

'We must rid the village of Salako's kind and his dirty way of doing business.'

'I will set a trap to clip his fangs, Baba.'

'*Bee ni* – yes?' asked his father, avidly leaning towards him.

'This night,' he said conspiratorially, 'when I speak about Kayode and Asabi...'

'*Bee ni?*'

Stolen Sacrifice

River Ogun
20 March 1761
Sunset

Darkness had fallen. Fast hooting wood owls injected a sombre note into the proceedings. Dressed in a pale *buba* and *sokoto* for the warm airs, Taiwo wore a symbolic brass bracelet and carried a burning palm torch. Ahead of his family and Chidike, the Igbo storyteller, he walked through a darker wedge of rainforest towards the River Ogun. Affected by the lament from his torch-laden relations, he halted briefly on the track to wipe his tears. Gazing through a gap in the canopy at the starry heavens, he muttered, 'Only the gods know where you stand this night, Kayode.'

'*Bee ko bee ko*, my son,' said his mother, catching up with her son. 'Them who snatch him know where your brother stands this night!'

Falling silent, he walked on hand-in-hand with his wife.

Nearing the river, the track opened onto a clearing fringing the water's edge and bathed in the incandescence of the full moon. Even a green grasshopper was visible. In ritual expectation of kidnapped escapees, flaming palm torches were set in the ground twenty paces apart, contouring the eastern bank for as far as his eye could see. As well as the colours of the *bubas* worn by the villagers, he could clearly make out his friends' faces. *Gele* headpieces jutted above the crowd like branched antlers. In his *fela* hat, *buba* and *sokoto*, Salako looked menacing in the moonlight.

Scowling at the sight of his *oluwa*, Taiwo turned away to watch the proceedings.

Beneath a moonlit sky the villagers had formed a horseshoe facing the portly *Bale*, who had his back to the river. Others came in ones, twos, threes and family groups. All wore a brass bracelet around one wrist, similar to those worn by the worshipers of Oshun, the god of the river. Above the rushing waters, a soft choral harmony splayed through the night air from Ake's songsters, more of whom were still gathering to augment the mournful saga of the kidnap:

Kith and kin were laughing.
Elegbara's – *Devil's – work was done.*
Billows of white darkness trampled the yellow sun.
Blood of kinfolk pour to a different place.
The night draws near and we see not your face…

The croaking of the big olive-green Pixie frogs leapt to a crescendo above the crickets. Strangely, he was disturbed by the clamour. Branches were unexpectedly shaken in the shadows on the edge of the glade, followed by a furious scrabbling across the forest floor. Aware that *kiniun* – lions – were on the prowl, he took a deep breath. Coupled with the distressing vigil, his uneasiness grew. Biting his lip, he swallowed and grasped his wife's hand.

'Eleven years, Sade,' he sighed, 'since that great walk through the rainforest with Kayode and Asabi to seek out the *Sese* bean from the Bariba in the far north of Yorubaland. With the bean in our posses-sion, we saved our family. Over many many suns facing many dangers with lots of laughter, I truly got to know my brother. We were all so much younger then.'

With tears in his eyes, he embraced his wife.

'You lessened my sadness, Sade,' he said, stretching out at the hazy figures of his children. 'Wild days with Kayode and Asabi are never far from my head. Your uncle Kayode was a beloved brother and a very great man.'

Stepping aside, the *Bale* watched five white-robed Mogbas file solemnly along the riverbank. They carried a gift to *Oshun* of a symbolic pottery dish filled with white stones from a river bed. In added obeisance to this female deity of the rivers, they tossed offerings of honey, mead, palm wine, pumpkins and perfumed oil into the dark running waters while chanting her refrain:

I am the honey-sweet voice of the waters.
I am the flowing of a woman's cloth as she dances her life.

With a flourish, the principal Mogba, an elderly white-haired man, threw the sleeves of his white *agbada* robe over his shoulders. Shuffling to the centre of the arena, he cleared his throat raucously until he gained silence. Raising his voice in prayer above the gentle backdrop of song, he was mournful. 'O merciful *Oshun*, god of the rivers and of the ocean,' he cried. 'Ake implores you who travelled with the Yoruba to distant lands, comforting them in the belly of the slave ships that took them far away from their homeland. We beg you to tell them that even now we wait for them. We love them still. We wept blood with the anguish of their disappearance. Wherever they are, whatever they may be doing, we wish they are not suffering. *Oshun*, we beseech you to bring them all safely home to Ake. All through this night in the Vigil for the Taken, we stay on the riverbank to remember our terrible loss. So that all peoples may know of our stolen sacrifice, we implore you to acclaim our stolen kinfolk, the noblest souls of all. Ask of us what you will, for a shameful wound bleeds in Yoruba hearts this day.'

'*Bee ni. Bee ni*,' cried the villagers.

Hot salty tears rolled down Taiwo's cheeks.
Again and again, the Mogbas chanted *Oshun*'s refrain:

I am the honey-sweet voice of the waters.
I am the flowing of a woman's cloth as she dances her life.

The chanting gradually faded. The torch-lit ceremony began.
Tugging his arm, his mother said, 'I not see well, Taiwo. What they doing now?'
'They are about to shout out the names of our stolen kinfolk,' he replied. 'Then we talk of our memories of our kidnapped, until all fifty-two names have been spoken of. It is Ake's tradition now.'
'Who speak for our family?'

'Baba ask me to speak for us, Iya. I go when they call me.'

A short while later, a stentorian voice cried out, 'Taiwo of the family Sodeke!'

Striding past the *Bale* and peevish Mogbas, Taiwo faced the villagers.

'Two lives were ripped from my family,' he shouted. 'I, Taiwo of the Sodeke family, speak for my brother Kayode and our adopted sister, Asabi. You all know Kayode. You called him the Cat of the Forest. He was a loving son and my best friend. To this night we still do not know where they were taken. I pray *Olorun* bring them back to us. They linger in a hell for slaves. Is it not a nightmare not to know what has happened to your family, your blood roots and your motherland? You are my neighbours and know me to be a man of my word. I will not rest until I find out what happened to them.'

Pausing to let his words sink into the heads of his audience, he turned to the *Bale*:

'A crime has been committed against the Yoruba,' he said angrily. 'What have you, our *Bale*, done about it? Not much. Not enough. Not anything. On the shores of Badagri, they say *Alafin* Agboluaje sells his people to white men they call Portuguese and English men. Who dares censure a King? I have even heard that his lesser kings have received white men on the coast in the *Alafin*'s Eko Palace. This brutal trade goes on undisturbed — selling Yoruba to whites in exchange for powerful *opas*. Black selling black to black is lawful. That stinks like shit. Slaves are big business for rich Yoruba. Black selling black to white is evil and spawns from the juju of *Elegbara* – Devil. Our stolen never come back and our people still disappear. Next big attack on Ake and the slavers will empty our village of people. We will all be turned into slaves.

'I have warned you again and again, *Bale*. This night I scream at you. Pluck out the *eba* – cassava dough – wedged in your ears. Purge our area of the whites with a force of trackers and fighters. Ambush the slavers! Free their slaves! Did I not take such action with Kayode? We found and freed Asabi from English slavers. Wake up, citizens of Ake! Cleanse the forests in our district! Never again will we be taken by white surprise! Respectfully, *Bale*, I beg the council to support my cause. And I swear to turn every captured white slaver into a slave!'

Cries of delight spilled from the applauding villagers. Even the usually po-faced Mogbas were smiling.

Striding bullishly into the grassy arena with hands on hips, Salako glowered around at the hushed villagers. Tossing his head contemptuously at Taiwo, he growled, 'And who will pay your fighters?'

The hostility in Salako's manner inserted a barbed tenor into the gathering. A light gust whisked through the clearing stirring the leaves. Collectively, the villagers held an anxious breath. Wood owls, the messengers of secrets, discharged a series of loud fast hoots.

Calmly turning to the *Bale*, Taiwo replied matter-of-factly, 'The village must foot the expense. Have we not all suffered at the hands of white slavers?'

Villagers applauded.

'Huh!' said Salako scathingly. 'Your fighters won't bring back my beloved father and sister!'

Gritting his teeth and glowering at his *oluwa*, he was in no mood to yield.

'Tell us about your beloved father and your sister, Salako,' he said impertinently. 'Tell us, your neighbours, what you have done to find your beloved in all these years? Nothing! What have any of us done for any kidnapped? There comes a time when we cannot dodge what must be done. This petition must not fall on deaf ears!'

'Why should I spend my hard-earned cowries on something without profit? You are foolish, Taiwo. You think you get an easy fight against the white men? You get more than that, my friend, you get all out war! Wars turn men into animals!'

'White men make slaves of people of our blood, Salako!' he spat indignantly. 'Ah ah! You think that is like eating *gari*? A shameful tragedy befell Ake. We have let it go unanswered. Wars may turn men into animals, Salako. Doing nothing turns them into slaves! Is that how you want to remember your beloved sister and father — as slaves? We did nothing to the white men who plotted with our Kings. They started this war when they attacked Ake. From that time the white men have gone on buying and kidnapping the Yoruba. Pull your big fat head out of your *agbada*, Salako — we have been at war since that attack!'

Salako's mouth fell open. To be addressed by his *iwofa* in such a manner in front of all his neighbours was the greatest humiliation.

Blundering forwards through the long grass, Taiwo's mother cried, 'Ah-Ah, Salako! The monsters in you disgrace the Yoruba.'

Cheers and clapping greeted her fury.

Shrugging off the hostility, Salako ambled over to a fallen trunk, slumped down and slipped into a sullen silence.

Strolling across to his sulking *oluwa*, Taiwo whispered, '*Alakoro ki isa ogun* – one who wears a coronet must never flee in battle.'

Grunting angrily, Salako turned his back on him.

For the remainder of the long night, while sipping spring water and praying to the gods and goddesses of the Yoruba, Taiwo shared cherished memories of Kayode, Asabi and others with his family, friends and neighbours.

At last, the night drew to an end. Heartened by the shimmering sunrise, he sat on the bustling riverbank, alone with his loving recollections of Kayode and Asabi. The Vigil for the Taken was over for another year.

The sun was nearing its peak. Red-breasted jet-black malimbe birds were foraging in the trees. In the noonday heat, the village pulsated with talk of slave caravans. Visiting neighbours with his father and Chidike, and armed with a gourd of palm wine, Taiwo's spirits rose at the almost unanimous support for his pre-emptive undertaking.

Strolling mutely by with friends, Salako glowered at him. Taiwo scowled back.

Responding to the demands for action by citizens, the *Bale* hurriedly sought the approval of the Elders of the Council. By mid-afternoon he had likewise obtained the sanction of the Mogbas.

At the end of a hot historic day, the odours of change wafted about. A crowd gathered before the imposing mud-brick residence of the mayor. Easing his way to the front, Taiwo joined his father and the storyteller.

Waddling onto the carved white mahogany verandah, the double-chinned *Bale* prepared to announce the decision of the Council. Pompously flinging the sleeves of his white and gold-trimmed *agbada* robe over his shoulders, he spoke in a gravelly voice.

'Your Council regrets not ridding our area of this white plague,' he said with vexation. 'Our failure to do nothing has been a great mistake. We will raise a volunteer force of fighters. They will be well-armed and well-fed. Taiwo will lead them. By order of the Elders, Taiwo's *iwofa* status is hereby cancelled!'

Salako's mouth crashed open. Spluttering furiously, he elbowed his way to the back of the crowd. Following in his wake, his companions grumbled in hushed voices, daring not to challenge the Council's sacrosanct judgment.

Dismissing the boorish protest, the *Bale* shook his head.

'Salako is not prepared to forsake his *iwofa*'s cowry debt for the benefit of the village,' he said irritably. 'His loan to Taiwo's father will thus be repaid by the village. Everyone will be taxed to make up the sum. Citizens of Ake, I beg you to take heart. Your Council will not stand idly by. To carry out this task we must have a plan. Come stand beside me, Taiwo. Tell us of your strategy.'

This false-hearted *Bale* seeks to evade responsibility, thought Taiwo scornfully.

Mounting the verandah and taking a deep breath, he addressed the assembled.

'England's white men will kill anyone who meddles with their traffic,' he said. 'Their deadly *opas* will stop any attack on the open savannah. We will ambush them in our friend, the forest. When we sight a slave column our assault will begin. Secreted in trees and bushes over many days, we will pick them off with poison darts, one by one. Starve them of sleep and sap their strength. In the weak glow of the crescent moon, we will take the rest before they can raise their *opas*. Give them reasons to scream for their God! Men of Ake, we go to rid our shores of white men! Who is up for this task? Who go with me?!'

Rowdy applause and a multitude of hands shot into the air.

Taiwo stepped off the verandah. Slipping in between his father and the storyteller, he grinned. His father smiled broadly, swollen with pride.

The *Bale* raised his arms for silence.

'On your behalf, citizens of Ake, the Council thanks Taiwo and our courageous volunteers. *Olorun* will esteem our campaign, protect our fighters and give us victory. Your Council urges you all to give our hatchling force your support. Heed my words, citizens of Ake. English men have kidnapped fifty-two from our village to sell in their slave markets. No white man skulking about shifting sands on strange shores can change that. We Yoruba are an ancient people — the children of the great god Sango. Conquering peoples and lands from here to the lands beside the Ashanti proves we are a great nation. This day our heads hang heavy with the shame of our defeat at the hands of white men. Our fighters are eager to exact revenge. Our roots go deep in our motherland! This red earth is in our blood! In our language and traditions lies our strength!'

Boisterous clapping and rousing cries greeted the *Bale*'s stirring speech.

'Your rascally *Bale* speaks well on this occasion, Taiwo,' Chidike said with a frown. 'He stir the people's spirits. Sounds like he mean what he say. His friend Salako stokes his own fire, for he lose big this day. Tread carefully near Salako my friend. A cornered rat—'

'First time I see Salako I tread with care,' said Taiwo. 'At last he stands almost alone. He have only his friends and his half of this two-faced *Bale*. The village bands against him. In any tongue that is very alone. For the first time the village aches to strike back at the whites.'

Keeping his eyes on the sullen-faced Salako, he whispered to his father, 'The pig lost one *iwofa*, Baba,' he said, holding up five fingers. 'He will lose five more this night.'

'Salako simmers,' sneered his father. 'Look at the oaf — even now he plots revenge. All night long at the Vigil he heard the bitter truth for slaving his *iwofa*. His neighbours scorned him till sunrise. Tell me Taiwo, how he lose his five *iwofa*?'

'They will volunteer to fight,' he said, smirking.

Grasping his arm with excitement, his father grinned.

'Is that what you mean when you say you clip his fangs? Salako know his *iwofas* volunteer?'

'When Salako find out he will plot revenge,' said Taiwo. 'We are ready for anything he throws. I tempt his *iwofa* before the Vigil. I warn them that they can die on this mission. You should have seen them, Baba. Five skinny *iwofa* fling down their machetes laughing and skip out of Salako's fields. Give them plenty food and the sleep of the gods to get them strong. We need them to be hard — very hard. Then, we need them angry enough to walk for days carrying an *ogbo* to thrust it coldly into white slavers. For that task they need full bellies.'

'The *iwofas* have fifty-two reasons to be heartless, Taiwo. What now?'

'In a few days we will enter the forest with trackers seeking a slave column. We will panic the whites night after night. Keep them awake, sap their strength and when they sleep, we take them with an ambush. We can let not one get away from here. Never again will they take us at will. Never again will England's men take us by surprise.'

Bending towards him, his father lowered his voice, 'Rainforest cover a big big province, Taiwo. To find a slave column will be like searching for a grain of sand in the Sahara desert. We must narrow your search. The *Oso* – sorcerer – will help you find a column in the forest. Through the *Oso* we will get the help of mystical powers. Say nothing of this in the village. Come, Chidike.'

Frowning deeply and scratching his head, the storyteller asked, 'Who is this *Oso*? Where is he? What he do?'

'The *Oso* is a juju priest who trades with the dark forces and he live in the forest,' said Taiwo. 'He is skilled in the mysteries of sorcery and consults the *nipa esu oros* – satanic spirits. Kofo, the village *asewere* – lunatic, is his assistant, who drifts around all day, drooling and babbling *isokuso* – gibberish. He is revered by all for his crazy wisdom.'

'Crazy wisdom?'

'Kofo act and gabble like an idiot, Chidike,' he said, shaking his head. 'But this *asewere* know what is going on. His unearthly visions grant him senses wise men cannot grasp. I know not how. Is Kofo truly crazy? I know he have frightening revelations. Long before that terrible day, he warn the village with a tale of a kidnapping raid by white men. Except for me and my brother, no one in the village had

ever sighted a white man. Mocking his 'ghosts', the Mogbas called
Kofo crazy. Just like he foretold, the white men attacked with their
fierce *opas* and kidnapped fifty-two villagers. The *Oso*, the Mogbas
and the villagers have vowed not to make that blunder twice. Now
when we have a crisis we listen to Kofo.'

'When we meet this *Oso*, leave the talk to me,' said his father
firmly.

Nodding his understanding, Taiwo continued to walk.

Stumbling for some distance along a patchy track on the edge of
the forest, Taiwo followed his father between soaring trunks. The sun
touched the horizon. It was cooler and darker amidst the tangled
foliage. The harsh scolding calls of the *okin eyes* – paradise flycatchers
– put him on edge.

Turning off a dusty track, they entered an open glade encircled by
spreading flame-of-the-forest trees bearing large orangey-red flowers.
At the heart of the leaf-strewn clearing was a round stone house topped
by banana leaves. Waving from the verandah was a jolly middle-aged
woman with a boy and girl. Pigs, goats, a cockerel, chickens and two
horses roamed inside a fenced-off enclosure.

The air suddenly turned icy.

'Dark forces infest this place,' whispered the storyteller.

Rubbing his arms for warmth, Taiwo shivered.

'I burn with cold,' he hissed. 'Feels like the cradle of sorcery.'

Under the branches of a flowering *awusa* – walnut tree – across the
clearing, Kofo squatted amongst fallen leaves. Chanting inharmoni-
ously, he prepared and lit palm torches. Delineated by white stones,
the *Oso*'s altar was laid out a few steps away. At either end were two
calabashes containing smouldering splinters of walnut wood secreting a cedar-like scent. In-between lay the long bill of an ibis, staffs
of sapele, iroko and ebony woods, a leather *fela* hat decorated with
cowry shells, and the shrivelled remains of animals amid knives and
other dark objects. At the heart of the display was a calabash holding
a trussed-up red-feathered fowl.

Clutching his arm, the storyteller hissed, 'Look!'

In the fading light, the *Oso* shuffled towards a small intense wood
fire. He was masked by a garish headdress in the shape of a monstrous

human head, from which sprang a hoop of two Gabon vipers eating each other. Clad in a scruffy black ground-length cloak, he raised his arms above the flames and mouthed an incomprehensible incantation. Turning ominously towards them, a pacific voice came from behind the mask.

'*Joko* – Sit down.'

Dropping to the ground, his father sat cross-legged facing the sorcerer on the opposite side of the fire.

Disturbed by the *Oso*'s grotesque features in the firelight with his hushed tone of voice, Taiwo held his breath. Recalling his father's instructions, he stepped back beside the storyteller.

Shuddering momentarily, the *Oso* removed his mask. In the light of palm torches, the unmasked man was wiry, sharp-eyed, bald and softly spoken.

'*Ekasan*, Baba Taiwo – Good afternoon, father of Taiwo,' he said warmly. 'A long walk through the forest makes for an empty belly. You must eat and drink.'

'*Ekasan*, Oso,' said his father respectfully. 'Your hearty welcome is food enough. Any small small thing you have will be plenty.'

'Rest your old bones my friend,' said the *Oso*, sitting down and pouring liquid from a bronze flagon into four wooden cups. 'We have *eba*, fish and soup. While my *iyawo* – wife – prepares the food, we will honour your visit with fresh palm wine.'

Rubbing his belly, Taiwo grinned at the storyteller.

'*Adupe* – Thank you, *Oso*,' said his father. 'Long time since I come to your house.'

'Baba Taiwo,' said the *Oso*, pulling himself upright and inhaling thoughtfully before chuckling. 'You must have a big big reason to drag your aged carcass from Ake through the challenging *igbocgan* – forest – to my poor poor *ile* – house.'

'Sorry to trouble you, *Oso*,' said his father apologetically. 'You is right. It take much to haul my old bones this far into the forest. My coming here is grave, *Oso*. Ake's timid Council have finally stumbled into courage and made a decision. They have tasked my son with a dangerous mission for the village. To fulfil this action I need the help of your mysterious talents.'

'Council's decision not yet travel this far into the forest, Baba Taiwo,' said the *Oso* dismissively. 'But me know why you come.'

'Ah Ah, *Oso*. I have not told you why I come.'

'You seek white men forcing black prisoners through the forest,' said the *Oso* impassively. 'You come to know just where you can find them.'

'How you know that?'

'Spirit house,' muttered the *Oso*, pointing a skinny finger at a conical mud-brick hut standing alone in the glade. 'Spirits tell me you come to me this day.'

'I see,' said his father, frowning thoughtfully. 'They tell you where we find white men in the forest in days?'

'Give me time, Baba Taiwo,' said the *Oso*. 'I will implore the spirits.'

Beckoning his assistant and kneeling, the sorcerer donned his headdress and picked up a bronze knife.

Walking once around the altar slowly, Kofo grasped the quivering chicken. Handing the sacrificial prey to the sorcerer, he slumped beside the fire and continued chanting.

Slitting the chicken's throat between thumb and forefinger, the *Oso* drained the blood from the convulsing corpse over the leafy ground between them. Tossing white *iyefun* – fine powder – at the blooded leaves, he sat back on his haunches to study the settling particles.

'*Dide dide* – Rise rise,' he urged.

Nothing happened. Time trickled by. A fast hooting owl whooped eerily. Then from nowhere came a cold gust. Suitably agitated, the leaves crackled rowdily and lifted crazily off the ground to form a knee-high symmetrical ring a stride in diameter. For a short time the leaves stayed hovering, noisily and ominously. On some baffling command, they began spinning around with ever increasing rapidity, filling the torch-lit glade with a low sinister rushing sound.

Open-mouthed at the spine-chilling spectacle, Taiwo looked around. The storyteller's eyes bulged with alarm. His father remained impassively focused.

Taking off his headdress, the *Oso* bellowed at the leaves in an unearthly voice:

'*Lati duro*! – Stop!'

As strangely as they had soared off the ground, the leaves plummeted. Instantly, the rushing sound faded.

Silence echoed around the glade.

Awed by the jarring experience, Taiwo gulped.

'*Oso* read only leaves flecked with blood and *iyefun*,' his father whispered.

Holding a palm torch, the sorcerer pored painstakingly over the leaves until at last he delivered a faltering verdict:

'Seven days from this day… white caravan…pass through forest… near Ajero village. I see seven white men with *opas*…holding 'bout twenty slaves… March three days from Ake …*agbede ariwa oun iwo ooun* – north-west – to Ajero forest. Your son will come upon their camp on the fourth night in a woodcutter's grove.'

'Ah Ah, *Oso*!' cried his father. 'Is you sure?'

'He will find them where I say,' said the *Oso* confidently.

Stopping his chant, Kofo leapt to his feet, gabbling wildly and unintelligibly.

Looking quizzically at his father and the storyteller, Taiwo scratched his head.

'You hear what Kofo say?' the *Oso* asked.

Frowning deeply, his father shook his head.

'He say before six full moons have come and gone, you will hear about your son Kayode.'

Dropping his cup of palm wine in amazement, his father leaned forward.

'Ah Ah, *Oso*!' he said. 'Kofo say that?!'

'Kofo got crazy wisdom my friend,' said the *Oso*, gently taking his father's hand. 'Kofo see what we cannot see. He hear what even I cannot. His crazy *iyeinu* – mind – communes with untainted spirits. If he say you get word, you get word. Now we eat.'

Washing his hands in a proffered bowl of water, Taiwo whispered into his father's ear, 'Not possible Kofo's crazy *iyeinu* remember Kayode,' he said. 'All day the fool sits around the village talking *isokuso* – gibberish. Sometimes he not even know his own name. Yet he know about Kayode.'

'If Kofo be right we hear 'bout Kayode in six full moons — then his crazy *iyeinu* be a wise one,' said his father brusquely. '*Oso* has guided you to the place for ambush. Leave soon, my son.'

'I will, Baba.'

The Reckoning

Stumbling through rainstorms for three days, Taiwo's weary volunteers arrived on the edge of the shadowy Ajero forest. Clenching his jaw, he raised his eyes. Black clouds whirled across the noontime skies. Blinded by the downpour, he peered into the forest of towering trunks. Ghostly ground mist swirled through the undergrowth and over decaying leaves strewing the forest loam. Worse still, the way before them was beset with mud.

Slowed by the high humidity and sheets of water gushing from the heavens, his clothes were also sweat-sodden. Scanning the bushes while taking a break, he spotted a drier overgrown track.

'Follow me,' he said, doggedly hacking at the sodden vegetation.

Under the shelter of the canopy, the deluge subsided. Leading the tracker and nine volunteers, he turned for the woodcutter's grove, the direction, distance and location of which had been furnished by the *Oso*.

Given a choice of Ake's volunteers by the *Bale*, he had picked a tracker, five former *iwofa* and four others, all of whom he believed had good reason to be cold-blooded in combat. Included in his assault force was the tracker, Sokoya; the champion bowman, Korede; and farmer, Adeyemi, the acknowledged expert with poisons. In addition to gourds of palm oil, his men each carried an *ogbo* – heavy cutlass, a *jomo* – short sword – and a heavy black palm bow with poisoned arrows. To strengthen their solidarity, he had insisted they take an oath in blood. Around a large fire attended by the Mogbas on the night before they departed the village, each man cut his forearm with the same knife and let his blood drip onto the fire. Brandishing *ogbos* above their heads, they vowed:

'We will kill any white man we find in the forest with prisoners.'

So as not to reveal their presence on the outskirts of Ajero village, he skirted the hamlet. On the other side, he grew aware of rising tensions. Hearing petty squabbles erupting, he knew they needed a respite to rally morale and focus minds. A good distance along the track, he called a halt and squatted with them under the large fronds of a dwarf palm.

Gratitude blazed from his eyes as he nodded at the soaked faces. Sniffing the air, he scanned the location.

'I love the song and earthy stink of the rainforest,' he said, as if he were ambling through flowery slopes on a sunny afternoon. 'Here, we rest and eat. Now I can tell you about the *Oso*'s prophesy.'

Waving his keen-edged *jomo* above his head, an impatient *iwofa* growled, 'Then we go after a big caravan.'

Dismissing the suggestion, Taiwo said, 'See the flowers over there with yellow petals spotted with red?'

'I see them,' said the *iwofa*.

'It is the *onaye* from which we get poison for arrows. Adeyemi needs handfuls. We will all pick a lot for him.'

'How it work?'

'It stop *okan* – the heart.'

'Me know what *onaye* do, Taiwo,' bragged Korede the bowman with a derisive snigger. 'It so powerful, it tell we to go after a big caravan.'

'We be a small force,' said Taiwo fiercely, 'so we take a small caravan.'

Raising no further objections, the fighters began picking *onaye* petals.

Ducking under the dark green glossy leaves of a young sago palm, Adeyemi brushed aside mosses, fungi, twigs and leaves. Fisting a bowl-shaped hollow in the soil, he dropped in six handfuls of *onaye* petals. With studious concentration, the dour-faced farmer began mixing and mashing ingredients for the bane. With eyes fixed on his malefic activities, Taiwo heard only the wind and the soggy song of the forest.

In due course, the farmer gave the deathly substance a final stir.

'Dip arrow tip in paste,' he ordered.

'How far to woodcutter's grove?' asked Taiwo.

'Four to five *ibusos* – miles – from here,' growled the tracker. 'We get there 'fore sunset.'

Rain was still falling when they set off through the forest heading north. The dense canopy kept them fairly dry. Going ahead of the tracker and a single file of men, Taiwo plodded deeper into the dark sultry labyrinth of hardwoods. Excepting the rustling of foliage, a stumble and the odd cough, not a word was uttered for the remainder of the afternoon. Finally, he sighted the entrance to a large grove that was open to the sky. A solitary rundown hut stood at the far end close to a tidy mound of piled trunks.

Secreting men in the bushes dotted around the woodcutter's grove, he settled down with Korede on the thick bough of a drooping almond tree. Hidden in its luxuriant branches, they held an uninterrupted view of the clearing.

Quietly slotting an arrow into the string of his bow, Korede whispered, 'Will this caravan arrive like the *Oso* prophesised, Taiwo?'

'It will,' he said confidently. 'We will stalk a small caravan for days, catch them off guard, and each night send two to their God.'

The rain stopped. The whine of crickets soared.

The fourth day was hot and clammy. A crowned eagle circled high above as a noisy flock of large grey parrots settled in the canopy. Clouds of mosquitoes were on the wing. Concealed in the undergrowth, Taiwo's fighters eked out their rations. On the verge of sunset, the wait was ended.

'Look, the *Oso* was right,' hissed the bowman. 'A man comes.'

Peering down the broad grassy track leading to the grove, Taiwo's hand tightened around his bow.

Glancing nervously from side to side, a wiry bare-chested tracker in worn breeches tottered into the open with a levelled *opa*. Strolling not far behind him was a tall, pony-tailed, tricorn-hatted white man in a filthy camel jerkin and breeches with a slung *opa*. Two sedan chairs followed, borne by a manacled prisoner on either end. Soon after came a staggering column of eighteen sullen prisoners, with two shouldering a brass-studded leather-domed trunk between them. Strutting up and down and flicking whips over bare skins, eight surly sweating white men with slung *opas* controlled the human procession.

Whispering in the bowman's ear, Taiwo was cold, 'Prisoners are Yoruba, Korede. Take out the white men in the chairs.'

'Why them?'

'Do it,' he snapped. 'Leaders ride, followers walk. We cut off the head.'

Stepping out of his chair, a blond-haired portly white man wearing a sleeveless red jerkin and brown breeches removed his tricorn hat. Wiping his jowls, he cast hostile eyes over the prisoners. Jabbing his finger at a striking bare-breasted young woman in a loincloth, he pointed at the forest.

Grabbing hold of the intended rape victim, the tracker bent down to remove her shackles.

Suddenly, Taiwo's bowman loosed an arrow. Shrieking and flinging his arms into the air, Blondie crashed to the ground. Letting go the shackled ankle, the tracker sought refuge behind the sedan. Levelling their *opas*, Blondie's startled companions fired a volley in varied directions at the forest. Dazed by the explosions from the *opas*, the captives cowered on the ground.

Sitting up hesitatingly with a scowl, Blondie gripped the shaft stuck in his boot. Yanking it out, he acted as if he had been merely stung by a bee. Warily rising to his feet, he scanned his mates' angst-ridden faces. Suddenly guffawing, he shouted, 'Sambo's blind. He's got no grey tackle to shoot straight.'

Surprised by Blondie's survival, his companions roared with laughter.

Vexedly shaking his head, Taiwo jeered in a hoarse, furious whisper, 'One big fat white target and you strike his foot. I thought you be Ake's finest bowman? Ah Ah. The man still lives!'

'Wait,' said Korede, calmly raising his hand. 'Watch what that dead man do. Adeyemi is a master of his dark craft. White man soon find out he be more than pricked by my arrow. Poison finish the deed an' spread panic.'

Stiffening in mid-laugh and gasping for air, Blondie clawed at his throat. Crumpling to the ground, he thrashed crazily about. Shuddering abruptly, he then lay still.

'*Eni* – One,' whispered Taiwo. 'He pay with his life for my brother, Kayode.'

'I need make only a scratch, Taiwo. Poison take the man.'

Dispatching a second arrow, Korede shrank back into the foliage.

'*Eji* – Two,' he said, without emotion.

The arrow glanced off the hairy arm emerging from the second sedan chair and struck dirt. Gripping his arm and yelping, a small bearded man dressed in a sleeveless black frock coat tottered a few steps from the chair and collapsed.

Two men lay dead.

Spewing curses, six white men fired muskets wildly at the forest. Thoroughly incensed, three others beat the cowering prisoners and then shackled them to a bat-infested kapok tree.

'We stalk the white men from this night, Korede,' said Taiwo menacingly. 'We kill every night.'

A half-moon cast disconcerting shadows across the unsettled grove. Seated around a table close to their prisoners, unintelligible white men quarrelled angrily.

According to plan, Taiwo's elated fighters repaired to a copse close to the grove identified the day before. Backed against the trunk of an *isin* – akee apple tree, he was resolute.

'Give the whites no sleep,' he quietly insisted. 'Grind them down. While eight of we sleep—'

'Let us sleep now, Taiwo,' said the farmer, stretching and yawning.

'You get plenty of sleep when you get back home, Adeyemi,' he said sternly. 'While eight of we sleep this night, two will take a turn to keep them fretting. For the two awake, stay that way. For them who rest, sleep lightly. We finish them off over three nights. Be on your guard. White men are daring with their deadly *opas*. They come even in the night. First they have to find us. Now we go back to the grove. Me and Korede take first turn to keep them alert.'

Following close on his heels back to the almond tree, the fighters scattered into the undergrowth.

Dropping into the space inside a flowering thorn bush, Taiwo sat with the bowman until the torch-lit caravan quietened. A cloud suddenly shrouded the moon and darkened the clearing. Dropping into the undergrowth, the bowman crawled away on a self-appointed mission. Heart pounding and holding his breath, sweat ran down Taiwo's temples. Soon, the bowman rose from the *koriko* grasses beside the sedan chair. Emptying a gourd of *epo* – palm oil – over the leather contraption, the bowman crawled back into the undergrowth and shortly materialised beside him inside the flowering bush. Closing his eyes with relief, Taiwo exhaled.

Wrapping an oil-soaked wad tightly around the tip of an arrow, the bowman set it alight and let fly at the sedan.

The contraption burst into a searing smelly inferno.

Startled by the incident, the two white guards screamed for their companions. Then, cursing furiously, they set about kicking the prisoners. With no water on hand to douse the blaze, the chair was left to burn. Holding a palm torch, a long-haired man walked to the edge of the forest to relieve himself.

'Help him pass his water in hell,' said Taiwo, pointing.

Drawing back his bow, Korede released the dart.

The arrow thudded into the man's buttock.

Discharging an anguished scream, he dropped to his knees with the barb jutting out of his buttock.

'Dead man on his knees,' whispered Taiwo.

Gathering around the casualty, his bickering comrades attempted to render aid. Fingering the arrow shaft stuck in his posterior, the stricken man wailed, 'Help me! Niggers done for me. I don' wanna die.'

The man stayed transfixed on his knees in the moonlight until, at last, he crashed face down in the dirt.

Agog with fury, his companions again fired volleys over the heads of the prisoners into the dark forest.

'*Eta* – Three,' hissed the bowman.

'Come,' whispered Taiwo, pulling the bowman deeper into the bush.

'*Koriko* grasses very dry after a long hot day,' he whispered.

'*Koriko* grows tall around the hut and tree trunks,' added Korede mischievously.

'Send arrows into the *koriko*.'

'Going to be a long long night for them whites,' said the bowman, preparing *epo* wads for his arrows.

Shortly, two fiery missiles struck the ground beside the hut. Fanned by a light south-westerly, the tall dry grasses erupted in a blaze.

'Stop them flames reaching them tree trunks,' someone shouted.

'What them white men say?' asked the bowman.

Shaking his head, Taiwo chuckled softly, 'I not know their tongue. It be something like put out the fire?'

White men and their tracker frantically beat the flames until the grasses were left smouldering.

At that moment, two fighters arrived for a turn at the harrying watch.

'We put one down,' said Taiwo. 'Give them a terrible night.'

'Sleep good, Taiwo,' whispered a merry voice in the dark. 'We keep them fully awake.'

First light dawned with a blood-streaked sky above the clearing. Shafts of warm sunlight woke Taiwo in the flowering bush. Rising to his knees and parting the bushes facing the caravan, he grinned.

Bleary-eyed, bedraggled and plainly lacking sleep, two white men were sluggishly folding up the table. Six shaky others unshackled the prisoners from the tree. Constantly stretching and yawning, they unslung their *opas* and decamped. Abandoning the undamaged sedan chair and its rotting bloating occupant, they whipped twenty-two captives into a column and staggered off down the track into the shadowy forest.

During the following two nights, six white men were sent to their God. Regardless of their losses, the surviving white men and the tracker persisted with shepherding the prisoners in a southerly direction. Nearing sunset on the third night, two jumpy white men made camp in a small leafy glade.

Scanning the encampment through dense foliage, Taiwo turned and shook his head at his comrades.

'*Esan lati ku*! – Nine dead!' he exclaimed. 'Yet they be still bent on making for the coast. White men got crazy courage. They will see not one more day.'

Scowling, Korede asked, 'What kind of men be they?'

'Men who do not give up so easy,' he said dolefully. 'That why after more than *apo kan odun* – one hundred years – they be still here buying and kidnapping Yoruba people. Tell me, Korede, how can so few white men cow and trick so many Yoruba people on Yoruba soil for so long?'

''Cos corrupt white men trade with corrupt black kings,' said Korede bluntly. 'An' white men use deceit with powerful *opas*. We answer with arrows and spears – weapons of ancient dead men. We must have *opas* and learn to use them.'

Pursing his lips impatiently, Taiwo snapped, 'We will free the Yoruba this night! We take them back to Ake in the morning!'

Carefully parting the bushes, Taiwo surveyed the activities in the caravan.

After gathering wood, the tracker built a large comforting fire. Slumped against the leather-domed trunk, two white men sat gabbling incomprehensibly and swigging from a bottle. Frequently shooting fearful looks at the forest, they were plainly edgy. Every snap or crunch from the forest had the pair on their feet firing *opas* into the dark.

Startled by the sudden appearance of an *iwofa*, the bowman recoiled and trod on twigs that snapped loudly in the dark. Swivelling *opas* at the forest, agitated white men fired. Flames exploded out of the *opas*. Instinctively, Taiwo dropped to the ground. An *iwofa* crumpled lifelessly without a sound.

With his eyes watering and his senses screeching with grief, Taiwo turned to the bowman aghast.

'*Ija* – War – has a price,' said the bowman firmly.

Seething with anger at the murder of a comrade, Ake's fighters scattered into the forest. Encircling the caravan, they dispatched a series of poisoned arrows at the white survivors, who were soon felled.

Catching sight of the white men's tracker dashing for the forest, Taiwo sent an arrow slamming into the tracker, propelling him into a tree.

'Traitor,' he snarled. 'Eleven white men are dead. Our friend lost his life. That treacherous tracker too had to die.'

Striding assertively into the fire-lit clearing, he helped the bowman unchain the prisoners.

Firstly prostrating in prayer to all the gods of the Yoruba, the freed men and women then made for the sanctuary of the bonfire and sat shuddering in torrents of tears. Ravenous since capture, they tore at the sun-dried meat and fruit and washed it down with water and palm wine.

Breathlessly opening the leather-domed trunk with the bowman, Taiwo began rifling through its contents. Underneath strange-looking garments he came upon two swords, six pistols, a worn silver clock-watch, a telescope, a mirror, clay pipes and unfathomable *awuruju* – junk. Distracted by laughter from the fireside, he stood up and stared happily at the scenes of jubilation. In the firelight, his attention was caught by three shiny wooden stocks of *opas* propped against a tree. On the ground lay leather flasks filled with black powder and bags of black iron balls.

'*Opas*,' cried Taiwo. 'We can strike at the English. First we find out how to use an *opa*. I get word from a trader from the land of the Ashanti about a John Connu. He say Connu live in a big castle along the coast with plenty of *opas*. He knows how to use them.'

'Ashanti dwell far far from here,' said the bowman, frowning. 'How we find this Connu?'

'To stifle this wicked traffic we must sacrifice, my friend,' said Taiwo.

'Sacrifice what?' asked the bowman, with a deep scowl.

'Time for a big journey along the coast of Guinea to find Connu's Castle,' said Taiwo. 'I lost my brother. You lost your mother. I seek revenge against the Yoruba kings and the English.'

'Hate serve two masters, Taiwo,' warned the bowman. 'One settles scores and the other destroys the hater.'

Averting his eyes, Taiwo was pensive.

'Look, look around that laughing fireside, Taiwo,' snorted the bowman. 'They so happy to be going home free.'

'Korede, rally our men to gather all the *opas*,' said Taiwo. 'We will carry them and this box back to Ake with us.'

'*Mo dupe lowo Olorun* – I thank God,' said the liberated men and women joyfully between mouthfuls of food.

Blinking back tears, a staggering realisation made Taiwo raise his head.

'We crushed the caravan, Korede!' he shouted, laughing loudly. 'Slavers is dead 'cos *opas* could not stop the poisons of the forest. From now on we ambush them in the forests, not on open ground. Soon, we will set out from Ake to stop another caravan. We do so 'til the caravans pass no more.'

'The *Alafin* is sightless to white slavers on the land of the Yoruba, Taiwo,' said the bowman rancorously. 'Villagers alone got to comb the forests, find the slavers and stop the caravans. We make it so they too scared to enter any forest.'

'We bury the *iwofa* this night,' said Taiwo resolutely. 'Come sunrise, we take our people back to Ake. Start after first light. Pass it on. Sleep now to be fresh for the journey.'

Dawn arrived with a pale blue cloudless sky. Piercing birdsong shot across the grove. Seeking carrion, a kettle of circling white-headed vultures drifted on the air currents high above. Grunting forest pigs rooted for fungi in the undergrowth. The heat was rising with the sun.

Standing on the path on the edge of the forest, Taiwo appraised the restive gathering. Twenty-two battered men and women were treading ground, impatient to get underway. Nine of Ake's task force kept watch. Smoke was still rising from the smouldering remains of the fire on which the corpses of two white men and the tracker had been dumped. Alighting on a woodpile, the cackling vultures hopped clumsily towards the baked carcasses.

Raising his arms for quiet, Taiwo smiled. Against the backdrop of the wakening forest, he spoke:

'We take you to Ake where you will be safe. It is three days from here. There you can rest. Our *Bale* will help you. Get well in Ake and then go back to your homes. White men have sullied our land. For gone *apo kan odun* – one hundred years – they have been buying our people from some of our kings and chiefs. When the white men cannot buy, they kidnap. That is how you come to be in shackles. We plan to kill the slave traffic in our area. You are free to join us against the trade of our kings who sell their own people to white men. We head now into the forest. Stay close and follow me.'

Shouldering the trunk as well as the *opas*, bags of black powder and black iron balls, the fighters fanned out around the column of freed souls. Following the brisk pace into the humid rainforest, they turned south-easterly for Ake.

Falling in behind the tracker, Taiwo was struck by a recurring thought.

'How did the *Oso* know that near Ajero village,' he said to himself, 'we would find what he said — the white man's camp in a woodcutter's grove. I must see this sorcerer again.'

And The Sea With All Its Madness

Aboard the Redemption
14 April 1761
13.30 hrs

The sea with all its madness had flung Jonas far from English shores. He had endured ten weeks of snow, ice and freezing conditions with gales and tumultuous seas.

Came the day a fiery sun appeared above the *Redemption*'s yard-arm. Auguring clearer skies, the wind shifted westward with the dropping sun and blew south-westerly from astern. Creaking and groaning with all sails set through the bright afternoon, large white-capped wavelets on a turquoise sea streamed against her barnacled sides.

In the warm tropical breeze, the barque surged through a pod of spotted dolphins. Close by the starboard side, he saw a flock of large-winged birds low over the water in loose formation. Behind the officers strategising with the Captain by the wheel, he leaned over the starboard poop rails. Long, brown, pendulous throat-pouched birds flew athwart the stern. He was captivated.

'Pelicans, Mister Guinea,' said the Second Mate, grinning. 'Bodes we be close to land.'

'Why thank you, Mister Miracle,' he said, laughing. 'I have not witnessed the like for many a year.'

Beside the Second Mate, he watched the flight of the fish-eating birds.

'Pardon me, sir, for I am intrigued,' he said. 'From where does your family name hail?'

'Miracle is Celtic, Mister Guinea,' replied the Second Mate affably. 'Miracle is Welsh for Meuric. Maurice to ye English. 'Tis easy to forget we Welsh own a different language and traditions. The name hails from the Isle of Anglesey, as do I. I trust you will tell me what rouses your interest?'

''Tis on an undertaking such as ours we may well be in need of a miracle,' he said, grinning. 'I vouch you be a right good omen, Mister Miracle.'

Laughing with the Captain and officers, the Second Mate said, 'A tot of rum on that, Mister Guinea.'

'A tot?' he asked. 'Nay, a tankard, Mister Miracle.'

'A tot of rum for all hands, bo'sun,' the Captain bellowed.

'Aye, Captain,' said the boatswain, grinning from ear to ear and dropping down the companionway.

A cry tumbled from the masthead. 'Land ho!'

'Where away?'

'Fine on the port bow.'

Turning to the prow, he saw the faint outline of the green mountain of Pertigua. A shiver shot down his spine. In sight of the land of his birth, the pinching in his turnshoes vanished. His thoughts fell on the flintlock pistols and Faith Bradshaw's letters of introduction.

'I pray Alexander Fairfax has gleaned the needed intelligence,' he said beneath his breath.

'We have made good time, Mister Guinea,' said the Captain.

'Doubtless due to your navigation, Captain,' he said, giving a slight bow.

'Our difficulties begin when we dock, Mister Guinea,' said the Captain. 'But I am confident we shall succeed. You are ready?'

'As ever as I can be, Captain.'

'Your gut feeling, sir?'

'Is it not all about instincts, Captain?'

'How so?'

'I believe that if a man feels he can do it, he can, sir,' he replied. 'If he thinks he can't do it, he can't. So if he thinks he can or cannot do to it, he is absolutely right. Somehow, strangely, I feel nervously certain. I am ready, Captain.'

Smiling and nodding, the Captain spoke to the Mate. 'What have you, Mister Hopkins?'

'Mount James, Captain. Hurricane Point lies three leagues to the west.'

'Westerly around Hurricane Point, Mister Hopkins,' said the Captain. 'Stand her off half a league. Anchor outside Darwin's Reef in the roads before Jamestown. Enter the Careenage at first light. Stay well clear of the lazarette anchored by the harbour entrance. I venture her contagious charges are justly quarantined.'

'Aye, Captain.'

'Mister Hopkins and Mister Guinea, a word in my cabin,' said the Captain. 'You too, Mister Miracle. Send for the sailing master.'

Five tense men gathered around the gimballed table inside the Captain's cabin.

'Gentlemen, we are on a noble enterprise,' said the Captain quietly. 'We cannot count on the silence of the crew. Rootless men with oftimes deviant ways can be easily bribed. Take Fingers Grabham, our apparently conscientious boatswain. A heavy drinker with peeling morals and more offspring than he can count could be easily induced to tattle with a measly tankard of ale. Grabham's not averse to taking a bit on the side. God knows who the fellow skulks with among his watch or the agents and harlots ashore. Hearken to my words, gentlemen. I informed the crew that Mister Guinea is aboard to assist our business in Pertigua. I want not a word to them apropos the runaways or Mister Guinea's true purpose, nor of our onward passage to the coast of Guinea. I shall inform them about that when we have cleared Jamestown.'

'Aye, Captain,' they said collectively.

Bending hesitantly forward, the Second Mate asked, 'Where do we meet with the runaways, Captain?'

'I expect Mister Guinea to furnish us with the coordinates for that rendezvous.'

Delivering a strained smile, Jonas said, 'I trust Mister Fairfax shall provide that in Jamestown, Captain.'

Turning to the sailing master, the Captain said, 'Once berthed, Mister Fernsby, there will be no shore leave until we have discharged our cargo. Then, I want our consignment of rum and sugar loaded post-haste. I want a fast turnaround, Mister!'

'Aye, Captain,' said the sailing master. 'A fast turnaround ye shall have.'

'By the time we have finished loading, Mister Guinea,' said the Captain, ''tis essential you have discovered the location of our rendezvous.'

'How long do we have, Captain?'

'Five or six days at the most.'

'With the luck of Saint Christopher, aided and abetted by Alexander Fairfax,' said the Mate cheerfully, 'we might obtain the intelligence in less, Mister Guinea.'

'I daresay, Mister Hopkins,' Jonas replied. 'Methinks in five days we—'

A shout from the masthead cut him short. 'Sail ho!'

The cry heightened the tension in the cabin.

'Where away?'

'Two points abaft the starboard beam!'

Given the capital penalty if their mission was uncovered, the shout galvanised all in the Captain's cabin.

Wracked with terror, Jonas joined the scramble up the companionway. Heart pounding, he arrived on the animated main deck.

Raising a shagreen-covered telescope to his eye, the Captain enquired, 'What do we have, Mister Hopkins?'

'A slight hitch,' groaned the Mate, lowering his telescope. 'An English man-o-war, Captain. On her present course I daresay she's making for Jamestown.'

'I agree,' said the Captain. 'Though I reckon when her commander sights us he will change course and come to inspect.'

'Besides an abnormal quantity of victuals and clothing that are well-stowed and which her commander cannot see, Captain,' said the Mate reassuringly, 'we have not anything else to hide. From his poop deck he will see only an ordinary English merchantman.'

'Belay that charade, Mister Hopkins,' said the Captain. 'Yonder captain may well possess intelligence of our intentions. Safer to presume he knows and we act accordingly. If you please, Mister Miracle, if we are closely approached by the man-o-war, I want the crew holystoning the decks.'

'Aye, Captain,' said the Second Mate, winding a short knotted rope around his knuckles. 'I'll have the decks whiter than a hound's tooth.'

'Belay the rope's end, Mister,' said the Captain firmly. 'Nay, act quite the opposite. And during our passage to the coast of Guinea, I want you to identify any member of crew agitating against the runaways. Then I want you to quietly assist that man to cultivate a more charitable manner towards our charges. God knows the runaways need and deserve it.'

'Aye, Captain,' replied the Second Mate, smiling thoughtfully and tucking the knotted rope into his pocket. 'I take your meaning, sir. I shall solicitously inculcate compassion.'

Leaning against the poop rails beside the red ensign jack, Jonas scrutinised the crew lining the starboard gunwales, rapt in the imposing lines of the warship.

'Frenchie an' pirates dodge the likes of her,' scoffed the carpenter. Inflating his chest, he crowed, 'Makes yer proud to see King George's Navy on the high seas. Britannia rules the waves, me hearties!'

'Aye,' cried Fingers Grabham, the boatswain, grinning. 'Right glad am I ter clap eyes on an English goliath. Now ye see why England rules the waves.'

If her marines board the *Redemption*, the flag-waving tars may well want to reassess that maudlin chestnut, thought Jonas.

Shielding his eyes from the glare, he shouted, 'Methinks the warship is altering course, Captain!'

Following his appraisal, the Mate said, 'You are right, Mister Guinea. I'd say the warship's on a bearing to intercept, Captain.'

The Captain raised the glass to his eye.

'Third-rate ship of the line. Seventy-four guns. Her lines give her balance between her firepower and her sailing qualities.'

Catching the sun glinting in the glasses sweeping the *Redemption*'s decks, Jonas trembled.

'Pray God, she does not order us to heave-to,' he said.

'I want no unusual activity on deck, Mister Hopkins,' said the Captain. 'A broadside from her will sink us. If she fires her signal cannon, heave-to and come smartly about.'

'Aye, Captain, that I will,' said the First Mate.

On the verge of sunset, the man-o-war came about onto a converging course in the crimson light. Flying the white ensign on her starboard yardarm, she drew within hailing distance.

Awed by a vessel that dwarfed the *Redemption*, Jonas examined the leviathan from stem to stern.

About one hundred and sixty feet long and forty-five wide, she was a three-masted naval fortress. Her huge black hull boasted two rows of white gunports with retracted cannons along the length of her two decks. On her main deck, red-coated marines and several hundred pigtailed Jack Tars lined the port gunwales. Beside the wheel on the poop quarterdeck, her bearded captain stood resplendent in blue frock coat with gold-laced buttons, white breeches and white stockings, with his starchy officers gathered around his portly self.

Cupping his hands, he bellowed over his port gunwale. 'Ahoy there! Captain Hezekiah Wainwright of His Majesty's Ship *Invincible*. Who are you and where are you bound?'

'Rowland Battersby,' yelled the Captain. 'Master of the *Redemption*. Ten weeks out of Gravesend bound for Jamestown with a general cargo.'

'Where are you bound after Jamestown?'

'Pool of London!'

Seeing the commander deliberate with his officers, Jonas's spirits fell. Skimming through a gamut of unpalatable scenarios, a long prickly pause ensued, during which time he heard the halyards rattling against the masts.

Re-emerging over his gunwale, the commander shouted, 'Good sailing, Captain Battersby!'

'Good sailing to you too, Captain Wainwright.'

The nightmare was over.

With a drawn-out sigh, Jonas wiped his brow. Shaken by the close encounter and sudden reprieve, he managed a faint smile.

Strained grins from the Captain and his officers told him they felt likewise.

Almost at once her sails billowed and the warship began drawing away. In what felt like moments she was out of hailing distance, well ahead of the *Redemption*, on a westerly course for Hurricane Point.

'That somewhat perfunctory inquisition was a little too easy for my liking, Mister Hopkins,' said the Captain suspiciously. 'Had I said we were bound for Guinea after Jamestown, I feel certain her commander would have ordered us to heave-to. Methinks we are on his watch-list, but he is not certain we are his target vessel. As I see it, as of this instant, we must believe the island's planters are expecting us. With the *Invincible*'s men at large in Jamestown, we must watch our step — especially you, Mister Guinea.'

'Aye, Captain,' he replied grimly. 'I note the added threat.'

'Bring her back on course, Mister Fernsby.'

'Back on course, aye, Captain,' the sailing master replied. Turning around, he yelled at the helmsman, 'Bear away!'

'Dead reckon from here on in, Mister Hopkins.'

'Aye aye, Captain.'

Second Dog Watch

The sun had dropped below the horizon. A waxing moon threw an ethereal glow over the sea. Pulling his cloak around his shoulders, Jonas beheld a black celestial bowl sprinkled with stars materialising through feathery clouds. Three leagues to port lay the rugged brooding silhouette of Pertigua. Spurred by a gusty south-westerly and a following sea, the *Redemption* surged on through the dark. Well ahead was the swaying masthead lantern of HMS *Invincible*. A few leagues beyond the warship lay the beacon at Hurricane Point.

Yawning quietly, Jonas looked across the poop deck in the flickering flame of an oil lamp. The silhouetted Captain raised his weather eye to the yards, grunted and addressed the Second Mate.

'Helm's yours, Mister Miracle,' he said. 'Mister Hopkins and Mister Fernsby, please join me in my quarters. Get some rest, Mister Guinea. We need you fresh on the morrow.'

'Aye, Captain,' he said wearily. 'I bid you good night, sir.'

'I have the ship,' cried the Second Mate. 'Steady as she goes, helmsman.'

'Steady as she goes,' repeated the helmsman.

''Fore you retire, Mister Guinea,' said the Second Mate, backed against the stern rail, 'I was wondering if you would share with me how you summoned the guts needed to accept such an endeavour. From where do you hail?'

'I mind not sharing my history with you,' said Jonas, steadying himself against the stern rail. 'I was sold at birth, Mister Miracle. I remember not my enslaved blood parents. I know not from which Yoruba village they came on the coast of Guinea. I know neither their affection nor how they looked. I know neither their names nor what became of them. I do know that I am of Yoruba blood.'

'Well blow me down, Mister Guinea,' exclaimed the consternated Second Mate. 'From your proprietary carriage to the cut of your jib, I could not tell you had suffered such despairing groundings.'

'I was sold to Captain Somerset and his wife,' continued Jonas. 'As a young house servant, I lived with them in Jamestown until we left for England. Before he died, the Captain gave me manumission and presented me to evangelists in Deptford. The Beechams took me to live with them, funded my education and trained me in the business of ship's chandlery. Given the challenging conditions for my kind in London and enslavement of them in Pertigua, I have indeed been fortunate. I come to Pertigua to give thanks to my God by helping free my people, Mister Miracle.'

'Why thank you, Mister Guinea, you have helped put my somewhat lesser misfortunes in a more meaningful context.'

Bidding the Second Mate a good night, Jonas went below to his cabin and flopped on his cot. The *Redemption* was nearing its destination. Keyed up by the imminence of such a landfall, he was also anxious about making contact with the runaways. Closing his eyes, he envisioned Mistress Beecham in the Prussian blue panelled dining room of Pilgrims, scheming with the mettlesome Faith Bradshaw. The island and its previous terrors materialised in his head.

'Pertigua affords a deified life of comfort for white men,' he murmured. ''Tis in truth a blood-soaked nugget set in an ocean of misery.'

Memories reeled through his head and tears blurred his sight as he yielded to self-pity. Bracing himself against the roll of the ship, he yawned. Kent and its oasthouses materialised in his mind's eye. Brushing her letter across his face, he smiled at the trace of eau de cologne that wafted from its pages. Its fragrance spoke of whispered promises in wild flower meadows surrounding Greensleeves. Picturing her taking off her clothes aroused him. His eyelids grew heavy. He would need his strength for the morrow. Yawning, he turned with a sigh to face the bulkhead and fell asleep.

Shouting startled him awake at first light. Blearily donning breeches, jerkin and turnshoes, Jonas stumbled up to the poop deck. Jabbing a marlinspike aloft, the Mate bellowed at the yardsmen up the main mast. They were in Jamestown harbour and the *Redemption* was drifting abeam to her berth by the Careenage.

Standing beside the helmsman watching the ship glide towards the dock, the Captain barked, 'Fore and aft! Stand by to make fast!'

Taking position against the stern rails, Jonas waited for orders. Warm breezes bestirred the red ensign and spry airs brightened his outlook. The temperature was rising. He patted his temples with a handkerchief. Peaking above an azure sea, a blood-red sun exposed a startling spectacle.

He gasped.

On the cobbled dockside, testy-looking white men paced around a huddle of squatting slaves. Under wide-brimmed fedoras, the overseers held whips and muskets. Silent and sullen and clad in tattered breeches, their charges were barefoot and bare-chested, with iron rings around their ankles.

Quivering with rage, he bit his lip.

Black-headed gulls cried excitedly around the topgallant masts as the ship docked. Yelling and flailing the slave gang, the overseers had the starboard breast ropes and springs speedily tethered to the dockside. That accomplished, they lashed and kicked the slaves back into a groaning, squatting huddle.

His legs buckled and he crashed backwards against the rails.

'Good God Almighty,' he exclaimed. 'Having been away for gone two decades, not anything on His earth could have prepared me for the wretchedness of this.'

Suddenly aware the Second Mate had been silently observing him all the while, he blinked back tears and stayed with his eyes fixed on the slaves.

''Twas at Cape Coast Castle, Mister Guinea,' said the Second Mate kind-heartedly. 'I witnessed a slave being executed by being cutlassed to death. I will not forget the dogged defiance in his dying eyes. Shook me rigid, it did. That once I saw it, I vowed not ever again would I do so. Before signing on for this voyage, I mulled it over a great deal with my family. My father believed that a conviction with moral gravity justifies its ends. I signed on for such a just cause, Mister Guinea.'

'Your father is a principled man, Mister Miracle,' he said, looking astern. Stiffening abruptly at what met his gaze, he rubbed his watery eyes.

Through the masts and yards of schooners, privateers, barques and brigantines, HMS *Invincible* was neatly tucked inside the harbour mouth at Deadpan. She was attended by a cluster of gigs and jolly boats. Even from that distance, he could hear the strains of a sea shanty from swaying seamen as they restocked rations, munitions, casks and cannonballs. A proscribed area around the warship was patrolled by sentries from her shore guard.

'The presence of the *Invincible* makes me edgy, Mister Miracle.'

'Methinks likewise, Mister Guinea.'

Surveying the bright, ramshackle, horseshoe-shaped port nestling beneath the lofty Mount James, a remarkable calm mollified him. On the opposite side of a wide cobblestoned road under the shade of a flowering tree, the timbered bell-tower of the Customs House caught his eye. On either side of the whitewashed structure, yellow-brown timber warehouses, varicoloured trading stores, taverns and whitewashed churches hugged the length of the road, lined with tall coconut palms. Snaking up from sign-posted T-junctions, roads meandered across the hills, past Georgian houses with landscaped gardens facing the harbour.

'Pertigua is clearly a prosperous colony,' he said. 'Fairfax has a bureau somewhere along the waterfront.'

Pointing up the hillside at a white Palladian building surrounded by regimented lawns, he asked, 'Yonder building, Mister Miracle?'

'Drake House, Mister Guinea,' replied the Second Mate. 'You are looking at the island's seat of government and the residence of Governor Curzon. A rich egocentric fop said to have the ear of the Prime Minister himself.'

'Then, sir,' said Jonas, smiling mockingly, 'methinks we best steer clear of this Governor's auricular attentions.'

The Second Mate grinned.

Hearing footsteps, Jonas turned around.

Striding up the gangway under an oversized tricorn edged with gold braid was a blotchy-faced portly officer. On his heels were two willowy men in tan jerkins, black breeches and black tricorns. Casting a look around the deck, the officer's cold grey eyes flickered when they caught sight of him and shifted grudgingly away.

Glancing nervously at the Second Mate, sweat poured from Jonas's armpits.

This corpulent officer suspects something, he thought.

Sporting a toothy smile, the Second Mate was cheery.

'Fret not, Mister Guinea,' he said quietly. ''Tis the harbourmaster for the Captain. Comes to clear the ship and levy harbour dues. The chief tally clerk attends to agree Bills of Lading with the Mate. That freckled one is the wharfinger, who with our boatswain will supervise the unloading of our cargo: the hogsheads of brandy, brass pans, casks of pewter and firkins of tallow for barter.'

Ineptly snapping his heels and delivering a stiff wheezing bow, the harbourmaster gasped, 'Permission to board the *Redemption*, Captain?'

Crossing the deck with extended hand, the Captain said, 'Permission granted, Mister Thistlewood.'

'After the tempests you have surely endured, sparkling airs welcome you to Jamestown, Captain,' said the harbourmaster. 'From whence did you sail?'

'Ten weeks out of Gravesend.'

'A speedy voyage, Captain,' said the harbourmaster, nodding across the dock. 'Yonder lies the barques *Osprey* and the *Mary Jane*, dismasted four days past. I trust your passage was not as eventful?'

'Rain, sleet, wind and tempests, sir.'

Sweeping his podgy arm around the harbour, the harbourmaster was hearty, 'Then welcome to an agreeable berth, Captain. You have docked in Pertigua on a glorious day. 'Twill do you and your crew a power of good to restore in our healing climes. May I ask how long you intend to stay in port and where you are bound when you clear Jamestown?'

'I will be in port for a week and bound for Gravesend afterwards, sir. May I enquire why you ask?'

''Tis more than idle curiosity, sir,' said the harbourmaster readily. 'We're conducting a survey of shipping in our waters to determine the expansion of the dock.'

'Come, Mister Thistlewood, let us conclude our business in the comfort of my cabin,' said the Captain. 'I can offer you a fine Madeira while you levy port dues.'

'Why thank you, Captain. Lead the way.'

The two officers dropped below decks.

Nodding at them and scowling, the Mate lowered his voice. ''Tis a tad strange that the harbourmaster of an isolated godforsaken little harbour should be interested in our destination after clearing Jamestown. Determining the expansion of the dock is a half-witted pretence if ever there was one.'

'Methinks his query raises questions,' said Jonas. 'Especially by the conspicuous way he appeared not to notice me. 'Tis as if he were simmering with notions.'

'Mayhaps we can seek from our harbourmaster the whereabouts of Alexander Fairfax,' said the Second Mate. 'He will be likely acquainted with the citizens hereabouts.'

'Hogwash, Mister Miracle,' said the Mate brusquely. 'Such a bungle could imperil Fairfax. Showing interest in anyone in particular invites reprisal on that person. On an island of despots such as this, everyone knows everyone. We come to Pertigua to activate a premeditated project. Giving away our hand is not part of that agenda. After breakfast we shall follow orders and go ashore, Mister Guinea. Probe the mettle of the enemy so to speak.'

'Gladly, Mister Hopkins,' he said anxiously. 'Methinks that would be wise with such little time. I pray it will not prove problematic to locate Fairfax.'

'Five days, Mister Guinea. We must find our man and make contact with the runaways in that time. The *Redemption* must sail in five days.'

Thursday began with a clear, hot and airless morning. Hammering, holystoning and yelling resounded around the harbour. Behind the Mate by the gangway, Jonas tucked a pistol down his breeches and scanned the port. Grubby white fishermen huddled on the dockside gutting fish whilst laughing gulls sat on the water squabbling over fish guts. Horse-drawn carriages with wigged gentlemen trotted along the

Promenade Road. Shouting erupted from a long rectangular wooden shed on the opposite side of the harbour.

'The Auction House,' said the Mate, visibly discomfited. 'Go nowhere near that building, Mister Guinea. A slave auction has just begun. Your Letters of Manumission?'

'I have them, Mister Hopkins. Fret not, sir, I am bent on being gone from this place.'

Accompanying the Mate at a little after ten o'clock, he walked uncertainly down the gangplank onto the cobbled dock. Striding past seamen, dockyard workers and three black men dressed like himself, he was struck by the lack of interest in him — a black man dressed like a white, in blue frock coat, matching breeches and black shoes with silver buckles. Stacking barrels in sweat-stained breeches, skeletal slaves stole incredulous glances at him. The affronting contrast could not have been starker. Tightening his lips, he glanced from side to side with mordant unease.

These tormented men bestir my twelve terrible years on this island, he thought.

Stride for stride with the Mate, he crossed the road.

'Even as a free man, Mister Hopkins,' he said, 'this island would be a somewhat terrifying place for me. I could not ever be certain I would not wake up in chains. Such is providence. Shall we tarry at that tavern by the Customs House? We might identify a cooperative pigeon. And as well we can savour the rum.'

'A fine mindset,' the Mate chortled. 'But leave the questions to me, Mister Guinea. 'Twould not be good to call attention to your elocution and manner. They will see you as impudent. Will ye heed my counsel, Mister Guinea?'

'Aye.'

Tapping his nose, the Mate winked and lowered his voice.

'Act deferential when you speak to me in front of white men,' he said. 'Around these parts they be not familiar with your black breed: educated, well-spoken and well-heeled.'

Cocking his head in momentary consideration, he grinned. 'I trust your judgment, Mister Hopkins, and methinks you are right. Though I might add that on account of my blackness and letters of introduction, I trust that in the looming contact with the runaways and Mister Fairfax, I and not you shall lead the dialogue.'

'Methinks you're not a novice in the ways of white men,' said the Mate, chuckling. 'But your colour and letters of introduction undoubtedly improves our chances. You make a mighty fine accomplice, Mister Guinea.'

Intrigued by the Mate's reasoned assessment of his person, he smiled and said nothing.

Falling in behind the Mate, he entered the *Savannah*, a bright yellow-ochre weather-boarded tavern. The cool buff interior streamed with light from windows facing the harbour. Tainting the sea airs was the overpowering stench of rum, tobacco and opium. Joshing with slubberdegullions of the port, rich bombastic gentlemen sprawled in planter's chairs with glasses of punch. Sat around three bottle-littered tables, hatted overseers played cards. A warped Queen Anne walnut longcase clock with crooked hands leaned against a wall at the farthest end. At a refectory table, poker-faced gentlemen were immersed in business transactions, shuffling sheaves of red-ribboned papers.

Settled at a round cherry-top table near a window looking out on the harbour, he turned around on an impulse. Plodding towards them was a pocket-sized character with grey hostile eyes fixed at him.

Drawing the cheroot from between his lips, the stranger addressed the Mate.

'Good day to you, sir,' he said, puffing out his chest and drawing himself up to his full four feet. 'You be looking at Silas Beadle, innkeeper of the Savannah. Who be this nigger then?'

Infuriated, Jonas simply frowned at the Mate.

Deadpan and tight-lipped, the Mate swivelled and coldly appraised the innkeeper.

'I dinna catch yer name, sir,' said the innkeeper, with a Cheshire cat grin.

'I did not give you my name, innkeeper,' said the Mate, dismissively scratching his neck. 'Hopkins is my name, Mate of the *Redemption*. And he is my friend — a free man with papers to prove it.'

'I meant no offence, Mister Hopkins,' said the innkeeper awkwardly, bestowing a smile rooted in a mandarin crease. 'Ye cannot be too careful in these difficult times. Round these parts, there be the Mongoose Gang an' three free niggers dressed like 'im. I met one jus' once an' he was—'

Raising his hand, the Mate interrupted.

'I am sure you have met many men, Mister Beadle,' he said dismissively. 'We took no offence. My friend and I want a flagon of rum and two goblets. I have a question for you.'

'A fine flagon right away, Mister Hopkins. An' what else might you be wanting?'

'The address of one Alexander Fairfax. I am told he resides hereabouts.'

'You come to the right tavern, Mister Hopkins,' said the innkeeper. 'Them at refectory table, they be acquainted with Fairfax. Make your inquiry with them. They be right 'appy to help you. I'll sen' over me boy with a worthy flagon.'

'Thank you kindly, Mister Beadle,' said the Mate, scowling at the departing proprietor.

'The Mongoose Gang, Mister Hopkins?'

Bending forwards, the Mate spoke quietly, 'See them well-fed, well-clad and hatted black men loitering by that warehouse over yonder?'

'Aye?'

'The Mongoose Gang. Freed men waged to hunt down runaways.'

'Cockeyed regimes construct cockeyed remedies, Mister Hopkins,' he said, shaking his head with chagrin.

'It grieves me that English men could wash their hides in this obnoxious trade, Mister Guinea.'

''Tis grief enough that such traffic could be spawned by a human mind at all, Mister Hopkins.'

'Thaddeus when we're ashore, Mister Guinea.'

Smiling thoughtfully, he said, 'Then Thaddeus it shall be, Mister Hopkins, and Jonas to you, sir. Although mayhaps not too loudly around these parts.'

A grubby bug-eyed lad with curly flaxen hair placed goblets and a flagon on the table.

'Rum, Mister,' he said, making a speedy exit.

'To our runaways, Jonas,' said the Mate, taking a swig.

'Aye,' said Jonas.

'Methinks 'tis time to get some answers from those men,' said the Mate, rising to his feet. 'You will be safe where you sit, Jonas. That impertinent innkeeper will by now have blabbed to all that you are a free man. They will still give you a wide berth.'

Mindful of his own anxious breathing, he turned to the harbour.

I like not the strain of being alone near anonymous white men, he thought. I pray they give me no more than a glance.

Minutes later, the Mate slumped back into his chair and heaved a sigh.

'Thus engrossed in their mercantile machinations, they paid scant attention to me or you,' he said. 'But we have what we came for — the address of Fairfax. We shall seek it out when we're done here. Not to draw attention to ourselves, it would be wise not to leave too soon.'

'More rum, Thaddeus?' he asked, filling both goblets.

'Aye, Jonas.'

On the north-eastern end of Promenade Road they turned into a bright flowery courtyard. At the top of a rickety wooden dog-leg staircase, Jonas arrived at a weathered oak door with a skewed plaque bearing the carved name: Alexander Fairfax, Esq.: Shipping Agent.

Knocking sharply, he waited.

'Enter!'

Opening the door, he stepped into a poky two-windowed weatherboard office. Musty odours of paper and tobacco assailed his nostrils. A polished mahogany tall case grandfather clock stood inside the door. Heaps of documents and vellum scrolls, a brass binnacle compass and models of barques bordered three Windsor armchairs.

Seated at a mahogany kneehole desk was a fine-jawed tanned man in his early forties. Such was the silence that squeaks from his striped-barb quill across notepaper were evident. In the middle of the day he was dressed in a brown silk banyan and a raspberry silk nightcap. Rounding off his fastidious persona, a smouldering marbled clay pipe dangled from his lips.

A veritable English dandy, thought Jonas.

'Good day, sir,' he said. 'We seek Mister Alexander Fairfax.'

Raising his head, the agent frowned.

'That is I,' he said coldly. 'And what do you require from me?'

'Jonas Guinea, at your service, sir,' he replied. 'And Thaddeus Hopkins, Mate of the *Redemption*.'

Suspicion purled from the agent's narrowed eyes and his manner said much the same. Pulling the pipe from his mouth, he leaned back in his chair.

'Should they mean something to *moi*?' he asked dismissively.

'My name may not, Mister Fairfax,' he said calmly, tendering Faith Bradshaw's letter of introduction, 'but my credentials should mean something to you.'

Putting his feet lazily onto an upholstered patterned hassock, the agent took the letter. Without looking up, he mumbled, 'Have a seat.'

Taking the chair, Jonas perused the chart-lined walls of the unusual office.

Suddenly guffawing, the agent stood up with outstretched hand.

''Tis good to meet you in the flesh, Mister Guinea,' he said eagerly. 'A pleasure, Mister Hopkins. I regret the frosty reception, gentlemen. A body cannot be too careful in these unstable climes. I have been keeping watch for you these past weeks. I had to be certain it was you. Right glad am I that you are safe. And I have to say 'tis indeed a privilege to participate in such an audacious project. Day after day, I witness the atrocities on half-starved men, women and children. I fancy a chance to strike back at the trade.'

'Glad to make your acquaintance, Mister Fairfax,' he said, beaming. 'Mistress Bradshaw spoke of your invaluable assistance during the dangers she faced in the uprising. And I have to say, sir, she spoke most warmly of you. I trust the League's plans progress as planned?'

'You have sailed into an uneasy era on a troubled island, Mister Guinea,' said Fairfax ruefully. 'Right now, the Governor and Matthew Fleming are raising Cain. They have men keeping watch for certain vessels. I cannot for the life of me—'

'Has the *Redemption* been mentioned?' he interrupted.

'Only as one among others,' said Fairfax, shaking his head. 'They know not which vessel they seek. Every ship entering the harbour is closely scrutinised. Be in no doubt, Mister Guinea, your free black person will have been verily noted. I will vouch for you if necessary. Be on tenterhooks, gentlemen. Black and white firebrands and informers lurk everywhere. Methinks it would be better not to tarry hereabouts in daylight hours. Below to the side of this house is the door to my lodgings. Return here at nine o'clock this night. We can down a fine wine and strategise — away from prying eyes. After that Mister Guinea, you can regale me with the social intercourse and well-being of Mistress Bradshaw.'

Rising to his feet, Jonas smiled thoughtfully.

'Till nine o'clock, Mister Fairfax,' he said.

''Tis providential we met so promptly, Mister Fairfax,' said the Mate. 'We have little time and a great deal to accomplish.'

In higher spirits they returned to the *Redemption* to report to the Captain.

Night tars were clustering along the waterfront. Slack waters augured peace. Gripping the stern rails with disquiet while awaiting the Mate, Jonas scanned the port. On the moored vessels and in the waterfront houses, the oil lamps defined the quaint horseshoe contours of the darkened harbour. From the shadows he heard the chatter of muted voices. Breezes sent halyards, blocks and tackle rapping against masts and spars. Above the sounds of the haven, he could hear the pounding in his chest.

At ten minutes to nine, he left the ship with the Mate under a gibbous moon, bound for the agency. Crossing the dockside road near a tavern, he heard a grating rendition of *The Handsome Cabin Boy*. Feeling blacker than the night, he strode along the cobbled thoroughfare. Dodging drunks who appeared to lurch towards him, he quickened his steps. To evade anyone following at the intended turning, he pulled the Mate sharply into the agent's courtyard.

Startled by a figure in the shadows, he gasped, 'Good God!'

Suddenly, Fairfax stepped into the moonbeam across the doorway.

Exhaling with relief, Jonas wiped his brow.

Heaving a sigh, the Mate chuckled inaudibly.

'Follow me, gentlemen,' said Fairfax, stepping through the front door and leading them down an oil-lit passageway.

Entering the withdrawing room, Jonas smiled.

Right down to the garniture decorating the cabinets, the chamber was elegant. Floored with red oak boards, it was lined with polished cherry-wood panels and candled brass sconces. There were three box-sash windows with harbour views along the opposite wall. Bottles of rum and Madeira and three goblets sat on a round polished mahogany dining table. Beside them lay a copy of *The Female Quixote* and an unfurled sea chart of Pertigua. In front of the middle window on the floor, a brass Persian astrolabe revolved inside a fruitwood stand. A walnut-veneered grand pianoforte straddled the far end, bearing the copperplate imprint: *Bartolomeo Cristofori. Florence.* Given the flamboyance of the man, he was not surprised by the presence of such an august musical instrument.

Eyeing Fairfax's white silk jabot, embroidered silk frock coat and white breeches, Jonas raised his eyebrows at the Mate.

I might have guessed Fairfax's abode, like his person, would defy credulity, he thought. I like his dissenting ways.

'An exquisite chamber, sir,' said the Mate.

Pointing at two brown quilted leather wing chairs either side of a grandfather clock, Fairfax threw a winning smile.

'Be seated, gentlemen, we have much to consider,' he said, decanting dark rum into three goblets. Very carefully, he drew heavily embroidered silk curtains over the windows. 'Now we have privacy. At present, mistrust in Jamestown is rife. Tickled am I to encounter you so timely. Shall we raise a glass to your speedy departure then?'

'Aye, Mister Fairfax,' he said, laughing and raising his goblet. 'The Captain itches to quit Jamestown. Inasmuch as Mister Hopkins and I would be happy to stretch out in the ease of your capital lodgings, the fraught atmosphere around these parts counsels us to be gone forthwith.'

Laughing at his droll rejoinder, Fairfax lowered his voice.

'Of late the town has been agog with startling gossip,' he said. ''Tis said an imminent raid for slaves is expected on the plantations. 'Tis supposed to be led by the French in conspiracy with pirates. Given such tidings, the militia and the overseers scurried for their muskets. Matthew Fleming's harbour watch began accosting citizens. Jamestown is at present braced for a fight. 'Tis all a duplicitous ruse to justify their actions of course, for as we know, 'tis really the *Redemption* they seek. Fortunately as yet, and even though they have a shortlist, both the Governor and Matthew Fleming are not the least bit certain of the name of the vessel they are after.'

Downing a swig of rum, the Mate asked, 'What of our runaways?'

'Twelve shall be awaiting you in Deception Bay, Mister Hopkins,' said Fairfax, pointing a manicured finger at a position on the chart. 'Zachariah, who has my utmost trust, is our go-between. I stumbled into him smuggling for the rebels in the uprising. One night he was surprised by a Redcoat patrol. He escaped and arrived at my door seeking sanctuary. I gladly obliged. A few days later, I was ambushed by rebels. His intercession saved me from their hangman. Following the defeat of the rebels, I rescued him from the executioner's flames. Somehow, gentlemen, it puts a contradistinctive slant on one's affairs when a slave saves a white life on a slave island. Zachariah has proved to be a first-rate friend and mediator with the runaways.'

Putting down his goblet, Jonas asked, 'Will Zachariah be with us this night?'

'Nay, Mister Guinea. He visits the runaways near Deception Bay.'

'When can we meet him?'

'The night of the morrow. Come for supper at eight o'clock. Zachariah will be here at some point. Owned by the port authority for some years now, he contrived his way to be trusted. A trustee has liberty to roam within Jamestown's precincts and the privilege to live with a woman of his choosing. However, on pain of death he is prohibited from consorting with slaves.'

'Where does he lodge?'

'Near the dockhead in a topsy-turvy shack which cannot be missed,' said Fairfax. 'In a yard on his roof he keeps vegetables, pigs and goats. Lives with his woman and scrabbles together enough to meet their needs. The man has taken considerable risks for the League's enterprise and has well-earned his berth on the *Redemption*. During the uprising, Mistress Faith and I came to depend entirely on his wits for food and shelter.'

Wearing a thoughtful smile, Fairfax lifted his goblet.

'Now tell me, Jonas Guinea, about the fetching Mistress Faith,' he said with a raunchy chuckle. 'Her correspondence has borne a curiously heady note of late. And her letter of introduction carried a certain, shall we say, unrestrained appeal.'

'She was in fine fettle when last I saw her,' he replied. 'Indeed, she looked wholly content with her rustic surroundings.'

Taking a sip of rum and disporting a smile tainted with suspicion, Fairfax said, 'I wonder why?'

Without equivocation, Jonas said, 'Methinks her recovery from the uprising and tranquil years on her Greensleeves estate appear to sustain her contentment.'

'Thou sometimes lend a comforting shoulder, no doubt?'

The fellow flaunts his unrequited affections, thought Jonas. It would be imprudent to confess my feelings for Faith. I have witnessed the demeanour of white men when a black beds a white woman and the other way around. On either side of the colour bar, a potent concoction of abhorrence and inadequacy arises. Jealousy could well make him sabotage his efforts in this mission.

Throwing a swig of rum down his throat with a smile, he tip-toed out a response. 'I am merely her good friend, Mister Fairfax,' he said dispassionately. 'I find Mistress Bradshaw to be one who keeps her own counsel.'

Visibly relieved by his response, Fairfax raised his goblet and said, 'Mistress Faith Bradshaw!'

'Aye,' he chorused with the Mate.

'What of the Flemings?' Jonas asked hesitantly.

'Since the uprising, at the instigation of Matthew Fleming,' said Fairfax, 'the overseers uphold order with transformed vigour across the island. Having succeeded his bedridden father as Pertigua's principal planter, the cold progeny administers his family's estates with remorseless cruelty. As his first gory adjunct, he ramped up the carnage across the island. Oftimes along Promenade Road there are bloody executions of so many slaves that the cobbles run red. On sighting the bodies of their kinsman, the slaves teeter on the edge of another uprising. It leaves one distraught.'

Incensed by what he heard, Jonas leaned conspiratorially towards his accomplices.

'This interminable trafficking in human beings,' he said emphatically, 'motivated a resolution of the League in London to explore ways and means to reverse the trade. Our presence here, in fact this enterprise, is the first such test. In truth, methinks our efforts will not impede the trade. But, it might crack the elemental crust of this inhuman commerce. It will prove to like-minded shipowners that by adopting this way of doing things, they as well can find and free runaways.'

'I am of like mind, Jonas,' said the Mate.

Enlivened by the evening's camaraderie, Fairfax pulled out a small oval table swathed with baize. Opening a drawer with a vulpine grin, he extracted clay pipes and a silk pouch containing dried green leaves. Crumbling the leaves and packing three pipes, he passed them around.

'Savour a therapeutic remedy of these isles with me, gentlemen,' he said, laughingly lighting his pipe. 'Indulge in my prescription for soothing the spirits and loosening inhibitions. We can as well partake in a wager or two.'

Appointing himself banker, Fairfax dealt cards across the baize for a game of Pharo. Coloured stones were co-opted as chips, valued at one penny to one shilling each.

Swigging rum and then a toke of his pipe, Jonas's senses began to swirl. Hazy miasmas obscured the chamber and the clock appeared to throb. Swaying woozily from side to side, he squeaked:

'My senses are somewhat befuddled, gentlemen. Methinks you flaunt monstrous filamentous noggins.'

'Your woolly head swamps this reeling chamber, Jonas Guinea,' said Fairfax, giggling girlishly. 'And you have the jaws of a whale, Mister Hopkins.'

Guffawing and rocking in his chair, the Mate woozily babbled, 'One in the eye, on the nose and in the bread-basket.'

Frowning at the Mate's perplexing comment, Jonas then smiled at Fairfax.

'I whiff foggy colours,' chortled the Mate. 'Met a buxom Irish wench once after a stormy passage from Guinea...' Suddenly, he dropped snoring onto the arm of the chair.

'Tut tut,' said Fairfax. 'Methinks Mister Hopkins has taken a leave of absence.'

'And without consent,' said Jonas, laughing.

Befuddled and weak-kneed, he stayed like a statue lodged in a garish fug.

Whelmed with high jinks, high spirits and side-splitting laughter, the long night drew to a close in birdsong.

Pax Africana

17 April 1761
20.00 hrs

Beneath a swelling moon, Jonas walked with the Mate into the shadows of Promenade Road. Arriving at the agent's abode, he was eager at the prospect of meeting Zachariah. At the first sight of the man in the curtained withdrawing room, he swallowed deeply.

Only luck and tutoring separates us, he thought. There but for the grace of God go I.

Stepping forward, Fairfax was effusive.

'Allow me to present my steadfast friend, Zachariah,' he said.

With a broad smile, Jonas shook his hard, calloused hand.

Of medium height and in his late forties, Zachariah was a lean, gaunt, furrowed-faced figure with the smell of audacity and eyes dulled by lassitude. Bare-footed and clad in frayed jerkin and breeches, he looked incompatible with the fineries and decoration of the candlelit chamber.

With a gap-toothed smile of stupefaction, Zachariah eyed his blue silk frock coat, breeches and silver-buckled shoes.

'You be no slave,' he said with mock disbelief. 'Dressed in fine white-man clothes — you be this Jonas Guinea then?'

Tendering his letter of introduction, he smiled.

'For you from Mistress Faith,' he said. 'Aye, Zachariah, I am Jonas Guinea. In truth, it has long been my aspiration to meet you.'

Sitting down, Zachariah opened the letter.

'Twelve runaways await you in Deception Bay, gentlemen,' said Fairfax. 'Asabi leads them. She was the woman of Kayode, known in these parts as Captain Sodeke, the rebel leader who perished in the uprising. Sodeke fought Governor Sir Anthony Ashley to the bitter end and lost. Providentially in his wake he had scattered his seditious imaginings on the restless plantations. So much so, I believe the slaves presently disguise signs of mutiny. I ask myself if there were a revolt, has Governor Curzon the military force to suppress it?'

'Has he?' asked the Mate.

'I think not.'

'Do the slaves know that?' asked Jonas.

'I think not.'

'An excellent moment to inform them,' said the Mate dryly.

Raising his head and waving the letter, Zachariah said, 'You live in England, Mister Guinea?'

'Aye. That I do.'

'You see Mistress Faith?

'Aye. That I shall.'

'You tell she 'bout Zachariah. An' ask she to come see we in Guinea!'

'I shall,' he said. 'I shall as well tell her of the risks you have taken in this dangerous venture. Most touchingly, she spoke of your many deeds and she did as well tell of—'

Coughing sharply, Fairfax broke up the dialogue.

'Shall we be seated gentlemen?' he said. 'We are here to agree the rendezvous and the—'

Belligerent banging on the front door echoed down the passageway.

Raising a finger to his lips, Fairfax leaned towards them.

'Stay quiet, gentlemen,' he said, lifting a lantern and making for the door. 'I shall send them packing.'

Rattled by the intrusion, Jonas looked at each man in turn. Beads of sweat burst from Zachariah's temples and his eyes bulged. The Mate had turned pasty white.

Hearing the front door unbolted and creak open, Jonas felt his ears straining.

'Sorry for troubling ye, Mister Fairfax,' he heard a voice growl. ''Tis Jasper Fetcham of the Harbour Watch. We be after Zachariah. Nigger should be at his lodging. His black hide been seen round these parts. He been here with thee?'

'What, lost another slave, Mister Fetcham?' mocked Fairfax. 'Tut tut tut, Mister Fetcham. Owners ship in slaves and ye swagger about losing them.'

'I got a clear conscience, Mister Fairfax.'

'Then you clearly possess a terrible memory as well, Mister Fetcham. Did ye not once fetch slaves for your master that did not correspond with his tally book? You mislaid slaves then did you not?'

'An honest mistake for a body who canna read, Mister Fairfax,' protested Jasper Fetcham. 'How was a body to know tally clerks fetched me the wrong number o' slaves? And that Zachariah can read an' write? Reading makes him more slippery than most. Forsooth! What dim-witted body learned a slave to read?'

'Perchance a body who knows all the facts, Mister Fetcham,' Fairfax chortled. 'Take your men and scour the waterfront; he may be night fishing in the crannies by the Auction House. He comes to take my consignment to the waterfront on the morrow. I myself find Zachariah eminently reliable.'

'Even so Mister Fairfax, keep yer doors an' winders bolted,' said Jasper Fetcham. 'Me an' my men will keep a sharp lookout for the edicated rascal.'

Hearing the front door bolted, Zachariah slumped back in his chair and let out a soft groan. Jonas heaved a sigh and mopped his brow. The exchange had shaken him.

Smiling imperiously, Fairfax resumed his seat and downed a hearty swig of rum.

'Fret not, Zachariah,' he said reassuringly. 'Fetcham won't show his face again this night.'

Tossing a splash of rum into his goblet, the Mate broached the subject of the *Redemption*'s recognition signal.

'In daylight,' he said conspiratorially, 'the Union flag will be at the main topgallant mast. At night, two lanterns, one directly above the other, will be lashed to the bowsprit. We'll send a gig ashore at first light.'

Zachariah beamed.

'To help you make we out at night,' he said, 'we raise two lights side by side.'

'Remember this too, Zachariah,' said Jonas quietly. 'I am told that with favourable winds the *Redemption* will anchor off Deception Bay — three days from now. We will send a jolly boat to Heddon's Mouth for you. Fret not if we're late. At such time we may well be dodging the privateers or the Navy. Hide among the rocks, my friend. We shall not sail without you.'

Venting a jubilant shriek, Zachariah's eyes glistened.

'We wait like hawks on the wing for a chance to get out,' he said in a breaking voice. 'Hope sits on the horizon mocking 'em with Guinea dreams, 'til 'em lose hope in the nightmare. Now there be hope for twelve — a drop. We be waiting on the shore for the *Redemption*, Mister Guinea. Then we wash our names from the blood-sands of Pertigua.'

Awestruck by the man's articulate analysis of his lost years as a slave, Jonas raised his goblet and said, 'One drop grows to a torrent!'

'Aye!' they cried.

Leaning back in his chair, Jonas exhaled.

'How long have you been on this island, Zachariah?' asked the Mate.

'Tell us, my friend,' said Jonas. 'We know not anything about how you have survived on the plantations and in the cane fields.'

It was as if Zachariah had long been waiting to give his testimony to the first man who would listen. A reservoir of pain burst and out poured his tale. Until the early hours, he described his hellish existence during forty odd years on the plantations. As a boy, he had survived the treacherous crossing. From then, he suffered the tortures doled out day after day by overseers until the youth quaked with despair and rage. The man was fiery and wounded, until the subterfuge of the League fell into his ears. Joy invaded his life and expectation blazed from his eyes.

Distressed by Zachariah's account, Jonas dabbed his cheeks. Paradise for this soul begins and ends on the shores of Guinea, he thought.

The Mate stayed pensively tight-lipped.

The evening ended on a sobering note. Nonetheless, the League's hitherto inconceivable *Pax Africana* — to reverse England's slave trade — was toasted with rum, Madeira and clay pipes.

Jonas's primary contact had been achieved and plans were proceeding. His coastal rendezvous was in the offing.

Sitting on the edge of the cot in his cabin and bracing himself

against the roll of the ship, Jonas penned two letters to England —
one to Mistress Beecham and the other to Faith.

The *Redemption*
Pertigua
17 April 1761

My dearest Faith,
How I have yearned for your companionship these past months.
My time at Greensleeves was made all the more delightful in
the company of your friends. Tender memories of your person
alone with mine continue to fortify me. As well, I love thee.
From the instant we parted on the carriage drive, not a day
has passed that I do not think of a joyful homecoming amid
thoughts of times to come. I have reread the warm sentiments
in your letter countless times and still I find them to be most
rejuvenating. 'Tis warm in these climes. 'Twill be hot on the
coast of Guinea. Be assured of my diligence. I am well and embroiled entirely in our quest for abolition. As I pen these words
the *Redemption* stands well out to sea and is imminently set to
embark our runaways, following which we are bound for the
coast of Guinea. Captain Battersby is indeed a first-rate Master
of a well-found vessel.

Your letters of introduction have indeed resolved much of what
we need and condensed our stay in Jamestown. In the affable
company of my appointed escort ashore, Thaddeus Hopkins, the
Mate of the *Redemption*, I have just returned from a most uplifting
evening in the lodgings of Alexander Fairfax, who introduced
Zachariah. I found both men to be everything you said of them —
daring, dependable and determined. I now understand how they
earned your confidence. Again I ask how a genteel soul encounters
such wonderful recalcitrant fellows. Our plans to liberate twelve
runaways have been established through Zachariah, who plans to
be among them going home to Guinea.

I most fervently hope and trust that you and the Parson will
visit Mistress Beecham. I wish I was there with you to help the
League and its willing hearts organise petitions to Members of

Parliament for the abolition of slavery. I will as well write to
Mistress Beecham.

By the time my words reach you, dear Faith, the *Redemption*,
God willing, will be nearing the coast of Guinea and then be
homeward bound. I love you and dispatch my ardent affections
across tempestuous waters.

Loving thoughts from foreign shores,

Jonas

To assist its arrival in her hands, he would give his letters to Captain Battersby, who would entrust them with an old shipmate, the
Master of the elegant barque, the *Merilyn*, bound for Sheerness in the
morning.

Conspiratorial Airs

It was a warm silken day. A rain shower had fallen in the early hours, and the earthy aromas heartened Matthew Fleming as he trotted along the carriage drive. Cheered by the welcome of swallows flitting from the eaves of the Great House, he dismounted. His sister was giving orders to a messenger by the front door. After a feisty night with Harriet Beaufort, and following his ride from Nonsuch Hall on Little Pertigua, he was now tired and preoccupied.

'She plagues me to marry,' he muttered to himself. 'Certainly she is spirited and satiates my appetite. She is presentable and well-connected, but will she settle? Having revealed the extent of her estate, I am confident Father will judge our combined holdings an excellent match. I feel luck is with me this day.'

'Stable your mount and see cook for victuals,' he heard his sister tell the messenger. 'We shall send a reply with you.'

'Thank 'ee kindly, Mistress Fleming,' replied the messenger, doffing his cap. 'I be a mite famished after me long ride from Jamestown.'

Leaving the messenger, his sister walked towards him with a quizzical smirk.

'What amuses the lass?' he asked himself.

'An exquisite day after a licentious night no doubt, dear brother,' she laughed suggestively. Wrinkling her nose, she embraced him. 'She is smeared all over you.'

'Hush your mouth,' he said, laughing. 'Harriet intrigues me so. She may well be the next Mistress of Augustfields.'

'Why am I not surprised by your intelligence, Matthew? Harriet has been in hot pursuit of you with the delicacy of a strumpet. 'Tis fortuitous then that the febrile firebrand and I are friends. I can abide the match. She will keep you happy — at least in bed. Enough prattle of your tryst. Even as you and that hussy were cavorting, our suspect vessels put in to Jamestown.'

'What, all three vessels? And Jonas Guinea?'

'Let me give you the messenger's report.'

Pausing in his stride, he listened to her tidings.

'We must act without further ado,' he responded. 'Father must be told at once.'

'Father is on the upper verandah with Mother,' she said.

'We must inform them this instant,' he replied. 'And try not to get the old folks unduly excited.'

Playfully poking her tongue at him, she took his arm and walked into the house.

On the upper verandah, the old man was sprawled on a planter's chair. He was in high spirits. Their mother sat giggling beside him, her tapestry cast aside. Goblets in hand, the couple were basking in a slave-free view of papaya and banana trees and flowering bougainvillea.

'Good day, sir, and to you too, madam,' said Matthew, perching on a chair. 'We have just received word from Silas Beadle, innkeeper of the Savannah tavern.'

The old man's face clouded.

'What's the unctuous scoundrel peddling?' he growled.

Flouncing across the verandah, Mary clapped her hands gleefully.

'Beadle says the *Oriel*, the *Phoenix* and the *Redemption* are finally all told in the harbour,' she said. 'The *Oriel* docked on the day last past.'

Bending forwards with a quizzical expression, her mother was abrupt.

'They have been previously identified, Mary,' she said. 'Is that all he brings?'

'Beadle did proffer an intriguing bit of tittle-tattle, mother,' said Matthew. 'He received in his tavern the Mate of the *Redemption* with a well-dressed free nigger — who spake not a word and appeared to conduct himself like a servant.'

Sitting bolt upright, the old man was clearly agitated.

'Is this a Mate with a mere servant,' he asked rhetorically, 'or is he a Mate with Jonas Guinea disguised as a servant?'

'Beadle says the nigger gave not anything away, sir,' said Mary. 'But the Mate asked for Alexander Fairfax.'

Scowling deeply, the old man exclaimed, 'Fairfax the shipping agent? Methinks you jest, Mary. 'Tis hard to believe that that fashion plate possesses the nerve to partake in a slave-raiding conspiracy.'

'Fairfax acts lightheaded, sir,' said Matthew. 'But I have never been convinced. He even appears fickle and giddy, which harbours a perfect disguise. Sanctioned by the powers that be, he is up to his neck in smuggling. In truth, he has a cunning hand and would stop at nothing to further his interests. Methinks he even betrays activist sympathies.'

'Fiddlesticks, Matthew,' said Mary, giggling dismissively. 'Fairfax is a delightful dandy with an odd manner and clean fingernails.'

'There may lurk a darker side to his grandiose and flirtatious ways than accords with your liking, Mary,' her mother cautioned.

'Fairfax heads Mary's salon of foppish flirtees,' said Matthew, grinning. 'And despite what you say, dear sister, I shall take no chances. I shall set the harbour watch on that sagacious poseur around-the-clock. The messenger awaits orders in the kitchen. We shall send Beadle instructions to carry out a clandestine search below the decks of all three vessels. Methinks the guilty Master will be transporting an unwarranted quantity of rations for a ship's crew — perchance for the Guinea-bound moonlighters?'

'Messenger's belly should be stuffed by now,' said the old man. 'Grab him before he drops off. Pack him on his way with your orders for his master. Rumour has it that in a private room in his tavern, Beadle has opened a molly house.'

'A molly house!' cried Mary, grimacing with disgust. 'Cross-dressing elegance stripped of all caution. Besides unnatural acts against God and man in obscure corners, Beadle will soon have Jamestown wading in sodomite mollies. Sir, I do declare that despite the isolation of this Great House, I cannot fathom how activities in Jamestown tumble into your ears.'

Tossing his head at her, the old man laughed. 'Watch what you say, lass. I hear that eminent names and one or two of our friends are among Beadle's clients.'

''Tis true, sir, Beadle has opened a molly house,' said Matthew, laughing quietly. 'And what with his profligate titled patrons, a tidy profit he will make too. Nevertheless, I shall set a close watch on the *Oriel*. I did hearsay that her Master has been sighted in matey dialogue with Fairfax on several occasions.'

'If your suspicions about Fairfax are right, Matthew,' said Mary soberly, 'then the Master of the *Oriel* most certainly warrants a close eye.'

'And should that anglicised nigger prove to be Guinea,' reiterated the old man, 'seize him when he is alone and burn his Letters of Manumission. That will be no easy matter. He has the law and highly regarded white men on his side. Hearken to me, my children. After his ship has sailed to rendezvous with the runaways, make certain you catch him red-handed. You had both best leave right away for Jamestown to confer with Governor Curzon.'

'In truth, sir,' stressed Mary, 'I do not believe that that servant can be Jonas Guinea. The man you have described strikes me not as one who would risk showing his black face on these islands.'

'Believe me when I tell thee, Mary,' said the old man forcefully, 'Guinea's wits are as wily as the best of white men. The nigger is well educated; he's a thinker and understands the white man's ways. He has been raised by erudite evangelists, whom I met over a long discomforting supper. A nigger with an opinion is bad enough. One with a penchant for activism parading a benign attitude is positively unhealthy.'

'And most certainly detrimental to our interests,' said Mary.

'Think carefully, Mary,' said Matthew softly. 'Where did the harbourmaster say these three vessels were bound after clearing Jamestown?'

'England, Antwerp and Brazil,' she replied.

'Whatever their masters divulged of their destinations,' said Matthew. 'One is a lying deceiver for he sails for Guinea — but which vessel?'

'I fancy the *Oriel* or the *Phoenix*,' she replied.

'I feel certain 'tis the *Redemption*,' said the old man. 'I sense it in the marrow of me.'

'I am with Mary on this one, sir,' he said. 'Come sister, we have an appointment in Jamestown. In Drake House we shall acquaint the Governor with what we know and reconcile our strategies. Somehow, sometime, someone will let something slip. Treachery is in the air. Even your shadow leaves you when you're in darkness.'

Traversing Raleigh's Passage with his sister through the airless afternoon, he was heading for the island of Little Pertigua. Rowed across Drake's Sound by a four-man crew, they then boarded the family's two-horse carriage retained at Fort Patrick on the north-east peninsula of Pertigua. While rattling away from the garrison along the dusty road, he re-evaluated the mission. Late in the afternoon in Jamestown, they sighted Drake House. Soon they were rolling between its tall wrought-iron Georgian gateposts.

Alighting from the carriage, Matthew hurried with his sister past footmen along a wide passage until he reached the maple highboys standing either side of the open withdrawing room door. He smiled at what met his eyes.

Predictably worse for wear, the Governor was cradling his head in his hands by the card table. His Excellency was taking hard tea with the war-scarred, bemedalled and barrel-chested commanding officer of the Redcoat garrison, Colonel Daniel Entwhistle.

After presenting himself before his executive staff and their wives during the ambrosial harvest of 1758, Governor William Curzon's striking looks had focused glad eyes until the final sentence of his inaugural address:

'I expect my summons to be promptly complied with,' he had said disdainfully, as if he were addressing schoolchildren.

Parading himself as a man of honour, Curzon was unfortunately mired by his grubby profession: politics. Furthermore, his winsome features were flawed by arrogance, in the eyes of many, with the exception being Matthew's doting sister.

The longcase grandfather clock chimed four o'clock.

Wobbling to his feet with outstretched hand, the Governor beamed.

'Begads Matthew and the fragrant Mistress Mary,' he said, putting a hand to the table to steady himself. 'Your appearance indeed heartens me. Your being here is timely. You are of course acquainted with Colonel Entwhistle. Come, be seated and assist us with a question pertinent to these times, which is the unlawful freeing of runaways. But first a restorative after your tiring journey.'

'A right good day to you, Colonel,' said Matthew. 'Father sends his warmest felicitations, William. Methinks a goblet of your punch would refresh. We departed Turtle Island the instant we received word from Silas Beadle. I trust, after what we have all learned from the recent dockings, we are all persuaded that the vessels we seek are now assembled in the harbour.'

'That we are, Matthew,' said the Governor, looking at each face in turn. 'Methinks 'tis time we do battle. Gentleman, and you as well, Mistress Mary. This morning I received disturbing intelligence regarding the buccaneer Hawthorne Read. Her vessels, the *Antelope* and the *Black Watch*, have anchored in a cove on the north coast near Ocean Bay. I sent for Hezekiah Wainwright of the *Invincible*, who has expended a great deal of time seeking her whereabouts—'

'Pirate or no pirate!' spat the Colonel, 'a mere woman cannot give us much trouble!'

'Forget not, Colonel Entwhistle, that the spawning of Hawthorne Read was in itself an offence,' said the Governor. 'Calico Jack Rackham was her father, who as you know was hanged in Port Royal, November 1720. Her buccaneering mother, Mary Read, pled the belly to delay execution, gave birth to a wicked little pirate and then escaped by dying in jail in April 1721. Of late—'

Mary retorted, 'I pray the wicked little madam speedily joins her kinfolk!'

'Of late,' continued the Governor, smiling at her comment, 'the aforementioned daughter has cut a gory swathe through the Indies, stealing naval sloops, marooning crews and plundering merchant ships. We have on our hands a thoroughly wicked handful. I intend to dispatch Captain Wainwright on a commission to apprehend Hawthorne Read. 'Tis unfortunate that the *Redemption* and the *Oriel* are as well on the verge of sailing. Gentlemen, we require all hands to the tiller. Matthew, is it still your intention to sail with the *Invincible* to identify Jonas Guinea after the arrest of the vessel?'

'Aye it is,' he replied firmly. 'Moreover, I wish to purchase Jonas Guinea from the Crown.'

Certain they all knew that Guinea was lawfully a free man, Matthew noted the discomfited looks before anyone spoke.

''Tis agreed,' said the Governor without emotion. 'Guinea will be auctioned and the Crown will be the beneficiary. The *Invincible* sails this night. Wainwright has consented to your berth aboard his ship. Vex not, Matthew, Mistress Mary will be kept out of harm's way here in Drake House.'

Daintily dabbing her brow, Mary smiled coquettishly at the Governor.

'I daresay I shall, William,' she said.

'A-as well, M-Matthew,' stuttered the Governor, plainly stirred by Mary's response, 'my men have sighted two niggers, one aboard the *Redemption* and the other on the *Oriel*. Either one could be Guinea.'

'Trust me, Mister Fleming,' said the red-faced Colonel. 'I have a battery of eyes on both vessels as we speak — with a clocklike watch reserved for shipboard niggers.'

'Father decidedly supports the arrest of affiliates of the League and signally the likes of Guinea,' said Mary imperiously. 'He will look very kindly on your pertinacity, Colonel.'

'Why thank you, Mistress Fleming,' said the Colonel, turning beetroot red. 'They shall not escape. This very night I will lead a detachment of musketeers for a foray on the north coast. Come morn, between my armed force ashore and Wainwright's cannons at sea, we shall have Hawthorne Read, her pirates and any loose runaways. If not, the Navy will have its work cut out to pacify the pirates and the runaways simultaneously. I daresay, Mister Fleming, you have still to locate the runaway's rendezvous, except that it is someplace on the north coast?'

'An acute observation if I might say, Colonel,' said Matthew testily. 'You can likewise be reassured that on and off the north coast, Captain Wainwright and your musketeers will not skirmish alone. They will be assisted by our overseers on shore and our privateers at sea.'

Pausing to mull over Matthew's statement, the Colonel grinned.

'Dying alone never did suit a body,' he muttered.

Clapping his hands and stamping with delight, the Governor said, 'Capital, sir! I daresay—'

There was a knock at the door.

'Come!'

Gliding into the chamber, the liveried butler announced, 'Captain Wainwright of the *Invincible*, Your Excellency.'

Scrutinising the podgy, bushy-bearded officer entering the room, Matthew narrowed his eyes.

I can see why the Admiralty gave him a man-o-war, he thought. A nautical cutthroat if ever I saw one.

At first glance, Wainwright looked a regular naval officer in blue frock coat with dress sword. But cauliflower ears and a flat-bridged nose with broad fat tip said he was a rank pugilist.

'We're drawn against a heartless trollop, but nobody's fool, Governor,' cautioned the Captain. 'After cleaving a murderous passage across the Indies, she has dropped anchor in Pertiguan waters — her greatest error. I shall harry and take the fornicating little hussy at first light. After noon, we shall set about apprehending the runaway vessel.'

Turning to the bullish-looking bearded officer beside him, he said, 'My First Lieutenant, Mister Hawksworth.'

'Many compliments, Captain Wainwright,' said the Governor, handing the man a wax-sealed scroll. 'Your orders, sir. Allow me to present Mistress Fleming and her brother, Matthew Fleming, whom I am happy to inform you is on standby to join you on the *Invincible*. We have much to do and very little time.'

''Tis indeed delightful to make your acquaintance, Mistress Fleming,' said the Captain, flourishing a bow. 'I have been given a first-rate account of your father's activities in this matter, Mister Fleming.'

'The honour to meet you is mine,' said Matthew, dipping his head. 'I shall pass on your generous compliments to my father.'

'I do declare that my regard for your pater is immeasurable,' said the Captain, 'for 'twas he who ensured Pertigua's stability and governance after the uprising. It gladdens me heartily to provide his son with a berth aboard my vessel. We sail this night with the tide, sir.'

'I hear your exploits in the Caribbean have not gone unrewarded, Captain Wainwright,' flattered Matthew. 'I am gladdened to be in your company aboard the *Invincible* for this action.'

I only hope, thought Matthew, the man does not discharge his duty in as lumbering manner as he looks.

Dispensing rum into a row of goblets, the Governor was good-humoured.

'I would like your company at a reception I am giving at seven o'clock,' he said. 'I have invited the masters of the nine merchantmen in dock as well as the best of the town's ladies of the night. Certain ladies among their number have been primed to coax out the name of the League's vessel from the masters. We may well learn something to our advantage. 'Tis said—'

Interjecting with a scowl, Mary quietly enquired, 'Hawthorne Read poses a far greater threat than that of the League, does she not?'

'Sink me, Mary!' cried the Governor pompously. 'You may not be aware that Europe's navies have grown too widespread and lively for buccaneering in the Indies. Piracy is consequently on the wane — but not it seems for this bloodthirsty little madam. Fret not, for we shall take them both. So raise your goblets to the termination of the skulduggery of Hawthorne Read as well as the League Against the Importation of Negroes.'

'Aye,' they all cried.

The clock struck seven o'clock.

Masters of the docked merchantmen began to drift into the withdrawing room. Ladies of the evening dispersed around the chamber.

The Last Supper

Storm petrels and red-billed tropic birds struck for the darkening horizon. Barques and fishing boats stood well out from the cliffs and rocky shore. In a dying blaze of colours, the hazy sun was sinking in the sea. Feathery airs augured good fortune.

Turning away from the setting sun, Asabi's belly gurgled with the meaty aromas entering her nostrils. Looking around, she smiled.

Half a mile east of the runaway stronghold of Freetown, a suckling pig was being spit-roasted on the wooded cliff-top grove, set on a rocky promontory overlooking Ocean Bay. Roasting odours wafted on silky gusts. Celebrating their very last night on the island of Pertigua, her comrades sat joshing around a heartening blaze.

Straddling a basalt boulder behind her son, Asabi pondered on the hazards of the night hike ahead. Despite her many reservations, she kept her misgivings to herself. Beaming around at her companions, she listened to the bombastic talk.

'…Dig it yerself I sez ter overseer,' said Abraham. 'An' fetch me grog when yer done.'

Laughter resounded around the crackling fire.

Rising to his feet and trotting out a doubtful tale, Moses ended by saying, 'I trip 'im up an' overseer pitch 'eadfirst into cesspit. 'E now call shit 'ead. It do 'im good fer some of the shit were 'is. I sez man get close to 'isself.'

Roars of laughter were followed by spirited banter.

With her lips by her son's ear, she whispered a roll-call of the historic assembly:

'Tomba go by hisself, then be One Night an' her man Moses, Zachariah an' his woman Sheba — who be on this island for gone thirty years, Isaac an' his woman Rebekah — who be jus' one year on the island 'fore them break out of plantation, an' now she with child. Them three by bushes over there be Abraham, Rachel an' Eve, they be going home alone. We twelve bound for Guinea. Everyone 'cept you, Abi, were born on the coast of Guinea.'

Opening his eyes wide with surprise, Abi's smile lit the dark.

Despite the noisiness of their festivities, she was certain they would draw no special attention. In Freetown, sixty-odd runaways subsisted in small interdependent groups. Dotted around the surrounding area were factions like hers, uniting under her leadership when it concerned the defence of the stronghold itself.

'This night like no other, Abi,' she said. 'I tremble with joy to set foot on the shores of Guinea and to see Ake again. Yet I be pining for Truelove.'

Bidding farewell to him had harrowed her. It was ten years since their first meeting. Her eyes watered at the memory of the irksome character she met with Kayode during her escape from Tamarind Trees. Since the death of Kayode, he had become a steadfast companion whom she had grown to respect and love. Before this chance to go back to Guinea, life without Truelove had been unthinkable.

'I quit being Captain an' not tell a soul,' she said, stroking her son's forehead. 'I feel I betray friends. When we not seen, they think we be captured or dead. Only Truelove know an' he take what he know to his grave.'

Desperate to see her motherland, she had happily relinquished her position as Captain of Freetown. Even after so many enslaved years away from Guinea, she was certain she could still find her way from its slave-littered shores through the rainforests to the village of Ake. She would raise her son among her people on the soil of her motherland.

People were taking rowdy turns rotating the suckling pig and sweet potatoes.

'Slave ship brings we to this island starving,' said One Night. 'Look at we leavin' for Guinea with full bellies. Fat white pastor in plantation church talk 'bout Last Supper, when he not hungry an' we starving. You give we chance to quit this wicked island, Asabi. At this last feast, my sister, you play jes Messiah. An' remember, Thomas not 'ere to give you up like he did Jesus!'

Applause and laughter shook the fireside.

Waving her arms for silence, Asabi spoke with resolution:

'We be the first to flee this evil land. We soon be free o' this nightmare. Forget your hate 'cos it baffles your wits. Think only o' *Redemption* an' the morrow. Them we leave behind will think we is dead or captured. We came to this island empty-handed an' we leave as we came. Where we sail to on this *Redemption*, others will follow. We mus' get to Deception Bay by nightfall of the morrow. From Heddon's Mouth, we get boat for *Redemption*. When we walk this night, keep sharp look out for Redcoats an' the Mongoose Gang. An' for *Olorun*'s sake, stay close.'

'Wise words, Asabi,' said Zachariah solemnly. 'That way we live to see Guinea.'

'Follow me, Asabi,' said Tomba. 'Me know hidden trail down to Deception Bay. We fill our bellies, smother fire leaving no smoke an' walk by moonlight. Redcoats 'fraid of the night.'

'Frit o' dark skin mek white man frit o' the dark,' said Moses, sniggering and cutting a thick wedge off the roast pig.

'Fear strips yer guts,' said One Night, munching sweet potato.

'It do,' said Moses.

Outward Bound

The Redemption
Careenage
Jamestown
25 April 1761
22.00 hrs

Awaiting departure, Jonas stood anxiously against the rails behind the officers on the poop deck. His ten days on the slave island had been fraught. At all times ashore he had had to be in the company of officers from the ship to prevent him from being apprehended alone. Glad to be vacating its harrowing atmosphere, he pondered the perils ahead.

'To reach Deception Bay and the runaways,' he muttered beneath his breath, 'we will need to outmanoeuvre the *Invincible* and the island's privateers. We will as well need luck.'

Raising his eyes skywards, he prayed for good fortune and favourable conditions. Shouts inside the harbour mouth by Deadpan drew his attention to the lanterned activity around the man-o-war. Alarmed, he approached the Second Mate. 'Methinks the *Invincible* is slipping her moorings, Mister Miracle.'

'You're on your toes, Mister Guinea,' said the Second Mate, turning to the warship. 'That she is. Goliath slinks out to sea. The riskiest element of our mission begins.'

'I pray she does not surprise us in Deception Bay,' he said.

'Captain Battersby is a shrewd old seadog, Mister Guinea,' reassured the Second Mate. 'Having outmanoeuvred a few seventy-four-gun pirates, he can well outwit the likes of the *Invincible*.'

Striding onto the poop deck and casting his eyes up the shrouds, the cloaked Captain turned to the Mate.

'What have we, Mister Hopkins?'

'Ready to sail, Captain,' said the Mate.

'Cargo, Mister Miracle?'

'Rum barrels are secured in a well-ventilated hold amidships, Captain,' said the Second Mate. 'Jute bags of brown sugar are stowed and battened down in the forward hold. All openings to that hold have been sealed.'

'*Invincible*'s making way, Captain,' said the Mate.

'Was that the innkeeper Silas Beadle I saw on my gangway?'

'Aye, Captain.'

'What did the weasel want?'

'I forbade him entry, Captain,' replied the Mate. 'Innkeeper was all eyes and exceedingly keen to see below decks. Would you not agree, Mister Guinea?'

'Indeed I would, Mister Hopkins,' said Jonas. 'Beadle is a philistine, Captain. I believe he was snooping on another's behalf — mayhaps even to assess the abnormality of our provisions.'

'My very thoughts, gentlemen. Having observed a few potential agents eyeballing the *Redemption* these past days, we shall take no chances. With the *Invincible* on her way, Mister Hopkins, we sail within the hour.'

'Aye, Captain.'

'Turn her around, Mister Fernsby.'

'Aye, Captain,' said the sailing master. 'All hands on deck! Let go fore and aft breast ropes.'

Spurred by the prevailing westerly breeze, the *Redemption* pivoted slowly on her after back spring, creaking and groaning, until her bowsprit pointed at the harbour mouth. There she lay alongside the dock, quiescent for an hour in the moonlight. Then, her lines were cast.

Suddenly a man from the waterfront dashed for the Customs House yelling, 'The *Redemption* sails!'

Jolted by the cry, Jonas narrowed his eyes. He could feel the unseen eyes scouring the ship from stem to stern.

'Foresails, Mister Fernsby,' said the Captain calmly. 'Let go the after back spring.'

A southerly gusted into the foresails. The *Redemption* was making way. Soon, she was passing the *Oriel* hoisting her sails and the vacated moorings of the *Invincible*. In the roads outside the harbour mouth, she began pitching in the swell of the Caribbean Sea. Though she was not a flyer, he was heartened by her fair turn of speed. In less than half an hour, Darwin's Reef lay off her starboard beam.

Gazing hard astern at the contours of the island, Jonas pursed his lips with irritation.

'Yonder isle harbours such brutality, Captain,' he said, 'yet appears infuriatingly innocent in this light.'

'Indeed, Mister Guinea,' said the Captain. 'And let us not keep our runaways waiting too long. Mainsails, mizzens and topgallants, Mister Fernsby! You have the ship, Mister Hopkins.'

'I have the ship, Captain,' repeated the Mate.

Striding to the stern rails, the Captain addressed the officers on the poop deck:

'Gentlemen, we sail into dangerous waters to break the slaver's *cordon sanitaire*. In the scales of history our kind will come to be called abolitionists. I want you to bear in mind that what we convey from this island, we do for a just and noble cause. Be in no doubt that though our efforts go against the slaver's grain, it will make not even a hiccup on the trade in slaves. Nevertheless, I am convinced that the Good Lord will look favourably on what some English men do in these outrageous waters. I fundamentally believe freeing slaves to be our moral duty. Pray God we do not founder.'

'Amen, Captain,' said Jonas, with the officers.

'I can just make out the *Invincible*'s lantern, Captain,' said the Second Mate. 'She is hull down about two leagues ahead.'

'Easy your helm,' said the Mate to the helmsman.

Piercing screams from red-billed tropic-birds flying over the main topgallant amplified the unease Jonas felt. In the sturdy westerly, Darwin's Reef fell half a league astern. Pulling his cloak tightly around him, he looked out to sea.

The Captain buttonholed the sailing master by the mizzenmast, 'Douse lanterns on sighting Hurricane Point, Mister Fernsby. We must not make it easy for the *Invincible* to get a fix on our position.

Hide the *Redemption* in any mists you detect. Keep her well astern of the warship, but keep her in your sights. Alert the crew. Tell them where we're headed, especially the bit about the bonus for an extended voyage.'

'Aye aye, Captain,' said the sailing master eagerly. 'The crew will be mighty gladdened. A bonus should moderate any errant attitudes towards the runaways.'

'Jury-rig a mast with stays in the cutter, Mister Miracle,' said the Captain. 'Locate a lighted lantern atop. Weigh her down with appropriate ballast and set her adrift when we have Hurricane Point on our starboard beam. Drifting away from our position in this moderate westerly, she will act as the *Redemption* by proxy.'

'An inspired deception if I might say, Captain,' said the Second Mate.

Turning aside, the Captain said, 'After we disembark our runaways on the coast of Guinea, Mister Guinea, we shall be bartering for a cargo.'

'I was well-versed by your owner, Mister Puddlewick, that you would be seeking gold, sandalwood and ivory, Captain.'

'Your presence could prove an advantage in our barters along that coast, Mister Guinea. Methinks in some villages and towns, white men fast outlive their welcome among people of your hue.'

'Indeed, Captain. In view of your concerns, sir, I am at your service and will gladly assist you in any way I can. And I daresay that akin to here in Pertigua, the temperature on the coast of Guinea is more conducive for my tropical kind. Perforce, in England my black fingers quite dally with numbing cold.'

Chuckling loudly, the Captain said, 'And I see those same fingers are getting the hang of working ship and careening her bottom. I want you to get to know her ropes as well, Mister Guinea. We have storms ahead. See the boatswain. We'll be at sea for a while yet.'

'I shall do that, Captain.'

A stiff gust scoured the deck.

'There's an icy nip in that breeze, Mister Miracle,' said the Captain. 'You have the ship. After embarking our passengers and when we're well out to sea, rig storm-sails and square away for heavy weather.

Mister Hopkins and I shall be in my cabin. Call me when you sight the Three Apostles.'

'Aye, Captain, I have the ship.'

Nearing midnight, Hurricane Point lay a league astern. Dolphin Bay was off the starboard beam.

'Take a trick on the helm, Mister Guinea,' said the Second Mate. 'Helmsman shall be standing close by.'

'Aye, Mister Miracle.'

'Steer east-nor'-east, Mister Guinea,' said the helmsman.

'East-nor'-east,' he answered.

Grasping the wheel, he looked at the compass and then up at the masthead. He shuddered at the power of the *Redemption* clawing the nautical miles under a full set of sails. Momentarily, he felt he held the League's project in his hands.

'With good fortune,' he muttered, 'we will soon be meeting with our runaways.'

Manchineel Tree

It was yet warm and past midnight. Under a lustrous moon, Asabi and the runaways started out along the clifftop. A warm south-easterly breeze soothed her anxiety. Beckoning her son, she dropped back behind Tomba who was following a rudimentary track only he could see. As if endorsing the big man's judgment, the young star-whites waved gawkily hither and thither either side of the track. To the north, miles out to sea, she picked out the guano-covered granite stacks of the moonlit Three Apostles. Though the waters were sweet-tempered now, she felt a sharp drop in the temperature of the freshening gusts. It augured a tempest in the making.

'I pray we board the *Redemption* 'fore this storm breaks,' she said.

'We will,' said Tomba without stopping.

Five miles along the rock-strewn grassy terrain, Tomba stopped for a break beside a basalt boulder close to a poisonous full-crowned manchineel tree. Slumping down against a boulder with the others, Asabi sat some fifty feet above the mile-long shores of Ocean Bay. Bordered by a strip of mangrove forest the length of the shoreline along the cliff face, white men could only access the bay by sea. She had often wondered about the secret route used by a few runaways from the clifftop down to the seashore. It had lately come to her ears that they had also found a way through the labyrinth of mangroves and across its sometimes fast-running streams.

Sitting upright, she asked, 'How we drop down to the mangroves from here?'

'Me show you,' said Tomba, pointing to a clump of bushes. 'We drop down over there an' hit the shore at daybreak, Asabi. We slip 'cross sand at the bottom an' into mangroves. We be well outta sight 'fore sunrise.'

Seeing no way off the clifftop, she frowned.

'I hear soldiers somewhere over there,' she said, anxiously pointing to the west. 'We got to be in them mangroves 'fore daylight my friend.'

'Them whites wake the dead,' sneered Tomba quietly. 'An' me know why them devils make camp. 'Fraid them fall over cliff edge, them camp on flats till sunup. Soldiers hunting us take more care, Asabi. Them know we here or hereabouts. Keep your musket and powder dry in the mangroves. An' watch out for snakes.'

Fifty feet below, the ebbed tide had yielded a long sandy moonlit shore.

Striding over to the silhouetted manchineel tree, Tomba sank to the foot of the broad trunk. Pulling aside a dense clump of tree branches, he revealed a sloping recessed rock ledge.

Gasping at the means of escape, she asked, 'Down there?'

'All the way to the shore, Asabi,' said Tomba proudly. 'I put branches back soon as we all go through. You go first.'

Shafts of daylight were filtering slowly across the sky.

A fifty foot sheer drop yawned to her left. Leading the way to the top of the rocky incline, she stepped onto a stone-littered dusty surface. Heaving a deep breath, she leaned into the rock face. Putting one foot gingerly before the other, she began her faltering descent. Time ticked agonisingly by until the ledge ran out, about ten feet shy of the shore. She jumped onto the sands followed by her son. Last to drop was Isaac and his pregnant Rebekah, aided by Tomba, making up the fatigued body count.

An orange sun peeked above the horizon. The heat began to rise.

Hawthorne Read

HMS Invincible
Fortitude Bay
26 April 1761
04.30 hrs

Cries of nesting birds merged with the waves crashing against the ponderous cliffs of north Pertigua. Roosting on high ledges, guillemots and dumpy razorbills cried noisily at the appearance of the small task force. Led by His Majesty's Ship *Invincible* and two privateers, the flotilla sailed into Fortitude Bay. In the early light, Matthew Fleming was with the watch on the poop deck when two pirate vessels drifted into view. Anchored under the long shadows of Ashley's tower at the top of a steep hill, the buccaneers lay directly ahead.

'That tower was constructed by Governor Ashley, a friend of your father, Mister Fleming,' said Captain Wainwright. 'It housed a garrison of four men and two cannon and served as an early-warning post during the conflicts with the French and Spanish. Not presently required, 'tis now deserted.'

'Ashley was a scrupulous Governor, Captain,' said Matthew.

Despite imminent action, Wainwright vaunts icy fibre, he thought. Thank God he is on our side.

Silhouetted against the rising sun, Matthew singled out the *Antelope*. The brigantine, moored a short distance ahead of the *Black Watch*, was said to be the barque of the pirate leader.

'On either one of those two vessels,' said Captain Wainwright quietly, 'the tea-drinking Hawthorne Read should be on her guard and alert. Given no grog, gambling or carousing is allowed aboard her vessels, one would assume the crew slept lightly. Yet we are this close and not a soul has stirred. Given all that, Mister Fleming, I judge that surprise is the one element Hawthorne Read has not bargained for.'

Smiling discreetly behind his hand, Matthew eyed the officer.

Fresh from hearing of Wainwright's Machiavellian skills in Drake House, he was in no doubt that the impending action would be prosecuted with the fervour expected by the Lords of the Admiralty.

The fortified trinity slipped quietly into the bay below Ashley's Tower. At ten cables, the pirates swayed obliviously at anchor.

'You are right, Captain,' whispered Matthew. 'The lack of lookouts on any of the barques displays certain arrogance.'

In grim contrast, the *Invincible* was bristling with eyes and ears. With her fighting complement of three hundred and eighty seamen and eighty Redcoats, he expected few problems at such close quarters.

'Clear for action, Mister Hawksworth,' said Captain Wainwright calmly to the First Lieutenant. 'Load, elevate and run out your cannon. And given that you are here, Mister Fleming, you should hear this as well.'

'Aye, Captain,' replied Matthew.

Drawing closer, he listened to the Captain's orders.

'Instruct the signal-lieutenant to signal the privateers that they must open fire with us,' said the Captain. 'As we pass, we will give the *Antelope* a broadside. Then we'll rake her quarterdeck with grapeshot. That ought to have them prancing a jig. The privateers must help us account for the *Antelope* by catching her in our crossfire. Then together we shall set about the *Black Watch*. Is that clear?'

'Aye, sir.'

'Have men set to arrest Hawthorne Read, Major Gaston,' said Captain Wainwright. 'And have your musketeers open fire when we are within range.'

'We have grappling irons ready, Captain,' replied the Redcoat officer. 'Read will not escape. We will take her alive.'

'See that you do, Major,' said the Captain. 'We need a prominent example for the gallows.'

Turning to the gun-captain, he said, 'Open fire when she comes within range, Mister Gore. No warning and no quarter until they surrender. The element of surprise should ensure that our fatalities are kept to a minimum.'

Holding his breath at five cables distance, Matthew could feel his heart pounding.

Even under strong sunlight, nothing stirred on the decks of the seafaring felons. All the while, the *Invincible* and the privateers drifted closer on the tide. In the closing moments, he envisioned Harriet Beaufort on horseback and his sister in the arms of Governor Curzon.

The Captain's brittle voice shattered his daydreams.

'After the broadsides,' said the Captain to the First Lieutenant, 'order the gun-captains to fire at will.'

'Aye aye, Captain.'

Gun crews elevating their cannons with handspikes echoed across the bay. It seized Matthew's attention. He heard the clap when the coin was pushed under the breech and a snap as gun-captains cocked the lock. The cannons were ready and the outlaws slept on. Tensing as he awaited hostilities, he could feel the hairs on the nape of his neck rising.

At a range of two cables, the *Invincible*'s starboard cannons resounded with a broadside. Cannonballs almost dismasted the *Antelope*. Grapeshot carried away the shrouds of her lower rigging. By the main mast alongside the signal-lieutenant, Matthew saw the pirates burst onto their quarterdeck.

'Fire!' shouted the Redcoat officer.

Eighty muskets opened up. Hot shot blistered the air and cut the buccaneers down in their stride. A few reached the cannons and began to load. Panic-stricken others began firing muskets wildly astray.

Going hard about, the *Invincible* continued the dismantling of the *Antelope* with another broadside. Cannonballs toppled her fore and mizzenmasts. Entirely dismasted, the *Antelope* heeled to port when the wind shifted to the southeast. Holed above the waterline, the brigantine ducked briefly beneath the waves. Admitting tons of water and with her crew abandoning ship, she creaked and groaned and righted herself to sit half afloat.

Men are dying in that floating coffin, thought Matthew grimly.

A lookout shouted from the crow's nest:

'The *Black Watch* escapes!'

Through his telescope, Matthew saw the *Black Watch* some distance away under a rapidly expanding set of sails. Standing cutlass in hand on her quarterdeck, Hawthorne Read was conspicuous by her black locks, vermillion shirt, jet-black tricorn with purple feathers and a defiant grin.

'Avast saving the dregs floundering in the water, Mister Hawksworth,' snapped the Captain. 'Leave them to the privateers. From here on in, concentrate all efforts on the *Black Watch*. After we capture her, we shall set about giving chase to the *Redemption* and the *Oriel*. Those fanatics shall not get far.'

'Deck is secured and we are set to pursue the *Black Watch*, Captain,' said the First Lieutenant.

'Casualties?'

'None dead and none wounded, Captain.'

'And Hawthorne Read?'

'Aboard the *Black Watch*, Captain,' said the First Lieutenant. 'I saw the brazen hussy myself.'

'Apprehend her, Mister Hawksworth,' said the Captain. 'She will make an excellent specimen for a public execution. How many of her crew did we pluck out of the water?'

'Boatswain has yet to report, Captain,' replied the Second Lieutenant.

'They are to be kept in irons at all times in the foc'sle peak,' said the Captain. 'Pass that on.'

'Aye aye, sir.'

'While we prepare to get hard on the tail of the *Black Watch*, Mister Fleming, will you join me in a beverage in the Great Cabin?'

'Certainly, Captain.'

'Signal the privateers,' said the Captain to the First Lieutenant. 'Send my compliments and instruct them along these lines: the prisoners shall be put on trial two mornings hence and will hang that same afternoon. We shall meet up with them in Jamestown on the morrow.'

'As you wish, Captain,' said the First Lieutenant, nodding at the Second Lieutenant.

'We have no prize but a wreck that could obstruct navigation,' said the Captain. 'If she is still afloat when we return to this bay, I want you to sink her with cannon fire.'

'Aye aye, sir,' replied the First Lieutenant.

Entering the Great Cabin, the Captain exclaimed, ''Pon my soul, Mister Fleming, the pirate was asleep! And she kept no lookout even though she knew King George's men were on her tail.'

'As bold as brass, Captain Wainwright,' said Matthew. 'Hawthorne Read has plagued our coasts for too long. 'Tis high time her gallivanting ways were terminated.'

'The capricious little wench should be hung, drawn and quartered,' said the First Lieutenant, 'to send an unequivocal message that piracy on the high seas will suffer the ultimate penalty.'

A steward arrived bearing a tray with noggins of rum.

'My judgment too,' said the Captain. 'Hawthorne Read has acquired a lamentable penchant for surviving. The seafaring princess has succeeded in piracy for so long because she kept order with a hard hand. She was finally winkled out because of overconfidence. 'Tis fortunate that our prisoners will all be begging for mercy. Some must hang. Plantation owners are on the lookout for indebted white men to work as overseers. White men will fetch a keen price. After we dispatch the *Black Watch*, I intend to overhaul and stop the *Redemption* and the *Oriel* to inspect what they carry. With fair winds and following seas, we should be back in Jamestown in less than forty-eight hours.'

Entering the cabin, the Second Lieutenant nodded to the Captain.

'Gentlemen,' said the Captain, 'let us return to the poop deck.'

Given his fresh sea legs, Matthew strode more confidently back up to the poop deck to witness naval tradition.

The rising sun was hovering above the horizon when the signal-cannon sounded. A puff of smoke drifted lazily across the *Invincible*'s foredeck. White-headed gulls sprang off the yardarm to skim over dolphins darting across the bow. Reefing-jackets flapped in the breeze and in line with glorious tradition, sailors of the *Invincible* and Redcoat marines of the Pertigua Foot Regiment lined the decks. Bobbing in a myriad of prancing wavelets, the man-o-war was under way.

Gazing up the mainmast from the poop deck, he was awed by the dexterity of the upper yardsmen. Catching the wind almost at once, her freed mainsails flapped in the stiffening easterly and her prow was lifted by the waves. Topgallants, jibs and staysails bulged. Initially snagged by the main-top-sail yardarm, the vast coarse red burlap mainsail shook free and swelled until she was full and by. In a blaze of red sails and white gunports in stark contrast to her black hull, he thought the *Invincible* presented a formidable and stirring sight. Outside the sanctuary of Ashley's Tower, she ran with the surging tide of the Atlantic, her mainsail driving her on the heels of the *Black Watch*.

'Nothing brings tears to a man's eyes,' said the Captain, ''til he sees the might of England on the high seas.'

'Aye, Captain,' said the First Lieutenant. ''Tis a sight that makes a body proud to be an Englishman.'

Turning anxiously astern, Matthew grew preoccupied.

'Where are the *Redemption* and the *Oriel*?' he muttered to himself. 'They must not be permitted to filch even one runaway.'

Stealing Away

At the foot of the cliffs on the north-west corner of Ocean Bay, Asabi gazed along the shore. On the edge of the strip of mangrove forest fringing the shore, the runaways squatted for a break. Suddenly explosions rumbled from the west.

She froze.

'Cannons?' asked Tomba, frowning.

'Quarrelling whites,' she said dismissively. 'They use muskets 'gainst runaways, not cannon.'

Ducking below the mangrove canopy in the early light, she looked around. It was a jagged, contorted forest with spreading green crests straining skywards. Jutting red roots, anchored in deep black stinking mud, buzzed with insects.

Dismayed by the density of mangroves, she stood up and gritted her teeth. Cupping her son's face in her hands, she sought to reassure him.

'Vex not, Abi,' she said. 'Keep close in the mangroves. Soon we stroll in the sun on the shores of our motherland.'

'We do, Ma.'

Glancing around, she accounted for twelve souls.

Springing into action with palm fronds, Tomba skilfully blurred all footprints in the sand. Backing the group into the shallows of the red mangroves, they were quickly swallowed up in a dark tidal jungle of dense thickets.

Squelching ankle-deep in mud, she shuddered. Humming with sand flies, the clammy habitat echoed with mangrove cuckoos, trickling waters and the muffled ocean. Screened from sunlight below the leafy canopy, she felt safer and pulled her son close.

''Bout a mile o' hacking ahead, Asabi,' panted Tomba, waving his machete before him. 'We mus' walk an' chop through the red, black an' white mangroves 'fore nightfall. When we see the button mangroves, then we be by Deception Bay.'

'Not far to go then?' said Zachariah light-heartedly.

Hacking at the mangroves, a testy Tomba snorted, 'Idiot!'

'We reach Deception Bay in daylight,' Asabi snapped, glowering at her companions. Smiling at Rebekah, she said, 'Baby good, sister?'

'Baby she glad to be goin' home, Asabi,' replied Rebekah, stroking her barely swollen belly. 'Me got Isaac wi' me. Me family goin' home.'

''Ow you know baby she, woman?' asked Isaac.

Giggling behind her hand, Rebekah replied, 'Woman know.'

'You blessed, Rebekah,' said Asabi. 'Your child be born free in our motherland. When we reach Guinea, our children spoil like fruit if we let them.'

Raising her machete, she continued wading through the sludge and slicing at the foliage.

Spinning abruptly to his left and striking a branch with his machete, Tomba cried, 'Snake!'

The reptile's head plopped onto the mud. Mudskippers scattered from the convulsing fangs.

Recoiling with fright, Asabi shivered and spat, 'I hate snakes!'

Yielding to short breaks throughout the day, they hacked, walked and clambered over, under and around thick roots. At long last the sun touched the horizon.

Weary and sopping wet, Asabi staggered out from the fruiting button mangroves behind Tomba with her son close by. Out of breath, she dropped wearily onto the southernmost shore of Deception Bay. Moments later, she sat up to get her bearings.

Heddon's Mouth lay a half-mile across the sands of Deception Bay, hidden inside its northern headland. The wind was up and frisking with the flood tide. Out to sea, a flock of brown pelicans were on the wing. Stars and a bright moon showed up in the fading light.

'Be soon dark, Abi,' she said softly, heaving a sigh at the thought of the sanctuary afforded by nightfall.

'Night be a good friend, Ma,' whispered Abi.

Suddenly, frenzied muffled curses burst from her companions.

Rising to her feet, she spoke sharply, 'Not time to fight! Let we go!'

Grasping her arm, Zachariah cried, 'Rachel not 'ere, Asabi! We look all over. She gotta be back in them mangroves!'

'Rachel?' she asked angrily. 'Lost on a walk? You got no eyes? We sail across the mighty ocean to coast o' Guinea an' we start by losing Rachel on an island. What we lose next — our heads? Who volunteer to go back to find her.'

Infuriated by the pathetic bungle, Tomba shook his head and turned away muttering oaths.

An awkward silence fell upon the runaways. Above the seabirds and the staccato of wind, discomfited breathing was evident.

Examining each face in turn, it was clear that no one was eager to look for Rachel. Breaking the jarring silence, she said, 'Abi and me go back to find her. Rachel be not far. *Redemption* not yet in sight.'

Annoyed by the sighs of relief from her companions, she embraced Tomba tightly.

'We meet you at Heddon's Mouth,' she said to her dearest friend.

Grasping her shoulders affectionately, Tomba implored her, 'Be at Heddon's Mouth. Go swiftly my sister, for the tide turns. We walk Guinea shores together. Be at Heddon's Mouth, Asabi.'

'We be there, Tomba.'

Closely trailed by her son, she ducked back into the mangroves.

The lower limb of the sun dropped below the horizon.

In less than a half mile and with the last vestiges of daylight, she came upon the mud-caked, bedraggled woman straddling a thick root and rubbing her head. Clutching a musket, Rachel was about to retrace her steps back to Freetown.

'Me at tail end,' she gasped. 'Me trip up, bang me 'ead 'gainst root an' me get knock out.'

Suddenly pulling them into the shadows, Rachel's hand shot up.

'Shhh,' she whispered. 'Me hear soldiers on clifftop.'

Cocking her head, Asabi heard the clatter and regulated steps of a militia on the move.

Peering up through the moonlit canopy, she whispered, 'There be ten or twelve soldiers. They going same way as we. We got to reach Heddon's Mouth 'fore them. Keep eyes on the clifftop. Let's go. The tide comes in.'

A Historical Rendezvous

The Redemption
Off north coast of Pertigua
26 April 1761
18.00 hrs

Before leaving his cabin, Jonas scribbled an entry in his daily journal:

> The wind continued fair until mid morning when it came round more to the eastward. It blew pretty fresh with a great swell and head sea, which made the vessel roll and pitch very much, and despite gaining sea legs made me very sick.

Sailing away from Pertigua and displaying no lights, the *Redemption* was four leagues off the Three Apostles on a north-easterly course. She was running before the wind in a moderate sea with a stiff easterly in her sails. Taking a final look along the darkening horizon against the glints of the dying sun, Jonas left the forepeak with the Second Mate.

'When will the *Redemption* change course for Deception Bay, Mister Miracle?'

'Methinks Captain will turn ship about when he is certain we have shaken off the *Invincible* and the privateers. Thus far this day, Mister Guinea, it has been a close call and it might yet get a lot closer.'

Before reaching the poop deck, Jonas heard the sailing master give orders to come about.

'All hands on deck,' he shouted. 'Lee braces.'

Rapt against the stern rails, Jonas kept his eyes on the bowsprit. As anticipated, veering slowly through a wide arc onto the starboard tack, the ship settled on a south-easterly course heading for Deception Bay. The low-lying moonlit shore retreated for about one hundred yards from the water's edge to mangroves and a lofty cliff thickly covered with trees.

'Prepare the recognition signal for the runaways, Mister Fernsby,' said the Mate quietly, 'and have the boatswain take soundings.'

'Recognition signal assembled and set to hoist, Mister Hopkins,' replied the sailing master.

'As soon as the anchor bottoms, Mister Miracle,' said the Captain, 'take the jolly boat and crew around the northern lip of Deception Bay. Proceed to Heddon's Mouth. 'Tis marked on the chart. Fetch the runaways off the shore and return post-haste. Is that understood?'

'Aye aye, Captain.'

In the shadows of the poop deck, Jonas wiped his neck and brow and recalled the past day's proceedings.

In the dark early hours of that morning they had been shadowed by two privateers. Weaving in and out of the mists, they had slipped their pursuers. A little after sunrise, cannon flashes from Fortitude Bay had seized his attention. Startled, along with the officers on the poop deck, he had trained his telescope towards the action.

''Tis the *Invincible*, Captain,' the Mate had said. 'She has caught and surprised Hawthorne Read. Officers from the *Invincible* boasted of this action in Jamestown.'

'Aye, Captain, I heard the loose talk as well,' the sailing master had said. 'But it appears the slippery virago has been finally snared in a cross fire. Unless Read quickly surrenders, her buccaneers will be cut to pieces.'

Hurriedly wiping the eyepiece of his telescope, Jonas had focused it on the action.

Close range cannon fire was dismantling the closer of two anchored pirate vessels — a brigantine and a barque. Through billows of smoke, the engagement resembled a histrionic seascape. The hot-blooded actuality of battle had left him aghast. For more than an hour, cannon fire, splintering timbers and screams had been carried on the wind until the brigantine was half-sunk and drifting. Meanwhile, the barque had weighed anchor and was fleeing on a north-westerly course. The *Invincible* set off in pursuit, though a good distance in the wake of the barque.

'I'll wager 'tis the *Black Watch*, the vessel of Hawthorne Read, that has escaped,' the Captain had said.

'Thank God the *Redemption* sails south-east, Captain,' Jonas had said, sighing.

'Nay, you can thank your Captain for that, Mister Guinea,' the Captain had chuckled. ''Tis fortuitous she sails after the *Black Watch*. Let us pray we don't encounter the *Invincible* with our runaways. We are far from clear of her interest. When she has apprehended the *Black Watch*, she will be on the hunt for us. And I might add that that man-o-war is a flyer. We must be far from this coast before she returns.'

'I as well pray we are gone before then, Captain,' he had said.

Daylight had come and gone since the *Invincible*'s action in the early hours. For some time after the onslaught, the *Redemption* had stayed well out to sea and out of reach. Now she was labouring through moderate seas on course for Deception Bay.

Steadying himself on the mizzen halyards, Jonas inhaled as he stared intently into the dark. Mesmerised by the images in the silhouette of the looming island, he visualised Faith Bradshaw dallying coquettishly in a simple sage-green dress. Late on that afternoon, the sun was still in the high meadows. Blood-red heads of great burnets dotted the grassy banks. In buoyant spirits amidst tufts of violet-striped oval eyebrights, she had voiced her feelings.

'I adore thee, Jonas,' she had said softly. 'And I adore the hue of thee.'

Her affectionate admission matched his yearning to be loved by a woman of his choice. Although he thought she secreted little, he had recalled a peculiarity of her gender. Mindful that it was the custom for women of her ilk to have a confidante with whom they shared much, he was curious as to whom that might be. Came the moment when he was next to the open withdrawing room at Greensleeves, studying a portrait of her mother by the noted painter, Arthur Devis. He had overheard a heart-to-heart with her abettor, Parson Merriweather.

''Tis time I settled, Parson,' Faith had quietly divulged. 'I feel ready to settle. I have found he with whom I wish to grow old.'

'I have reason to suspect that he is Jonas,' the Parson had said with a chuckle. 'Our company proprietor owns a fetching affection for you. For what it is worth, my lass, methinks he is as well ready to set down roots. You two make a right good colourful match.'

He had grinned at the Parson's comment. Yet four thousand sea miles from England's shores, he could still smell her bosomy secrets on the sultry airs. On a rolling barque approaching a moonlit island in cramped conditions, he was comforted by the notion that she envisaged her years with him.

'I vow to get back to her unscathed,' he whispered to the winds.

Sudden shipboard activity brought him back to the poop deck. Soundings were being called and relayed to the Captain in hoarse whispers. Men were scurrying up the ratlines, across the yards and the main deck to haul up and furl the mainsail. Orders were being rendered in hushed voices.

'Man the main clew-garnets and buntlines,' shouted the sailing master. 'Ease away the main tack and bowline! Haul up to windward!'

Looking around the ship, Jonas sighed.

Two oil lanterns, one directly above the other, had been lashed to the bowsprit. With muffled activity, yardsmen were speedily reefing in. Roughly two hundred yards off the northern tip of Deception Bay, the *Redemption*'s anchor plunged into the sea for a standing moor. Amidships by the starboard pinrails, men were feverishly lowering the jolly boat. Splashing down on the water, the craft was hurriedly boarded. Six oars were slipped into padded rowlocks. At once urging his crew, the Second Mate spoke crisply.

'Prepare to give way,' he commanded. 'Give way together.'

Pulling inaudibly for Heddon's Mouth, the jolly boat was rowed away, tossed towards the shore on small choppy waves. Soon the craft was swallowed up by the dark leaving the soft rhythmical clunk of oars.

The *raison d'être* for the League's enterprise was on the threshold of success.

Leaning against the bulwarks, Jonas raised his telescope. Scanning the shore, he quaked when he thought he saw something stir along the clifftop.

'I sense movement on the clifftop, Captain,' he whispered.

'Douse the recognition lanterns, Mister Fernsby,' said the Captain. 'We have no further need of them. Mister Miracle is on his way. We must presume the runaways are standing by. Make certain the lookouts are not snoozing, especially those aloft.'

'Aye, Captain,' replied the sailing master.

'Keep your eyes peeled along the cliff as well as seawards, Mister Guinea.'

'Aye, Captain.'

Scouring the horizon, Jonas gulped and lowered his telescope.

'I see the lights of a vessel to the north-west, Captain,' he whispered anxiously.

'Keep a close eye on her,' said the Captain curtly. 'That is an order, Mister Guinea.'

'Aye, Captain.'

'Prepare to receive our passengers, Mister Hopkins,' said the Captain. 'Be alert for any faint hearts among the crew.'

'Aye, Captain.'

'A tot of rum for all hands when we're clear of this coast, Mister,' said the Captain.

'Aye, Captain.'

Cornered

Ocean Bay
26 April 1761
22.00 hrs

Challenging in daylight, the mangroves were treacherous by moonlight. Held fast against strong tides, the entanglement of roots and cloying mud made for a laborious passage for the trio. Keeping muskets above the flooding water, progress was a sweaty stolid crawl. Coming to a large break in the mangrove canopy, Asabi heard illtempered English voices. Looking up the rock face, horror rippled down her spine. Sited on a crag on the clifftop with an unobstructed moonlit view of the mangrove clearing and the shore, the Redcoats had set up a watch.

'Soldiers,' she hissed, pointing upwards. 'Shhh.'

Robbed of the camouflage of the canopy, she knew they could not make it to the opposite side of the clearing without being seen. Unless the Redcoats moved off and soon, they would be trapped in the mangroves and on the island. Sweat and anger gushed down her temples at the notion of failure.

'We get so close,' she muttered, shaking her head and chewing her lip. 'The *Redemption* will sail 'fore we reach her.'

Suddenly, amidst much yelling, a volley of musket fire exploded from the clifftop.

Ducking below the mangroves, she whispered, 'Heads down!'

Grasping her arm, Abi whispered, 'Who them shooting at, Ma?'

'Not we. Shhh.'

Tapping her on the shoulder, Rachel whimpered remorsefully. 'Sorry me make trouble for you, Asabi.'

'I could not leave you behind,' she whispered. 'Nuff talk, we talk on ship. Jus' now we got to get to Heddon's Mouth 'fore them Redcoats.'

'How long we stay 'ere, Ma?'

''Til Redcoats get their fat backsides off clifftop,' she replied gruffly.

Now and then, she heard musket volleys spewing from the cliff top.

Peering above the canopy, she beheld muskets firing out to sea. Gazing past the peninsula of Deception Bay, she saw musket balls kicking up spumes of water yards short of an anchored vessel. She caught sight of Tomba clambering from a small boat up its side. Then, Tomba waved at the mangroves from the deck.

She spluttered, 'Redcoats are shooting at the *Redemption*!'

The signal-lanterns on the vessel suddenly disappeared. She was horror-struck.

Despite the alarming implication of doused lights, she was happy for her friend Tomba. In chains, they had arrived on the *Pelican* in Pertigua from the coast of Guinea. At this frightening moment, she knew he would be going back home to the coast of Guinea without her. Shock and grief razed her spirits. Tears blinded her sight. During all her years on the Pertigua, this was the closest she had come to her motherland. But while the village of Ake was drifting away into an abyss, she was satisfied that the strategy had succeeded. Nine runaways had fled to Guinea.

'Kayode be glad for Tomba an' heart-broken for we,' she said, pulling her son close. 'He waved at we from the *Redemption*!' Woebegone, she slumped against a mangrove root, muttering, 'Too…late…for… we…'

Wiping her cheek, stroking her brow and taking her muddied hands, Abi spoke tearfully. 'I so sad too, Ma. Let we go back to Free-town.'

Masking her bitter disappointment, she stroked his cheeks.

'When Redcoats get their bottoms off clifftop, we make for Free-town,' she said. 'Our chance to leave this wicked island is gone. We lose all.'

'You still got me, Ma,' consoled Abi.

'An' me love you,' she said softly, kissing his cheeks.

'Me make place to sleep,' said Rachel, bending down to entwine spindly mangrove branches into a hammock to keep them above the incoming tide.

Yet again, peeking above the mangroves to assess the calamitous situation, Asabi angrily bit her lip.

Billowing sails saw the *Redemption* making way, leaving a sturdy moonlit wake on the surface of a choppy sea. Desolation raked through her. She collapsed onto the hammock nursing a dark pulsating ache. Pulling Abi and Rachel close, and her musket closer, she fell asleep.

Decamping Redcoats woke her at dawn.

Poking her head above the mangroves, Asabi scanned the Atlantic Ocean and then peered along the clifftop. The *Redemption* and the Redcoats were nowhere in sight.

'We will not look back an' we got no time to weep,' she said firmly. 'Be glad for Tomba and laugh with me for them who getaway. Runaways do well this day. We defeat this island's wicked order.'

Clapping their hands, Abi and Rachel laughed softly.

On reaching the deserted clifftop in improved humour, she set a brisk pace for Freetown. Her thwarted escape focused her thoughts entirely on the morrow. No longer would she dream about the village of Ake and the shores of Guinea. She would not see them again.

Not knowing when another group of like-minded white men would again mount such a venture, she rendered a decision. 'Pertigua will forever be home. An' on this island we will grow roots, Abi.'

'We build a life, Ma.'

Cheered by her son's optimism and yearning to see Truelove again, she was also consoled by the fact they would not be slaves on any plantation. They were still runaways but at least they were free.

Departure

Logging the embarkation of runaways in his journal, Jonas wrote:

27 April — Mister Miracle's jolly boat was fired upon from the shore. Two of his men suffered flesh wounds. Three runaways failed to appear. Thus we did take on board five men and four women. I note the names they furnished: Tomba, One Night, Moses, Zachariah, Sheba, Isaac, the pregnant Rebekah, Abraham and Eve. Late last past night, we sailed with said nine runaways, bound for the coast of Guinea.

Considerably bedraggled and fatigued, nine hearty spirits applauded the *Redemption*'s crew all around and then partook of celebratory tots of rum. Given the sole language allowed on the plantations, they speak and understand English very well. The hammocks slung on the fore 'tween deck were new to them. As was the fare of boiled salt beef, boiled peas and bread, which they eagerly devoured before they slumbered. The Captain was eager to issue them with fresh apparel. Joyfully beats my heart to be with the runaways we have saved from the unspeakable horrors of the death plantations. All that is left to do is to land nine souls on the shores of Guinea – *Ad majorem Dei gloriam.*

In these contrary seas, we have seen the *Invincible* once only — Thank God. We continue to keep a keen watch for her and—

There was a soft knock on his door.

'Aye?'

'Och, Mister Guinea,' said a Scottish voice. 'Captain wants ye on deck.'

Hurrying topside during the lull, Jonas joined the Captain and the Mate on the poop deck.

'I have sent for a delegation from our runaways, Mister Guinea,' said the Captain, grinning. 'Methinks you will want to become better acquainted with our charges. Come, we shall greet them in my cabin.'

Thus far, thought Jonas, the League's commission has been successful. So much so, entering the Captain's cabin he could feel the muted jubilation. Sitting on the oak banquette beside a buoyant Mate at the rectangular gimballed table, he grinned.

Perched on an ox-blood leather chair at the head, the Captain dispensed Madeira into a row of goblets.

Raising his goblet, Jonas grinned. 'The coast of Guinea and a fair wind,' he said.

'Aye,' they all chorused.

A tall, bald-headed, broad-shouldered character strutted into the cabin in fresh breeches and jerkin. He was followed by two shorter men dressed likewise. The stench of the plantation wafted into the cabin. All bore wheals on their arms and legs, had missing teeth and showed gaunt signs of undernourishment. Visibly relieved, they steadied themselves against the roll of the ship and nodded their gratitude.

Startled by the big man in the moonlight of the previous night, Jonas had thought he was a brute, clawed and grim-lipped. In the light of day, he was warmed by the man's charm and affability. Catching the big man scrutinising him, he smiled. Clearly astonished by the sight of Jonas, he frowned and then gave him a slow faltering smile.

Rising to his feet grinning, the Captain extended his hand, 'Captain Battersby, Master of the *Redemption*, at your service. Allow me to introduce Mister Hopkins, the Mate, and Mister Jonas Guinea, who together with others in London helped plan your escape. It gladdens me to tell you that the *Redemption* is here to take you home. Who will speak for you?'

Stepping forwards, the big man shook the Captain's hand vigorously.

'Tomba,' he said, laughing quietly. 'Name be Tomba, Captain. This be Zachariah and this be Moses.'

'We meet again in freedom, Zachariah,' said Jonas, smiling.

'Aye, Jonas Guinea,' said Zachariah, pumping his hand. 'You keep your word.'

'We three speak for all,' said Tomba, smiling heartily at Jonas. 'And we wanna say we have not got nuff words to give you thanks. We suffer for years on plantations. We thank God we be free from graveyard o' Pertigua. Just now, Captain, we be broken-hearted, 'cos three friends get trap in mangroves. Them not make Heddon's Mouth. We shed many tears for them. We be happy to help work *Redemption*, Captain.'

'Please be seated, gentlemen,' said the Captain, pointing to the padded banquette.

Confused by the Captain's gentle manner, Tomba visibly hesitated.

Disturbed by the big man's insecurity, the Captain was mortified. 'An unforgettable experience, Mister Hopkins,' he said reflectively, 'to witness the response of freed men to the unacquainted experience of kindness and the epithet of gentlemen.'

'Aye, that it is, Captain,' agreed the Mate.

Man's cruelty against man, thought Jonas pensively.

Suddenly breaking into a broad grin, Tomba nodded to his companions.

'You be very kind, Captain,' he said, sitting down beside his friends.

Clasping his hands in supplication, the Captain bowed his head.

'Let us give thanks to God,' he intoned sombrely. 'O Lord, we thank thee for the watch you have kept on the *Redemption* for the deliverance of your people from the death camps of Pertigua. Most fervently, O Lord, we beseech thee to liberate the slaves from that violent territory. 'Tis true that English men helped fashion the wicked regime of plantation slavery together with men from other nations. 'Tis true as well that many English men object to the very notion of slavery. The men of the *Redemption* are such disciples. As we carry out your good works, O Lord, we trust you will watch over us on our voyage to the coast of Guinea and on our return to our loved ones in England. Amen.'

'Amen,' they chorused.

In his mind's eye, Jonas saw Faith Bradshaw happily chatting while picking apples in a Kent orchard.

Raising his head thoughtfully, the Captain addressed the runaways.

'We can, alas, do not anything as yet for your three friends,' he said sympathetically. 'Where shall we set you down on the coast of Guinea? Doubtless you were in Pertigua for innumerable years. I am bound to ask if any of you can remember from whence you came along that coast?'

A disquieting issue, thought Jonas.

Looking the Captain warmly in the eye, Tomba confidently replied, 'Badagri, Captain. You can put we down on the shores of Badagri.'

'Badagri be Yoruba, Captain,' said Zachariah. 'We be Yoruba. We find way home from Badagri.'

'We do,' agreed Moses. 'Badagri good place to set we down.'

Mindful of the expected report to the League in Deptford, Jonas said, 'May I seek clarification, Captain?'

'Aye, Mister Guinea, indeed you may.'

'What happened to your three friends, Mister Tomba?'

'Woman get lost in the mangroves, Mister Guinea,' replied Tomba. 'My bosom friend, Asabi, she go back with her son to look for woman. Redcoats trap 'em in mangroves an' stop 'em getting back to Heddon's Mouth.'

'Some day,' said Jonas resolutely, 'we will return to fetch them.'

'You intrigue me, Mister Tomba,' said the Mate impulsively. 'Can you remember your language that has not crossed your lips after so many years in captivity? Are you certain you will remember your people? Will you find them?'

Slapping the table, Tomba laughed aloud.

'Forty years cutting cane helps a man forget his motherland, Mister Hopkins,' he said. 'Hope play no tricks 'cos it turn into stranger. That helps a body real good. Forgetting eases the pain. Been gone 'bout ten years. Forget much of me tongue. I learn quickly. Motherland and family still burn deep in my soul. I know me find them.'

Captivated by the big man's confidence, the Mate thanked him with a nod and a smile.

'Except for the woman with child, Mister Tomba,' said the Captain, 'your people can be trained to work ship by the port and starboard watches and then they can stand watch. I trust that will satisfy your request?'

Tomba sprang to his feet

'Thanks be to you, Captain, we free and we happy to be going home,' he said with watery eyes. 'That mean we free to do what we want. So we free to choose to work ship.'

Glancing at the Captain and then the Mate, Jonas turned pensive.

Before me is the human evidence of the League's slave-freeing enterprise, he thought. I can already hear freedom changing their language.

'Methinks we have outwitted the privateers for now, Captain,' he said, sighing. 'An inconceivable shipload of travelling companions will make for an unforgettable passage.'

'It shall indeed, Mister Guinea,' grinned the Captain. 'Your men can work the sails, Mister Tomba. Your women can perform tasks on deck. See Mister Hopkins.'

The ship rolled queasily to starboard.

Turning a dun complexion, Tomba was woozy. 'Sound good to we, Captain.' He glanced as his sick-looking friends. 'We see Mister Hopkins.'

Responding to the sickening dilemma of his guests, the Captain shot to his feet.

'Follow me, gentlemen,' he said.

Arriving on the poop deck with the Captain, Jonas felt the drop in temperature.

A frosty easterly whistled ominously through the rigging. Dark bases of storm clouds stretched low across the skies and raindrops spattered the decks. Soon the seas streamed through the scuppers. Spume scurried down from the crests of the big Atlantic waves. The ship shuddered.

Throwing up over the port gunwales into the wind, Tomba and his companions were drenched with the spewed contents.

'Here endeth the primary lesson of the sailor, Mister Miracle,' shouted Jonas above the wind. 'Do not anything into the wind.'

'Methinks you have been observant, Mister Guinea,' said the Second Mate, grinning.

Wiping his mouth with the back of his hand, Tomba was drolly repentant.

'We really sick over each other when we ship-in as slaves to Pertigua, Captain,' he said, guffawing. 'Sweating in them cane fields make we forget 'bout that. Now we are on the way home, we free to be sick as gentlemen.'

'Break out boat cloaks for the new crew members, Mister Miracle,' chuckled the Mate. 'See that the companionways have been cleared, Mister Fernsby. And batten down the hatches. We're in for a stormy passage.'

'Aye aye, sir.' said the sailing master. 'Storm sails are rigged.'

'See that our runaway crew wait below till this tempest subsides.'

Off watch that night in his cabin, Jonas wrote in his journal:

Port watch: Tomba, One Night, Moses and Zachariah.
Starboard watch: Sheba, Isaac, Abraham and Eve.
Our exceedingly joyful passengers have been much sickly. They will find their sea-legs. I like Tomba. If his mindset and physique is to go by, he must indeed have been a sharp-witted strapping young fellow when he first saw Pertigua. He would have lived every day for escape. I see fatigue and sorrow in his eyes, yet he seems alert and surprisingly displays little bitterness. Methinks I feel a bond growing between us.

During the following five weeks, succeeding storms and gale force winds denied him opportunity to make Tomba's acquaintance. Late one morning, becalmed in the horse latitudes, he encountered the big man on the forepeak, perched on the windlass and gazing at a mirror-like ocean.

Backed against the gunwale, he said quietly, 'Methinks you look burdened, Tomba.'

'I tell this to you, Jonas,' said the big man, staring forlornly out to sea. 'I sell slaves an' pay for my wicked sins slaving on the plantations. My spirit is much vexed for Asabi. It were she who plan escape. And she get stop in mangroves an' lose *Redemption*. Asabi will never walk

the shores of Guinea wi' me. So I will carry sad words to village o'
Ake to tell 'em o' Kayode. He be son of Ake and Asabi's man. I will
tell 'em 'bout big uprising he make with Asabi. 'Ow he lead runaways
to victory. 'Ow runaways quarrel and suffer defeat. How Kayode take
his own life.'

Rapt in the big man's account, Jonas shook his head sadly. 'I was
encouraged by the uprising, Tomba,' he said softly. 'Did you ever
meet Mistress Bradshaw?'

'I first see she when she come to China Lights Great House for
feast,' said the big man, rising to his feet. 'I meet she few times during
uprising. I get Zachariah. She be his very good friend.'

Deprived of wind, the burlap sagged on all three masts. With little
to do in the noonday heat, a combined get-together was taking place
on the main deck. Spry with his fiddle, the carpenter sang shanties that
flowed across the deck. Hatted seamen sat about the deck, swapping
tales and laughing with the returnees. Others were splicing rope,
stitching sails and whittling wood. With few friends among the crew
and having shunned the returnees, Fingers Grabham, the brooding
boatswain, was propped against the mainmast. On the poop deck, the
Captain and his officers ambled languidly about.

Minutes later the big man returned with Zachariah in tow.

'I tell you about Mistress Faith,' said Zachariah, slumping on the
deck and grinning.

Cross-legged on the warm oak foredeck with a flagon of water,
Jonas sat with the two men through the airless afternoon.

'First I ask a question, Jonas,' said Tomba.

'Aye?'

'You be Yoruba?' asked Tomba.

'Aye?'

'Your face look so,' said Tomba. 'You be born in Pertigua. Most
slaves on that island be Yoruba.'

'So what be your Yoruba name then, Jonas?' asked Zachariah.

For a moment he was mortified. Having been sold before he was
even aware of himself or his slave parents, he had no answer. He had
never known his Yoruba name. Apart from the island of Pertigua and
England he had stepped on no other land mass. Moreover, he had

known no other language than English. Why does shame overwhelm me so?

'Jonas Guinea is the only name I have ever known,' he said awkwardly.

'You have woman and children in England?' asked Tomba.

'A woman aye,' he replied. 'No children as yet.'

'She be a white woman then?'

'A very fine white woman.'

'Not good 'cos she white,' said Zachariah curtly. 'Black with white don't mix. Come to Badagri with we, Jonas. I get you fine black Yoruba woman with big pum-pum. Now that Mistress Faith, she be a very fine woman with—'

Chuckling at his mention of Faith, Jonas changed the topic.

'Zachariah sounds white to me,' he teased.

Rocking with laughter, Tomba lifted the flagon of water.

'White owner name me,' said Zachariah, laughing derisively. 'Zachariah be slave name. I dump it. Me and me woman, Sheba, we go with Tomba to his village, where we free to carry Yoruba names. We leave all white things on that wicked island.'

Cheered by the warm fellowship, Zachariah aired his account of Faith's involvement in a slave escape from her stepfather's plantation. On the issue of slavery, Zachariah believed she made known her leanings with her deeds. Along with Alexander Fairfax, she sided with the slaves in the uprising and saw them in victory. After the island was recaptured by the Redcoats, she sailed for London, intent on carrying on the fight against slavery.

Certainly from his intimate acquaintance, Jonas knew her to be fiercely opposed to the ethic of white superiority, which she believed categorically spawned turmoil. Moreover, her expressions of love for him in the high pastures and the way she loved him as a man added credence to her beliefs. He smiled at the vision of her collaborating over petitions with Mistress Beecham at Pilgrims. And he was equally heartened by Tomba's effusive condemnation of slavery and his resolve to stir up the Yoruba against the English and Yoruba slaver traders.

I pray the Yoruba heed Tomba's words, he thought.

A strong southerly suddenly filled the sails at twilight.

'All hands on deck,' yelled the sailing master. 'All hands on deck.'

The Wretched and The Wronged

Coast of Guinea
29 June 1761
05.30 hrs

With all sails set, the *Redemption* was bowling along with a stiff breeze on her port quarter.

'Land ho! Land ho!'

'Where away?'

'Dead ahead!'

Turning to the prow from the stern rails, Jonas shaded and strained his eyes for his first sight of *terra firma* in two months.

The lone silhouette of an unfamiliar cape slipped slowly onto the horizon against the rising sun. Simultaneously, a spectacular V-formation of great white pelicans passed overhead heading out to sea. The heat was rising.

Patting his temples with a handkerchief, he scanned the coterie on the poop deck

Lowering his eyeglass, the pony-tailed Captain mopped his brow and beamed.

'Methinks we have the coast of Guinea in our sights, gentlemen,' he cheerfully proclaimed. 'I reckon about ten days to the Slave Coast from here, God willing. Lay a course for Badagri in the Gulf of Guinea, Mister Hopkins. And by the grace of God our returnees shall disembark on those shores.'

'Amen to that, Captain,' said the Mate, smiling. 'Returnees will be right anxious to hear. Mayhaps in Badagri we can barter our hogsheads of English brandy, pans, pewter and firkins of tallow for gold, sandalwood and ivory. And even a few days of time ashore?'

'We attain our stipulated cargo and time ashore is granted, Mister Hopkins,' said the Captain. 'After provisioning, we shall take the *Redemption* home. I want a sight at noon, Mister Miracle.'

'Aye Captain,' said the Second Mate, smiling. 'On such a historic occasion, Captain Battersby, I will give you a textbook latitude.'

'See you deliver your usual, Mister Miracle,' said the Captain. 'Stand her well out, Mister Fernsby. We don't want to go aground after the gamble we have taken to get us this far.'

'Nay Captain, we don't,' chortled the sailing master. 'Steady as you go, helmsman.'

Backed against the poop rails in the brightening light, Jonas gazed at the speck of land.

'The cradle of my forefathers where Parson Merriweather cut his teeth,' he murmured.

Gripping the rails, he appraised the big man. Rooted to the poop deck ogling the fragment of land with glistening eyes, Tomba clapped his hands.

'Home!' he cried exultantly. 'Me see motherland! Me come home! *Olorun* be praised!'

Moved by the big man's euphoria and by the tangible proximity of the Guinea coast, Jonas let out a long sigh of contentment. 'Barring an act of God, my duty is done.'

'Amen,' said Tomba heartily.

Then, he felt warm tears trickling down his cheeks. Yet, gazing astern at the wooded shore, he was maddened.

'Many many years ago, some men and women of my flesh and blood were bludgeoned onto ships sailing to Pertigua,' he said. 'Having long hungered to tread the land of my blood, I am filled with rage, my friend. On account of the slave trade, I know not to which Yoruba family I belong in Guinea. I fear the anger deep in my soul, for I am a man with a mangled history. Methinks the truth is that slavery blights Guinea's peoples. We know not the consequences for Guinea, England and Pertigua that will surely follow long after the slave trade has ended. Methinks 'tis reasonable to ask why some men seek to build and enrich England from the toil of black slaves? And why do some black kings and chiefs of Guinea sell their people, thus continuously impoverishing their own kingdoms?'

'Greed,' snapped Tomba indignantly. 'Greed mek men do it to get rich. Look what wicked things me done. An' me truly suffer for me sins.'

The rough-edged state of the big man and his flimsy breeches as well reminded Jonas of their difference in circumstances. A loving family, a comfortable London house and a profitable company fashioned conflicting emotions. In startling contrast to the quest of a destitute returnee seeking a vague destination somewhere on the coast of Guinea, his prospects were positively gilded.

Nearing the soil of his ancestors, he was suddenly beset by cries from his enslaved parents. Yet, he felt an outsider in their motherland. Veritably he was a tormented descendant bent on bearing witness to the crimes still taking place in his unfamiliar homeland.

Scowling at the looming peninsula, he seethed. 'Skulking along that shoreline are men like they who kidnapped or bought my parents. But for that contemptible fact, the ancestral lands of the Yoruba would have been my birthplace. I would not have been born a slave on the island of Pertigua and freed into a borrowed life in London.'

Grasping his shoulders, Tomba looked into his eyes.

'Cos o' you an' your friends, Jonas, some o' we back home again,' he said and then burst out, 'you be a true Yoruba man who done right for we Yoruba!'

Clutching the gunwales with pride at the acceptance of his belonging, Jonas lowered his eyes thoughtfully onto the wavelets. Then, he remembered that the big man had confided his slaving transgressions in a convincingly repentant manner.

Attempting to mollify the big man, he said, 'You have paid your dues, Tomba, and need no longer—'

Cutting him short, the Mate pointed at a promontory.

'I fancy that headland be Cape Mesurado, Mister Guinea,' he said. ''Tis the Grain Coast from where farmers extract the 'grains of paradise' — the seeds of the melegueta pepper, used in the victuals of the Mohammedans and the people of these parts, as well as them of Brazil and Portugal.'

Glancing quizzically at the officer, Jonas looked away and smiled to himself. This Mate suspects my turmoil and kindly disrupted us, he thought.

'Ten weeks from Pertigua and we are set to land the returnees, Mister Hopkins,' he said, smilingly changing the subject. 'Once more the *Redemption* shall be a common trading vessel and free from arrest. Will ye recognise Badagri, Tomba?'

'I know she when I see she, Jonas,' said Tomba, nodding confidently.

'Badagri lies on the Slave Coast, Mister Tomba,' said the Mate, grinning. 'Barring a skirmish with pirates along the way, we will first pass the Ivory Coast and Gold Coast. When we sight Cape Coast Castle, we will be approximately six days from Badagri.'

'White men destroy me family when they mek me slave, Mister Hopkins,' said Tomba. 'They not got power to destroy shape o' the coast. Only *Olorun* can do that. I know Badagri when I see her big shore.'

'You have come back home and I am unbelievably gladdened for that, Tomba,' said Jonas, grinning broadly. 'The League's endeavour has been a godly and proven project, Mister Hopkins.'

'Aye, Mister Guinea,' said the Mate. 'The *Redemption* has this day blazed a trail for the mission to abolish slavery. Many more endeavours like ours will be needed to sap the life-blood of the slave plantations. 'Tis much work to do. Right now we are making for the Cape of Three Points and Connu's Castle. Hearken back to this day in your twilight years, Mister Tomba. Ye can then give your grandchildren a fresher account — how some other white men and a Yoruba friend sailed from England to put right a wrong.'

Smiling at the Mate's account, Jonas turned his eyes to the thickly wooded coast.

'I tell you what me tell my people, Mister Hopkins,' said Tomba seriously. 'I tell them 'bout greedy men who sail from England to buy we like animals from black kings. They work we as slaves. Then I talk 'bout the men from the *Redemption* who sail from England to bring we back. *Olorun* work in ways that mek complete mystery to me. I tell the Yoruba that white people like black people, Mister Hopkins. Like we, England got some bad fruit.'

Smiling warmly, the Mate spoke softly. 'I cannot differ with your opinion, Mister Tomba.'

Six days later, the *Redemption* passed Cape Coast Castle without incident. A further nine days sailing found her in the Gulf of Guinea nearing the shores of Badagri.

Daylight arrived brightly with the rising sun. The wind fell to a breeze and the seas moderated to a long swell.

Sighting two dozen vessels at anchor across the bay, Jonas knew his mission was approaching its end. In the increasing light he could make out a fleet of canoes bearing provisions and captives scuttling between ships and the sweeping sandy shore. Euphoria came with the light wind. Leaning over the port gunwales of the poop deck, he sighed gleefully and looked along the deck.

Suddenly, flinging his hand towards the shore, Tomba was agog.

'Badagri!' he screamed. 'I see Badagri! I see Badagri!'

Like a contagion, his cries sped across the *Redemption*. Returnees materialised along the port rails on the main deck.

Scanning the deck with watery eyes and a lump in his throat, Jonas muttered, 'The wretched and the wronged.'

Zachariah had his arm around Sheba. Heavy with child and sparkling with joy, Rebekah was draped around Isaac. While cuddling One Night, Moses began loudly telling her how happy they were going to be in their new life. Lining the gunwales, the returnees were babbling giddily, whirling about and dancing in ecstasy. Silent for much of the voyage, the unattached, Abraham and Eve were gleefully pointing out features along the shore. The ship's crew were captivated by the high spirits of the returnees and simultaneously by the conclusion of the hazardous element of the voyage. Soon, the *Redemption* would once more be a common trading merchantman.

'I know she when I see she!' cried Tomba, leaping up and down. 'An' I see shore of Badagri!'

Beaming on the poop deck, Jonas shook hands with the Captain and his delighted officers.

'Well blow me down,' said the sailing master, scratching his head. 'For many years Tomba's been gone from Badagri, yet he crosses a vast ocean and still remembers the sands from where he were snatched.'

''Tis Badagri sure enough,' said the Second Mate, lowering his telescope. 'Our destination and the end of our mission is an agreeable sight.'

'I have long dreamed about disembarking returnees on the coast of Guinea, Mister Miracle,' said Jonas, shaking his head in wonder.

'You prayed for a miracle, Mister Guinea,' said the Second Mate, beaming. 'You got a Miracle to get to Guinea.'

Laughing with the officers, Jonas said, 'A tot of rum for that, Mister Miracle.'

'A tot all round once we have anchored if you please, Mister Fernsby,' said the Captain. 'Anchor close to shore but a good distance from any vessels of the Royal African Company. That moneyed concern has age-old arterial connections with the authorities and plantation owners in Pertigua.'

'Aye aye, Captain,' said the sailing master. 'I shall be on my guard.'

'No doubt ye will want to go ashore with the jolly boat, Mister Guinea,' said the Mate.

'I must tread the soil of my motherland, Mister Hopkins,' he said, grinning. 'With the Captain's permission, of course.'

Raising his telescope and slowly scanning along the arc of the sandy windswept shore, Jonas gasped. He stared in disbelief upon a long-established site of slave embarkation.

Dense rainforest spilled along the crest of the shoreline. Decaying hulks lay skewed in the shallows of the eastern shore. Masts and spars, barrels and rotten planking littered the white sands. To the west, serried ranks of semi-naked and manacled captives stood massed on the vast expanse of sand waiting to board canoes for the anchored vessels. Whip-wielding slave masters sloped about the sands, casually kicking their charges. Even from that distance he could hear the wailing and groaning columns of humanity.

Quivering and lowering his telescope, he turned to the Captain. 'Besides the slaves cowering on the Jamestown dockside, sir, a more soul-destroying sight I cannot imagine. Lest our returnees get mistaken for escaped prisoners, should they not be escorted safely off this shore?'

'Badagri is the Gomorrah of wickedness, Mister Guinea,' snarled the Captain scornfully. 'From these shores, Englishmen shipped captives away from their land, forcing disgusted Englishmen to ship them back.'

'Many years ago, Tomba walked through Badagri's Gate of No Return, Captain,' he said quietly, 'yet against all the odds he has come back. And my friend Parson Merriweather once gave benedictions over departing slaves, yet he is now an avowed member of our League. Methinks they give rise for optimism in the morrow.'

'Aye, Mister Guinea, you are right,' said the Captain. 'To stop the abomination of slavery is the morrow we must advance. Be so good as to see our returnees safely off the shore and out of harm's way, Mister Miracle.'

'My greatest pleasure, Captain,' said the Second Mate heartily.

Excitedly readied beside the Second Mate, Jonas stood at the top of the Jacob's ladder. Saddened by the exodus of the returnees, he was simultaneously overjoyed to be stepping foot on his earthly heritage. Even so, he was moved to tears by the leave taken of the returnees by the Captain and crew. Bonds had clearly been formed. Sniffling could be heard on both sides.

Movement by the mainmast caught his attention. The boatswain, Fingers Grabham, pulled Tomba gently aside and shook his hand. Deck chatter fell to whispers. The cry of seagulls was suddenly apparent. Beside the Second Mate, Jonas held his breath and watched.

Giving Tomba a whittled replica of the *Redemption*, the boatswain was forthright.

'I want you to have this keepsake, Tomba,' he said sincerely, 'so you can in the years to come hark back to a wondrous voyage. When we met I did not have kindly words for the likes of you and yours. I confess I had feared them of your skin. That was before I came to know thee. Yours has been a life wasted by my rich countrymen. 'Tis much the same men have done for the poor likes of mine. Your people showed goodly courage fleeing the plantations, Tomba. You all got guts. We'll not meet again in this life, my friend, but I'll remember thee warmly.'

'A wise voyage end wi' laughter an' a sharp man get respect, Mister Fingers,' said Tomba with a gap-toothed smile, vigorously pumping his hand. 'I like your words, my good friend.'

Heaving a collective sigh, the congregation on deck burst into a laughing lively hubbub.

'Methinks this leave-taking is somewhat uplifting, Mister Miracle,' said Jonas, steadying himself against the main-top backstay. 'Take our erstwhile blinkered boatswain. Do you recall his bigotry at the start of our passage?'

'Aye,' said the Second Mate.

'After that discomforting debacle,' continued Jonas, 'it takes mettle to openly express regret to another and shake his hand. I am heartened. Oddly enough the League's scheme was devised in a house called Pilgrims. When our returnees stand again on the sands of Badagri with that God called the motherland, our League would have realised a worthy action. The members will be gladdened by the events of this day. And not only shall I not ever forget our returnees, I shall truly hold Tomba and Zachariah in my affections. Methinks such an outcome is uplifting.'

'In all my born days, Mister Guinea,' said the Second Mate, shaking his head with quiet amazement, 'not ever before have I partaken in such a just and perilous project. Our League has forged a weapon with which we can galvanise the like-minded. On many a night in my home on the isle of Anglesey, my family gathers around the hearth with cups of mulled wine. On the next such occasion I shall be honoured to recount the *Redemption*'s escapade to liberate runaways.'

Jonas smiled.

The sun was nearing its zenith. Tomba and his companions clambered boisterously down the Jacob's ladder. Nine jubilant returnees, four rowers and the Second Mate settled themselves in the jolly boat with Jonas.

Standing at the top of the ladder, the Captain was uncharacteristically impassioned, 'Fare thee well, men and women of Guinea. We came to right the wrong that was done to you. We have completed our mission. Ye have proved right hearty shipmates. May the Gods of your motherland protect you and carry you home safely.'

When the bobbing craft was under way, Tomba rose wobbly to his feet and cried out:

'Fare thee well, Captain. Our spirits rise with the eagle; to laugh with the sun and dance with God. We thank you for what you have done. We see out our days under Yoruba skies. We pray you mek safe sail to England, Captain.'

From the stern-thwart, the Second Mate gave orders, 'Oars!'

Spry pristine notes from a fiddle sprang from the main deck. Turning around, Jonas saw the crew lining the gunwales, with the ship's fiddler standing tall on the main hatch bowing a soulful melody. Weathered voices floated across the waves:

'Fare thee well men and women of Guinea,' cried Captain Battersby.

'Fare thee well,' bellowed the ship's crew.

Ploughing through the surf, the jolly boat finally grazed the fine white sands, coming to rest a good quarter mile from the slave columns lining the shore.

Springing into the shallows, Jonas waded up the shore.

'I walk in the steps of my ancestors to touch the hand of God, Mister Miracle,' he said ecstatically. 'This land has seemed for long a fantasy of my making.'

'What lies before us is justice in action, Mister Guinea,' said the Second Mate. 'I cannot fathom the anguish of being torn from my kinfolk. Or what I would feel about their enslavement.'

'In London I keep the shame and anger to myself, Mister Miracle,' he said ruefully. 'It has fashioned a visceral resolve to put an end to the slave trade.'

'To sign on for this expedition, Mister Guinea,' said the Second Mate, 'I had to put aside my anger and revulsion of the trade.'

'You did indeed, Mister Miracle,' he said, smiling. 'Though I warrant when you rediscover that anger, you will hurl it at the door it belongs.'

'Aye Mister Guinea,' replied the Second Mate with a knowing smile. 'I best attend to Tomba and the returnees. They have all agreed to help him find his village and rest there. You can well imagine that he is itching to be on his way.'

Walking up the shore to the crest, Jonas arrived at a wide dusty track. Sitting alone on a barrel with his back to the rainforest, he surveyed the bay. Shackles, spiked collars and other unspeakable implements of cruelty protruded from the sands. The mass of captives on the shore was simultaneously growing and shrinking. Arriving slave caravans were snaking down from the rainforest and spilling onto the sands. Canoes were being relentlessly loaded before heading for the anchored vessels. Wielding whips and muskets, white and black cabiceers brutally supervised the human consignments.

'Systematic trafficking in prodigious proportions,' he muttered.

Jesting with the frock-coated Second Mate and four pig-tailed seamen, Tomba and his companions, in fresh jerkins and breeches, arrived at the top of the sandy shore.

Jonas rose to bid farewell to his erstwhile shipmates. One by one he solemnly embraced all nine.

'I will be forever overwhelmed by you and the strength you must have had to endure the terrible years on the plantations,' he said. 'That is all behind you. I know not the trials that stretch before you. But know ye this, you are now much stronger and free to choose your destiny. You have all taught me so much. That no matter where we are born, we are all still Yoruba. And your return to our motherland has given me fresh hope. I go back to England humbled by our meeting and an improved resolve. I shall not ever forget you.'

'If me baby be boy, we call him Jonas,' said Rebekah with sincerity.

'An' if baby be girl, we call her Jonas,' said Isaac, laughing.

'Tell Mistress Bradshaw that Zachariah be truly happy to feel the sun in his homeland.'

'We go to Badagri Town,' said Tomba, embracing him with tears in his eyes and a tremor in his voice. 'You look fine in white man's frock coat, Jonas. You look better in *agbada*. Be wi' us. You Yoruba like us an'…'

'In England, my family await my return,' he replied, smiling, 'And I very much want to see them.'

'Farewell Jonas Guinea — Son of the Yoruba,' said Tomba. 'We will meet again.'

With his head reeling, Jonas wiped his eyes and blew his nose. I have heard Tomba's last words to me in this life, he thought forlornly. I know I will not ever again lay eyes on him.

With the Second Mate and crew of the jolly boat, he stayed waving until the group had passed a giant *abura* tree and disappeared into the forest.

'Son of the Yoruba,' he said to himself, with watery eyes. 'I have not ever been called Yoruba, though 'tis heart-warming to be accepted by my own without conditions.'

'We have prevailed in our contest with the elements, Mister Guinea,' said the Second Mate, laughing. 'Shall we attend to another pressing matter?'

'Is this matter risky, Mister Miracle?'

'Now let me see,' mused the Second Mate, teasingly scratching his head. 'Maybe the trivial matter of bartering for a cargo and getting our backsides back to England.'

''Tis a risk with appeal, Mister Miracle,' he chuckled. 'I like it. I as well hanker after a woman in England.'

'You have certainly kept very quiet about your woman, Mister Guinea,' said the Second Mate, winking and pointing at the waiting jolly boat. 'After you…'

Smiling broadly, Jonas stepped into the clinker-built craft and made no reply.

Soon they were pulling for the *Redemption*.

Barely had Jonas stepped on deck from the Jacob's ladder when he was met by the Captain.

'Our mission is well-accomplished, Mister Guinea. Set course for Cape Coast Castle on the Gold Coast, Mister Hopkins. The super-cargo-in-residence is an old shipmate. Ye old sot will help sort out our barter for gold, ivory and sandalwood. Stow it in the after hold, well away from the rum and sugar.'

'Aye, Captain.'

'All hands on deck,' yelled the sailing master. 'All hands to the sails.'

Heavy-hearted, Jonas gazed desolately astern beside the Second Mate on the poop deck.

'Torrents of fire and torrents of darkness will plague this land before the light,' he said.

Staring at the receding shore of his motherland, he felt the heart-beat of the Yoruba. It belonged to him, by colour, by history and by blood. Yet this motherland was unknown.

'Tis true I feel a stranger in my mother's land, he thought.

'You are Yoruba and this is your motherland, Mister Guinea,' said the Second Mate kind-heartedly. 'But could you live on the coast of Guinea?'

'And why not?' he countered defensively.

'Books!' said the Second Mate with a straight face. 'A man like you could not live without books.'

'Though it grieves me to say so, I cannot deny that, Mister Miracle,' he said, smiling. 'But as well, I could not live without friends. In London, I have met many for whom my colour matters not a jot, a few of whom have become good friends. By some I am merely tolerated. Yet others expediently recall that Guinea is where I belong. They say, do you not pine for your motherland, Mister Guinea?'

'How do you reply?'

'I pine for my country whenever I leave her.'

The Second Mate rocked with laughter.

'I cannot deny the distressing actions against them of your hue, Mister Guinea,' he said with a knowing look. 'I am Welsh. I have myself encountered and witnessed English intolerance towards the Welsh. We continue to have our fair share of disputes. Through I suspect that England has many quarrelsome years to pass through before colour matters not. I hope what we have just achieved with our returnees marks a step along the way.'

Smiling at the Second Mate, Jonas said, 'As well as liking your optimism, Mister Miracle, I agree with your analysis.'

That night the *Redemption* ran before a gale with high following seas. Battered and bruised she recovered over the next six days with a strong following breeze to Cape Coast Castle. Six tranquil days elapsed during which time Jonas assisted the officers in haggling for a cargo.

Alone in his cabin, he made an entry in his journal on 30 July 1761:

...At 13.30 hrs – fully laden the *Redemption* dropped her moorings. But for the non-appearance of three returnees, we mercifully disembarked nine. They will establish themselves in

Tomba's village and make expeditions to discover their own. I shall inform Faith that Tomba will journey to the village of Ake to take the report of Kayode to his family. All things considered we have an excellent outcome to our mission. Barring the appearance of pirates, pray God we make a speedy passage to England. I yearn so much for my beloved Faith. What glad times we shall have...

Striding onto the poop deck the following morning, he stopped, wiped his brow and gazed fiercely astern at the receding Cape Coast Castle. Grimacing at the bastion of pain, he pondered aloud, 'How many men, women and children have staggered through your Gate of No Return?'

'I fear a horrendous number, Mister Guinea,' said the Second Mate.

'It takes a mere spark to turn a flicker into a flame, gentlemen,' said the Captain quietly. 'With others we must provide that spark. Thank God our duty here is done, morally and profitably. Methinks we have witnessed enough on this coast. Set course for England, Mister Hopkins.'

'Aye, Captain,' said the Mate gladly. 'West by south, helmsman.'

'Aye aye, Mister Hopkins,' growled the helmsman with a smile. 'West be south it be.'

Homeward Bound

Start Point
South coast of England
7 October 1761
03.30 hrs

Pitching in choppy seas, the *Redemption* stood a league off Start Point, an exposed promontory running nearly a mile out to sea. Stiff breezes sporadically scourged the deck in the early morning. Dark swollen clouds hung threateningly.

For the next seven days through nigh-on glacial conditions, heavy rain showers and reduced visibility, she limped up the English Channel with a moderate westerly veering north-west. Nine days elapsed before she rounded North Foreland. Trimming her sails, she entered the estuary and beat up the calmer snaking waters of the River Thames. Given the stiff airs, only foresails were hoisted. Shortly, dense flocks of mallards, geese and waders were taking flight and landing on the marshlands lying along the bank on either side. After nine turbulent weeks at sea from the coast of Guinea, the *Redemption* was nearing port. It was the sixteenth of October 1761.

Tightly wrapped in a boat cloak, Jonas walked the main deck with the Mate, the officer of the watch.

'Before we reach Fort Gardens I have to say this, Jonas,' said Mister Hopkins, halting in his tracks. 'Not ever before have I partaken in such a gallant challenge. And you made a right able shipmate. Tarry the night at the Three Daws and raise a tankard with me. Though somewhat bawdy, the hostelry boasts a snug cot, grand fires, fine ales and victuals. 'Tis a rumbustious watering hole for Jack Tars and smugglers living on the brink.'

'How so?'

'Press gang always arrives to find an emptied tavern,' said Mister Hopkins, laughing. 'Given the alarm by the innkeeper, seamen and smugglers skedaddle down five staircases and out of two entrances. Methinks it won't be long before the Lords of the Admiralty dispatch two press gangs on a raid. 'Tis said that a princess called Pocahontas was buried nearby in bygone times. In truth, Jonas, 'tis a smuggler's paradise. And 'tis in the Three Daws, Pridmore, the shipping agent, awaits the return of our vessels. He has been ordered by the Captain to see you safely back to Deptford, you being a man of colour and all. A well-earned feed, raise the roof, a good night's rest and you can leave early in the morning.'

'As a member of your crew I have been guided by your good counsel, Thaddeus,' said Jonas, with a heartfelt tenor in his voice. 'For that I give you many, many thanks. And for your companionship during such difficult moments in Jamestown, you have my deepest friendship. Methinks you disport an enticing flier for this Three Daws. How could I not but be drawn by your invitation?'

Drifting into view, peeking from behind and above the town of Gravesend, was the mill on Windmill Hill.

Turning his thoughts from Tomba and the coast of Guinea, he wondered about Pilgrims. I ache for you, Faith, and long for your company, he thought.

Within the hour on an overcast day in Fort Gardens, back springs and breast ropes were quickly secured to the dockside bollards.

Heaving an elongated sigh, he noted the time.

It was four o'clock. He had been gone eight months and sixteen days. He was a carriage ride away from Pilgrims and from Faith Bradshaw. On the horizon lay the uncertain crossing of Blackheath.

Bidding farewell to Captain Battersby and the sailing master, he exchanged addresses with the Second Mate. Disembarking with his gear and boxed pistols in Fort Gardens, Jonas trudged with the Mate the quarter mile to the Three Daws. After paying a shilling for bed and supper, he picked out the rotund shipping agent easily, sitting alone near a glowing hearth.

Having shed not an inch of girth, Pridmore was as he remembered. Oozing out of a black frock coat and with his buttocks drooping over either side of a chair, the rubicund-faced man was leafing through a bundle of documents on a small card table. Rising unsteadily to his feet, the shipping agent smiled.

'It gladdens me to see ye back safe in home waters, Mister Hopkins,' he said. 'I see ye made it back undamaged then, Mister Guinea.'

'I heeded your counsel, Mister Pridmore,' he replied, chuckling.

'And what was that?'

'You said not to falter, Mister Pridmore. I did not.'

Slapping his thigh, the shipping agent laughed.

'Vex not about our journey, Mister Guinea,' he said. 'This time we be crossing Blackheath in daylight when Isaac Darkin be sleeping with a strumpet.'

'Your confidence is heartening, Mister Pridmore,' said Jonas, crossing his fingers behind his back.

At sea for the best part of a year, he succumbed with the Mate and the shipping agent to a night of Gleek – a card game of tricks and bluff – with sea shanties, pitchforked eels and tankards of ale. In high spirits for the promised morrows with Faith, he was tinged with a faint disquiet that had been troubling him all evening. He retired to his cot.

'I will ask for her hand,' he muttered, 'if she has not already promised it to another.'

Frazzled from the *Redemption*'s perilous Guinea adventure, he turned over and closed his eyes.

A slate-grey sky hung over a sodden day. The freezing air was driven by a biting wind.

Slipping out of the tavern at the crack of dawn in his boat cloak, Jonas's face iced up. Crossing the market square outside the Three Daws, he climbed unsteadily into the waiting carriage. Inside the draughty interior, he dumped himself down opposite the shipping agent.

'I carry primed pistols, Mister Pridmore.'

'You'll not be needing them, Mister Guinea. I foresee no mishap crossing Blackheath. Save for the time lost for a change of horses, you'll be in Pilgrims for supper.'

Sticking his head out of the window, the shipping agent cried, 'Away with you, Mister Pritchett.'

Lurching forward, the carriage set off over the cobbles of Crooked Lane. Soon they were trundling along the stony Overcliffe above Chalk Pitts, through the slumbering village of Northfleet and out onto the London Road.

Drawing his cloak around him, the shipping agent grinned.

'You being at sea an' all, Mister Guinea, I daresay you don't know the talk on England's lips?'

'Mayhaps you might acquaint me with the gossip, Mister Pridmore.'

'We have a new King,' said the shipping agent. 'Prince George was married and crowned King.'

Looking out of the window and stifling a yawn, he asked, 'When did this happen?'

'Georgie boy was married on eighth of September and crowned George the Third on the twenty-second in Westminster Abbey. Someone was clearly in a hurry. Of German extraction, Georgie boy sought to distance himself from his Hanoverian roots in his accession speech to Parliament. Born and educated in this country, he said, I glory in the name of Britain. Methinks Georgie boy will fit right in.'

'Whom did he marry?'

'Some German woman.'

'German?'

'Aye.'

'May I be candid, Mister Pridmore?'

'Aye you may, Mister Guinea.'

'And I do so with much respect.'

'Aye?'

'Why was an Englishwoman not deemed fit to be Queen? Besides, I thought the English were at loggerheads with the Germans?'

'You clearly do not understand the contrary mindset of the English, Mister Guinea,' said the shipping agent, chuckling. ''Tis true we are commonly at odds with the Germans and the French. As far as our leaders are concerned the people are, on the whole, a passive people. And as such, if our betters say we must accept a German King or

Queen, we will. Even the poor will make merry with street festivities. In the main, we accept the dictates of our rulers. I know 'tis unjust, yet I am still proud to be English.'

Feeling he had taken his inquiry as far as the tribal circumstances allowed, Jonas fell thoughtfully back into his seat. Observations by a black man about English society are generally frowned upon, he thought. I tread carefully on questions of the monarchy.

'Naturally, Mister Pridmore, I do wish His Majesty and his Queen good fortune, a long life and many heirs.'

'I presumed your respect for the ways of another, Mister Guinea,' said the shipping agent, smiling.

As promised, the crossing of Blackheath passed without incident. Indeed the entire journey was uneventful. Soon they were on the chaotic Highway. Half-mile along the thoroughfare, they stopped outside Pilgrims behind a waiting carriage.

Picking up his gear and boxed pistols, Jonas stepped onto the cobbles.

Poking his head out of the window and shaking hands, the shipping agent was warm-hearted. 'You be the first of your kind I have met, Mister Guinea. Indeed, I have learned much from our encounters. And I am glad for it. Considering your perilous venture on the high seas, I am right glad you made it home safe. I bid thee a heartfelt farewell, Mister Guinea. You make a right fine black English gentleman. I hope we meet again. I go on to Greenwich to meet Captain Battersby at Mister Puddlewick's abode.'

'I have to thank you, Mister Pridmore,' he said.

'Aye?'

'On our way to join the *Redemption* in Fort Gardens, your tactful honesty made for a most thought-provoking passage. I shall not forget the tutoring you gave me regarding self-protection on the King's highway. I am certain we shall meet again.'

Turning around, he gasped and then laughed. Mistress Beecham stood on the top step of Pilgrims with a broad smile. Charged with success, he bounded up the steps. Venting a prolonged sigh, he dropped his gear. Sobbing and laughing at the same time, she embraced him.

'My beloved son, praise God you are home safe!' she exclaimed. 'Right glad am I to hold thee again. Come hither and tell me everything. There is much for you to know. Before this night is over, you must hear about the West Indies Sugar Cartel and our suspicions of the Flemings. Now let me look at thee.'

'By the grace of God I continue to breathe. I am most certainly glad to be back with you in Pilgrims. After supper I shall tell you what I learned about the Flemings' activities in Pertigua.'

'Come Jonas, first you must tell me all about the *Redemption* and the runaways. You arrived just in time too. Reverend Whitehouse is our house guest, as is Mistress Bradshaw. The smitten mistress has been with us this past week and is set to depart in the morning for Kent, though I daresay your appearance may well change all that.'

Giving him a slow unskilled wink, she laughed. Bashfully averting his eyes, he grinned.

'On second thoughts,' she said, 'I shall tell her coachman to pasture her horses. Methinks she may not be leaving in the morning. Come, we are in the withdrawing room.'

Opening the door, he drew a sharp intake of breath.

Goblet in hand, Faith Bradshaw stood beside the affable clergyman with her back to the hearth. Wearing a simple close-bodied honey-coloured silk gown and with twists of jet-black curls framing her soft features, she was even more arresting than he remembered. His heartbeat quickened.

'Not a soul could deny you are dazzling in such an eye-catching gown, Mistress Faith,' he said, smiling at her. 'I am delighted to be in your company again. And yours too, Reverend Whitehouse.'

Inching towards him with a playful look in her eyes, she stretched out her hand. Kissing her fingers and raising his head, he looked into her dark eyes.

''Tis good to see that your thorny deeds have not dulled your charm, Jonas,' she said, in a soft coquettish voice. 'And I have to say your seafaring appears to have fashioned a spirited look in thee. I have so longed for your company. And to think I was set to return to Kent in the morning. Sadly being somewhat under the weather, Parson Merriweather cannot be here to drink you under the table in welcome. But no doubt he has reserved you a bottle of special vintage. I know you must be terribly fatigued. I myself will deny sleep itself to hear the account of your expedition to Pertigua. 'Twould mean me tarrying one or two more nights, Mistress Beecham?'

'Your chamber is prepared, my dear,' said Mistress Beecham with a knowing smile. 'Stay as long as you wish, my dear. I have sent your coachman to pasture your horses and retire for the evening. Tuppence will attend to his needs.'

Raising his hand, Jonas said, 'I shall keep you all in suspense not an instant longer—'

'Aye, Jonas, do tell,' said Faith, taking his arm.

Handing him a goblet, Mistress Beecham said, 'First get this brandy down you.'

'As you all know, Captain Battersby had planned to ship twelve runaways,' he said, taking two hearty swigs of brandy. 'Nine runaways made it to Deception Bay and sailed with the *Redemption*. Despite running the gauntlet between the naval patrols and Redcoats on the shore, you will be happy to learn that all were landed safely on the sands of Badagri on the coast of Guinea. When we bade the return-ees farewell, the League's objective had been accomplished. Before I forget, Mistress Faith, Tomba and Zachariah send you their esteemed regards. Not exactly with those words but that is what they meant...'

Mistress Beecham giggled. Faith smiled her gratitude.

'I do believe that among other necessities,' he said dryly, 'the plantations truly forgot to furnish the slaves with a tutored education.'

'As well as a long list of provisions,' carped Reverend Whitehouse, inhaling snuff off the back of his hand.

'I must add, Mistress Faith,' continued Jonas, 'that your friends Alexander Fairfax and Zachariah proved indispensable. We could not have succeeded without them. And with the grace of God guiding the Captain and crew of the *Redemption*, I can report that our enterprise was an unbridled success.'

'Amen,' said Reverend Whitehouse.

A round of applause echoed through the withdrawing room, followed by clinking glasses. Merrily raising her hand, Mistress Beecham beckoned all to the dining room. Euphoria and good humour flooded the warm chamber. Soon, the candlelit table was laden with a tureen of turnip soup, dressed artichokes, rabbit stew, boiled potatoes, bread and Portugal cakes.

'To celebrate your return, Jonas,' said Mistress Beecham, nodding at the housekeeper, 'I traded some wine with a garlicky Frenchman doing business with the Chandlery.'

Uncorking a bottle of Chateau St Emilion, Tuppence Honeypenny filled the goblets.

'My son is home from the sea,' cried Mistress Beecham, gleefully raising her goblet. 'I toast thee for a blooded effort that took some pluck, Jonas. Let us as well drink to the League's unprecedented venture outside these isles.'

Vigorous clapping shook the dining room.

The reunion supper effervesced with the textures and berried aromas of the rich red wine.

'A finer wine I have not ever tasted,' said Jonas. 'My thanks to you all for such a heartening welcome.'

'I received your letter on the day the Puddlewicks came for tea, Jonas,' said Mistress Beecham. 'I was much gladdened by it, though you did pen a few lines that at times left me reeling and fatigued with fret.'

'I heard not a word from thee,' said Reverend Whitehouse light-heartedly before pulling out his Bilston Battersea Truth enamel snuffbox. 'But I was somewhat reassured when my name was mentioned in your letter to Mistress Beecham.'

'What with the domestic fripperies of Kent, Jonas,' said Faith, 'your letter arrived like a mango from the tropics. I shuddered reading your stormy oceanic images, though I was heartened by and concurred with the sentiments you expressed.'

A grin darted across the visage of Mistress Beecham, who glanced at Reverend Whitehouse, who winked and hurriedly took pinches of snuff. Shyly averting his eyes, Jonas felt beads of sweat running down his temples.

''Twas warm in those climes,' he said, smiling sheepishly and wiping his brow.

Tapping her goblet with her fork for attention, Mistress Beecham leaned conspiratorially forwards and spoke with lowered voice:

'We have been informed that the West Indies Sugar Cartel intends to send agent provocateurs to break up public gatherings wanting an end to slavery. I should add that Matthew, the scion of the Fleming family, is in London. Jeremiah Puddlewick overheard him at Bootle's Gentleman's Club. Apparently, the weasel heir acting on behalf of his bed-ridden father was asking rich friends to subscribe to a fighting fund for the Cartel. This dastardly fund is for the express purpose of disrupting anti-slavery meetings and all opposition to their trade.'

'Opposition is certain to grow,' said Jonas.

'Aye it will,' said Mistress Beecham. 'Rich men continue to prosper and they ignore the forces hostile to their trade. But I suspect they dread a combining of elements of the populace opposed to their immoral business. Antagonistic voices are slowly cohering. However, we need to reconcile the profits from the *Redemption*'s voyage. As agreed, investors shall receive equal shares, including you, Jonas. But we must decide what to do about the Flemings and their skulduggery. That said, I think you will all now appreciate why I have requested an Extraordinary meeting of the League.'

'Methinks you did right, Mistress Beecham,' said Reverend White-house. 'We need to thrash out a strategy before the Flemings' writ gathers momentum.'

'Aye,' said Jonas. 'A meeting of the League is crucial. In Pertigua, I learned that it was on the orders of Randolph Fleming that privateers were sent to arrest the *Redemption*. I was to be taken alive.'

'And to think we once entertained Randolph Fleming to supper at this very table,' sneered Mistress Beecham. 'His only saving grace was his charming French companion, Monsieur de La Fontaine, whose etiquette was beyond reproach.'

'According to Alexander Fairfax,' said Jonas, 'the Flemings and the West Indies Sugar Cartel have a growing list of anti-slavery targets. Our League sits near the top.'

'We must assume that by now,' said Reverend Whitehouse, 'the Flemings know the *Redemption* was involved with the recent libera-tion of runaways. But I suspect they have not the evidence as yet. If my estimation of the man who came to supper is accurate, Randolph Fleming will not leave it at that. I daresay in his son, the apple falls not far from the tree.'

'I did hear something that will surely come to challenge England's men of letters,' said Mistress Beecham, almost in a whisper. ''Tis said the new King's consort, Queen Charlotte, is of black blood.'

Frowning deeply at Mistress Beecham's startling tidings, Jonas asked, 'Is Her Majesty not white-skinned?'

'She does appear so,' said Reverend Whitehouse, sipping wine. ''Tis said that she is descended from a branch of the Portuguese royal family. Her ancestry is said to be traced back to a thirteenth-century ruler, Alfonso the Third, and Madragana, his Moorish lover.'

'Does that mean their heirs will carry traits of Moorish blood?' asked Jonas with mounting perplexity.

'Mayhaps,' said Reverend Whitehouse, chuckling and sniffing snuff. 'Unfortunately the good Lord did not furnish me with the science of the hereditary traits of procreation.'

'A pity He did not provide you with such,' said Mistress Beecham dryly. ''Twould have been interesting to see in the fullness of time if the traits in question came to pass or be acknowledged.'

'Aside from the affairs of state, important as they are,' said Faith Bradshaw, 'there are others diversions Mister Guinea has been without in his long absence. You like cricket do you not, Jonas?'

'As much as I understand the game.'

'I wager you did not know that my county of Kent trounced Essex this past June?' she asked teasingly.

'Why that must have passed me by, Mistress Faith,' he said sportively. 'I don't recall it being raised by anyone during our meetings with the runaways.'

Giggling at his droll response, Faith took a sip of wine and winked.

'I did hear the result was somewhat dissimilar to yours, Mistress Bradshaw,' said Reverend Whitehouse, chuckling. ''Twas announced in the County Cricket Journal: eleven men of Kent versus the best eleven of Essex. I believe the game was never ended, methinks because of war.'

Clapping her hands gleefully, Faith laughed.

'Men are so much better at cricket, Reverend Whitehouse,' she said frivolously. 'And the outcome is almost always definitive. To recover your health, Mister Guinea, you would do well to rest and recuperate from the effects of your gruelling expedition. I can think of nowhere better than the comforting attractions and meadows of Kent. Would you not agree, Mistress Beecham?'

Energised by her proposition, Jonas raised his goblet and smiled.

'I am of the same mind, Jonas,' said Mistress Beecham. 'With the assistance of Reverend Whitehouse, I am happily content to administer the chandlery for a few more weeks. Kent's rural curiosities and pastoral diversions should alleviate the angst from the horrors you have witnessed. Given the weighty decisions and activities that lie ahead, a respite at this time would make good sense.'

Jonas closely eyed Mistress Beecham and Faith Bradshaw in turn.

How effortlessly they seem to agree, he thought. Methinks much has been said in my absence which has brought them close. Perchance as well they are agreed on other anonymous matters.

'My gratitude for your concern, Mistress Faith,' he said, giving her a crisp bow. 'A rustic sojourn would certainly counteract the glacial and spartan conditions on the *Redemption*. 'Twould be my pleasure to accompany you to Kent on the morrow.'

'Parson Merriweather and I shall be glad of your company, Mister Guinea.'

Following the port, the homecoming celebrants retired.

In the throes of the warm reception, he ambled wearily to his bed-chamber.

How much does Mistress Beecham know of my feelings for Faith, he pondered. On my return from Kent, we will continue managing Thomas Beecham, Chandlers. By then, affairs between Faith and I will hopefully be much clearer.

Meadowlands

Greensleeves
18 October 1761
15.45 hrs

Gazing at the rolling pastoral landscape from the carriage, Jonas heaved a sigh of fulfilment.

In the crisp chilly air, falling amber leaves littered the furrowed track and the hawthorn hedgerows bordering the Greensleeves estate. Earthen odours of banked brushwood heightened his felicity. It was autumn in Kent. The woods were on the turn and the trees had begun the wait for spring.

''Tis a joy to be back at Greensleeves,' he said, taking Faith's hand. 'On the *Redemption*, I yearned for the meadowlands and the wildflowers. To forestall any doubt, Faith, I want you to know that I love you. 'Twas many months ago we had the mission to Pertigua obstructing our morrows. Pertigua is now behind us. Thus the years ahead are ours.'

'Methinks we can take up where we left off,' she said unequivocally. 'I as well want you to know my love for you is unconditional. Though I have to say I would far rather have you and your adventures on home soil. I cannot love you in small lumps, Jonas.'

Nodding his appreciation of her heartfelt avowal, he smiled and sighed happily to himself.

At long last I have what I seek, he thought.

From half a mile he could see wood smoke spiralling from the mansion house. The carriage shook as it swung between stands of pollarded willows either side of the carriage drive. Twilight beckoned. Juddering to a standstill before the entrance, he smoothed his muslin cravat and frock coat. Unlatching the carriage door, he stepped out and helped Faith onto the stony drive. Bustling from the house, the housekeeper approached the carriage. Parson Merriweather stood wobbling against the door frame.

'I suspect our Parson is well sozzled,' said Jonas.

'Creature of hard habit,' said Faith, smiling.

Bounding past the housekeeper in his haste to greet them, the cleric's straggling hair splayed out like that of a mystic.

'A thousand and one greetings, Mistress Faith, and in such a fetching gown,' said the Parson gleefully. 'As well, I might add, you seem exceedingly cherished with the proverbial suspect ensconced in your carriage. Welcome back to Greensleeves, Jonas. After your incursion into seafaring, slavery and risky assignments, whispering meadows and bosoms of contentment await you around these parts.'

''Tis inspiriting to be with you again, Parson,' she said, shivering and smiling infectiously while pulling back the hood of her cape. 'There is a frosty nip about and 'tis going to rain. Let us repair to the withdrawing room for a pre-prandial beverage.'

Entering the warm candlelit hall, Jonas sighed.

'Outward bound in heavy seas and freezing conditions off North Foreland,' he said, 'I craved for thee, your cheer and the airs of Greensleeves.'

'We are all delighted you are here, Jonas,' she said, smiling.

Pausing in the doorway of the withdrawing room, he looked around beaming.

The chamber was as he remembered: stone mullion windows, flames in the inglenook fireplace, the flowering aspidistra, and the screech and timbre of the polished oak floors underfoot.

'To touch again the silk embroidery of these walls stirs memories.'

''Tis heartening you feel so, Jonas,' she murmured.

'I can see by the cut of your jib you fulfilled your mission, Jonas,' said the Parson affectionately. 'Congratulations on an extraordinary accomplishment. It reminds me of my younger years on the wild shores of Guinea. Quite by accident the day last past I chanced upon the George and Dragon on nearby Speldhurst Hill. I shall take you. 'Tis a thirteenth century inn with roaring log fires, hefty oak beams and an excellent port...'

''Tis comforting to see your libational tendencies are in such rude health, Parson,' said Faith, laughing. 'And 'tis most reassuring to be back in your trust, Mistress Bracegirdle. After such a fatiguing passage we are in dire need of refreshment. We shall take supper here in the withdrawing room as soon as cook has it prepared.'

'We got no warning for the time of yer homecoming, Mistress Bradshaw,' said the housekeeper. 'I set a decanter and glasses on the card table. Yer might like to partake of a warmed brandy or two while supper is prepared.'

Sitting down beside her on the Chippendale sofa, Jonas addressed the merry cleric.

'To answer your question, Parson, the *Redemption* fetched nine runaways and landed them on the shores of Badagri. Watching Tomba and his friends disappear into the rainforest will be forever etched in my head. In all my born days, I have not ever experienced such spiritual composure as I did at that moment. Nine wrongs had been righted.'

''Twas on the lawless aboriginal shores of Badagri I committed my greatest transgressions,' said the Parson without emotion.

'Transgressions, Parson?'

'Aye, transgressions,' replied the Parson repentantly. 'As the representative of the Church, my ambition blinded me to the inhumanity of my ministry. I violated God's law by delivering benedictions over them being shipped to Cape Coast Castle and onwards to plantation slavery. My blessing was a contemptuous transgression, for it furnished slave-owners with moral justification for their dark deeds. I confess I knew what I was doing. As ye both well know, since that gory uprising in Pertigua, a doctrinal cataclysm reversed my erstwhile beliefs.'

'True absolution can be found only on the other side, Parson,' she said sympathetically. 'But your associating with the League and investing in the mission to liberate slaves puts you firmly on the right side of Judgement Day. What else is there to know? We have changed. You have changed. Time, circumstance and recovery of a moral code have seen to that.'

A poignant silence greeted her statement.

Then, Jonas heard the soft patter of raindrops. Supper was served under a half-moon peeking between cloud banks, its vaporous light casting otherworldly shadows onto the windows. Carrying his glass to the round beech table, he sat down and noted the unusual collection of George the Second Irish silver cutlery. A pair of old French cherub gilt candelabra lit the table.

Into the chamber swanned two maidservants, bearing platters of roast goose, carrots, peas, celery and boiled potatoes, to be followed by cook's own lemon syllabub. With the aroma of the baked bird wafting into his nostrils, his belly gurgled loudly. The Parson smirked.

Gobbling voraciously until at last he swallowed his final mouthful of syllabub, Jonas dropped his spoon and dabbed his mouth with a napkin.

'I have to admit that after the mildewed victuals aboard the *Redemption*, I needed a gastronomic deliverance,' he effused. 'You must allow me to thank your cook for a delicious goose and a truly life-affirming feast.'

'Then you must indeed after supper,' she said happily.

Decanting red wine into three glasses, the raconteur in the Parson surfaced.

'Some months past,' he said, 'I happened upon a French wine merchant in Winchelsea—'

Openly sniggering, she said, 'Did you happen to happen upon this said wine merchant inside a tavern, Parson?'

Acknowledging her mockery with a nod and a wink, the Parson soldiered on, 'Anticipating your triumphant return, Jonas, I bought a few bottles of Chateau Boyd-Cantenac Margaux from this said Gallic vintner. An excellent vintage from a Bordeaux wine estate. Savour its fragrance of liquorice, flowers, oak and earth and—'

'A fine bouquet indeed, Parson,' said Jonas, laughing and wiping his lips. 'I—'

'Before I forget, Jonas,' interrupted the Parson. 'In the past two weeks, HMS *Deptford* of fifty-guns departed from Deptford Dockyard.'

Puckering her brow, Faith asked, 'And why might that be of significance to Jonas?'

'In line with the experiments to ascertain longitude at sea,' replied the Parson, 'a ship-of-the-line has been commissioned by the Board of Longitude. Under orders, she has sailed for Jamaica carrying John Harrison's timepiece.'

'They clearly plan an examination of Harrison's timepiece over a distance of four thousand miles,' said Jonas. 'Given my vested interest, I keenly await the Deptford's return with the results of the trial.'

'What vested interest have you, Jonas?' she asked, clearly mystified.

'Certainty of longitude will expedite sailing passages, Faith. It will make more certain the delivery of cargoes and give import to ship timetables. Certainty will as well stimulate fresh investment in shipbuilding. That should in turn greatly increase trade for chandlers like me.'

Greeting his explanation with a broad appreciative smile, she sipped wine.

Barking burst out on the carriage drive. A man could be heard bellowing at the dogs.

'Sneddon, the gamekeeper,' she said.

Eerie hoots echoed through the chamber. Cocking his head towards the window, Jonas frowned.

'Barn owls by the stable block,' she said. 'Even they will more than hoot at what I have to say this night.'

Shifting in his chair, Jonas was intrigued.

'And that is?' he asked.

''Tis become abundantly clear, at least to me,' she said, pulling herself upright, 'that we of the League must modify our tactics. What is absent is that most salient of questions: how to inform not just the few, but the entire populace? Hitherto, we have attended small gatherings and addressed many small meetings espousing abolition. To win the empathy and support of the population, I say we need to do more. By way of a profusion of handouts we should make the populace unequivocally conversant with the ghastly truth of the slave trade. We must produce a series of petitions promoting abolition. Thereafter, people can formulate their own petitions in growing numbers. I believe voices against this grisly trade are growing in number.'

Frowning deeply, the cleric asked, 'Petitioning whom exactly?'

'Members of Parliament, the Lords Spiritual,' she replied, count-ing on her fingers, 'not forgetting the Church and certain members of the intelligentsia. But—'

Shifting uncomfortably in his chair, the Parson growled, 'Many of the rascals you have just mentioned are slave-owners.'

'If you allow me to finish, dear Parson,' she said insistently, 'the majority of petitions shall come from the populace. Governments know 'tis not wise to dismiss an informed populace that as well feels powerless.'

'Only the Commons carries the power to abolish England's slave trade,' said the Parson. 'The petition to the Members should consequently carry most weight. But since they are not likely to vote for a statute that is against their own vested interests, I'd say your line of reasoning is difficult to fault, Mistress Faith. What say you, Jonas?'

Just then, in his mind's eye, he was envisioning the slaves he had seen cowering on Jamestown's dockside when the *Redemption* was docking.

Stroking the back of his hand, she spoke softly. 'Come back to us from your travels, Jonas. What say you?'

Shaken out of his reverie, he craned forwards and lowered his voice. 'Methinks the League should assemble a group of influential friends from among the politicians. Naturally, you and the Parson are better placed than I to ascertain who among their number harbours anti-slavery sympathies.'

Acknowledging his tact, she gave him a broad knowing smile, as did the Parson.

'Messrs Puddlewick, Drinkwater et al,' Jonas continued, 'could mayhaps encourage like-minded shipowners to employ similar meth-ods to the *Redemption*. 'Tis been made amply clear that the Commons will entertain not even a sliver of legislation on abolition. Petitions can, however, publicise the cruelties of the slave trade to countless cit-izens at once. Given persistence and time, Members of the Commons should by and by begin to hear from an informed, irate populace. I, as well, believe that there is sufficient empathy and goodwill in England to bring that about. I may never live to witness the end of this trade but, by God, I will die trying.'

'Likewise, Jonas,' she said.

'Amen,' said the Parson.

Lightning suddenly flashed across the withdrawing room windows. Thunder crashed directly overhead. Rain fell in torrents, cascading from the eaves. As unexpectedly as it came, the rainstorm slackened.

Shut out by the wanton looks in evidence, the Parson made his excuses for an early night.

Minutes later, hand in hand, they mounted the stairs. Lovingly, she led him into her candlelit bedchamber. A banked log fire flickered in the fireplace behind a tapestry-panelled fire screen. Eau de cologne wafted faintly in the warmed room. Between two windows, an ornately carved four-poster stood head to the wall. Aged curtains fell to the floor, decorated with the thin leaf stems of the Indian tree of life. And so intense were the block-painted colours, thought Jonas, the brushstrokes might have been made that very afternoon. Above the sound of wind and rain, he could hear his breath. Distracting himself, he picked up the gift-wrapped bottle of Chateau Bellevue St. Emilion from the bedside table and smiled.

'When the *Redemption* was thrown about in precipitous waves, I prayed to God and while doing so, I yearned for you,' he said. 'We must first thank God we are as one again. And with this special wine, we must drink a toast to our bright morrows.'

''Tis a wine for nurturing unspent energies, my love,' she whispered. 'You plan no more absences, do you?'

'I do not.'

'Then, my precious, our morrows truly begin this night,' she whispered, running a finger slowly down his nose and onto his lips. Aroused by her soft touch and her sentiments, his spirits soared.

Uncorking the bottle, he filled two goblets and passed one to her, steadily holding her gaze. Taking a mouthful, he untied his muslin cravat and unbuttoned his jerkin before leaning forward and brushing his lips against hers. With a sip of wine and a delicate kiss, she stepped back and gracefully disrobed.

By the glow of a solitary pillar candle, they slipped between the bedclothes to begin making good a long aching separation. And given the length of his absence, time slipped slowly by. Satiated, they fell back, talking in hushed tones into the early hours.

When a previously unarticulated subject was raised concerning the animus of some on the issue of black consorting with white, she was emphatic:

'Our liaison contravenes no laws.'

Slipping on a painted cotton banyan, he sat up against the headboard. Lying on her back in cream silk nightgown, she put her head in his lap.

'Can I raise a delicate matter, Jonas? I will understand if you wish not to speak of it.'

'Ask what you will, my dear.'

'The wound across your back?'

In the candlelight, she saw the flicker of anger in his eyes. Then, she felt him relax.

'I was born a slave and raised on Captain Somerset's plantation,' he said in a soft, firm voice. 'When I was about four, I started work in the gardens of the Great House. At about ten years of age I was transferred to the cane fields picking up the cane cuttings. I need not tell you of their violence. When I was about twelve, Somerset took me from the fields and made me his house slave valet. The beatings stopped. On the day I received this wound, Somerset was away in Jamestown. Conveniently, the head overseer declared that a floor I had scrubbed was not spotless. Stringing me to a frame for punishment, he gave me twenty-four lashes. Expertly, he laid virtually every stroke across the same site. The pain was such that I passed out and did not recover for three days. I bear an ever-present salutary reminder of the abuse of power. The sting and humiliation of that lash has not ever left me to this day.

'Somerset bequeathed me manumission, much to the head overseer's chagrin, and took me to England before he died that year at his sister's. As a free man in the days before I sailed for England, I would stroll cheekily past that overseer eating a mango, or slumped in a planter's chair with a mug of sarsaparilla. Believe me when I say

I have seen greed for power at work. I know what it means to be a slave.'

Baring his right shoulder to her, he said, 'In view of the promises we have made each other, I will hide not anything, not even my slave brand from you.'

Sitting up, she made out inch-sized letters *CS* burned into his shoulder. Tears welled into her eyes. Caressing his face, she lowered her voice. 'I promise thee that you will never know humiliation again. They will have to take me first. I will love thee and fight for thee, Jonas Guinea, 'til I can no longer draw breath.'

The ferocity in her eyes left him in no doubt of her troth.

Tenderly taking his hand, she said, 'Let me tell you about an intriguing exchange I had when last I visited Pilgrims...'

Noting a hesitation in her voice, he chuckled. 'Oh to have had an ear buried in the withdrawing room wall.'

'Without prompting from me,' she said, putting her fingers to his lips, 'Mistress Beecham and Reverend Whitehouse counselled me most precisely.'

'Counselled? About what or can you not say?'

'Given the hurry of your departure, you may not know that they both wholeheartedly support our union.'

'No doubt without reservation?'

'No reservations,' she reiterated. 'On the question of black with white, they believe there is no such thing as adulterated blood, only adulterated attitudes and adulterated hogwash.'

'I could not agree more,' he laughed.

Sitting up, she continued, 'And I quote — no matter what doubting mouths mutter, take from life what will make thee happy, or be crucified on the cross of time, regret and the mores of society. And by all means have children. Brown and bonny they will be as well. No matter what the hue, children don't need or want the earth — they just need love. Providentially, there is a sufficient kindness about our neighbourhood as well — unquote.'

'Tell me, Faith, what do you believe?'

'I believe that they who abhor our liaison cannot possibly fathom the feelings I have for you. A woman in love can bear many torments, in fact more than most men. Moreover, I believe that what a child needs most are loving parents, a loving home, good victuals, a rounded education and good family friends, which we can amply provide. Do you want children, Jonas?'

'I heed not what the doubters say,' he said, taking both her hands. 'When they condemn, they do so out of an ignorance with which they incite fears about contamination of English blood. I have as well heard a few blacks say consorting with white contaminates black blood. I believe both opinions are a recipe for intolerance. Given the influential sceptics about, we must trust one another unconditionally, so that our union prospers to write good memories. You are all I need. I know I can make you happy. Will you promenade with me down the aisle, Faith?'

'Marry a first-rate tropical spirit like you, Jonas? Aye! I will marry thee. I love thee so much I cannot bear even the notion of another separation.'

'God-willing we shall beget some naughty children,' he said, smiling.

'At least two,' she said.

'And since we are of like mind,' he said, 'separation enters not to my head either.'

Flinging her arms around him, she drew him close.

'Aye, Jonas Guinea, I will marry thee gladly. We shall make of our morrows what we will. And when I carry your seed in me, I shall do so with love and pride. Mistress Beecham confided she wants to see you wedded and believes you are ready for family life. Though I am Catholic, I am happy that Parson Merriweather and Reverend Whitehouse will jointly officiate in the Methodist church in Deptford.'

'I have always had the love of Mistress Beecham,' he said. 'I love her as my mother. She knows me very well. Both clergymen have my trust. They have proved good friends for many years. I am more than ready for wedlock and will put all my energies into making ours a happy union. Our offspring will see to that. With what I have saved for such an event, I can amply provide for us and our family.'

'Not forgetting I am as well financially independent, so I can and will contribute. Between us we make a good match and shall make a good marriage. And we shall continue furthering the abolitionist cause of the League.'

Taking her hand, he said, 'You have my word on it.'

The first rays of dawn peeked from the edges of the curtains.

Ake

Coast of Guinea
30 October 1761
10.00 hrs

The sun was climbing inexorably into a blue sky. At the forest edge, twittering groups of red-headed malimbe birds were foraging in the low trees. Earthy odours were yet rising in the sun. It promised to be a hot day.

Slumping down for a break on the leaf-laden river's edge, Tomba wiped his sweating face on his cotton *buba* and *sokoto* – shirt and trousers. Scanning the glade by the splayed foot of a towering *abura* tree, he was tired and feeling the heat. Alert to the prospect of being taken by slave traders on his expedition, Zachariah, Moses, Isaac and Abraham had thought it safer to travel with him. At first light they began by following the meandering course of the River Ogun from Abeokuta. Nearing midday, Tomba and his companions had reached the giant tree beside the track said to lead to the village of Ake. Heeding their groans, he was aware they were beginning to wilt.

Rising abruptly to his feet and ready to set off down the track, he tried to cajole them.

'Sit on your bottoms all day if you want,' he said brusquely. 'Yet you claim you came to honour a promise. You won't do that on your backsides. You forget you lose many years enslaved to white man. An' yet you say you honoured to make this big footslog to tell final words o' big story that begin many years ago. You come to shine light on Kayode's life in his village where he from. It be too late to go back now. It be painful tale we carry to his family. We owe 'em blood duty to put end to their long suffering.'

'Not easy to be messenger of heartbreak, Tomba,' said Zachariah, standing up.

'Worse to keep it in yer head,' Tomba growled.

'Kayode's people lucky,' said Moses reflectively. 'It be possible his be first family of we sold to find out.'

'In Ake we seek out the house of *Bale*,' said Isaac. 'We get his help to meet Kayode's family.'

'You quiet, Abraham,' said Tomba, turning around.

'I was thinking a man's belly tell 'im what 'is body needs,' said Abraham ruefully. 'We eat what we feel like 'cos we free to do so. This day in Pertigua, overseers will force slaves to eat shit an' cut cane an' then cut them with the lash. I will not ever forget I lost most me life in them cane fields.'

'Now you free to play big fool 'cos you free to do so,' said Tomba, laughing and slapping him on the back.

His companions guffawed.

Turning off the loamy red track snaking from the rainforest through an area of tufted *koriko* grasses, he arrived at a cleared area of forest inhabited by a collection of mud-brick huts and houses surrounding a large red-soiled rectangle.

'My gut say this be Ake,' he said.

A short distance to his right, a brawny bald-headed man shouldering a hefty bundle of wood strode out of the forest making for the village.

Drawing level with the carrier, he gave him a broad smile. 'My name is Tomba,' he said in broken Yoruba. 'Is this the village of Ake?'

'This be the village of Ake,' said Babarimisa proudly, puffing out his chest. 'You be looking at the village blacksmith.'

'We come from Badagri Town,' said Tomba. 'We seek Sodeke family to bring 'em big big *irohin* – news. You know 'em?'

'I know everyone,' said Babarimisa. 'Sodeke is like blood to me. From Badagri you say? You walk a long long way. I take you right away to meet Baba Sodeke.'

Beside the blacksmith, they stopped under a tall acacia tree. Across a wide pathway stood a dark-red mud-brick house with a low conical roof of plaited banana leaves. Yellow bush daisies lined the foot of the dwelling.

'That is the house of Sodeke,' said the blacksmith, pointing. 'Come meet the family.'

Turning to his companions, Tomba beckoned them.

Walking down the side of the house with the blacksmith, he came to a large mud-walled, well-groomed grassy compound. A group of people were sitting under a spreading mango tree.

An elderly woman was in a chair boasting carved arms, dressed in an indigo *buba* and *aso iro* — a cloth wrapped from the waist to the feet. Beside her sat an aged, white-haired man. They were in laughing banter with two younger men in cotton *buba* and *sokoto* perched on carved stools. At the sight of the visitors, the elderly man rose to his feet with difficulty.

'*E'karo* Baba and Iya,' said Babarimisa, prostrating. 'I bring strangers to see you. They have travelled all the way from Badagri Town.'

'*E'karo*, Baba and Iya Sodeke. My name is Tomba,' he said, and then introduced his companions. 'We have come to bring you big *irohin* about your son Kayode.'

At the mention of her missing offspring, the old woman leapt to her feet, clapped her hands and cried out, '*Olorun* has answered our prayers!'

'Bit late,' said the old man tersely. 'We been praying long enough.'

'*E'karo*, Tomba,' said the old man warmly. 'Ah Ah. Your coming was foretold. The *Oso* say we will hear about Kayode before six moons have come and gone. He was right. After such a long journey you and your friends must be hungry. Come, Tomba, eat and drink with us. Meet Taiwo his elder brother and our Igbo storyteller friend, Chidike.'

Embracing a tall thickset round-faced man in his forties, Tomba felt heartened. Recognising Kayode in his elder sibling, he grinned and nodded.

'Come sit, my brothers,' said Taiwo, pulling out stools for them all.

'Tell me, Tomba, where is my beloved son?' said the old woman, her voice breaking.

Heeding the pain in her eyes and the deep furrows of her brow, he sat down at once and quietly began his tale.

'From the shores of Badagri,' said Tomba, 'your son was chained with me an' Asabi on the deck of a slave ship called the *Pelican*. In the shit and sickness on that vessel, I get to know him well. He tell me 'bout Taiwo an' Asabi an' the expedition for the Sese beans. *Pelican* sails for over *eji osu* – two months. When she reach the island of Pertigua, we were whipped down to the plantations. In them wicked fields we cut cane day after day an' year after year. So much the whites love sweetness, they used our backs to get it. In just *eerinla osu* – fourteen months – Kayode break out o' plantation with Asabi. After he escape everything on island change.'

Chapter by chapter through the breathtaking afternoon, Tomba sketched the frightening saga of their stolen years. Throughout his account, the old man and his wife sat with tears in their eyes, hand-in-hand in silence.

Ending his wide-ranging account, Tomba said, 'When Kayode mek big uprising, he fill slaves wi' 'ope an' fight. We call 'im Captain Sodeke. 'E lead us in many fights 'gainst Redcoats an' we win. At end o' last big battle over many days, my heart break when me see 'im seize by Redcoats. I not see 'im again. Faster than lightning 'e were put on trial. In the blink of an' eye them find 'im guilty an' 'e were judge to burn alive. To not scream wi' agony burning to death in front o' slaves, 'e tek 'is own life in prison wi' poison. 'E cheat Redcoats—'

'How Kayode cheat Redcoat?' asked Taiwo indignantly. 'He dead.'

"Is body dead, Taiwo,' said Tomba triumphantly, 'but 'e not dead fer we. Your brother's courage lives in 'is friends an' many many slaves. 'Is kind now feared by whites in Pertigua. So let we give this to you,' he said, taking their wizened hands in his. 'Captain Sodeke gave we runaways big dream. An' 'e make 'is vision come true. We 'is friends mek this long walk to give thanks to you, his Baba and Iya, fer borning a mighty spirit. Like an *abura* tree, your son lived a giant life.'

Giving an anguished shriek, the old woman collapsed sobbing.

Assisted by the storyteller, Taiwo carried his mother gently into the house.

Wiping his eyes, Tomba felt the cavernous silence from his companions behind him.

Tears welled into the old man's eyes. Stock-still and upright, he sat gazing fiercely into the distance. At times, his hoary eyes seemed to well with pride, while at the same time telling the tale of one who had lost a treasured son in terrifying circumstances. Then, as if by some imperceptible command, drops toppled over the lower lids and rolled down his cheeks.

'At least we know,' he said softly. 'White men will not ever know 'bout pain an' suffering they give my people.'

Affected by the searing torment in the eyes of the wizened elder, Tomba crumpled.

'Now we know that freedom not ever free,' he sobbed. 'Freedom, my friend, ask a steep price.'

Heads bowed, his companions sat with watery eyes.

Turning to his son, the old man was composed.

'Take Chidike and help me send word to all the family, Taiwo. Tell them to come right away. Tell them we know what happened to Kayode and Asabi. The women can prepare food for Kayode's friends while we arrange a place for them to sleep. In a few *ose* — weeks — we will give you horses to ride back to Badagri, Tomba.'

Rising abruptly, Taiwo left the compound along the side of the house.

'Come, Tomba,' he said.

Sitting in front of the dwelling under the acacia tree with the storyteller and Tomba, a grieving Taiwo said, 'At last we know what happened to Kayode.'

A watery film slipped over his eyes. Dropping his face into his hands, he burst into gut-wrenching cries. Then, raising his head, he spoke to the storyteller.

'Our wait is over, Chidike. We will never forget Kayode or Asabi. *Olorun* have them safe in his keeping. When you go, Tomba, we will ride with you to the coast and then make journey to Connu's Castle.'

'Why you go to Connu's Castle?' asked Tomba, frowning.

'To learn how to use the *opas* we captured from the white slavers,' said Taiwo. 'Then if they ever come again we will give them a sea of red.'

'I go with you,' said Tomba, smiling. 'I know John Connu if he be still living.'

'With a common cause an' blood of the Yoruba, Tomba, we go as brothers,' laughed Taiwo. 'Let we go and tell the family, Chidike.'

A Winter Romance

Pilgrims
Christmas Day, 1761
18.00 hrs

Snow had been falling all day. Now and then, swirling flurries swallowed up the Highway. Helped by the winds, snowdrifts built up around the houses and along the thoroughfare. The branches of the plane trees sagged under the weight of snow and ice. Muffled up to the eyeballs, passers-by stepped like ghosts through the mists.

In a white muslin cravat and teal fitted coat with matching waistcoat and breeches, Jonas Guinea was primed for Pilgrims' Christmas dinner.

Lighting the Yule candle above the hearth, he picked up his goblet.

We shall not have the wit of dear old Parson Merriweather this yuletide, he thought. His letter to Faith said he was confined to his cot at Greensleeves. I do hope he makes a speedy recovery.

Punch in hand and cocooned in the warm wood-panelled dining room, he surveyed the frozen Highway.

Given the freezing conditions, braziers, market stalls and shelters had been erected between the drifts along the thoroughfare. As well, the Quaker's street kitchens were dispensing hot soup and warm gingerbread to queues of beggars and prostitutes. I hope the tradesmen's Christmas boxes bring some comfort. A cold hungry Christmas is certain for some.

Putting down his glass and biting his lip, he shook his head with chagrin. To counter his discomfort, he shifted his reflection to a more promising event.

We are to be wed, he thought. I cannot quit the chandlery. Neither can Faith sell Greensleeves. Dividing married life between Pilgrims and Greensleeves, we shall make a good living from both. If we are blessed with children to sweeten our years, we shall as well stay curious.

'Matches! Matches!' cried a street hawker. 'Wan' any matches?'

'Wood, two bundles a penny!'

A breakneck price rise for an icy season, he thought. It was three bundles a penny the day last past.

The bells of St George-in-the-East struck six. The door opened.

Flouncing into the dining room, Grace Puddlewick flourished a glowing smile to the assembled. Sporting a red beauty spot and true to her fashionable self, she was attired in an extravagant salmon silk gown. She was followed by her bullish, ship-owning husband, Jeremiah, wearing a powdered wig and a plum-coloured fitted knee-length coat. Togged in a crisp white cravat, clerical bands and fitted black frock coat, Reverend Whitehouse appeared the archetypal parish vicar. Gliding smoothly into the chamber came Faith Bradshaw, painted and primped in a lilac silk gown, with a tightly-fitted bodice showing her figure to perfection.

'A woman primed to bewitch,' Jonas said beneath his breath. He smiled warmly at her.

With her lips curling slowly into a smile, she felt euphoric.

I will have babies with this man, she thought. We will raise a fine family.

Sidling across to Jonas, she bent close to his ear. 'Somewhere out there is the son I had with Kayode, who was sold into slavery by my stepfather. I want us to have many children and see them grow into men and women. As God is my witness, Jonas, I will dispatch anyone who so much as looks at any child of ours in any way I don't like.'

Looking intently into her unwavering brown eyes, he squeezed her hand and smiled.

As the guests fanned out around the Chippendale table, he sat down beside an ebullient Mistress Beecham, who was perched like a *grande dame* in an indigo gown with full sleeves and skirts. Faith sat opposite. Inside the hearth of the white statuary and green *verde antico* marble fireplace, heat was radiating from the blazing Yule log.

The candlelit chamber was redolent with festive tidings and good cheer.

'Oh my, Mistress Beecham,' cried Grace Puddlewick, her eyes gliding over the silver-set mahogany table. 'Cook has quite surpassed herself. A finer Christmas dinner I have yet to see.'

Half the table groaned under silver platters of roasted cod and fried sole with oyster sauce, a sirloin of roasted beef and roast goose, a tureen of pea soup and an orange pudding. The other half of the table was filled by two brace of roasted wild duck, a fork of lamb, salad and mince pies filled with poultry, meat and dried fruits, with a fine plum pudding at the centre.

Wobbling like blancmange, the housekeeper, Tuppence Honeypenny, dispensed Château d'Angludet wine into sparkling colour-twist stem goblets. Clumsily, she dropped onto a chair by the fireplace.

Rolling his eyes jokingly at the housekeeper, Jonas gave her a warm smile.

Clasping his hands together in prayer, the clergyman turned to Faith Bradshaw.

'I trust my Catholic sister,' he said genially, 'will not mind my using a Methodist prayer for a Protestant celebration?'

''Tis still a prayer, Reverend Whitehouse,' she replied, dipping her head graciously.

'Methinks John Wesley's *Rule for Christian Living* is most pertinent before we commence this bounteous feast,' said the clergyman, licking his lips and bowing his head.

'Firstly let us offer a prayer for the wellbeing of our dear friend, Parson Merriweather,' he said. 'May he make a very speedy recovery.'

'Amen,' said the assembled.

'Let us pray,' said the clergyman.

'Do all the good you can,
By all the means you can,
In all the ways you can,
In all the places you can,
At all the times you can,

To all the people you can,
As long as ever you can.'

'Amen,' chorused the assembled.

'Most appropriate in the circumstances, Reverend Whitehouse,' said Faith, smiling broadly.

'As long as ever you can,' the sloshed housekeeper chortled. ''Tis a commonly sought ambition, Reverend.'

'Happy Christmas to you all,' said the clergyman, raising his goblet. 'And may I add my congratulations, Mistress Bradshaw, on your impending nuptials with Mister Guinea.'

Wobbling to her feet without warning and raising her goblet in her shaky hand, the housekeeper slurred, 'To Mishtress Bradshaw and Mishter Guinea.'

'Why thank you, Mistress Honeypenny,' said Jonas, smiling benignly at the housekeeper, who slumped back down onto her chair.

'All the world's a stage when all eyes are on you,' said Mistress Puddlewick, 'as they will surely be at your wedding ceremony. Bask in the honeyed warmth of your dear friends.'

Simultaneously raising their goblets, everyone cried:

'Faith and Jonas!'

'A bane on any who would oppose the union,' said Mistress Beecham.

'They stand about as much chance of hampering our match,' said Faith merrily, 'as they do preventing me from devouring this feast.'

Laughter enveloped the dining room.

Taking a sip and then exchanging goblets, Jonas and Faith toasted each other.

Without further ado, the guests began to load victuals onto blue and gold Derby porcelain dinner plates.

'This Château d'Angludet has an excellent bouquet, Mistress Beecham,' said Reverend Whitehouse, with the snooty airs of a sommelier.

'And a full body to match,' said Jeremiah Puddlewick, downing a mouthful.

'Dandy tipple I have to shay,' slurred the housekeeper, giggling.

'A toast to Parson Merriweather,' cried Mistress Beecham, raising her goblet, 'and to the *Redemption*. We thank you deeply for your vessel's significant participation, Mister Puddlewick. Were that not so, we might not be presently toasting the forthcoming nuptials.'

'Aye,' they all cried, raising their goblets. 'A toast to Faith and Jonas!'

In that instant the clatter of forks against plates resounded around the chamber. For a short time silence reigned as the first mouthfuls were consumed.

Beaming around the chamber, Jeremiah Puddlewick addressed Jonas:

''Twas not so long ago that we were bidding thee farewell, Mister Guinea. Heartfelt congratulations on your blooded escapade with the *Redemption*. Captain Battersby gave a first-rate account of your contribution and of your outward-bound sickness and seawater curative. I am told you even witnessed the *Invincible* in action? Must have got somewhat heated out there. Primarily, I yearn to hear of the tactics and subterfuge employed to ascertain the whereabouts of the runaways. We may need to employ them again.'

'After we are married, Mister Puddlewick,' said Jonas, forking a wedge of lamb and dried fruits. 'I will gladly furnish you all with a detailed account of my observations, suggestions and such at Greensleeves.'

'Aye,' said Faith graciously, dabbing fried sole into oyster sauce, 'we keenly anticipate you all visiting us at Greensleeves. No doubt by then, Parson Merriweather will have recovered and be keen to display his prodigious acquaintance with the ales of Kent.'

Grins, smiles, chuckles and camaraderie flowed around the table.

'Methinks matches like yours augur an agreeable and intriguing revolution in English society,' said Mistress Puddlewick thoughtfully, impaling a large piece of roast goose.

'Yet we must not ignore that there are those who denigrate the match of a white woman to a black man,' said the clergyman, picking up his goblet. 'Intermarriage remains a decidedly contentious issue for some. Mercifully, they most certainly do not count among our friends.'

Sipping wine and glancing at Faith, Jonas winked. Grinning, she raised her goblet to him.

'I have to say, Mistress Bradshaw,' said Jeremiah Puddlewick, 'that when we learned of your betrothal to Mister Guinea, we were delighted. Before another word could be uttered, Mistress Puddlewick set about arranging her wardrobe for the occasion. And I would have you know you can count on me and Mistress Puddlewick to be of sturdy support to your union.'

'We thank you, Mister Puddlewick, and you as well, Mistress Puddlewick,' said Jonas, raising his goblet.

'I could not agree more with Reverend Whitehouse,' said Faith, tapping her goblet against others. 'We thank you all heartily, dear friends, for your kind support and good wishes.'

'A Happy Christmas to you all,' said Mistress Beecham, hoisting her goblet in the air.

'And a Happy Christmas to you, Mistress Beecham,' everyone chorused.

'Antithetical to your prayer, Reverend Whitehouse,' said Mistress Beecham, tearing off a leg of wild duck with her fingers, 'is a preposterous article I have just read in the London Chronicle. It accuses black people of using mixed marriages as a means of, and I quote, washing the Blackamoor white, unquote.'

'That is a most uncouth judgment,' said Mistress Puddlewick disdainfully. 'Most people appear not to care about mixed or any other matches. Methinks 'tis only the intolerant and class discriminating, curiously many from good society, who frown upon any mixed match of colour or class. Regrettably, that minority have, as well, the means and access to publish their scare-mongering opinions.'

'May I remind you all that that good society is, as well, the very same society that proscribes women from conducting business,' said Mistress Beecham tartly, taking a sip of wine. 'There is much that is not fair. But I shall not dwell on them on this triumphant and festal season. Suffice it to say that unlike many newlyweds, Mistress Bradshaw and Mister Guinea have mercifully a chandlery and an estate to cushion them from the icy draughts of tribal politics.'

''Tis curious then,' said the clergyman, 'that it seems only them of good society who possess such duplicity and heartlessness as well possess the funds to own slaves.'

'They are as well the same ones,' said Jeremiah Puddlewick, sitting upright, 'who justify the existence of England's slave trade with all manner of claptrap. Let me summarise for you the arguments I have heard lately, promulgated by the pro-slavery advocates to win over popular support for the trade.'

'Oh do, Jeremiah,' said Mistress Puddlewick, clapping her hands approvingly.

Goblet in hand, the housekeeper suddenly lurched forwards garbling, 'What ish it they shay, Mishter Puddlewick?'

'They state,' said Jeremiah Puddlewick portentously, 'that the trade is essential to the accomplishment and prosperity of England. And that if we did not engage in the trade then others would. I find that a mightily fallacious argument.'

'As do I,' said the clergyman, taking a large piece of poultry-filled mince pie. 'Recently, I have listened to comparable drivel in a church hall. A Member of Parliament told his audience that Africans are already knee-deep in slavery, thus transporting them from their motherland provides them with better prospects. Most chillingly, he said that Africans are inferior and are unsuitable for any other work except slavery. Is that not bald-faced encouragement for all and sundry to sail down to the coast of Guinea to snatch any black person they meet?'

Spooning a portion of plum pudding, Jonas agreed.

''Tis indeed, Reverend Whitehouse,' he said. 'In addition to your contention and contrary to what we know, pro-slavery advocates sally forth with the falsehood that the environment on the slave-ships is first-rate and that slaves are not maltreated on the plantations unless they are disobedient. I myself know the terror and barbarous conditions slaves suffer. Were he present, Parson Merriweather would doubtless confirm such.'

'Moreover,' said Jeremiah Puddlewick indignantly, 'pro-slavery advocates argue that slavery is accepted in the Bible, with which they can bring the black peoples closer to God. It defies credibility that the misinterpreted Good Book lies at the heart of their expedient politics.'

'That England depends on slavery is in itself lamentable,' groaned Reverend Whitehouse, putting down his goblet to take pinches of snuff. Then, he proceeded to unfold a sheet of paper. 'Despite the League's meetings of protest and addressed gatherings, not anything has changed. Pray, let me quote from a pamphlet published by the pro-slavery lobby in London as far back as 1749:

> 'The most approved Judges of the Commercial Interests of these King-doms have been of the opinion that our West-Indian and African Trades are the most nationally beneficial of any we carry on... That Traffic alone affords our Planters a constant supply of Negro Servants for the Culture of their Lands in the produce of Sugars, Tobacco, Rice, Rum, Cotton, Fustick, Pimento and all our other Plantation Produce: so that the extensive Employment of our other Shipping in, to and from America, the great Brood of Seamen consequent there-upon, and the daily bread of the most considerable of our British Manufactures, are owing primarily to the Labour of Negroes.'

'I have not heard anything so preposterous for quite a while,' said Faith, irritably fanning her face. 'Can they not see that there are sub-stitutes for this ghastly trade? For instance, instead of slaves, why not trade Africa's spices and hardwoods, gold and ivory for English man-ufactured goods like cloth, rope, tools, ironware and liquor.'

'Surely,' said Mistress Beecham, filling drained goblets, 'if we deem slavery to be morally wrong, it is morally wrong whether oth-ers do it or not? 'Tis in no way an excuse, but I have lately heard that slavery among Africans is rather different from England's slave trade. And however misguided and 'tis as well not a justification, but are not their slaves mostly prisoners of war or sufferers of pun-ishment under their laws? And I'm told that those enslaved keep their names and identities. Furthermore, that enslavement does not extend to mire the next generation and the one after that.'

'Given ours and the League's long experience of gentlemen like Mister Guinea, Ignatius Sancho, Francis Barber and others,' said Mis-tress Puddlewick, 'all of whom are well educated, people of colour are patently not inferior and should be treated as equals.'

'As of this moment,' said Faith, taking a sip of wine and changing the subject, ''Tis reckoned that England's slave-owners number about six thousand families, companies and concerns. More or less, they own all of England's slaves.'

'But will the remainder of English men and women,' asked Mistress Beecham, 'share in the blame for a trade not of their making? We can agree that the trade is damaging to Africa and its inhabitants. By having their families continuously fragmented, do they not suffer all the more by as well being snatched from their homeland? Slavery is morally wrong. And an upright Christian nation like England should not be up to her neck in it.'

'What's more, from what passes before my eyes among the populace,' said the clergyman, unfolding a newssheet, 'the black and white poor are mostly friends, not rivals. That morsel of intelligence has at least not been lost on Sir John Fielding—'

Interjecting, Jeremiah Puddlewick asked, 'Is he not that blind magistrate?'

'Aye.'

'Who, I might add,' said Faith, 'is as well the younger brother of Henry Fielding, the author of *Tom Jones*.'

'Oh I say,' exclaimed Mistress Puddlewick.

'As Henry Fielding's assistant, he helped establish the Bow Street Runners,' said the clergyman. 'In an article in the newssheet I hold in my hand, John Fielding notes that pursuers of absconding black servants find:

'... the Mob on their side, it makes it not only difficult but dangerous to the Proprietor of these Slaves to recover the Possession of them, when once they are sported away.'

'In the meantime,' said Mistress Beecham dryly, 'the common people of England are kept ignorant of the goings-on inside the slave plantations.'

'Our petitions shall help to put that right,' said Faith.

'We shall need petitions,' said Mistress Beecham. 'I recall that some years ago, to counter the incited furore over the numbers of black people in the city, the Lord Mayor of London issued an edict debarring them from company apprenticeships. And it is only because of me that Mister Guinea can act as co-proprietor of an English company. That should not be so. The Lord Mayor's edict is palpable nonsense. We shall need to lobby against that as well.'

It was gone ten-thirty.

Glancing at the clock and covering his mouth, Jonas yawned. Lowering his hand, he smiled lovingly at his wife-to-be.

Rising and making for the door, Mistress Beecham beamed at her guests.

''Tis Christmas, my friends', she said. 'Let's not dwell on the activities of a heartless trade on such a joyous occasion. Come, my friends. We shall have port with our games in the withdrawing room.'

'Aye 'tis a time for merriment,' said Mistress Puddlewick, merrily flinging up her hands. 'Lest the men commandeer our festivities with politics, a goblet of port and brandy over the plum pudding should serve to remind us to rejoice.'

'Though I see not the festive relationship between plum pudding and the Nativity,' said Faith, 'I do see the connection between brandy and quadrille.'

Clapping her hands, Mistress Puddlewick shook with laughter.

'Indisputably, Mistress Bradshaw,' she said joyfully, 'I am delighted that you as well appreciate the liquid incentives of yuletide.'

'Ash do I,' the tipsy housekeeper gushed.

In the lively conviviality of the withdrawing room during the final game of quadrille, the discourse returned to the forthcoming nuptials.

'Nathan Greensleeves was a close friend of mine for many of his years,' reminisced Jeremiah Puddlewick. 'Though I'm a poor substitute for your dear father, Mistress Bradshaw, I would nonetheless deem it an honour to give you away.'

'I am enchanted by your kind offer, Mister Puddlewick,' said Faith enthusiastically, 'and most heartily I accept.'

'Francis Barber will be my best man,' said Jonas. 'Having had his release procured by Doctor Johnson from the decks of the HMS *Stag* in the North Sea, Francis has returned to Gough Square as his valet.'

'We had a year of miracles in '59, thanks to our victories in the Battle of Lagos and the Battle of Quiberon Bay,' intoned the clergyman, like a veteran army officer. 'We have been officially at war with France since '56. I pray for another miracle. God knows when this war will end. Barber is fortunate not to have seen much action at sea during his service.'

'He will be better remunerated as a butler than as naval fodder,' said Mistress Puddlewick caustically. 'And given his manicured self, Francis Barber will make an excellent best man.'

'Of course you will marry on a Wednesday in the Christ Church Mission at which I shall officiate,' said the clergyman, grinning matter-of-factly.

Turning to Faith, who nodded, Jonas smiled beatifically at Mistress Beecham and then at the clergyman.

''Tis settled then,' said Mistress Beecham, clasping her hands with delight. 'You plan a May wedding. If that day be a sunny Wednesday, 'twould be most enchanting for the guests to stroll or carriage the half mile from the church along the Highway to a reception at Pilgrims.'

Glancing at Faith, Jonas smiled. Her eyes brimmed with affection.

'We thank you, Mistress Beecham,' they said in unison.

A little past one in the morning, all retired to their allotted bed-chambers.

At the window of his bedchamber in his nightgown, Jonas watched the occasional carriage trundle by along the Highway.

Soon, Pilgrims grew still and silent.

Slipping out of his door and along to her bedchamber, he closed the door softly behind him.

Wedlock

Wednesday
6 May 1762
10.00 hrs

Morning was cloudless, warm and summery. In the crowded Methodist Christ Church Mission on the Highway, an unusual wedding ceremony was being conducted by Reverend Whitehouse assisted by a clear-headed Parson Merriweather.

Looking radiant in a floral-patterned *robe a l'anglaise*, Faith smiled at her groom. Complementing his bride in an embroidered silk frock coat and matching breeches, Jonas took her hands.

Simultaneously turning to face the Reverend, they warmed to his words and promised, 'I do.'

Slipping the gold band onto her finger, they kissed.

Intoned by the Catholic Parson Merriweather, a heartfelt Nuptial Blessing concluded the simple ceremony. Afterwards, forty-two smartly-dressed guests filed out of the church behind the newlyweds.

Settling into a black and yellow lacquered landaulet, Mister and Mistress Guinea led a convoy of chaises down the Highway to the reception in Pilgrims.

Looking appreciatively over the served wedding fare, Faith sighed.

'Mistress Beecham honours us with this huge feast, Jonas,' she said. 'And I must say, 'tis fortunate Parson Merriweather made timely improvement to officiate this day.'

'Flabbergasted I am by this table,' he said, shaking his head in wonder. 'Like as Mistress Beecham has done throughout my years with her. Knowing there would be so many bottles attending the reception, the Parson could be nowhere else.'

'A certified certainty, Jonas,' she laughed. 'But I have to say 'tis a delight to behold the affection in which Mistress Beecham holds you. I hope you are as happy with my companionship as you have been with hers.'

'What you and I have is without rival,' he replied, smiling affectionately.

Hand-in-hand, they surveyed the fare laid out on long, silver-laid refectory tables spanning the dining and withdrawing rooms. Two Chinese blue and white platters held large turduckens – a boned turkey stuffed with a boned duck, which in turn was stuffed with a boned chicken. Tureens of mock turtle soup and roast legs of beef jostled with legs of pork, lamb and an assortment of roast vegetables and a host of sweetmeats.

Master of ceremonies and mother of the groom, Mistress Beecham was everywhere, directing servants and marshalling guests to their seats. Following flowery speeches in the garlanded withdrawing room, she soon had friends and members of the League, bewigged merchants, Captain Battersby and other shipmasters, insurers and smiling domestics eating and drinking and falling into rowdy banter. Sparkling with good cheer through the afternoon, they amused themselves with card and board games.

Squeezing his wife's hand and laughing, Jonas pointed out a familiar figure.

Wine bottle beside him and goblet in hand, a fuddled Parson Merriweather was sprawled on a long chair holding forth with a sea captain.

Shaking her head, Faith smiled.

Glancing across the chamber, he saw Francis Barber beckoning him from the windows. At twenty-six years of age, Doctor Johnson's valet looked a fine-boned fashion plate in a black silk frock coat. Refilling his goblet and informing his new wife, he threaded his way through the knots of effervescing wedding guests.

'You were a princely attendant this day, Francis,' he said, clinking goblets. 'I cannot thank you enough, my friend.'

'You have married well, Jonas,' he said, patting him affectionately on the back. 'Faith has had a marked effect on you.'

'How so?'

'Has she not improved your humour and tempered your manner?' asked Barber, chuckling softly.

'That she has,' he replied bashfully.

'You can both be sure of my best endeavours if you are ever in need, Jonas,' said Barber sincerely. 'Methinks we are all in the thrall of your Mistress Faith. Her appeal is compelling. Given the hostilities she witnessed in Pertigua's uprising, she is one of a kind. Having the stuff to survive a revolution, she most certainly has the mettle to silence any sharp tongues hereabouts. Thank God you both do. 'Tis most fortunate you have the resources to care for your well-heeled wife and to ward off cold winds.'

'In general, Francis,' said Jonas dispassionately, 'the prime function of the black in the employ of the rich is to be a turbaned decoration. Marriage to a white woman is bound to raise eyebrows in some quarters. Thus, if I wedded a white woman, I needed to wed one of conviction — one made of stern stuff, who would brook no criticism of our union. And as you so observed, Francis, I am fortunate to have the funds as well as friendships like yours to fall back upon. That reassures me greatly.'

'Despite some disapproving looks that will be cast at your match,' said Barber confidently, 'I am certain Faith is equally capable of standing her ground and withering their looks with expressions of her own.'

'Faith is of great comfort to me,' said Jonas reflectively. 'In all my thirty-four years, Francis, I have not ever been the recipient of such passion. And given the fervour of her affections and of her proven capabilities, I love and trust her entirely.'

'I trust I will be as lucky as you, Jonas,' said Barber quietly. 'To make some sense of the wasted life I have led, I need to establish myself. To realise my resolution, I have let go the hate I stockpiled cutting cane as a slave in Jamaica. Hatred had kept me alive in those sugared fields. Hate had steered every step I took. It grew heavier with the years and it hampered me. But now I have let hate go so I can travel light in this life. Following my service under the Navy's despotic officers, I resolved to transcend this life of servitude. Thus I intend to acquire letters that will better my prospects and my standing.'

'You have a plan, Francis?'

'Indeed,' said Barber confidently. 'I propose to firstly further my education with the help of the good Doctor. Given my position in Gough Square, I can save enough for a cottage. Then, I as well will look for a hand in marriage. Given the scarcity of women of our kind in the metropolis, I know the odds against meeting one are not good. Nevertheless, I hope to make a good match regardless of her skin.'

Arm-in-arm with Mistress Beecham, Faith suddenly appeared beside them.

'A good match did I hear someone say, Jonas?' she asked playfully. 'You tire of me already my love?'

'Not anything could weary me of you, dearest Faith,' he said, kissing her cheeks affectionately. 'We were musing on the colour of a match for Francis. He was of the view that it depended on who he was more likely to meet.'

'I did hear that of the black populace in London, Francis,' said Mistress Beecham warmly, 'there are said to be about thirty or forty like you and Jonas who are not slaves or in domestic service. I know not if any of the few are women.'

'Correct me if I am wrong, Francis,' said Faith light-heartedly, 'but I do seem to recall seeing significantly more white women than black women in London Town. Methinks such manifest evidence suggests the more likely outcome. After all, 'twould be a tad difficult to fetch a woman from the coast of Guinea for the purposes of wedlock.'

'If I might say, Francis,' said Mistress Beecham, laughing, 'a fine-looking catch awaits your match whatever her hue.'

'You are too kind, Mistress Beecham,' said Barber. 'I was wondering if this would be an inappropriate moment to ask if I could help compose and distribute your petitions? And following Jonas's extraordinary account of the *Redemption*'s exploits with the runaways, I am keen to become a member of your League. As you know, even before your visit to Gough Square Doctor Johnson was supportive of your League's activities and, as well, continues to speak strongly against the trade. Such is his detestation of the slave trade, the good Doctor will not so much as even let me buy food for his cat.'

'Why ever not?' asked Faith quizzically.

'Doctor Johnson is unyielding on this point,' replied Barber. 'He believes and I quote, 'tis not good to employ human beings in the service of animals, unquote. Suffice to say he procures all food for his cat himself.'

'Given the attitudes of present company, Francis, your request to join the League is agreeably accepted,' said Mistress Beecham. ''Tis said that even King George is against the abolition of the slave trade. So you see we can well do with an extra pair of hands. Mayhaps you can keep the good Doctor acquainted with our petitions, our meetings and our activities.'

'Most certainly, ma'am,' said Barber, giving a slight bow.

'Tis good my wife is fond of Francis, thought Jonas.

'When shall we have the pleasure of your company at Greensleeves, Francis?' asked Faith. 'We shall be leaving for our honeymoon on the south coast in the morning. We shall spend a week at the Old Ship Inn in Brighton. Then, we journey on to Greensleeves and shall return to Pilgrims in a fortnight. Mayhaps by then you can furnish us with a date for your visit?'

'You have chosen the most auspicious season of the year for your marriage,' said Mistress Beecham. 'May is the emerald month for a honeymoon. Everything is in blossom. And after the noxious environment of His Majesty's Navy, Francis, I guarantee the salubrious airs of Kent will be more to your liking.'

'Before summer begets long shadows, Faith,' said Barber, smiling broadly, 'you will find me at the gates of Greensleeves.'

'Methinks we ought to rejoin our guests,' said Mistress Beecham, extending her goblet for a top-up of Madeira. 'We have a long night ahead and I have so much to celebrate.'

Arm-in-arm with Mistress Beecham, Francis Barber strolled back to the festivities.

Parson Merriweather was still ensconced in the long chair in a corner of the withdrawing room. Utterly still, the rebel cleric had his eyes open in a seemingly lifeless stupor.

Beckoned by the shipowner and Captain Battersby to the opposite corner, Jonas settled down on the Chippendale sofa beside his wife.

'I thought you should know, Jonas,' said Jeremiah Puddlewick quietly. 'The day last past, Captain Battersby and I ran into Matthew Fleming in Bootle's Gentleman's Club. He was intoxicated of course.'

'At last the Prince of Darkness himself ventures out into the open,' said Jonas. 'Does he plan anything against the League? Mischief can be his only reason for vacating the misappropriated amenities on his island paradise.'

'Fleming questioned us most closely on the *Redemption*'s whereabouts after clearing Jamestown,' said Captain Battersby. 'I might add his suspicions were barely concealed.'

'Fleming was eager to know why you were aboard the *Redemption*,' said Jeremiah Puddlewick. 'I told him you were born on the island and possessed connections useful to my business in Jamestown. By the look in his eye, I'd say he did not believe us. The man's a poltroon. He knows that without proof he cannot accuse white men who he suspects liberated his slaves. So he has turned his wrath against the only one he could, you. Fleming has you in his sights, Jonas. Primarily, the man's a slave-trader. Given his malice against black people and despite the fact that you are properly a free man, he will have you abducted if chance allows. And he would most likely arrange that chance. Henceforth Jonas, be vigilant on the streets and alleyways, particularly in shadowy locations. Go not anywhere on the streets or near the dockyards alone.'

Throwing a discreet glance at his wife, he saw that her eyes held unease. He was perturbed. Grasping her trembling hands, he sought to hearten her.

''Twill not be possible to get near me,' he said, endeavouring to relieve her anxiety. 'Fleming's thugs will have to first get past the men of the chandlery. And I have known them for the best part of my life.'

'That is all very well while you remain inside the premises of the chandlery, Jonas,' she said. 'And when you venture out?'

'Moreover the close proximity of slave-owners like Fleming should help disturb the sentimental among London's anti-slavery lobby,' said Jonas, changing the subject. 'I trust it will rid them of the prevailing inclination to romanticise the plight of enslaved Africans. With respect to present company, methinks the League's forthcoming leaflets for London's citizens should describe the inhumanity of plantation slavery to those who can read with words and those who cannot with pictures.'

'My sentiments precisely, Mister Guinea,' said Captain Battersby. 'But I do agree with your wife, we will need to keep an eye on you.'

'You must take your turn, Captain Battersby,' said Faith hotly. 'Matthew Fleming will have to first get past me. I have known the man from childhood. If he as much as bats an eyelid at my husband, I shall make him rue the day he ever again laid eyes on these shores. Now,' she said, heaving a long sigh, 'that is the only threat I have uttered in a long, long while.'

I have wed a fellow traveller, he thought, beaming at his wife.

Laughter resounded through the chamber. The Chippendale grandfather clock struck the half-hour. It was three-thirty in the morning.

Rising wearily to her feet and yawning, Mistress Beecham opened her ivory fan. Fanning her face and revealing the inscription *How to Play Whist and not lose your Temper*, she said, 'I have been captivated and wonderfully fatigued by your nuptials. My dear departed Thomas would have been overjoyed to witness this day. Now I must haul these old bones to my cot. I bid thee newlyweds and merry friends a splendid good morning.'

Guffawing followed her departure.

Rising to his feet, Jonas faced his wife.

'Wish our guests as you hold my hand tight,' he said aloud to her.

Joining hands and facing the guests, they spoke in unison:

'Good night all, to all a good night.'

A roar of laughter and applause rang in their ears. They walked quickly up the stairs to embark on their first night of marriage, leaving Parson Merriweather dead to the world on the long chair.

Laying her head on his chest beneath the covers, she caressed his neck.

''Tis challenging for black citizens on the streets during the day,' she whispered lovingly, 'but 'tis mightily hazardous at night. The threat posed by Fleming's thugs is not an issue we can take lightly, Jonas.

Our dreams would come to nought should anything awry happen to thee. For my sake, when venturing outside Pilgrims or the chandlery, I want your promise you will take a man with you wherever you go.'

Noting the anxious timbre in her voice, he drew her closer.

'I give you my word, my love,' he whispered, stroking her brow. 'Hereafter I shall be exceptionally watchful on the streets. And I shall at all times carry a sword cane. I shall as well conceal one of Mistress Beecham's flintlock pistols on my person. That should help discourage their zest.'

'And don't you go getting yourself injured, my love,' she whispered, yawning.

'I shan't,' he said, closing his eyes.

Dark Mind Within Me

Rain was falling heavily. The salubrious environs of Piccadilly were cold, wet and blustery. Rainwater swamped the gutters and spilled across the cobbled road. Running through the surface water, the clatter of carriage wheels turned into a splashing rumble. On both sides of the street, penniless pedestrians scampered for shelter in the doorways, while the well-heeled huddled beneath oiled umbrellas.

Pulling his cloak snugly around him in his draughty carriage, Matthew Fleming muttered to himself. 'Samuel said London is where we meet the others. His letter said that the abolitionists are stirring. And that an influential coalition is required to spearhead the fight to preserve plantation slavery. 'Tis intriguing to ponder who might be among the little cabal he has pulled together.'

Raindrops petered out. His jolting carriage stopped beside an elegant white and honey-coloured townhouse on Piccadilly.

Stepping onto the wet cobbles and eyeing the building, he grinned. A gathering of slave-owners arranged by a Member of Parliament bodes well, he thought.

Behind a black balustrade stood a four-storey Palladian building with French adornments and two gate-perched lamp standards. Waiting at the top of half a dozen steps was Samuel Davenport. Dressed in an embroidered frock coat, the gnarled-looking thirty-eight-year-old remained the Member of Parliament for Aylesburn. Branded by his broad smile and unsightly squint, the politician appeared relieved to see him.

'Why Matthew,' he chortled, giving an affectionate backslap, 'yet another expedition to the Old Country inside a year. Can ye not keep away then? Come in, dear boy, come in. While you down the excellent Madeira I procured for your visit, I shall apprise you of the current conditions.'

Following his host to the first floor, he entered the high-ceilinged, lime-green and gold withdrawing room. Gladly flopping into a George II wing armchair, he sighed.

''Tis good to be in this bodacious chamber again, Samuel,' he said, laughing. 'O the hell-raising nights these walls have witnessed. Acknowledging the grim forecast detailed in your letter, I sailed at once on the *Swift* from Pertigua. She's a flyer and made the passage to England in eight weeks. I daresay you have arranged a suitable meeting place?'

'Many thanks for your speedy response, Matthew,' said Davenport. 'Steadfast, my butler, will fetch refreshments. Then we leave by landau for the Blackheath Golf Club. You might not know that, in addition to the Royal Exchange, the magnificent greens of this Masonic little golf club serve as the principal location for slave trading agreements and coalitions. Our luncheon appointment is with William Beckford, the Lord Mayor of London. You and he have much in common. With three thousand slaves working his twenty-two thousand acres of cane in Jamaica, he has much to lose if abolition came about. Thus he is keen to help establish a fund for subverting the anti-slavery irritants. I said you would be interested in such a scheme. We shall tarry this night with my friend in Greenwich. You should as well know he has invited some spicy fillies.'

Rubbing his hands excitedly, Matthew grinned.

A little after one o'clock, they arrived outside the village of Blackheath. Beneath an overcast sky, Davenport's black and yellow landau trotted onto the wide carriage drive of Greenwich Lodge, the grand Restoration clubhouse of the Blackheath Golf Club.

Charmed by the manicured courtyard and surrounding greens, Matthew walked eagerly to the entrance hall.

Traces of opium, tobacco and the piercing whiff of coffee were evident inside the mahogany-panelled antechamber. His eyes smarted and his nostrils twitched.

Depositing his cloak with a liveried attendant, Matthew looked around.

'A first-rate setting for such an assignation, Samuel,' he said.

Servers were bearing trays in and out of the smoky dining room. Stepping into the large lively dining room, Davenport led them to a corner by the windows overlooking the greens. Two frock-coated gentlemen rose to their feet beside a silver-laid round mahogany table.

Sniffing with high regard, Matthew was heartened to be among his kind.

'May I present Matthew Fleming of the West Indies Sugar Cartel,' Davenport announced. 'And may I present the Honourable William Beckford, Lord Mayor of London.'

In his fifties, tall, bewigged, long-faced and sporting a fleshy nose, Beckford smiled broadly and shook his hand.

'It grieves me to hear that my dear friend, your father, has taken to his sickbed, Mister Fleming,' he said cordially. 'I trust the warm airs of Pertigua will speed his recovery. Pray remember me to him on your return. I have sorely missed his company, as well as his good counsel. Permit me to introduce my good friend, John Julius Angerstein. Dabbles in insurance and suchlike, and as well owns sugar estates on the island of Grenada.'

Matthew eyed Angerstein with interest.

Reputed to know all who mattered among the great and the good, he looked about thirty, of German extraction, slightly built with sharp eyes and a ruddy-cheeked, sickly demeanour.

'Aye, Mister Fleming,' said Angerstein, chuckling. 'Your father's absence has left a hole in our golfing circle and our card set at Bootle's. Pray give him my compliments. And pray tell him that on my passage to Jamaica in August, I shall pay him a visit.'

'Father will be delighted to hear of your warm wishes, sirs,' said Matthew, courteously bowing. 'And your visit would most likely raise his spirits, Mister Angerstein.'

Atingle with the affection for his father and basking in reflected credit, he sank into his chair at the table.

Forthwith, the establishment's liveried servers dispensed the victuals with a showy flourish. Claypot grouse and roast vegetables was

followed by a trifle pudding, downed with bottles of Rouge du Chateau Margaux.

Being the representative of the West Indies Sugar Cartel, Matthew
was buoyed by the talk about the fight against abolition.

'As I see it,' said Angerstein, sipping wine and looking intently at
each man in turn, 'we must use handouts and newssheets to publicise the gospel of the light work, lodgings, spiritual guidance and
good conditions we provide for our slaves. At stake is our slave traffic,
which is the bedrock of England's trade in rum, sugar, cotton, tobacco and coffee — which I believe, gentlemen, is the heart of England's
commerce.'

'I have a darker mind within me,' said Beckford emphatically. 'We
shall not abide even the thought of an interruption to our trade. Put
some stick about for a curative before this yet budding threat gathers
momentum. Gentlemen, we cannot let them disrupt our way of life.
Enough is enough. I suggest we set up a fund to sponsor agents to
hinder the stirring anti-slavery resistance. At present they have no
great figure to draw public attention to their cause, but a few are
rearing their heads. Some fifty Members of the Commons own slaves
or have a monetary interest in a plantation. Between the politicians
and ourselves we will invite others to contribute to the fund. Who
says Aye?'

'Aye,' they said in unison, clinking glasses.

'What else should we do and who do we inveigle?' asked Davenport, munching a forkful of grouse. 'For we cannot ourselves be seen
doing anything improper.'

'Nay, Samuel, neither needs we,' said Matthew matter-of-factly,
taking a sip of wine. 'By employing *agent provocateurs*, we can plead
plausible deniability, for we will not be anywhere in the vicinity. From
arm's length, we shall disrupt and sabotage the activities of anti-slavery
assemblies. Furthermore, we shall employ the said *agent provocateurs*
through a third party. I know a man who has just the man.'

'I like your philosophy, Mister Fleming,' said Angerstein. 'Through
handouts and newssheets, we can enlighten the populace with the
report that anti-slavery activists are bent on sabotaging England's
commerce. That should give them something to suck on, especially

since if abolition becomes an Act, they will get laid off. And while we're about it, we should tell the priests to ask their gluttonous flocks if sugar in their tea, cakes and puddings jogs their memories.'

Begirded by much camaraderie, luncheon ended with a hearty toast with port. So much so, Beckford invited Matthew to join them for dinner at Bootle's on Friday the twelfth — two nights hence.

'We can conclude the specifics of our fund, Mister Fleming,' said Beckford with a knowing smile, 'in the cosseted comfort of Bootle's.'

Throwing his cloak around his shoulders in the antechamber, Matthew beamed at his friend.

'My heartfelt thanks for such excellent connections, Samuel,' he said heartily.

'After such a first-rate collaboration, Matthew,' said Davenport, 'we could well do with a night of scandal and debauchery by Greenwich Park.'

It was freezing in the courtyard. The light was fast fading and stars began peppering the darkening cloudless sky.

Satisfied with the day's events, Matthew climbed into Davenport's landau. They were expected for supper at a house on Crooms Hill near Greenwich Park, owned by the rich slave-owner, Duncan Campbell, with whom they would also be lodging the night.

With the horse-driven vehicle rolling away from the Blackheath Golf Club, he stared out of the window and pictured Harriet, his wife of six months. Her full-bosomed image loomed large. He smiled to himself. With child three months before he sailed for England, she was due to give birth after he returned home. Thousands of miles from Turtle Island, he was free to cavort with wine, frilly women and opium, his favoured medication. Slowing momentarily, the driver flicked the reins and cracked on.

'We have one irksome faction of concern, Samuel,' he said quietly, 'and one man specifically.'

'Who are they and who is he?' asked Davenport.

'The faction is the League against the Importation of Negroes from the Coast of Guinea,' he said. 'And the man is one Jonas Guinea.'

'When last I visited you on Turtle Island, you were apoplectic about this Jonas Guinea. You could not lay hands on him or the *Redemption* then. On my return to England, I made discreet inquiries. Let him be, Matthew. Guinea is no fool. He did not arrive in England on the day last past. Trading as he does in ship's chandlery, this nigger is a free man on English soil, co-proprietor of an English company and has connections to a number of influential friends. Were something to happen to him, awkward questions would be asked in the wrong quarters akin to disturbing a hornet's nest. As well, I know that that little League associates with the likes of some outrageous free-thinkers. The Oxford Methodists would raise hue and cry. Nay man. But you must have every vessel leaving your island scrupulously searched for any do-gooders trying to copy the *Redemption* in springing slaves.'

'I shall do as you say, but I still mean to take Guinea,' he said doggedly. 'To witness that nigger cutting cane would raise the spirits of my sick father.'

'Thomas Beecham, Chandlers, boasts a rope loft and is renowned for its hemp rope,' said Davenport, with a wayward glint in his eye. 'You could call in on Pilgrims on the pretext of placing an order for hanks of rope. Once inside, you can then assess the scoundrel and his concerns from close quarters.'

'Buy rope and then what?' he snapped.

'Surveillance, dear boy, surveillance,' said Davenport, tapping his nose with a podgy finger. 'If one plans to conquer a citadel, one does so by scrutinising its fortifications from within. From what you ascertain on your visit to Pilgrims, you will then be far better placed to foment a strategy for Guinea's capture. It won't do to have a nigger strutting about acting like a white man. It sets a somewhat bad example to the others.'

'Care to join me on a visit to Pilgrims before I return to Pertigua?'

'Indubitably, Matthew, I shall be delighted to accompany you. Two pair of eyes so to speak. We can decide what we do about Guinea afterwards. Now, tell me of your delectable sister, Mary.'

'You are incorrigible, sir,' said Matthew, laughing loudly and shaking his head. 'You well know that in matters of the heart, unlike her female contemporaries, Mary is an enlightened spirit and holds her own counsel.'

'Such a pity,' said Davenport longingly.

Halfway up Crooms Hill the carriage halted outside the residence of Duncan Campbell.

Angry Airs

Wednesday
24 November 1762
Noon

It was freezing, damp and overcast. Sulphurous smog and wood smoke drifted over the industrious parish of Deptford. Nifty with the reins of Samuel Davenport's covered landau, the cracker driver threaded a route between the carriages along the Highway.

'The conditions make for a cold encounter,' groaned Samuel Davenport.

'The conditions prove not anything,' replied Matthew Fleming. 'Taking Guinea by surprise gives me cause enough for good cheer.'

Clenching his jaw, Matthew scrutinised the bustling, overcast thoroughfare.

Suddenly slowing, the landau juddered to a halt near a hanging copperplate sign: Thomas Beecham, Chandlers. The establishment was a long two-storey brick-built factory possessing a highly regarded rope and sail loft behind a facade of six large Georgian windows.

Surprised by the size of the chandlery, Matthew pushed open the carriage door.

'A gilt-edged nigger,' he snarled, raising his eyebrows.

'A nigger with capital is decidedly unsettling,' said Davenport.

Stepping onto the cobbles with the politician, Matthew paused. Nodding his head at the adjacent double-fronted detached Georgian house, he asked, 'Pilgrims?'

'Aye, Matthew, 'tis the abode of the devil himself.'

'And as well, I believe, the residence of Mistress Alice Beecham,' added Matthew. 'I am reliably informed that like her late husband, the woman is sharp-tongued and not one to be trifled with.'

Passing by a myriad of blocks and tackle of varying sizes inside the entrance, the walls and ceiling of the substantial shipshape chandlery were populated with knives, cleats, marlinespikes, anchors, belaying pins, holystones and all manner of things nautical. Hanks of hempen rope and rope yarn stood in seamanly piles on the floor. Brass binnacles with compasses lined the back wall.

'Good afternoon, gentlemen,' said a podgy waist-coated clerk respectfully. 'May I help ye, good sirs?'

'Matthew Fleming and Samuel Davenport, Member of Parliament,' said Matthew, sniffing superciliously, while fastidiously brushing invisible specks off his frock coat. 'My good man, be so good as to inform Mister Jonas Guinea that we wish to make a purchase. Namely untreated natural hemp rope, ten of two hundred foot coils of four-strand twisted.'

'Right away, sir,' said the Clerk of Chandlery, walking briskly away.

Moments later, hearing crisp footsteps from another door, Matthew turned to see a tall, slim and striking black man in a black frock coat.

'Guinea,' whispered Davenport.

Shaking hands with his enemy, Matthew stepped back to take stock, as did Jonas.

This frock-coated nigger exudes self-assurance and arrogance, he thought disdainfully. Methinks a thoroughly unwholesome combination for a black. He needs bringing down a peg. By the looks of him, he's nobody's fool.

Eyeing Matthew's oleaginous features, Jonas observed an average-looking, brown-eyed white man with a round head and manicured sideburns.

Besides hanging and flogging slaves, he thought, what can a feckless dilettante like you want with rope? I like not what I see in your pompous manner. And I like even less your fat ugly friend.

'As I said to your clerk, Mister Guinea,' said Matthew condescendingly, 'I wish to procure untreated natural hemp rope, ten of two hundred foot hanks of four-strand twisted.'

'Most certainly, Mister Fleming,' said Jonas courteously. 'And while you wait for your order to be amassed, gentlemen, pray join me next door in Pilgrims for a goblet or two. Our clerks will administer and make up your order.'

'Why thank you, Mister Guinea,' said Davenport with a strained smile. 'You are too kind.'

Stepping into the hallway of Pilgrims, Jonas effected introductions:

'May I present my wife, Mistress Guinea. My mother, Mistress Beecham. And I believe you are acquainted with our house guest, Mistress Greenwood.'

Bowing graciously, Davenport discharged a perfunctory smile.

Setting eyes on Rose Greenwood, who had cruelly spurned his premarital advances, Matthew's heart sank. A fresh, radiant virago of ill-substance if ever there was one, he thought. Furthermore, irked by the notion of black hands on white skin, he had nonetheless shaken Jonas's hands with a gracious smile.

Entering the withdrawing room, he savoured the heat radiating from the hearth.

'White wine, gentlemen?' asked Mistress Beecham.

He took a seat with his glass on the Chippendale sofa beside the politician. 'The quality and variety of goods in your chandlery from one of your hue is impressive, Mister Guinea. I do indeed appreciate the foundation of your reputation.'

'Thank you, Mister Fleming,' said Jonas, smiling at the backhanded compliment. 'Your praise should properly be directed at Mistress Beecham and her late husband.'

'Who as well, I might add,' said Faith distractedly, 'founded the League Against the Importation of Negroes from the Coast of Guinea.'

'In other words, Matthew,' said Rose acerbically, 'a staunch opponent of your Cartel.'

Turning purple, Davenport exploded into a coughing fit.

Patently waiting on the politician to recover his equilibrium, Jonas bowed.

'All of which was certainly known to your father, Mister Fleming,' he said, 'whom I had the pleasure to converse with during a compelling evening in this very chamber.'

Tutoring has tainted this black with presumptuous and impertinent airs, thought Matthew. Confidence suits not his kind. And what turned the Greenwood vixen into an abolitionist?

'I believe you were observed on the *Redemption* in Jamestown in the past year, Mister Guinea?' asked Matthew, almost as an aside.

'Aye, I was in Jamestown, Mister Fleming. Was that against England's or the island's laws?'

'Nay, Mister Guinea,' said Matthew with a strained laugh. 'Four months on the *Redemption* to spend just a few weeks in Pertigua? Did you not find your voyaging somewhat out of the way and a little fatiguing for such a short respite?'

This pasty fox hides angry airs and his cold eyes attest to it, thought Jonas, cracking a taut smile at his tormentor.

'My connections in Jamestown were judged essential by Captain Battersby,' he said impassively. 'I agreed to act as his liaison on that one voyage for which I was handsomely recompensed. Why do you ask?'

A rehearsed answer if ever I heard one, thought Matthew, narrowing his eyes.

'When the *Redemption* cleared Jamestown, Mister Guinea,' he asked, as if addressing a Board of Inquiry, 'in which direction did she sail? For after the harbour mouth, the said vessel appears to have vanished. 'Twas suspected that she was in fact making for the coast of Guinea.'

'The coast of Guinea?' asked Jonas, frowning deeply.

'The ocean is a somewhat big environment to find one lone vessel, Mister Fleming,' said Mistress Beecham dismissively. ''Twould be akin to seeking a needle in a haystack.'

'Mayhaps your men were distracted by mermaids,' said Rose frivolously.

Glancing in her direction, Matthew mustered a thin smile.

'I cannot understand why you did not sight her,' said Jonas, frowning and scratching his head. 'To answer your question, Mister Fleming, the *Redemption* was going about her lawful business on a course bound for Gravesend. Or have you evidence to the contrary?'

'There can be no evidence to the contrary,' said Faith, smiling and shaking her head. 'My husband could not have journeyed to the coast of Guinea, Mister Fleming. He arrived from Pertigua when we expected. Is that not so, Mistress Beecham?'

'Aye, that is so, Mister Fleming,' said Mistress Beecham. 'And delighted we were to have him back safely with us.'

'I was myself on the *Invincible*, Mister Guinea,' said Matthew suspiciously. 'During the *Invincible*'s patrol along the north coast that morning we sighted not a speck of the *Redemption*.'

'I know not why, Mister Fleming,' replied Jonas. 'We were sailing the same waters in fairly close proximity. Yet you say you did not sight us? 'Tis only now I realise how you could have missed the *Redemption*.'

'How so, Mister Guinea?' said Matthew, smiling sardonically.

'I do recall hearing that the *Invincible* was in pursuit of the pirate, Hawthorne Read, Mister Fleming,' said Jonas. 'Before the *Invincible* sailed, Jamestown's taverns were all agog about her proposed action. Mayhaps, you were probably in action against the barque of Hawthorne Read. Thus, so profoundly engrossed, you did not sight the *Redemption*.'

'Your lookouts might have been looking the other way or mayhaps in slumber,' said Mistress Beecham blithely. 'I cannot for the life of me understand why men aboard a vessel of His Majesty's Navy were asleep while on patrol.'

'No man sighted mermaids or was asleep on the *Invincible*, madam,' said Matthew irritably. 'Jamestown's harbourmaster alleged the *Redemption* was on a clandestine course bound for the coast of Guinea with runaways on board. If his suspicions are proved true, the Master of the *Redemption* would be guilty of piracy on the high seas, a hanging offence.'

Faith fixed her eyes on the politician, who closed his eyes and shook his head.

Drinking wine with a slave-owner and a duplicitous politician bequeaths a ghastly taste, thought Jonas.

'Even I would recall laying eyes on the coast of Guinea, Mister Fleming,' he said facetiously, 'or seeing runaways strolling the decks of the *Redemption*. I can assure you the Master of the vessel is God-fearing and is guilty of not anything, save going about his lawful trade.

Throughout my somewhat instructive voyage I witnessed not anything untoward on his vessel.'

''Tis a reasonable opinion, Matthew,' said Davenport in a pacifying voice. 'The harbourmaster could not substantiate his suspicions with evidence. Methinks such a defining moment is an enigma of our times, Mistress Beecham. Mister Fleming cannot prove that Mister Guinea was pirating runaways. Conversely, Mister Guinea cannot prove that he wasn't guilty of such piracy.'

'Have you not promulgated misguided notions before, Matthew?' asked Rose casually. 'In Jamestown, did you not assault a cloaked gentleman for stealing wine when he was none other than the parish priest carting communion wine to his church?'

Blenching at the awkward memory, Matthew was unrepentant.

'An easy mistake in poor light,' he said curtly.

''Tis beyond me to fathom the reasons for the harbourmaster's allegations,' said Jonas. 'To the eyes of landlubbers like me, one sailing vessel looks very much like another.'

Thoughtfully putting down her goblet, Faith was composed.

'Have you considered mistaken identity, Mister Fleming?' she asked. 'Surely a man of your ilk and education appreciates the possibility?'

Politely bowing, Matthew smiled.

'Your words are as persuasive as your charm, Mistress Guinea,' he said without equivocation. 'Although unlikely, I admit such a possibility exists.'

So Rose Greenwood, daughter of a plantation owner, has turned traitor, he thought. On Pertigua, the prissy little madam belittled my proposal. She needs a strong hand. Yet now she stirs me. Wonder who beds her? And that Guinea is no fool. What is the point of education if anyone like him can have it? He knows I cannot accuse him directly without proof. Methinks 'tis time to wring more out of this uppity nigger and his women.

''Tis indeed good to see you again, Mistress Guinea,' he said. 'Before I left Pertigua, though I held no lengthy discourse with him, I did meet your father in Drake House at a planters' gathering.'

'Clearly my father did not know we would meet, Mister Fleming,' said Faith cordially. 'Or else you would have mentioned your contact with him when you arrived. I trust you found my father in rude health?'

'Rude health? Indeed he was, Mistress Guinea,' said Matthew. 'But he has, alas, been lately troubled by the insurrections he had to put down on his Tamarind Trees plantation. He was—'

Rolling her eyes with exasperation, Faith interrupted, 'What, yet another fiasco on Tamarind Trees? As you well know, Mister Fleming, I experienced the last gory disaster which nearly cost his life. Father has yet to fathom that slavery and mutiny will always be unsurprising bedfellows.'

'Lacking a moral code I can have faith in, Matthew,' said Rose impassively, 'you will understand that explosive natures and a penchant for brutality was the only currency I ever saw meted out on the plantations. I found my principles repetitively tormented.'

Blinking in disbelief at the candour of one he had thought of as being of marital substance, Matthew twisted his lips into a prickly smile and stayed silent.

'On your return to Pertigua, Mister Fleming,' said Mistress Beecham quietly, 'pray remember us to your father. With his delightful companion, Monsieur de La Fontaine, he did spend a most enlightening and memorable evening with us.'

'Gladly, Mistress Beecham, gladly,' said Matthew, smiling broadly. 'I shall be returning to Pertigua in a few weeks.'

I recall Father was most affronted by Guinea that evening, he thought.

'I trust our Members of Parliament are being swamped with petitions calling for the abolition of slavery, Mister Davenport?' asked Mistress Beecham.

Taken aback by the directness of her enquiry, Davenport spluttered. Speedily collecting his wits with a mouthful of Madeira, he countered by fudging.

'Er, I cannot recall seeing nor receiving petitions to that effect, Mistress Beecham,' he said, squirming with discomfiture. 'Being occupied in constituency matters, I have regrettably not attended the House of late. So I know not what appeals have been most recently received by the Clerk of the Commons.'

Dishonesty drips like sweat from this politician's flaccid lips, thought Jonas, and his odour is much the same.

Taking a ruminative sip of wine, Faith smiled and then enquired, 'If abolition came to a vote, Mister Davenport, would you give it your support?'

Reddening and twisting in his chair, Davenport was evasive.

'If such a motion found its way to the floor of the House,' said the politician smoothly, 'I would vote with my conscience.'

'As would I, had I a vote,' said Matthew, taking a lusty swig of Madeira.

'Conscience?' asked Rose, frowning.

'Conscience is an intriguing concept in the present state of England's affairs, Mister Davenport,' said Mistress Beecham with sagely scepticism. 'What if the motion, for instance, asked if your empathy was for the slave-owner's rights of ownership against the rights of black people to be free? How would you vote then? You see, I believe an honest conscience intrinsically would favour liberty.'

'If such a motion were presented to the House, Mistress Beecham,' said Davenport, 'Members would be allowed suitable time to study any such proposition.'

Ever the wily politician, thought Jonas.

'Surely with conscience they would not need time to study such a worthy proposition?' asked Rose.

'They need time to look at all implications of abolition,' said Davenport snappily.

'Methinks if any motion for abolition came to the floor of the House it would fall at First Reading, Mistress Beecham,' said Matthew. 'A significant number of Members are themselves slave-owners and plantation owners. Why would they vote against their own interests? As well, they are wisely aware that England's economy and continued prosperity depends on sugar.'

Frowning deeply, Jonas spoke quietly. 'At the expense of other peoples?'

Sniffing superciliously, Matthew replied, 'You are looking at an un-adulterated English patriot, Mister Guinea. I say England's interests above all others, especially the French.'

'Mayhaps 'tis high time Englishmen found a commodity less contentious with which to trade,' said Faith dryly.

'If only,' replied Davenport cordially. 'As we speak, there are Englishmen scouring the seas for such a discovery.'

'With luck,' said Rose cuttingly, 'Englishmen will hopefully discover a trade less cruel.'

''Tis difficult enough to have our millworkers slaving in northern cotton mills owned by Englishmen,' said Faith emphatically. 'But the buying and kidnapping of other peoples to be trafficked to plantations owned by Englishmen is decidedly offensive.'

'You are convinced that no such vote will ever occur, gentlemen?' asked Mistress Beecham, drumming her fingers on the arm of her chair. 'Yet why do I have a suspicion you visit Pilgrims to assess our League?'

''Tis veritably untrue, Mistress Beecham,' said Matthew feebly, crossing his legs.

'Were that true, then one might suspect that you fret about opposition, Mister Fleming,' said Mistress Beecham. 'I daresay you mostly fear the yet dormant awareness of the populace. At present, not many in the kingdom know about or understand the evils of the slave trade. I would have you know that in our quest for abolition, we of the League cannot match the finances available to you and your associates. That will not stop us from publicising the iniquities of your business. Nevertheless, you and Mister Davenport come to us somewhat preoccupied. Methinks you might—'

'I know not what you mean, Mistress Beecham,' protested Matthew, stopping her in mid-sentence. 'On good recommendation we came to procure a quantity of rope and—'

'To meet elements of the opposition, Matthew,' said Rose, succinctly finishing his sentence.

'Mayhaps you might be preoccupied,' said Mistress Beecham, amiably interjecting, 'because you wish to discover if we know about the slave-owners' plans to disrupt anti-slavery meetings. 'Tis my impression of your business and on this we might even agree. England's slave trade is owned by a minority of her middle and upper classes in collusion with her aristocracy — for some of whom, treason allegedly, seems only a matter of expedience. Methinks that minority of a minority truly fears the response of an informed populace.'

'Your judgment is somewhat difficult and disappointing, Mistress Beecham,' said Matthew, twisting uncomfortably in his seat. 'I had hoped we might find an accommodation between our respective beliefs and activities—'

''Tis 1762, Mister Fleming,' interrupted Mistress Beecham, 'and the occasion for accommodation evaporated from the moment the first slave was embarked. At that moment, in a feeding frenzy for profit, England was unwittingly divided by the slave-trading minority, for they disregarded the non-involvement of their countrymen. Responsibility therefore, for what I consider a crime, will in time be laid at the feet of all Englishmen—'

'That's a bit steep, Mistress Beecham,' said Matthew, butting in.

'As you well know,' said Mistress Beecham, ignoring his comment, 'at present the population is mostly ignorant of England's vast slave trafficking. But when acquainted with the iniquitous facts and galling conditions on the slave ships and no doubt the plantations, methinks they will most likely join with our League in petitioning Parliament to abolish the trade. Regrettably until then, Mister Fleming, you and your associates ply a valid business — in the eyes of the law.'

Glancing awkwardly around his listeners, Matthew felt a thorny silence settle in the withdrawing room.

The woman is foxed with persecuting opinions, he thought, examining her closely through narrowed eyes. I wonder if she is privy to covert intelligence of our conspiracy.

Winking furtively at his wife, Jonas turned and smiled at the discomfited politician, who averted his eyes.

Pouting in matronly fashion, Mistress Beecham tilted her head and nodded at Rose, who smirked.

Street vendors and the clatter of carriages on the Highway splintered the tension in the room.

'I-I-I don't recall mentioning any concerns about your League, Mistress Beecham,' stuttered Matthew, wriggling uncomfortably on his chair.

Endeavouring to regain his equanimity, he continued, 'Persuaded by the repute of your chandlery we came merely to transact business.'

'Much wayward tittle-tattle passes by these elderly ears, Mister Fleming,' said Mistress Beecham, chortling. 'But now and then something irksome takes root. Like for instance, the shenanigans between slave-owners and shipowners at the Blackheath Golf Club to hamper anyone hostile to their trade. I do believe that in those august confines, the froth about the feeble opposition is giving way to fears of a consequential anti-slavery campaign. I would have them know they are right.'

Visibly paling, Davenport gulped down a mouthful of Madeira.

Looking askance at the unsettled politician, Matthew silently exhaled.

Does this seasoned harridan, he pondered, allude to my luncheon with William Beckford at the Blackheath Golf Club? Or is she simply guessing?

'Truly, Mistress Beecham,' he said, recovering his masked surprise, 'we know not of any such conclaves. My time in England has been taken up with attending to my sugar imports and the affairs of my Augustfields estate in Yorkshire. For the past few weeks I have resided in Piccadilly as the guest of Mister Davenport. I daresay I will be in London not long enough to know who is or who is not conspiring with whom.'

Thank God he is departing these shores, thought Jonas.

'I was not suggesting that two such principled gentlemen as you would be party to such cabals, Mister Fleming,' said Mistress Beecham, shaking her head. 'Nay, I simply meant that we of the League are aware of surreptitious transactions in the Blackheath Golf Club and in the Royal Exchange.'

There was a knock at the door. Shuffling into the chamber, the chubby Clerk of Chandlery bowed courteously.

'Your consignment has been loaded into your carriage, Mister Fleming,' he said.

Accepting the invoice from the clerk, Jonas sighed with gratitude at the timely intrusion.

Heaving a silent thankful sigh for the appearance of the clerk, Matthew rose to his feet.

'We stand as equals either side of a great divide, Mistress Beecham,' said Davenport, smiling imperiously. 'But until Parliament declares otherwise, I daresay we shall all have to abide with the status quo. Shan't we?'

'Regrettably so, Mister Davenport,' retorted Mistress Beecham, with a tepid smile. 'But we do not have to like it. You must by now have appreciated that come what may, our League will sustain its campaign for an end to a destructive trade. You see, sirs, we of the League fundamentally believe that in the first instance, the very nature of slavery is in itself immoral.'

Smarting from her riposte, Davenport's haughty smile withered.

'Pray tell me, Mistress Greenwood,' asked Matthew, in soft supercilious tones. 'How can scribbling tedious petitions in smoky Deptford satisfy a high-spirited sun-worshipper like you?'

'Easily Matthew,' said Rose, giggling sarcastically. 'On England's shores foul air smells sweeter than the sundrenched suffering on Pertigua. I shall not ever again set eyes on those sorrowing plantations. Pray remember me to mutual friends. Did you know I can set traps for the wild mushrooms in Sussex?'

Shaking his head, Davenport frowned.

Suppressing a smile, Mistress Beecham turned briefly away.

'Your significant other, Mistress Greenwood,' said Matthew patronisingly. 'I don't believe I have had the pleasure of his acquaintance.'

'You probably won't, Matthew,' said Rose curtly.

She not ever mentions her admirer, mused Faith. Mayhaps he was Fleming's rival.

Such a whirlwind is she I have not ever even pondered on his identity, thought Jonas.

Settling his account, Matthew donned his cloak with a quizzical look and a chastened demeanour. Bowing stiffly, he felt thoroughly discomfited.

'I would have you know that the slaves we care for on our Pertiguan plantations, Mistress Fleming,' he said, 'benefit from superior victuals and environment than they did on the Slave Coast.'

Yet again an edgy hush charged the chamber.

'But they did not choose to be slaves on your plantations did they, Mister Fleming?' countered Mistress Beecham. 'You would not stomach such an abject state would you, gentlemen? Moreover, the Africans did not name the coast of their motherland the Slave Coast. English cartographers did so on their maps, which might suggest an apt classification for a dark purpose.'

Shaken by her scathing retort, Matthew's convictions were tinged by a fleeting uncertainty. Momentarily envisaging himself a cane-cutting slave, an entirely vexatious notion, he shivered with discomfiture.

'Given our unexpected visit, Mistress Beecham,' he said respectfully, 'your hospitality was utterly gracious. And I have no doubt the success of your chandlery is due entirely to your sterling efforts. Though your beliefs were forthrightly expounded, I still harbour the hope that in the fullness of time we might somehow resolve our differences.'

Turning with a steely look in his eyes, Matthew smiled through faintly bared teeth.

''Twas indeed arresting to meet you, your good wife and your mixed-match, Mister Guinea,' he said with frosty courtesy. 'Mayhaps one day we shall meet in Pertigua. Nonetheless, we bid you all a good day.'

Smiling inscrutably, Jonas stepped into the hallway and gave the faintest bow.

'With my many responsibilities here in Deptford, Mister Fleming,' he said with brusque civility, 'I have no need or time to return to Pertigua. Regarding your disquiet about the rising anti-slavery sentiments wafting about, I trust you will not forget the lessons of history.'

'And what might they be, Mister Guinea?' asked Matthew disdainfully.

''Tis impossible to quench the thirst for change when conviction raises its head,' replied Jonas. 'Having dined with your father, Mister Fleming, it has indeed been intriguing to make the acquaintance of his son. We bid you gentlemen a very good day.'

Shutting the front door firmly behind the visitors, four mouths heaved a collective sigh and returned to the withdrawing room.

'Those duplicitous villains are hatching a plot,' spat Mistress Beecham. 'I stake my bonnet on it.'

'I second that,' said Rose. 'The scheming scoundrel I know visits only when he wants something.'

Placing logs on the fire, Jonas chuckled.

'Such is the consequence of drinking with serpents.'

'Or being in close proximity to a duplicitous legislator,' said Faith, laughing. 'I glean a certain satisfaction knowing that Fleming, who believes he knows everything of the goings-on on Pertigua, knows not that my stepfather and I have been long estranged.'

Wiping his brow, Jonas heaved a sigh.

'Wilier guests we have yet to entertain. Methinks you are right, they have a plot afoot. Those innocent brown eyes of Fleming's camouflage a ruthless disposition. And that paunchy politician, who most likely bribed and bullied his constituents for a seat in the Commons, is one unprincipled reason abolition remains nowhere near the Statute Book.'

'Neither man is to my taste,' said Mistress Beecham briskly.

'Where Matthew Fleming is concerned, Jonas,' said Faith, taking his hand, 'watch where you tread. He and his companion are the epitome of men like my stepfather, who turn a profit from human trafficking. Given their suspicions about you and the *Redemption*, you are a scapegoat. For everyone else connected with your voyage is white.'

''Tis true, Jonas,' said Rose anxiously. 'You are an easy and exposed target. Without proof, Fleming would not dare accuse respectable white men openly. He risks being sued for slander.'

'My gut feelings tell me they have you in their sights, Jonas,' said Faith firmly. 'With the connivance of the church and state, the likes of Fleming buy and kidnap men, women and children up and down the coast of Guinea. Who will stop their slave-hunters snatching a black man or two off the streets of London? At all times when you leave Pilgrims or the chandlery, my dear husband, you must take a man with you for protection, especially about the docks.'

Presented with three anxious faces, he returned a grimace.

'Fleming shall not lay hands on me,' he said robustly.

'I would rather have you take two men, Jonas,' said Mistress Beecham, frowning. 'By flaunting his slave-owning credentials with such satisfaction, Fleming has quite made up my mind. Taking much comfort from the achievement of the *Redemption*, I say we should instigate another exploit with more runaways and fewer mistakes.'

Thumping the arms of their chairs, they replied in unison:

'When do we start?'

'Can I partake?' asked Rose excitedly.

'Aye,' three voices chorused.

'We start at once,' said Mistress Beecham eagerly.

'I shall pen a letter to Alexander Fairfax,' said Faith. 'And in case it had slipped your mind, my dear husband, we are newly married. As your wife, I forbid you from participating in this project by sailing to Pertigua on whatever vessel is engaged by the League.'

Veiling the lower half of her face behind a fan, Mistress Beecham giggled.

''Tis oft said that woman is master at home, Jonas,' said Rose teasingly. 'Why won't men admit such?'

Smiling affectionately at his wife, Jonas solemnly placed his hand over his heart.

'I promise,' he said, chuckling softly. 'What with the experience and understanding I gained during the *Redemption*'s voyage, I am better placed to be of use in the planning of this project. After all these years I have a wife and prospects of family. I shall not tempt providence twice.'

'I shall put pen to paper to invite our members to a meeting of the League,' said Mistress Beecham. 'Think of it. A slave-owner and a loathsome legislator, notorious for his support for England's slave trade, came to take surreptitious stock of us. After such close proximity to such animus, I am famished. What say you to a hearty supper with a bodied French wine?'

'Aye, let us raise a glass to a distasteful exchange,' said Jonas. 'With good fare, good cheer and laughter at Fleming's expense.'

'And may we spoil his half-baked plans,' said Rose raising her glass.

'I shall have a word with cook,' said Mistress Beecham, chuckling her way out of the room. 'Mayhaps we may yet even bake the other half.'

Pressing his lips lightly to his wife's cheeks, Jonas said, 'We have a great deal of work ahead, my dearest.'

Cupping his face in her hands, she flashed her eyes lustfully. 'Aye you have, my love.'

In the freezing mid-afternoon, with stowed hanks of rope, Davenport's landau rolled away from Pilgrims.

Absorbed in the endless rows of sometimes drab dwellings, Matthew snuggled deeper into his cloak.

'Guinea articulates well for a nigger,' he snorted. 'The scoundrel is intelligent and vigilant. 'Twill not be easy to take him by surprise. Unless we take action, his purported mother, his wife, the Greenwood vixen and that meddlesome League and their likes could well become a thorn in the side of our interests. I say we engage the top dog of London's slave-hunters, Solomon Festus. Pay him to deliver Guinea to the jail in the Poultry Compter and thence onto a vessel bound for Pertigua.'

'Capital, Matthew, capital,' said Davenport, chortling like a schoolboy. 'Solomon Festus is certain to snatch Guinea. After we land him on Turtle Island, your overseers can take the strut out of him.'

Clutching Davenport's cloak, Matthew shuddered. 'The thought of it, Samuel! The thought of black hands fondling her sickens me. How can a virtuous white woman marry a nigger?'

''Cos she's a harlot at heart, Matthew,' said Davenport. 'No respectable white woman would ever let a nigger touch her.'

Turning left at the end of the Highway, the landau headed towards the City of London.

Pondering out loud, Matthew muttered mischievously, 'I wonder if her hot-tempered pater knows of her mixed-up marriage. As well, we may have to do something about that interfering Greenwood trollop. I shall ascertain who squires the woman. He may not know she sides with abolitionists.'

'Even the hearth in the withdrawing of Pilgrims lacked warmth,' said Davenport petulantly.

Slave-Hunters

A crescent moon cast an eerie glow over the parish of Deptford. Gusts of swirling snow reduced visibility down the Highway. In the paltry light of two oil streetlamps, wraithlike shadows flickered all along Bottom Lane.

'Stop here if you please, Mister Plowright,' said Jonas, patting the driver's shoulder.

Ahead of his two strapping minders, he descended from the carriage.

Trundling off up the lane, the lanterned carriage turned right onto the Highway and out of sight. Silence returned to the narrow street.

Without waiting, Jonas strode absent-mindedly up the dim-lit lane towards the Highway.

Suddenly, a shrouded thickset figure wielding a quarterstaff stepped out of the shadows and blocked his path.

'Who the devil are you?' Jonas demanded.

'We come for ye, Guinea,' the figure growled.

His mouth dried. He heard laboured breathing from two men behind him. He was trapped. Instinctively drawing his sword-cane, he took his guard.

'Help! Help!' he shouted. 'Tapsell! Foggerty!'

'We're with thee, Mister Guinea,' shouted Foggerty, sprinting towards him.

A heavy object struck the top of his head. Crashing to his knees, he was momentarily stunned. Warm blood trickled down into his eyes and dripped onto the cobbles. Crushing hands suddenly pinioned his arms from behind. Horrified by the thought of enslavement, he was seized by rage. Violently struggling, he freed himself. Quickly thrusting his sword-cane blindly to the fore, he felt it cleave through soft tissue. Twisting his wrist as schooled, he extracted the blade.

'Ugggghhhh!' screeched the shrouded figure, dropping to the cobbles with a thud. 'Nigger stabbed me leg.'

Bloodied sword-cane in hand, Jonas staggered woozily to his feet with his head throbbing violently. Wiping blood from his eyes, he beheld a frenzied scene.

Waylaid by his minders, the other two wiry assailants were receiving a pasting against the wall of Pilgrims. The thickset mugger sat on blood-spattered cobbles propped against the wall nursing his punctured thigh, whimpering and shuddering involuntarily.

Watching the thrashing being meted out by his minders, a shiver skittered up Jonas's spine. He sighed with relief at his narrow escape.

'Slave-hunters,' he fumed aloud. 'Matthew Fleming had clearly not reckoned that I might have protection.'

Soon the beaten, winded muggers lay on the cobbles by the wall with his minders hovering over them. Even in that muted light, he could see that as well as shredded garments, the night's work had earned them a severe battering, a broken arm, a shattered leg and a perforated thigh.

'Not your finest night's work, I wager,' said Jonas scornfully.

Abruptly seizing a thug by the neck with one hand, Foggerty slapped his face several times with the other and then began to squeeze his throat.

'Who sent ye?' he growled menacingly.

'Festus,' squeaked the thug, desperately fighting for breath. 'Solomon Festus.'

Blinking the blood from his eyes, Jonas groaned, 'Solomon Festus the slave-hunter.'

'An' what 'em call ye?' snarled Foggerty, tightening his grip.

'Pipkin,' the man squealed. 'Tom Pipkin.'

'If we ever sets eyes on thee 'round these parts in this life, Tom Pipkin,' snarled Foggerty, 'we will drop yer all 'ead first alive in yer deep sludge on the Gravesend foreshore.'

Gurgling incoherently and his eyes rolling with terror, the rattled mugger nodded.

Grasping the third man and dragging him to his feet, Tapsell growled into his ear. 'Run back ter yer master. Tell 'im Mister Guinea ain't wanting to sail to sunny climes. Yer got that? An' ye be leaving Mister Guinea well alone. Yer got that?'

'I got yer,' said the trembling thug. 'We be leaving Mister Guinea well alone. Yer got me word.'

'Where ye be laying yer 'orrible little 'ead then, Tom Pipkin?'

'Got lodgings in garret...in Cable Street...... number twenty one... I swear it.'

Kicking the muggers hard in the buttocks, Tapsell snarled, 'Get along with ye. Ter mek sure ye stay away, me mates be at Cable Street this night ter break yer legs an' tek yer eyes out. Yer looked on Mister Guinea yer last.'

Shocked, befuddled and limping, the villains hobbled up the lane to the Highway.

'Now let's be seeing to thee, Mister Guinea,' said Foggerty.

Quaking and rearranging his torn cloak, Jonas forced a grin. Aided by his minders, he tottered painfully up the lane with furrowed brow and a throbbing head.

'Them slave-hunters won't be troubling thee again, Mister Guinea,' said Tapsell with a scornful laugh.

'Mister Foggerty and Mister Tapsell,' said Jonas, grasping their forearms and halting their progress, 'I have not the words to thank ye enough, gentlemen.'

'Well blow me down, Mister Guinea,' said Foggerty, scratching his head. 'I did not know that London Town could be such a perilous place for them of yer skin.'

Crashing into the hallway of Pilgrims, his arrival wrought consternation.

Seeing his bloodied appearance in the hall, Tuppence Honeypenny dropped a laden tray that clattered across the floor.

Hurrying into the hallway, Faith flung her hands to her mouth and shrieked. 'Ye gods, Jonas! Let me help you to the withdrawing room, my dearest.'

'Good God, Jonas, what has happened to thee?' cried Mistress Beecham. 'Mistress Honeypenny, pray fetch a bowl of hot water, a cotton bandage and ample cotton wads.'

Helping Jonas onto the Chippendale sofa, Faith stood up and grasped the hands of his minders. Struggling to keep control of her emotions and blinking back her tears, she spoke plainly. 'Mister Foggerty and Mister Tapsell, I am indebted to you for your speedy action in aiding Mister Guinea. On the morrow you must accept a token of our gratitude for your timely conduct.'

'Thank 'ee, Mistress Guinea,' said Foggerty. 'We be working for Mister Guinea for gone eight year. 'E can surely count on us.'

'We be getting along home now, Mistress Beecham,' said Tapsell. 'We be at work in the morn.'

'I truly thank you, gentlemen,' said Mistress Beecham. 'I bid thee a very, very good night.'

The door closed behind his minders.

''Tis a strange happenstance that Matthew Fleming visited in the past week,' bristled Mistress Beecham. 'Almost certainly bears the hallmarks of his handiwork. I shall fetch you a tonic, my dear Faith. And you, dear Jonas, are most certainly in need of a very large brandy.'

Patting a wet wad to clean his head wound, Faith sighed.

Jonas winced. He could feel her fury and sorrow. Taking her face in his hands, he sought to reassure her.

'Fret not, Faith,' he said firmly, 'such a trap shall not happen again. Having nearly suffered the loss of my liberty reminds me how precious freedom in this life is. I will heed this as a God-sent warning.'

Sitting tearfully down beside him and slumping onto his lap, she uttered a pained cry. 'What depth of hatred does Fleming have to want to enslave thee?'

'One born from a foolish sense of superiority,' he said scathingly. 'That way the man doesn't have to think.'

Sitting upright and wiping her eyes, she said, ''Tis fortunate we own the resources to shield you from the hunters, Jonas.'

Stirred by her protective nature, he drew her closer and kissed her brow. 'I was born a slave and arrived here free. As God is my witness, I shall not ever be enslaved again.'

Bearing a tray of brandy-filled glasses, Mistress Beecham returned with a flush in her cheeks and somewhat rejuvenated.

'We must implement a strategy to keep you safe, Jonas,' she said. 'Methinks in the meantime you'd best vacate Pilgrims for Greensleeves for a few weeks recuperation. Parson Merriweather would be glad for your company. He is fond of you.'

Crisis

Walking breathlessly into the withdrawing room, Jonas waved a letter.

'I have just received heartening correspondence from Francis Barber.'

'What tidings does he convey that has you so animated?' asked Mistress Beecham, raising her eyes from her newssheet.

'Granville Sharp has thrown his weight behind an escaped slave,' he said excitedly.

'My goodness!' exclaimed Mistress Beecham, dropping her newssheet. 'We must write to him at once to give him the League's support and—'

Bursting giddily into the chamber, Faith chattered eagerly:

'I met with Rose Greenwood and we had luncheon in Matilda Hockworthy's town house on Crooms Hill, Greenwich. Mistress Hockworthy then took us to Deptford to meet women from the evangelical churches, all of whom are opposed to the slave trade. There were many seamstresses and Quakers among their number. Following impassioned debate and a unanimous vote, they took the decision to form an association to be known as the Deptford Female Anti-Slavery Society.'

I wed a true fighter, thought Jonas.

Beaming at his wife, he asked, 'What activities does the Deptford Female Anti-Slavery Society intend?'

'The Quakers have long fought against slavery,' said Mistress Beecham. 'As ye both well know, my parents were both Quakers and consequently I hail from the Quaker tradition. Where does the Society meet so I might attend?'

'In the crypt of St Paul's Church in Deptford High Street,' said Faith, sitting on the Chippendale sofa to massage her feet. 'We will begin our mission by addressing assemblies of working women to inform them about the slave trade. Doubtless they will spread the word around their neighbourhoods. Moreover, we shall urge sailors at the dock gates not to sign on to slave ships, otherwise they will be signing on to unspeakable cruelty. We shall as well write petitions to all manner of pertinent bodies and to Parliament. We hope one day it will all amount to a boycott of slave-made goods. We believe a boycott is something women can bring about. Knowing we needed to finance our activities, we had a collection before our meeting was ended. Our collection produced five pounds seven shillings and tuppence in as many minutes. We being the best educated in the meeting, Rose Greenwood was elected chairwoman and I elected Treasurer.'

'Treasurer is a key position,' he said. 'Yet you seem troubled.'

'Leaving the church,' she said, clutching her shawl to her chest and shuddering, 'we encountered an angry mob that had clearly intended to disrupt our meeting. They had undoubtedly been swilling liquor in taverns before they combined. Fortunately, they arrived too late. Thank God. Waving their fists and hurling vulgarities and curses, they threatened us with a beating for meddling with their trade.'

'Since they have the effrontery to openly abuse and threaten women,' scowled Jonas, 'it tells us that the slave-owners have most certainly begun their campaign of disrupting abolitionist gatherings.'

'Indeed it does,' said Mistress Beecham, frowning. ''Tis comforting that working women with the least finances and least security are moved to make such effort for those more insecure than themselves.'

'A commendable argument, Mistress Beecham,' said Faith. 'Working women generally subsist in frugal conditions, yet still feel able to protest against injustice for others. Methinks given that mob, 'twould be wise for the Deptford Female Anti-Slavery Society to frequently change venues for our meetings. Where are our children?'

'In the library at their lessons with Mistress Tubworth,' he said.

He was in his forty-fourth year and she in her forty-eighth. In the years 1763 and 1765, they had been blessed with the births of Solomon and Olivia. Given the sometimes wretched conditions for most free Africans, he felt a lucky man.

Smiling to himself, he thought back to a warm summer evening in the high meadows near Greensleeves before the children were born.

Lying among tall grasses with her head on his chest, Faith had asked, 'What of the education of our children?'

Hearing the fretful note in her voice, he said, 'In view of the problems in the schools for some children of colour, I think we should firstly have ours tutored at home.'

'I am of the same mind. What if we have a boy?'

'He can attend Alleyn's School and then go to University.'

'If a girl?'

'Women are not permitted to matriculate to membership of a university,' he had said. 'Our daughter can be tutored until—'

'I do not want our daughter to attend a finishing school,' she fiercely interrupted. 'I will not have her saddled with deportment, etiquette and cookery.'

'Our daughter can receive tuition in reading, writing, arithmetic, science and Latin,' he had replied. 'Thus educated, she can be trained in the business of Thomas Beecham, Chandlers, until she marries. A tutor will cost us the princely sum of twenty-four pounds per annum per child.'

'A princely indispensable sum I'd say,' Faith had exclaimed. 'And I warm to the notion of raising a woman for commerce. 'Tis high time we changed the current state of the affairs of men.'

A woman of ambition, he had thought. Opportunity for women was her personal struggle, but he knew that being not a native son, he could not oppose the status quo. Nevertheless, he gladly embraced her parity for women. Given her determination on the issue, he had gazed lovingly at her and thought how relieved he was to be married to a woman of conviction. As well, he had very much wanted any daughter they had to be at least skilled in the practice of commerce.

Re-engaging with the events in the withdrawing room, he imparted his news.

'I have received promising intelligence from Francis Barber,' he said. 'Granville Sharp has taken on the case of a James Sommersett, an escaped slave. Recaptured and clapped in irons on the slave ship *Ann and Mary*, he is destined to be sold in Jamaica. I know not the particulars, but persons claiming to be Sommersett's godparents made an application for a writ of *habeas corpus* before the King's Bench. It was granted. Sommersett was freed on bail pending a hearing. The Chief Justice, Lord Mansfield, has ordered these persons to produce Sommersett before the Court on 21st January 1772.'

'My goodness,' said Faith, ''tis a matter of months away. What case do they make?'

'They declare that though colonial laws sanction slavery, English law has not ever authorised such. Only a new Act of Parliament can make slavery legitimate. Consequently, slavery has not ever been lawful on English soil.'

'If true,' beamed Faith, ''twould be the gladdest tidings I have heard in many a year.'

'My feelings exactly,' he said firmly. 'According to what I read in a tuppenny weekly journal, it became illegal to teach slaves to write in 1740, or being found upon the King's highway with a sooty face. With edicts like that and other legal mysteries crippling Sommersett's freedoms, 'tis imperative we help him win his case.'

'I suggest we dispatch a letter to Granville Sharp,' said Mistress Beecham, 'to offer the League's support and donations.'

'I heartily agree,' said Faith. 'And as well, I propose we establish a public collection for Sommersett's defence without delay.'

'Substantial contributions will be needed for a case that is bound to attract much press attention,' he said. 'Due to the consequence of the outcome, slave-owners will sponsor the cause of Charles Steuart, a Customs officer and Sommersett's owner.'

'A victory for Sommersett would indeed set a precedent,' said Mistress Beecham. 'Consequently, Charles Steuart's counsel will put his argument forcefully. I am certain Granville Sharp will see that Sommersett is defended by an equally persuasive counsel who will be costly.'

'We need money and lots of it,' said Faith resolutely. 'I am certain Rose Greenwood will agree to the Deptford Female Anti-Slavery Society making Sommersett's case our first endeavour. Women's associations will prove to be of great assistance furthering his just cause and collecting donations for his case.'

'We have to match the funds of the other side,' he said. 'To that end, Francis Barber and I will seek contributions from the black commune in Spitalfields and around the docks. And should we not convene a meeting of the League to solicit the support of the members?'

'Aye, Jonas, I shall write to the members this very evening.'

The door opened. A lissom, flaxen-haired girl in a red pinafore dress skipped into the chamber.

'Hello everybody,' said Olivia, waving her slate and giggling.

Laughing affectionately, Jonas embraced his six-year-old daughter.

'I have done my lessons, Papa,' she said with a big smile. 'I learn withmetic and poetwee.'

Running his fingers through her hair, Jonas said, 'I know a clever girl like you will want to read your beautiful poems to us after supper.'

Shyly putting two fingers into her mouth, Olivia nodded, took a few steps and fell into her mother's lap. At that moment, a boy with huge brown curls and a wide smile walked in, carrying a copy of *A Little Pretty Pocket-Book*.

Cuddling her eight-year-old son and gently pulling his chubby cheeks, Faith asked, 'Will you read to us after supper, Solomon?'

'Yes, Mama,' he said, eagerly waving his book. 'I read a poem call *Cricket*.'

Dressed entirely in a spinster-black gown, Mistress Tubworth, the tutor, walked into the chamber. Without ado and with delight, she tripped out a progress report. While doing so, her eyes danced with mirth and her russet hair slipped over half her long face.

Thanking her for the children's heartening improvement, Jonas bade a warm-hearted farewell. "Til the morrow then, Mistress Tubworth.'

'I bid you all a very good night,' replied the tutor.

'A very good night to you, Mistress Tubworth,' said Faith affectionately. 'Now, children, I want you to go and help cook get supper ready.'

'Yes, Mama.'

The Heart of the Matter

Greensleeves
Kent
Friday
3 January 1772
10.00 hrs

Dense white clouds blanketed the skies. Wintering lapwings headed easterly over the pastures around Greensleeves. Thawing hoarfrost had left a sparkling coat of dew on the leaves and grasses. Beset with thorns astride a tangled framework of branches, rows of denuded hawthorn hedgerows divided the fields. It was the third day of the New Year. Calm befell the carriage drive until the last member of the League arrived.

It was the Mate of the *Redemption*, Mister Hopkins. Strolling into the house with his friend, Jonas slapped him on the back, ''Tis good to greet my old shipmate.'

''Tis good to see my old shipmate.'

'For a family man ye look in rude health, Jonas,' said the Mate affectionately.

'Mistress Guinea manages a plenteous and lively household, Thaddeus,' he replied, beaming.

'Bit too much ratafia trifle, ay, my friend?' said the Mate, looking him up and down.

Patting his small potbelly, Jonas laughed. 'Kent's attractions have clearly not distracted your eyesight sufficiently. I can see we shall have to amend what you see during your visit. 'Tis been quite some time since our escapade on the *Redemption*. We are on yet another consequential mission, Thaddeus, but this time 'tis to help James Sommersett set a legal precedent.'

'Given the League's involvement in Sommersett's defence,' said the Mate, 'I daresay you will not be with us on the impending venture to spirit more runaways from Pertigua?'

'I daresay you are most observant, Thaddeus,' replied Jonas with a soft chuckle. 'I must manage the chandlery, for Mistress Beecham slows. And as well, Mistress Guinea and our children would disapprove of any such absence. Anywise, I am certain Matthew Fleming and the West Indies Sugar Cartel are on the lookout for me. My presence therefore would most likely imperil the mission.'

'Then I daresay we would be safer without you, Jonas,' said the Mate, stepping into the hall.

Pondering on the fate of James Sommersett, Jonas followed.

Mindful of slave-trading spies and *agent provocateurs*, Mistress Beecham had requested they move the gathering for Sommersett's defence to Kent, away from prying eyes and ears. Of the eighteen members of the League, twelve had confirmed their attendance at Greensleeves.

As well as Faith, Mistress Beecham and Parson Merriweather, Jonas was expecting Reverend Whitehouse, the banker Elijah Drinkwater and his lawyer son Aaron, shipowner Jeremiah Puddlewick and his wife Grace, Captain and Mistress Battersby and the Mate, Mister Hopkins.

'Snug in the Garden of England,' Faith had said, 'we shall be at liberty to plot unobserved.'

Closely followed by the Mate, Jonas entered the withdrawing room.

The frock-coated shipowner had just risen to address the members.

'Honourable Members,' said Jeremiah Puddlewick, looking solemnly around the table. 'As I see it, this is what we are up against. The Bank of England makes capital effortlessly obtainable for slave voyages to practically anyone who can crawl. As well, London's fifty banking houses offer, nay, indeed advance credit for slave trading, inducing even them without vessels to apply. England's slave trade, I fear, is escalating.'

''Tis true England's trade grows apace, sir,' said Jonas, 'and that initial trickle of slaves has indeed become a flood. Should we not, as a priority, acquaint the populace about this vast trade? I believe that the enormity and cruelties of England's slave trafficking has been deliberately kept from common knowledge by the slave-owners, the shipping companies, the sugar cartels and the Church. Methinks 'tis our bounden duty to rouse the populace with a profusion of disturbing handouts in both words and illustrations.'

'Are we not still liberating runaways?' asked Parson Merriweather groggily. 'I believe that as of the week last past, vessels emulating the *Redemption*'s runaway escapade landed one hundred returnees back on the coast of Guinea.'

Lively applause was summarily curtailed by the raised hand of the lawyer, Aaron Drinkwater.

'England's trafficking cannot be halted by shipping the people back to the coast of Guinea piecemeal,' he said loftily. 'Abolition will be determined by the votes of Members of Parliament. I would remind you all that many of these politicians are themselves up to their nostrils in slave trading.'

'Your analysis is irrefutable, Mister Drinkwater,' said Jeremiah Puddlewick. 'Foxes have no sympathy for the wellbeing of chickens.'

Sighing inaudibly, Jonas winked at Faith, who smiled.

Tapping her gavel on the table, Mistress Beecham interrupted the roving discourse.

'Honourable Members,' she said, raising her voice. 'Can we please turn our attention to the dilemma of James Sommersett? His case is due to be heard before Lord Mansfield at the King's Bench on 21st January. We know that, among others, Francis Hargrave has been retained as an advocate for Sommersett. Having entered Lincoln's Inn as lately as 1760, he is reputed to be unstinting in his efforts for his clients. Hargrave's perspective is encapsulated in his published line of attack: *An Argument in the case of James Sommersett, a Negro, wherein it is attempted to demonstrate the present unlawfulness of Domestic Slavery in England, 1772.*'

'My word,' exclaimed Grace Puddlewick. 'I have to say, 'tis a decidedly believable title.'

Chatter surged after Mistress Puddlewick's remark.

'Tis surely heart-rending that a man has to plead before another for a freedom illicitly taken, thought Jonas sombrely.

Mistress Beecham used her gavel to gain their attention, then spoke gravely. 'Honourable Members, Sommersett's case may well cost in excess of one hundred and fifty guineas which, I might add, is why we have gathered here.'

'Sommersett's case is upon us,' said Grace Puddlewick, throwing up her hands with alarm. 'We have no time to fritter away.'

''Tis fortunate then that a request for time to prepare arguments has been made by Sommersett's counsel to the Court,' said Aaron Drinkwater. 'Hargrave has been granted an adjournment. On the day last past, the postponement was the talk of the King's Bench. Sommersett's case will now be heard on 7 February 1772, which in turn affords us a little more time.'

''Tis essential Sommersett wins the day,' said Jeremiah Puddlewick vehemently. 'I propose we set up a Sommersett Fund with a target of one hundred guineas towards his defence. If we members give five guineas apiece towards the account, we should make up the shortfall from absent members and with donations. What with the generous collections from the populace and the evangelicals, I daresay that should help give Sommersett a fighting chance. What say you all?'

'A goodly sum to aid the cause,' said a delighted Mistress Beecham.

'Five guineas is a useful figure, Mistress Beecham,' said Elijah Drinkwater, carefully extracting from an embroidered silk wallet a white ten-pound banknote issued by Coutts Bank. 'I shall give ten for such a crucial action.'

'As shall I,' said Aaron Drinkwater, following his father.

Coutts Bank, thought Jonas, raising his eyebrows. The Drinkwaters are full of surprises.

'Honourable Members,' said Mistress Beecham. 'What say you all to at least five guineas apiece towards the Sommersett Fund?'

'Aye,' the members chorused.

The vote was unanimous. Some members gave five guineas and others proffered ten.

The door opened. Under a frilled mob cap and in a mushroom-coloured dress, Mistress Bracegirdle, the plump, absent-minded housekeeper, shuffled into the chamber scratching her head.

'Now let me see,' she mumbled to herself. 'I have it. Luncheon is ready to be served, Mistress Guinea.'

'Thank you, Mistress Bracegirdle,' said Faith, rising to her feet and smiling broadly. 'Honourable Members, please follow me. We can carry on our discourse over a fine sirloin and an excellent Chateau Gruaud Larose.'

Murmuring oozed from the bellies trooping into the dining room.

Fanning around the dining table, the members bowed their heads for grace. Typical of the amicable temperaments in the League, Reverend Whitehouse and Parson Merriweather respectively said a Methodist and a Catholic prayer.

'I foresee a time,' said Faith, as if uttering a prayer, 'when we shall not fear attack for openly declaring our abolitionist sympathies.'

'Hear, hear,' said the members.

The white soup was served in blue and white porcelain soup bowls.

'I hear that even the poor blacks of Canning Town have taken a collection for Sommersett's costs,' said Mistress Battersby. 'I pray Sommersett wins his case for 'twill be a goodly sight safer for black citizens on the streets of London.'

''Tis as well astonishing that since learning of the Deptford Female Anti-Slavery Society,' said Grace Puddlewick, 'I have heard of two other women's associations called the Mothers Against Slavery and the Charwomen's Anti-Slavery Society. Excepting present company, of course, there are those who believe that women have not the intellect or mettle to partake in such political activity. They say women have not the head for politics and the excitement might cause them to swoon.'

Laughing loudly with the members, Mistress Beecham quietened to disclose a little-known fact:

'Since 1761,' she declared, 'Quakers have been banned from owning slaves or buying slave-made sugar. Any Quaker who does not conform is disowned.'

'Oh that England should follow such a fine example,' lamented Grace Puddlewick.

'What say you, Mister Guinea?' asked Captain Battersby amiably. 'You are an African. Here in England or on the plantations, the African sits at the heart of the matter. You are among friends who very much welcome your opinion, sir? And I trust you will not be excessively diplomatic with your answer.'

The chamber quietened.

All eyes turned to Jonas. Glancing affectionately at his wife, he took a ponderous swig of wine.

'Captain,' he said, smiling and dabbing his lips with a napkin, 'I believe the relationship between poor black and poor white is generally a good one and sometimes smudged by contradiction. For instance, you have all heard some erudite agitators state that black people threaten the purity of the white race. How can that be? For 'tis reckoned that out of London's population of around eight hundred thousand, there are some twenty thousand black people. And how upon their immigration to England blacks might become intoxicated with freedom, grow indolent and unruly and take work away from the populace.'

''Tis the scripture of the firebrand,' said Captain Battersby mordantly.

'Precisely, Captain Battersby,' said Jonas. 'But have we thought about how they must feel seeing their kind savagely depicted on slave notices dotted around the metropolis? I know how I feel. Contrary to the duplicitous words from such agitators, there are some, like Francis Barber and I, who have encountered generosity and friendship. And I have to say we continue to do so.'

Nodding appreciatively at what he heard, Captain Battersby's smile narrowed his eyes.

'You have been nurtured in England for most of your life, Mister Guinea,' said Aaron Drinkwater with manifest regard. 'I daresay you understand the English from inside the citadel, so to speak. Because of your familiarity, what you say about England is food for thought. I shall indeed ponder deeply on your observations. Given the straits and dangers experienced by many of your colour, 'tis most heartening to hear that some have met with good companionship and kindness. Abolition, then, should bring a change for the better.'

Considering Drinkwater's characteristic caution, thought Jonas, I am heartened by his change of heart.

'Alas,' griped Reverend Whitehouse, 'England will not adopt the moral code of the Quakers. 'Twill be at least half a century before abolition becomes law. But I will campaign for abolition even though I may not see it come to pass.'

Picking up his glass, Jonas looked at Faith and nodded towards the door. Leaving the discourse in full flow, she followed him across the hall.

Redolent with wood smoke, paper, ink and leather, the library was warm and hushed.

'From the very beginning,' she said quizzically, 'Aaron Drinkwater was the sole member set entirely against the first expedition of the *Redemption* to free runaways. The man appears to have experienced a conversion from his earlier mind-set.'

'Methinks,' he said, sitting down beside her, 'the accomplishment of the *Redemption* ensured that outcome.'

'Was Drinkwater actually opposed to the venture?'

'Nay, my love. Drinkwater was simply afraid of failure and its terrifying consequences. The *Redemption* demonstrated that such an untested dangerous venture could be covertly and simply accomplished. We lost no man overboard, nor to arrest or musket shot, although two men did suffer flesh wounds. Unlike his father, Aaron Drinkwater is faint-hearted and dislikes getting his hands dirty. But the *Redemption*'s accomplishment supported by tangible evidence, namely his share of the profits from the voyage, certified his change of mind. It would seem that whatever is deemed impossible on this earth remains so until it is accomplished. Everyone then acclaims the victor, even the erstwhile faint-hearted.'

Sipping wine, she smiled and stroked his neck.

''Tis but another step towards abolition,' he said. ''Tis only on the verge of catastrophe do people have a mind to change.'

'Methinks the Sommersett Fund is a significant part of that,' she said.

He kissed her lips softly. 'We should rejoin the members.'

By four o'clock the gathering was at an end. Together with Mistress Beecham, the members boarded their vehicles for the journey back to London.

Watching the departing carriages with Faith, Jonas pondered aloud, 'I wonder if in the fullness of time anyone will remember the sacrifice and labours of the abolitionists?'

'Someone will,' said Faith softly.

'I hope so,' growled Parson Merriweather tersely. 'Someone will have to take responsibility for this little tragedy. Memory may well aid that.'

The League's Sommersett Fund had netted eighty-three pounds.

Henry Jackson

Limehouse
Monday
6 January 1772
08.30 hrs

In the hallway of Pilgrims, Jonas waited. Looking out the window, he watched a flurry of snow drift across the Highway. Just then, Francis Barber's hired carriage drew up outside.

Bidding Faith an affectionate farewell in the hallway, he stepped out onto the Highway. Carrying a linen haversack of provisions, he boarded the carriage with his minders, Messrs Tapsell and Foggerty.

'Pray inform the driver of our destination, Jonas,' said Barber with a welcoming grin.

'To the Deptford landing stage, driver,' he said.

'Across the Thames?' asked Barber.

'We take a wherry to Locke's Wharf on the Isle of Dogs. From there we hail a carriage for Narrow Street near the Limehouse Cut.'

Spurred on by the flick of the whip, the horse-drawn carriage sped off down the cobbled thoroughfare.

'Is Limehouse not a little chancy?' asked Barber, frowning.

'We go to visit Henry Jackson,' he replied, 'who has agreed to help us collect a donation for Sommersett from the black poor where he lives. As regards the hazards of Limehouse, we journey with Mister Tapsell and Mister Foggerty.'

Smiling and tipping his head respectfully at the minders, Barber enquired, 'Who dwells in Limehouse?'

'Poor whites share the squalid hamlet with eighty or ninety poor blacks and lascars. Working whites labour in all manner of trades. A few blacks work as servants to rich whites. To some extent, because of pro-slavery agitators militating against the black presence in England, most blacks can find only irregular employment as soldiers and sailors, watchmen, labourers, stevedores, cutpurses and beggars. I need not tell you, Francis, that we are fortunate.'

Nodding his agreement as they arrived at the Deptford landing stage, Barber smiled and stepped down from the carriage.

Leaving the wherry on the Isle of Dogs, they boarded a carriage hailed by the minders.

'Is Henry Jackson the secretary valet thrown from his lodging and service?' asked Barber.

'Aye.'

'Is that bag you carry for him?'

'Aye.'

'Your loyalty is truly heart-warming, Jonas.'

'Henry is a dear friend,' he replied.

'Henry was a fool to try his luck,' said Barber curtly. 'He should know that familiarity from the lower classes is offensive to the rich. In losing sight of his station, Henry crossed sacred boundaries. His experience in service should have told him that he was in the employ of an unreconstructed bigot.'

Accepting Barber's cuttingly accurate summing up of Henry's downfall, Jonas leaned forward.

'Since that tragic episode, Henry had to take any employment to feed and provide for his family. He found a position as secretary and manservant to the vicar of St Anne's Church in Limehouse. To supplement his income, for tuppence he writes letters and petitions about all manner of requests, principally for those at odds with their employers or the law. He says the black poor of Limehouse want to contribute to the League's fund for Sommersett's defence. Justifiably, they see Sommersett's fight as their fight and I might add, 'tis our fight as well, Francis.'

Momentarily thoughtful, Barber nodded.

'That it is,' he said solemnly. 'If Sommersett loses his case, the streets of London will be an even more dangerous locale for people of colour.'

Harbouring more than an air of discontent, Limehouse was a sulphurous maze of squares, dead ends and blind alleys. Noxious gases combined with wood smoke diffused the daylight. The atmosphere was tainted. Emptied slops added to the squalor and the slime in the gutters. Contagion festered in puddles and nooks and crannies.

'A hellish environment,' said Barber.

'The worst lodgings I have seen in London,' said Jonas.

Snow was lightly falling. Turning into Narrow Street, the carriage was obstructed by rambling pedestrians. Slowing to walking pace, the vehicle threaded its way along the bustling street. Besides the cries of the street traders and babble of the pedestrians, the thoroughfare shook with the rattle and screech of carriages, carts and overloaded tumbrils.

'Good God,' exclaimed Barber. ''Tis the nether world of the damned. Given Henry's former affluent location, how can he survive these conditions?'

'Slavery would seem to be more unbearable,' said Jonas impassively, staring out of the window.

Icy winds off the River Thames carried the stench of sewage. As well, Limehouse reeked of wet horses and manure. Piles of garbage lay rotting in the street. Lumps of excreta floated along an open drain running along the north side. Occasionally, hands emptied chamber pots out of windows onto passers-by, after which a ruckus ensued.

It was colder now. Pulling his cloak tightly around him, Jonas espied barefooted, matted-haired urchins in ragged jerkins and breeches pulling tricks on the tinkers, street traders and foot traffic. Given the noisy queues on the cobbles, the pie shop and bakery were clearly doing brisk trade.

Seeing Barber's continuing consternation at the dirt-besmeared hovels, he pressed his lips together and sighed inaudibly.

'Henry's fate could well have been ours,' he muttered.

Next to the newly opened Limehouse Cut, where the Lime Canal empties into the River Thames, the carriage halted. Set slightly back from the frozen cobbles of the narrow road, Henry Jackson's abode was the first of five decaying two-storey terraced cottages. Smoke was rising from its blackened chimney. Fronted by grimy studded doors with corroded strap hinges, the crazed dwellings had crumbling brick walls and knotty timber beneath tiled roofs sprouting foliage.

'Oh Henry,' Jonas sighed gloomily, seeing the disbelief that belaboured Barber. 'Henry could have fared much worse, he could have been sold.'

'As can we,' said Barber with chagrin.

Rattled by the humiliating truth, he grinned anxiously at his taciturn minders, Messrs Tapsell and Foggerty.

'Thank God we have you gentlemen,' he said, smiling at them.

'Yer safe wi' us, Mister Guinea,' growled Mister Foggerty. 'We got no liking fer sellin' 'umans. 'Taint godly.'

Leaving the minders with the parked carriage, Jonas stepped down onto the cobbles with Barber and the haversack. Pausing by the roadside, he scanned the dismal neighbourhood.

A community of tightly-packed rundown houses lined both sides of the street. He could see and feel eyes gawking through broken patched windows. Dressed in a sea-green woollen cloak and with Barber in a black roquelaire, he felt conspicuous. Passers-by were friendly, though a few baulked and gasped. Halting at the sight of them, a pair of blackened tradesmen grinned and waved at them from the opposite side of the street. Heartened by the kindly salutation, he smiled and waved back.

Proceeding to the closest cottage, Jonas knocked. Hinges creaked as the door was slowly pulled open. Clad in washed-out jerkin and breeches, an almost unrecognisable slim dark figure in his early forties stood blinking in the daylight.

''Tis me, Henry,' said Jonas, chuckling.

Recognition suddenly flooded the man's face.

''Tis indeed thee, Jonas,' cried Henry, throwing the door wide open. 'My dear friend, welcome to my humble abode. Let me take your cloaks. Though your letter said sixth January, you did not say what time to expect you. By chance, my employer the vicar has journeyed to Hampshire and has given me a few days off.'

Progeny of a married wine merchant and his African maidservant, Henry was born in a Clerkenwell boarding house. Given a classical education at a reputed Church school, he was aged twenty before he landed an excellent situation as valet and then as secretary to the rich shipowner, Ambrose Hennessy. Employed for gone twenty years, Henry's prospects looked assured until he was unceremoniously sacked.

Through many of his years at Thomas Beecham, Chandlers, Jonas had kept company with Henry for games of quadrille in withdrawing rooms and taverns. Both of contentious hue from comfortable circumstances, they became close companions. During an unforgettable sunlit stroll along the rural banks of the River Thames, he heard an explosive secret — Henry was having a hot-blooded dalliance with his master's daughter. Jonas was certain that the testy shipowner would have not ever countenanced any mixed match for his fragrant offspring. Luckily, the consummated affair bore no fruit and remained undiscovered.

On many a night with Henry in the Devil's Tavern by Wapping Wall, a hostelry of dubious reputation, he quaffed untold goblets of port and Madeira. In its dark wood-panelled confines, they composed informative newssheets and petitions for the League's campaign to abolish the slave trade. There was one night, invited to victuals in a certain moneyed dining room, they had afterwards repaired to the Devil's Tavern for strong alcohol to reflect on the bigoted remarks made in their presence by a few. Irrespective of the energies spent circumventing the narrow-minded, they had as well spent uproarious times with trusted white friends and colleagues.

Then came that terrible moment when Henry arrived in the Devil's Tavern, tearful, thunderstruck and tight-lipped with a curdled visage. Over the tavern's long, winding pewter counter, he trickled out the account of his humiliating expulsion from the residence of Ambrose Hennessy. Given that Henry had lived in considerable comfort for over two decades and had just been made homeless, he was plainly frightened of the morrow.

Church bells chimed nine o'clock.

''Tis getting late, my dear friend,' Henry had said fearfully. 'This night, I trust I will find shelter in a boarding house in Limehouse. I am really scared, Jonas. I know not how to live without the comforts. More than most, I have an education. I must begin again in Limehouse.'

Taking his friend's jittery hands, Jonas's voice had cracked when he spoke.

'I will miss you muchly, Henry,' he had said, pressing a folded five-pound note into his hand. 'Pray accept this small sum as token of my friendship. You are not alone, Henry. You can count on me. Let me know your whereabouts when you are settled.'

Like a dead soul with his haversack of worldly goods, Henry had stepped out into the icy night air. Cutting a tragic figure, he headed for Limehouse seeking shelter and hopefully a home. Bidding him farewell, Jonas had wondered whether Henry's imprudent tryst had played any part in his downfall.

''Tis good to be with thee again, my friend,' said Jonas, swallowing the lump in his throat. 'Of course you remember Francis Barber?'

Pumping their hands in the dreary candlelit hallway, Henry turned to the fair-haired white woman of waning good looks by his side. Though dowdily dressed in a shapeless brown smock and in her late thirties, her chubby presence illuminated the tiny passage.

'Mistress Lorna Jackson, my good wife,' said Henry with unbridled pride. 'After my dismissal, I would have been destitute had it not been for her coming to my aid. Alas, my friends, our children are away visiting their grandparents this day. You will meet them on your next visit. Come, we have a warm punch in the parlour for thee.'

''Tis indeed an honour to greet thee, Mistress Jackson,' said Jonas, smiling broadly and shaking her surprisingly soft, slender hand.

''Tis good to know our friend is in your trusting hands, Mistress Jackson,' said Barber, flourishing a gracious bow.

Giggling into her hand while bobbing a crisp curtsy, a soft Irish accent breezed from her lips. 'Why the pleasure be mine ter be sure, gentlemen,' said Mistress Jackson coyly.

Motioning to Barber, who was plainly moved by what met his eyes, Jonas followed Henry down a short passage to his best room. Its destitution shredded his senses.

A cast-iron cooking fireplace warmed the cramped, antiquated parlour. Daylight poured through a small window with open shutters. Dark odours of mildew tainted the smell of freshly baked bread. A cracked-faced clock in a lopsided mahogany carcase was perched on a rough-hewn, charred mantelpiece. The elderly timepiece said eleven. At the heart of the simple room, an earthenware jug and wooden mugs idled on a split oak table bounded by four broken chairs. Cooking utensils dangled down dank discoloured walls, as well as a cluster of garments, slave auction notices and a poster promoting the Mothers Against Slavery Society. A few feet away was a reasonably accomplished drawing of two smiling sons. In such straitened circumstances, a fashionable withdrawing room was by now for Henry a distant memory.

Masking his discomfiture, Jonas produced an unaffected smile and held out his present.

'Pray accept this small contribution, Henry,' he said softly.

Looking into the haversack, Henry raised tear-filled eyes.

'Brethren,' he gasped, wiping his eyes on the sleeve of his jerkin and then clutching his wife to his side. 'I have not the words to tell you how much your presence and your gift means to us.'

'Then say not anything, my friend,' said Jonas. 'Your company, wellbeing and laughter are enough.'

Filling mugs with punch, Mistress Jackson gushed, 'A toast ter 'Enry's dear friends, fer times gone by and fer good times ter come.'

'Aye,' they chorused, taking swigs of punch.

'Pray be seated, brethren,' said Henry. 'Methinks you have journeyed far in support of an action that may have far-reaching consequences. How fares brother Sommersett?'

'A writ of *habeas corpus* prohibiting Sommersett's removal from England has been granted,' said Barber eagerly. 'Sommersett is out on bail and appears before Lord Mansfield at the King's Bench on seventh February.'

'Bail for a slave must indeed be a precedent,' said Henry, puckering his eyebrows. 'What is the disposition of this judge on the issue of slavery?'

'I gamble ye did not know that Lord Mansfield's great-niece is black,' said Jonas.

'Mother of God,' cried Mistress Jackson. 'That be good tidings ter be sure.'

'I did not know that,' said Henry. 'But will such a fact influence Mansfield's judgment? Who is the lady? From where does she hail?'

'Dido Elizabeth Belle,' said Jonas, 'the illegitimate daughter of Admiral Sir John Lindsay and Maria Belle, an African slave. Debarred from raising her in his marital home, she was dispatched by her father to live in Kenwood House with his uncle, Earl Mansfield. Thus, instead of being enslaved on a sugar plantation, Dido Elizabeth Belle has been raised as a gentle Englishwoman on an estate. Such are the times. I trust any attachment to his great-niece will figure in the deliberations of his Lordship.'

'Sommersett needs every timely vagary in an uncertain wind,' said Barber. 'His freedom and mayhaps his life hangs on a thread. And we need every penny to support his case which methinks has implications for even the freed.'

'We got no time to waste,' said Henry, pulling on a faded frock coat. "Tis bitter outside. I say we finish our punch. Then we go to meet friends who will help raise a black donation to the Sommersett Fund.'

'Wi' the growing anti-slavery mood among the people, the Fund is bound ter draw support,' said Mistress Jackson quietly, knocking back a swig of punch. 'Men 'ttackin' them fightin' slavery is risin'. 'Tis at times gettin' a tad dodgy on the streets fer them 'gainst the trade.'

'I would welcome your thoughts, Mistress Jackson,' said Jonas, putting down his mug, 'about the feelings of the Limehouse citizenry on the issue of slavery.'

Taking a lusty swig of punch, she was forthright:

'In Lime'ouse we poor whites live a bit like slaves an' sweat like slaves at work. Most o' them I meet, o' the ones 'oo know 'bout the slave trade, 'ave sympathy fer slaves. It were jes' two day ago, traders passed the 'at roun' the penny market fer Sommersett. Seems more an' more white an' black poor an' workin' women's 'sociations is giving money ter Sommersett. In confidence like, Henry an' me work fer the cause. Regular an' real quiet like, he meets wi' black campaigners, men o' yer 'quaintance, Mister Guinea. On some evenings, I meet wi' the Limehouse Women's Anti-Slavery Guild.'

Rapt in her account and confidential disclosure, Jonas sat smiling admiringly at her.

'Your opinion is undeniably enlightening, Mistress Jackson,' said Henry, beaming proudly at his wife and then gently kissing her on both cheeks.

'Send away the carriage, Jonas,' said Henry. 'Your minders can wait here in the parlour. Mistress Jackson will give them soup, a warm drink, gin and good chatter. We may well be some time.'

'Thank you kindly, Henry,' said Jonas. 'I shall let the carriage go and bring our minders inside.'

Following Henry at a brisk pace, they walked a quarter mile along the towpath past the first great bend of the Lime Canal. Turning right by a canal side alehouse, they continued through a narrow alleyway into Ropewalk Gardens. Outside a squalid three-storey dwelling with a red door, they sidestepped a group of drunken sailors. Of varied ethnicities, the grubby sailors were shouting sea shanties and swapping obscenities with brassy women drooping out of the windows.

''Ow much?' yelled a pustule-faced sailor.

'Shilling for a quick 'un,' said a flabby sickly-looking woman.

'Shilling for me an' me mates,' he replied brazenly.

'Shilling each,' she said flatly, clearing her throat gutturally and gobbing phlegm onto the cobbles.

'Scumbag,' snarled the sailor, making for the red door. 'I got me bodily needs. Shilling it is then.'

'First floor on yer right me lovely fer rumpy-pumpy wi' a scumbag,' she cackled, drawing a flimsy discoloured piece of cloth across her window.

'Lady of diseased pleasure,' said Henry, grinning.

'Methinks,' chuckled Jonas, 'she won't be found in *Harris's List of Covent Garden Ladies*.'

'A fetid woman for a scabby seadog,' muttered Barber, sinking into his roquelaire. 'The well-dressed whores who make *Harris's List* are rather more fetching.'

'You have some experience then, Francis?' sniggered Jonas.

''Tis hard not to notice the harlots in doorways around Piccadilly,

Jonas,' said Barber, laughing. 'Methinks they might even have caught your eye.'

Grinning, Jonas made no reply.

Stopping in front of the house next door, Henry announced, 'Brethren, we are here.'

Taking a step backwards, Jonas surveyed the property.

The double-fronted three-story boarding house groaned with decay. Slate tiles were missing from the warped moss-ridden roof. Wet crumbling bricks lined the begrimed facade and weeds sprouted from deep settlement cracks. The lodging might have been considered derelict but for the hop jig, hornpipe and fiddle, the chatter and laughter purling from the residence.

'This house,' said Henry sadly, shaking his head, 'is the abode of two couples with two children, two childless couples, two elderly women sharing, two single men and two single women, both widows.'

Aghast at the number living in the crowded habitat, Jonas's mouth fell open.

'Come,' said Henry, knocking on the splintered door.

Moments later, a huge hawk-eyed jet-black man stood over him.

Clad in a frayed, fustian justaucorps coat with mariner's cuffs, the giant's big head was squeezed into a cramped Monmouth cap. Giving a broad smile, he spoke with a deep gruff island accent.

'Come in quick brudder. You stan' out there, 'Enry, an' you freeze them balls in English.'

'I bring friends I want you to meet,' said Henry.

Stepping back into the passage aloofly, the big man eyed them, hands on hips.

'They call me Breathless,' he said warmly, ''cos me mouth full o' words. You be them two fancy blacks o' the League 'Enry bin gabbin' 'bout. An' in such fancy white man dress too. I not met yer kind 'fore now. You black and friend o' 'Enry so you be brethren. You go wi' we an' 'elp collek fer brudder Sommersett.'

Captivated by the affable openness of the prodigious character, Jonas shook his big calloused palm.

'Jonas Guinea, one fancy black from the League.'

'Francis Barber, another fancy black from the League.'

Rocking with laughter, Breathless slapped his thigh and turned away.

'Come meet udders,' he said, ambling down the passage. Side-stepping children in swordplay with sticks, he beamed and opened a door.

The whiff of ale and rum and the reek of tobacco wafted into the passage. Daylight poured through a tiny window into the small room. Cheered by the heat emanating from the hearth and fitted beehive oven, Jonas's nostrils twitched at the trace of herbs. A crooked table stood in the centre of the chamber. It was littered with bottles, wooden mugs, petitions, clay pipes and curios from foreign parts. Huddled in a dark corner were rolled-up straw-filled mattresses. Rising from stools and smiling with extended hands stood two light brown men in their early thirties.

Taking the arm of the lanky oval-faced man with loosely crimped hair, Breathless made introductions.

'This be Tom,' he said. Pointing at the chubby-faced man with tightly curled black hair, he said, 'an' 'e be Jack. They jes' bin paid-off a barque on a passage from India.'

Tom carried out a playful inspection before speaking. 'You be lookin' right posh, brethren,' he said with a cockney accent. 'Methinks you done right good. I bet them snotty whites not see you same as them, you not being white like.'

'In truth?' asked Jonas.

'Aye,' said Tom.

'Some treat us as equals,' replied Jonas. 'Most pay us no heed and a few are blatantly hostile. Would you not agree, Francis?'

'Aye, I would, Jonas,' said Barber. 'And like you, Tom, danger dogs our footsteps every day.'

'Lest you be hoodwinked by the cut of our jib,' said Jonas, chuckling. 'We are confident our garments provide no more security for us than for beggars.'

'You jes' 'ave ter tread carefully in the fine parts you live, Mister Guinea,' scoffed Jack. ''Ere in the slums of Limehouse we live every day on the bone. 'Roun' 'ere whites' be too poor ter fret 'bout we. What yer 'ave ter watch out fer is yer footpads an' them not liking blacks. Most folks 'roun' 'ere be right neighbourly.'

'Until now,' said Barber, shaking his head with wonder, 'I had not appreciated just how many poor whites had befriended poor blacks.'

''Tis the time-honoured practice of the poor regardless of difference, Francis,' said Henry impassively. 'When people have less they share more.'

'Despite the difference in luck or complexion, my friends,' said Jonas with a heartfelt tone of voice, 'in the eyes of bigots we all look the same.'

'If an edicated body got 'nough grit ter climb white man's ladder,' said Tom, grinning broadly and looking directly at him, 'a body wi' luck wi' reach the top. Me wonder if Englishmen really like that.'

Laughing at the comment, Barber raised his eyebrows.

Smiling thoughtfully, Jonas changed the prickly subject. 'About Sommersett—'

'Brethren, we must be on our way,' said Breathless impatiently.

Spurred on by the urge to get cracking, they set off along Ropewalk Gardens for the first alehouse. Negotiating a labyrinth of alleyways, Jonas thought the narrow passages gave excellent cover for footpads. Passing the hat in diverse slum dwellings and alehouses, he was shocked by the evident deprivation. Rotting rats, cats, dogs and horses speckled the streets and lay in nooks and crannies. Carriages splattered putrid puddles over irate pedestrians. Tousled, skeletal urchins with pimpled faces pulled scraps from gaseous banks of rubbish.

On most streets, beggars clustered around braziers for heat, while toasting all manner of dubious fare. In dark dank rat-infested garrets, he saw them huddled in damp and blackened bare rooms. Sprawled in a stinking passage were two semi-naked bodies with grotesquely bloated death masks; woolly black hair said one was black. Had they expired *in situ* or had they been dumped? His wits reeled in the noxious atmosphere. The air was heaving with contagion. He found his afternoon to be a mind-numbing sojourn of donations, depravity, dirt, distress and death.

If ever hell existed, 'tis surely here, he thought.

Coupled with the threat from press gangs as well as numerous privations endured by common citizens, the blacks as well lived each day in fear of kidnap by the slave-hunters. In the alehouses and black dwellings, he was heartened by the response to Sommersett's bail. Pennies aplenty rolled in from the poor blacks of Limehouse. Poor whites as well put pennies into the fund. After about three hours, collecting donations came to an end.

Outside the final alehouse with his companions, Jonas looked into the sailcloth pouch.

'How much?' he asked.

'The black and white poor of Limehouse,' said Henry proudly, 'have donated fourteen pounds and sixteen shillings to the Sommersett Fund.'

Barber whistled.

'An astonishing figure from such circumstances,' he said.

Saddened by the fraternal leave-taking of Breathless and the seamen at their lodgings in Ropewalk Gardens, Jonas was buoyed by the sum total he was carrying back to the League.

'Tell yer League tha' this lodging be a safe house fer runaways,' said Breathless. 'They be needin' a place ter 'ide. Bring 'em 'ere. We pass 'em on ter white men 'oo forge papers ter make 'em free men.'

'Your secret is safe with us, Mister Breathless,' said Jonas quietly. 'We shall very soon need to use your safe house. I shall be in contact.'

By the time they reached Henry's cottage, daylight was waning. Icy gusts hurtled down Narrow Street. Soot swirled in the polluted air. Pulling his cloak tightly around him, Jonas gripped the pouch holding the Limehouse donation. Anxious about the journey back to Pilgrims, he sought out his escort.

'Carriages could spurn thee, Mister Guinea,' said Mister Foggerty impassively. 'In yer stead, me an' Tapsell will go on ter Narrow Street an' 'ail a carriage.'

'Many thanks, Mister Foggerty. As well, I thank thee kindly for your protection this day. We shall settle up at Pilgrims.'

Church bells pealed four o'clock.

Mortified by the damp impoverished environs of Limehouse, he craved for the clean bedding and nutritional comforts of Pilgrims.

Just about to depart from the cottage, he pressed a folded five-pound note into his friend's palm.

'I have known you for gone fifteen years, Henry,' he said in low voice. 'I shall always be there for you as you were for me.'

After bidding Mistress Jackson a warm-hearted farewell, he gave Henry an affectionate hug.

'We shall visit again soon, my friend.'

'Gratitude overwhelms me, Jonas,' said Henry, wiping his eyes. 'After I was thrown out, I lost all my friends, except for you and Francis. I thank you both for your steadfastness.'

On the point of departure, Barber pushed a folded five-pound note into Henry's hand.

'We must soon meet again, Henry,' he said, with a tremor in his voice. 'You can as well depend on me, my friend.'

Clattering up Narrow Street in a hired carriage, Jonas turned around. In the waning light on the cobbles beside his wife, Henry looked a forsaken figure. The sight was as much as Jonas could bear. Sitting further back into his seat with watery eyes, he gazed out of the window and fell into thought.

''Tis indeed a pity Henry forgot to hold back his education and intelligence from his employer's guests,' said Barber sympathetically. 'With fortitude, he has weathered his fall in status as well as the deprivations of Limehouse. Incredibly, he harbours no grudge for his ruin. But his fate serves to remind a body not to forget his place, particularly when in humorous banter with the moneyed.'

Cocking his head thoughtfully, Jonas nodded, smiled and quietly replied, 'Despite his impoverishment, Henry has two friends he can trust, Francis. As a result, our friend is rich.'

Adjournment

Deptford
Thursday
10 January 1772
16.30 hrs

'Farewell, dear Rose,' said Faith, embracing her oldest confidante. Opening the front door, she whispered, 'and someday you must tell me what changed your attitude to plantation slavery.'

'Not someday, dear Faith,' said Rose Greenwood with a calculating smile. 'I shall tell you all when we meet at the King's Bench for Sommersett's hearing. We must both keep watch for the announced date. After the proceedings, I shall be delighted to receive you and Jonas in Rye.'

'And we shall take up your kind invitation,' said Faith, smiling broadly. 'By the way, dear sister, I look forward to meeting your anonymous admirer. But as well you must promise to visit us in Kent.'

'I promise,' cried Rose, waving and laughing as her carriage rolled away.

Following her friend's departure, Faith entered the panelled ground-floor office. Finding her husband and Mistress Beecham reviewing the order books on the partner's table, she paused. Both looked up, gave her a warm smile and returned to the task in hand. Content to wait, she smoothed creases out of the embroidered bodice of her gown and ambled to the window. A light flurry of snow began to fall as she looked along the Highway. Her thoughts drifted back to the island of Pertigua and a glorious June day in 1751.

During a ride in a landau across her plantation, Rose had expressed her unqualified support for plantation slavery. One year after Faith's migration from Pertigua, Rose unexpectedly sold her plantation and freed all her slaves. What incident had transformed her into an abolitionist? She still would not say. But fitting her epiphany, she returned to Sussex and settled on her arable estate near Rye. And true to the resolve in her renaissance, she attended this morn's session of the King's Bench and brought word of the adjournment.

I must speedily share her report with Jonas and Mistress Beecham, thought Faith.

Engrossed in the legal opinions on Sommersett's plea, she was startled by an easterly rattling the windows and dumping a heap of snow. Shortly, the grimy cobbles submerged under a white fleece. Close to the windowpane, her breath fogged the glass. Tracing a smiling face on the pane, she stepped back to appraise her naive artwork.

Following tuition, Solomon and Olivia can take supper with cook and Honeypenny in the kitchen, she thought. Jonas and I have to talk about the disquieting indecision at the King's Bench. Mistress Bracegirdle has sent word from Greensleeves that Parson Merriweather had taken to his sick bed. As soon as the snows have melted, we shall leave the children in the care of Mistress Beecham and journey to Kent to see our dear friend. We have much to do before we leave.

Her recollection was disturbed by hammering on the front door. Thereafter, she heard the unexpected caller ushered into the hall.

'Who can be calling in such a bitter climate?' whispered Mistress Beecham.

Peering through the window at the snow-white steps, Faith said, 'I see not anyone at the front door.'

Hearing the soft knock on the office door, she turned and waited.

'Come in,' said Mistress Beecham.

Slower now, aged fifty-six, Tuppence Honeypenny shuffled into the chamber.

Smiling affectionately at the aging housekeeper, Faith winked furtively at Jonas.

'Mister Puddlewick calls,' wheezed the housekeeper absently, as if about to keel over.

'Show him in and pray fetch a decanter of brandy, Mistress Honeypenny,' said Mistress Beecham. 'Puddlewick's tidings must be pressing for him to venture out in such inclement conditions.'

Taking a chair at the table, Faith said, 'I wager Puddlewick comes with word of an adjournment for the Sommersett case.'

'Why say you?' asked Mistress Beecham, with a quizzical look in her eye.

'Rose Greenwood called by earlier,' she replied. 'My friend is unbelievably well-informed.'

'If what you say is true, Faith,' said Mistress Beecham thoughtfully, 'then considering Puddlewick has taken it upon himself to traipse some distance through the snows, who will have the heart to tell him we have already been made aware?'

'Not I,' said Jonas, smiling warmly at his wife and taking her hand. 'If Sommersett wins 'twill help put the slave-hunters out of business. But it may not mean that from thence England's black citizens will be lawfully free and can walk without fear of abduction.'

'That indeed may be the unforeseen consequence of a favourable judgement,' sighed Mistress Beecham. 'A positive verdict may change the law but will it change minds and attitudes?'

Sitting back with a perplexed smile, Faith puckered her brow.

'Unforeseen consequence, Mistress Beecham?' she asked. 'Call me cynical, but 'tis difficult to believe that there is anything unforeseen about the customary inactivity following a reluctantly enacted law. Were it not for the fact that—'

Bursting excitedly into the chamber, Jeremiah Puddlewick was agog.

'A good day to you, Alice,' wheezed the shipowner. 'I have sped post-haste from the King's Bench. Sommersett's action has been adjourned to another date.'

'On what pretext, Jeremiah?' asked Mistress Beecham, with a surprised frown. 'Adjourned to what other date precisely?'

'Mansfield's clerk deflected my inquiries regarding the delay with codswallop,' replied the shipowner with exasperation. 'The pompous fellow stood there spouting no end of juristic hogwash about the pitfalls in setting precedents. His Lordship, he said, had much to ponder on. Or much scheming to cobble together, I'd say.'

Smirking at the shipowner's jibe, Mistress Beecham proffered a goblet.

'Take the weight off your feet, Jeremiah,' she said affably. 'Come warm yourself with a tipple of brandy. French, I might add. I trust Mistress Puddlewick is in good health?'

'Aye, that she is,' said Jeremiah Puddlewick, taking a generous swig of brandy. 'Mistress Puddlewick entertains our grandchildren this day. She sends you her warmest felicitations.'

''Tis apparent to me that Mansfield vacillates,' said Faith scornfully. 'By employing delaying tactics he avoids committing himself on the question — should he set a precedent by freeing a slave? Given the disdain of the gentry and certain Members of Parliament to the unrest in the populace over the issue of slavery, 'tis clear to me that the Sommersett case has them and the slave-owners downright vexed. Is slavery lawful in England? Will Mansfield endorse colonial laws which have not an English legal equivalent? Methinks his slave-owning connections will pressure him to leave the answer to such awkward questions as at present — ambiguous. And we all know a great deal of political and mercantile skulduggery has been accomplished under Union Flags of ambiguity.'

'Could it be that this judge merely hesitates before crossing the Rubicon?' asked Jonas, playing devil's advocate. 'For he knows once crossed there is no going back. Thus he concocts an expedient pause, which has raised the expectations of both the pro- and anti-slavery lobbies. Against a background of voices hostile to the slave trade, he seeks to make a judgment—'

Jeremiah Puddlewick interjected, 'You have my undivided attention, Mister Guinea.'

'Furthermore,' continued Jonas, 'Mansfield knows that much of the gentry depend on the continuance of slavery. He is, as well, aware that noble sensibilities prefer the trade be not so overt and not so close to home — better in the far-off plantations. So you see his landed slave-owning connections may as well influence his decision.

Lord Mansfield stands at the gates of history. Methinks His Lordship is the man of the moment.'

'If perchance Mansfield finds for Sommersett,' said Faith, lowering her voice and looking solicitously at her listeners, 'and thus endorses the freeing of slaves throughout England, has anyone considered how his judgment will be enforced?'

'I do believe you have put your finger on an unconsidered aspect of these proceedings, Mistress Guinea,' said Jeremiah Puddlewick. 'How indeed will a favourable verdict be enforced? Who will be waged to stop the slave-hunters?'

A hush followed the shipowner's question.

Calmly fanning her face and then taking a sip of wine, Mistress Beecham broke the silence.

'Having to weigh bigotry against moral justice amid so much anticipation must tire His Lordship so,' she said sarcastically. 'I suspect there will be many more postponements before this issue is adjudged. Nevertheless, I have reaped much satisfaction from the report about the consternation witnessed inside the Blackheath Golf Club, which I must add was all about Sommersett. Their disquiet suggests to me that England's financiers are mightily disturbed by being dragged on the back of events to the brink of change. Methinks in the current circumstances, something has to give, however little. Mansfield's judgment will say a great deal in respect of which direction England is travelling — forwards or backwards. You will of course have supper with us, Jeremiah?'

'Alas, I regret I cannot, Alice,' said Jeremiah Puddlewick. 'Captain Battersby is expected this evening. I came only to inform you of Sommersett's adjournment. As we speak, my carriage waits to carry me on to Greenwich. However, Mistress Puddlewick and I would be charmed to have you all to luncheon overmorrow. Pray extend my invitation to Reverend Whitehouse?'

'Gladly,' said Mistress Beecham, rising from her chair. 'Thank you for bringing such a encouraging report. Until luncheon then, Jeremiah, I can barely contain my excitement to speak with Mistress Puddlewick again.'

Following the shipowner's departure, Mistress Beecham walked to the office door.

'I must have a word with cook,' she said. 'Can I leave you to bring together the Cumberbatch and Sons order and settle our books, Jonas?'

'I shall take good care of that order and our books,' replied Jonas.

Stretching across the table, Faith squeezed his hand.

'I shall keep you company, my dearest,' she said.

With Jonas summarising the order books, she studied the father of her children. I know he wearies so of the politics engulfing his colour, she thought. Though he has not ever said as much, he behaves as if our morrows are inextricably linked with Sommersett's fate. For the most part he masks his feelings, but I know him and I am certain he masks his anger, for my sake and the sake of our children. I recollect his words after he had proposed.

'On the streets and in good society, dearest Faith,' he had said, 'any children we have will likely be deemed strange at first. Methinks most will come to accept them, but some might reject them. In these testing times, we will need unconditional trust in our marriage. I love you, Faith. And I know I can make you happy.'

'I love you without conditions, Jonas,' she had replied. 'You of all understand the stormy history that beset my years in Pertigua. The insecure existence you have experienced on the streets of England mirrors mine in Pertigua. Irrespective of our difference, my love, we are bound by marriage vows because of love. Have we not then volunteered to furrow the same road?'

'Aye, that we have,' he had replied.

At times he seems beside himself with rage about the prospects for our children, she thought. Why do I feel certain the adjournment of Sommersett's case is but a mere hiccup? As well I feel certain Sommersett will win. Mansfield's adjournments suggest he will do what is morally right in the end. Methinks Jonas is right — Mansfield falters before he crosses the Rubicon.

Raising his head above the stack of order books, Jonas smiled and held out his hand.

'Let us go and hear the learning of our children,' he said.

Taking his hand, she noted the bulging veins along his temples. A certain symptom of private turmoil, she thought.

'Sommersett will prevail, Jonas,' she said, squeezing his hand reassuringly. 'We must keep an eye on the listing of his hearing and attend.'

'Most certainly we will,' he said firmly. 'I suggest that while we are with Solomon and Olivia we put Sommersett out of our heads. At nine and seven years, they are far too young to be saddled with the sordid state of the social order. Children should have time only for poetry, arithmetic, science and Latin and bringing laughter to all our lives.'

Bursting into laughter at the brevity of his stated manual for child-rearing, she cradled his face in her hands and kissed him.

Positive Law

Pilgrims
22 June 1772
08.00 hrs

Suffused in lambent shafts of midsummer sunlight streaming through the open windows, the withdrawing room of Pilgrims sparkled.

Dressed in a frock coat, Jonas rapped his fingers restlessly against the doorframe.

'Are you not ready yet?' he demanded impatiently. 'Reverend Whitehouse and Mistress Beecham await us in the carriage.'

Throwing on a red wool riding habit, Faith waved him away and pouted.

'Intolerance befits not this day, Jonas,' she snapped, taking a last look in the giltwood mirror above the mantelpiece. 'Can you not see that I am just about ready?'

Despite his tetchiness, he entered the carriage and traded hearty greetings. Prepared for an ordained legal spectacle, Mistress Beecham exuded brass in a grey silk hooded Brunswick gown finished with striped ribbon ornaments. Perched piously and plumply beside her sat Reverend Whitehouse.

The exhaustion in the carriage was evident to Jonas. Bloodshot eyes said it all.

Taking pinches of snuff and then tapping his cane against the driver's box, Reverend Whitehouse called out, 'Westminster Hall if you please, driver!'

Lurching forward, the aged carriage clattered off along the Highway.

Brushing off her husband's irritation, Faith looked thoughtfully out of the window.

'This day will be ours,' she said.

''Tis the day of reckoning, Mistress Guinea,' said Reverend White-house, sneezing.

'I cannot abide any further adjournments,' said Mistress Beecham, frowning at the cleric.

'Methinks a sunny day augurs good fortune,' said Jonas, smiling to himself.

'Monetary or otherwise,' said Mistress Beecham, 'I pray that all the pains and labours on Sommersett's behalf prevail. His case has been argued by five advocates before Lord Mansfield at three separate hearings between February and May. I believe that Mansfield might even be sympathetic. Methinks he has considered this matter long enough. This day he must hand down his decision.'

Attempting to ease the tension in the carriage, Reverend White-house took pinches of snuff and said, 'Let me acquaint you all with some particulars about Westminster Hall.'

'Pray tell, Reverend,' said Faith gladly.

A timely distraction, thought Jonas.

With the vehicle rumbling along the cobbled Embankment, the elderly cleric described the inner sanctum of the English Judiciary.

'You should know,' said Reverend Whitehouse with a pedagogic air, 'that the King's Bench is the Supreme Court of Common Law and sits in Westminster Hall.'

'When was it built?' asked Jonas.

'Circa 1097 by William the Second.'

'William the Red?!' exclaimed Mistress Beecham, frowning. ''Twas suspected the poor man may have been murdered.'

'Aye, that is so, Mistress Beecham,' said Reverend Whitehouse, pausing to acknowledge her comment with an admiring smile. After taking pinches of snuff, he sneezed noisily into his handkerchief. 'The reconstruction of Westminster Hall,' he said, blinking repeatedly, 'if I remember rightly, was commissioned by Richard the Second about 1393.'

'All well and good, Reverend,' said Faith. 'But why have such an edifice at all?'

''Tis alleged,' said Reverend Whitehouse conspiratorially, 'that William devised his extravagant venture to ram home to his new subjects the authority and magnificence of his rule.'

'Such is the certainty of naked power of a kingly nature,' said Jonas.

'Once inside,' said Reverend Whitehouse, as if in the pulpit, 'I want you to turn your eyes to the rafters. Up there you will see a spectacle of construction in the unsupported hammer-beam roof. Said to be the largest medieval timber roof of its age. 'Tis indeed an extraordinary masterpiece.'

Smiling at the cleric's outline, Jonas said, 'Thank you kindly, Reverend Whitehouse, for such an instructive moment on the makings of the King's Bench.'

Soon after, the carriage turned into Whitehall. Suddenly, a cacophony of voices fractured the air. Hansom cabs, gigs, landaus and stagecoaches were dropping passengers. Babbling crowds lined both sides of the chaotic thoroughfare. Finding a gap in the traffic, the carriage jolted to a halt outside the Palace of Westminster.

Astonished by the sizeable crowd outside the vast Gothic edifice, Faith exclaimed, 'Mother of God!'

Shaking his head in wonder, Jonas smiled thoughtfully.

Either side of the grand porch of Westminster Hall, two factions separated by philosophy, rank and wealth had established a no-man's-land filled with angry shouts and lewd gestures in-between. Outwardly disinterested in the legal proceedings, street vendors sold matches, stuffed beef and cheesecakes, gammons of bacon, scissor-grinding services, hot gingerbread, oranges, meat pies and love songs. Quilled top-hatted newspaper correspondents prowled around cajoling people for comment. Newssheet hawkers were thrusting gossiped intelligence into eager hands, while pro- and anti-slavery militants dispensed leaflets and pressed individuals for signatures on petitions.

Closing his eyes with incredulity, Jonas thought he could have been at a festival. Walking to the left of the grand porch, he joined the abolitionists on the cobbles. Heartily greeting Francis Barber, the Puddlewicks and Mister Miracle, the Second Mate of the *Redemption*, he scanned the gathering. Marvelling at the huge number of black and white anti-slavery supporters, his voice broke when he spoke. ''Tis a long held aspiration to see black and white consorting without rancour, as if a daily occurrence.'

''Twould be most interesting,' mused Mistress Beecham, 'to see if and how the journalists report this event in their magazines.'

'How can they fail to report such a noteworthy occasion?' scowled Faith.

'Better ask if they will report it all?' asked Mistress Beecham, looking around the faces of her listeners. 'For instance, will they state that men and women from the white and black poor came here in great numbers to the King's Bench to support a black stranger?'

'It has not gone unnoticed that if the white or black poor exhibit anything constructive,' said Reverend Whitehouse acerbically, 'journalists and their editors seemed to be prone to a skewed sleight of hand.'

Smirking at the cleric's contempt for the press, Faith was wayward.

'Why Reverend Whitehouse,' she said cheerily, ''tis comforting that a member of the clergy recognises the abusive politics employed by the newssheets and magazines.'

Shaking his head at her good-natured aside, Jonas grinned.

'I may be aging and about to expire so far as you can see, Mistress Guinea,' said Reverend Whitehouse with a teasing twinkle in his eyes, 'but I am not yet too harebrained or delusional to spot biased narratives.'

'Given the metropolis seems alive with slave-hunters,' said Jeremiah Puddlewick, 'it must have been risky and irksome for the black poor to journey to Westminster. The hundreds here for Sommersett confirms their interest and their determination. 'Tis said they have meeting places, public houses and churches, which must as well prove there is a budding and ordered black presence in London.'

'That is all true, Mister Puddlewick,' said Jonas. 'I can as well testify to such, as can Mister Barber.'

'I can indeed, Mister Puddlewick,' said Francis Barber. 'Intelligence about slave-hunters and the trade are carried by couriers between meeting places, public houses and churches where the information is dispersed. That is how so many came to be here at the King's Bench.'

'That being so,' said Reverend Whitehouse sagely, 'England must begin to think of black people as more than servants, vagabonds and beggars, for they are demonstrably capable of combining and effecting trades like others.'

'I am of like mind, Reverend,' said Mistress Beecham. 'But I am just as flabbergasted by the hundreds of the white poor who came to show their support for Sommersett.'

'Married to Jonas it might be thought that I have interest vested in what I am about to say,' said Faith. 'Grinding conditions are endured by the white poor, yet many of them clearly have concern for others. 'Tis patent, at least to my eyes, that by their numbers and donations they undoubtedly have sympathy for the African. Did you know that there are even white beggars who black up with crushed charcoal because they attract more donations from the citizenry? 'Tis not the white poor who buy and sell Africans and 'tis not they who profit. In England, slavery is clearly the livelihood of an affluent minority…'

Catching an encounter in the corner of her eye, she lowered her voice. 'Our divas meet at last! What a timely omen for such an occasion.'

Following her eye line, Jonas smiled.

On the edge of the crowd, Rose Greenwood was closeted in conversation with Grace Puddlewick. Wearing hooded and jacketed Brunswick travelling gowns — one of flowered silk with double sleeves and the other of pink satin trimmed with striped ribbons — they were clearly dressed to be noticed.

Turning away, Mistress Beecham giggled behind her hand.

''Twas an accident in the offing,' said Jonas, laughing softly.

Soon, the divas migrated through the crowd to join the members of the League.

Nodding across the cobbled no-man's-land, Jeremiah Puddlewick lowered his voice. 'Thither stands the opposition, Mister Guinea,' he said contemptuously. 'Fancy-coated pro-slavery advocates we call Oran Utang philosophers.'

Scrutinising the other side, Jonas scorned the well-dressed assemblage of slave-owners, shipowners, merchants, sea captains, frock-coated men and their women. Grating his teeth, he seethed, 'Oran Utangs are riddled with bigotry.'

'And wading in atrocities,' added Jeremiah Puddlewick tersely.

Stepping onto a small crate from the ranks of the pro-slavery chapter, a thin-lipped, taciturn, lanterned-jawed firebrand livened up.

'Tarry a while, good friends,' he cried. 'Hearken to the sayings of Barnabas Bumpkin. Hearken to the dire prophecy I give you of the morrow. England stands at the edge of a grim state, nay, a critical state of affairs. I will tell you why. No doubt, my friends, you as well will have been startled by the growing numbers of sambos on London's streets. Does their wild revelry at all hours not threaten the peace? Will they not in time come to blows with their neighbours? Moreover, if mixing and intermingling fornications are not speedily outlawed, England will suffer such a consequential sullying of white blood, she will spawn a generation who will not know who they are nor who they belong to—'

'Humbug,' yelled a cultivated stentorian voice. 'Mixed-bloods are like us and different only in colour—'

Interrupting the cynic's assertion, a purple-faced Bumpkin launched a furious riposte:

'Heed not bleeding heart abolitionists like him,' he bellowed. 'Loafing about airing gushy claptrap about sambos being like the white man. I say hogwash. White men do not roam around naked and live in mud huts. And where would we be without writing and books? Are these sambos not better protected and better fed on our plantations, where as well they are taught to read and write and be brought closer to God with the scriptures? Without the transformative benevolent largesse of English plantation owners and the Royal Africa Company, assisted by the benedictions of our clergy, the sambos would hack each other to pieces and starve on the dark unchristian shores of Guinea. Sambos with whom I have myself conferred told me they much prefer the plentiful provisions and sunny abodes on the plantations—'

Clapping erupted from the pro-slavery devotees.

'Wot a whopper yer old windbag,' yelled a cockney woman abolitionist. 'May yer be struck down wi' yer lie in yer mouth. I 'ear yer jes' got skin an' bone cuttin' cane on yer 'eartless plantations.'

Glowering at his irate heckler and waving her away, Bumpkin turned arrogantly back to his hushed audience.

'Contrary to England's wellbeing, my friends,' he cried, angrily jabbing a thick finger at the anti-slavery crowd, 'these traitorous abolitionists would prefer to hamper England's economy. They would prefer that we, their countrymen, starve. Despite their bellyaching efforts, our plantations manufacture bullion in the form of sugar, the profit from which is the bedrock of countless trades and estates. Without sugar, think of the ensuing rise in unemployment—'

'Hogwash,' shouted an refined voice. 'Sugar is a wage-free commodity. Slave-owners don't pay slaves! No wage bill means our economy thrives on the back of free labour!'

Visibly rankled by the line of argument, Bumpkin mopped his brow and inclined towards his audience.

'What's more, my friends,' he cried, changing his line of attack, 'how can we ever be certain of the allegiance of brown-skinned halfcastes to England? Mark these words and forget not that you have been so forewarned.'

'Black men, soldier, sail and die for England in her wars!' cried an irate voice. 'Does that not show enough allegiance?'

Applause erupted from the abolitionists.

'Balderdash to Bumpkin,' said Faith furiously. 'Our children know who they are and who they belong to and much, much more besides. Anywise, what has that to do with the Sommersett trial?'

'Bumpkin is an *agent provocateur* if ever I saw one,' said Rose tetchily.

Exhibiting uncharacteristic rancour, Reverend Whitehouse growled, 'When Barnabas Bumpkin departs this world, he need go nowhere else. For any man who bears such malice is already in Hell.'

Quivering with soundless rage, Jonas wiped his brow.

'Bumpkin overtures what is to come,' he said. 'Should Sommersett win his freedom, I suspect agitators plan to then unsettle the populace with misgivings about stealthy integration. Bumpkin seems to have conveniently forgotten an embarrassing truth, that the slave-owners among his audience mask double standards. Are they opposed to assimilation when they lumber onto slaves, leaving them with enough offspring to populate an island? They even auction the offspring.'

Out of the corner of his eye, he saw Faith curdling. He took her hand.

'Forgotten?' continued Mistress Beecham, snorting derisively. 'Since the fleshly assaults take place in the out-of-sight plantations, it sounds more like forgotten duplicity I'd say.'

Turning his head, Jeremiah Puddlewick nodded towards the porch.

'The hatted rake in the portal is the villain of the piece, Mister Guinea.' he said. 'Charles Steuart is Sommersett's owner, and 'tis he who initiated this action to force the return of his runaway slave.'

A stout frock-coated man a step below Sommersett's owner suddenly raised his head. The arrogant profile matched Matthew Fleming.

Glowering at his adversary, Jonas snarled, 'Why am I not surprised by his repellent presence?'

Furnishing a fake smile, Fleming gave a curt nod and with a contemptuous air, turned away.

Scowling and muttering, Mistress Beecham hissed, 'The ogre himself!'

'Pay Matthew Fleming no heed, Mistress Beecham,' said Faith furiously. 'Rose and I have known the tiresome maggot since our childhood in Pertigua. It takes little effort to identify all the parasites on a grain of sand. We well know his rich loathsome family. All by his ham-fisted potbellied little self, his pater, Randolph Fleming, almost single-handedly inspired Pertigua's disastrous uprising. Likewise, Matthew Fleming is shuddersome and as incompetent as his father. 'Tis certain this day one side or the other will leave this place disappointed.'

Sidling up with barely restrained excitement, the Second Mate of the *Redemption* pulled him aside and out of earshot.

'I came to alert you, Mister Guinea,' said Mister Miracle, softly panting. 'Solomon Festus has been sighted hereabouts. 'Tis said the slave-hunter anticipates an adverse judgment for Sommersett. If such should transpire, I suspect he and his thugs will most certainly spring into action. With so many black citizens in this crowd, slave-hunters would make good a rich haul this day. I have informed Captain Battersby. Fret not, my friend, I will stick close by thee.'

'Many, many thanks, Mister Miracle,' said Jonas, mopping his brow with relief. 'Once again I find myself in your debt.'

'What was that about?' asked Faith.

'I will tell you all at Pilgrims,' whispered Jonas calmly.

Suddenly, a beaky black-cloaked Clerk of the Court appeared on the steps of the grand porch.

'Hear ye. Hear ye all who own an interest in these proceedings,' he droned mournfully. ''Tis forthwith demanded of all witnesses, if he knoweth or hath anything to say in the matter of Steuart versus Sommersett before the said justices of the King, they are summoned this instant to attend.'

Properly and duly announced, the Clerk rolled up his scroll and strutted back through the porch, followed by animated attendees.

Leaning on his ivory-handled cane at the head of the members of the League, Reverend Whitehouse shuffled into the hallowed confines of the Court of the King's Bench. Sitting down he took pinches of snuff. Sandwiched between Faith on one side, and Rose, Mistress Beecham and the Second Mate on the other, Jonas shuffled along a pew, sat down and looked around the rapidly filling chamber.

'Reverend Whitehouse said many things about this being the largest hall in all England,' he whispered dryly to his wife, 'but he failed to mention the faultless render on six-foot-thick walls. Otherwise, Westminster Hall is as he described. Can ye not hear the gossip? This manor hums with conspiracy.'

'I wager Matthew Fleming's snout is by now deep in a trough of treachery,' said Faith. 'Plotting is linctus to him. 'Tis said that even his marriage was a conspiracy of two unscrupulous spirits.'

Suddenly, the door opened on the raised dais at the far end of the high-ceilinged cavernous chamber. Walking to his chair, the Judge bowed to the courtroom and, with a haughty flourish, sat down.

Hoarse whispers shot across the courtroom from all directions.

'Great heavens, Faith,' hissed Jonas, 'from this distance, the Judge looks like a deity from another realm!'

Giggling into her hand, Faith winked at Rose, who grinned.

Seated beneath a gilded canopy, the Judge's poker face peered out from under a full-bottomed wig. The sixty-seven-year-old bigwig of his day, William Murray, First Earl of Mansfield, was resplendent in a violet robe faced with silk, black scarf, girdle, and scarlet tippet. A row of functionaries sat sternly on the tier below.

Bemused by the panoply of costumed figures, Jonas surveyed the spectacle.

He counted at least fifty bewigged barristers taking up the first four pews. Turning his attention to the characters assembled behind the lawyers, he grimaced; the next three rows were occupied by elegantly dressed aristocrats, wealthy merchants and slave-owners.

'These pernickety villains act as if they are beyond reproach,' he snorted, clenching his fists. 'First they strip James Sommersett of his freedom. Then his counsel must win an action that seeks to return him to the plantation of his owner, permanently depriving him of his God-given liberty. What justice is in that? I wonder even if the notion of justice will ever apply to a man in Sommersett's position.'

'A good number of the gentry have built their fortunes from slavery, Jonas,' said Mistress Beecham. 'In a nutshell, with ill-gotten resources they have, as well, bought themselves a seat at the High Table. And since they could not admit they had committed a sin in the first place *vis-à-vis* Sommersett, a compromise of a finding for the defence inside the imposing location of the King's Bench is what they might accept, if Mansfield so decides. I harbour a sense that we may be about to witness a concession bundled up in judicial procedure and judicial hogwash to promote its significance. It may yet free the slaves on England's shores, but will it ease a bothered conscience?'

'Why, Mistress Beecham,' said Faith, 'I did not know you could be so cynical?'

'My dearest Faith,' said Mistress Beecham sagely, 'cynicism about the despotic is a demanded requirement. Cynicism helps neutralise their contempt for the African. Moreover, cynicism scorns the duplicitous arguments employed by some clergymen to justify their involvement in slavery.'

'Foreign spectators might think that our peoples have assembled to settle our differences with words,' said Rose acerbically.

'Not by the looks of Matthew Fleming et al,' said Faith briskly.

Over the heads in the courtroom, Jonas saw Fleming and his associates glancing disdainfully around.

As well as pro-slavery supporters, the remaining pews were brimful with abolitionists, mostly from the labouring class. Having come to witness what was at hand for them and their offspring, black Londoners crowded the four rows of the rear upper gallery. Members of the League filled the last two rows.

Chatter flooded the packed courtroom. Hereupon the stage was set.

'In this humble woman's opinion,' said Faith, 'the question for this court is simple. Is slavery lawful in England?'

Heeding a sudden decrease of chatter in the vast chamber, Jonas whispered, 'Methinks the event is about to get underway.'

Striding before the Bench, the Clerk of the Court produced a scroll with a grandiose flourish.

'In this Trinity Term on the twenty-second of June 1772,' he cried, 'we are convened to conclude the case of the runaway, James Sommersett, brought before your Lordship on a writ of *habeas corpus*. It should be known that the said writ was obtained by one Granville Sharp.'

Bowing courteously to the assembled, Lord Mansfield began to read his judgment:

'We pay due attention to the opinion of Sir Philip York and Mr Talbot in the year 1729, by which they pledged themselves to the British planters for the legal consequences of bringing slaves into this kingdom, or their being baptised; which opinion was repeated and recognized by Lord Hardwicke, sitting as Chancellor on the 19th of October, 1749, to the following effect: he said, that trover would lay for a negro slave; that a notion prevailed, that if a slave came into England, or became a Christian, he thereby became emancipated...'

Captivated by this opening statement, Jonas smiled to himself. Craning forwards, he listened more intently as the Judge droned on and on and on. Suddenly, he heard the words:

'...The state of slavery is of such a nature that it is incapable of now being introduced by Courts of Justice upon mere reasoning or inferences from any principles, natural or political; it must take its rise from positive law; the origin of it can in no country or age be traced back to any other source: immemorial usage preserves the memory of positive law long after all traces of the occasion; reason, authority, and time of its introduction are lost; and in a case so odious as the condition of slaves must be taken strictly, the power claimed by this return was never in use here; no master ever was allowed here to take a slave by force to be sold abroad because he had deserted from his service, or for any other reason whatever; we cannot say the cause set forth by this return is allowed or approved of by the laws of this kingdom, therefore the black must be discharged.'

A prolonged shocked silence reverberated around the courtroom.

Blinking repetitively with astonishment, James Sommersett looked helplessly about. Having escaped from his owner, the man had been hunted with dogs for several days. Recaptured, he was clapped in irons aboard a vessel bound for Jamaica. Bailed by white godparents, he was supported by the abolitionist, Granville Sharp. Moreover, he was defended by counsel paid largely from public donations.

Frantic whispers darted about the courtroom.

Smiling with an elated look that said he'd won the day, the aquiline-nosed Francis Hargrave rose to his feet. Successful by his early thirties, like all of Sommersett's lawyers he had given his services *pro bono publico*. Bowing politely to the Judge, the barrister beckoned his client down from the dock.

Keeping his eyes on Sommersett, Jonas held his breath for what was about to follow.

Dressed in fresh drab brown jerkin and breeches, Sommersett plodded half-smiling down the short stairs. For a lengthy moment, the echo of his booted steps peppered the hush that reigned over the courtroom. Stepping onto the floor, he pumped his counsel's hand with vigorous gratitude. Then, he gazed around, clearly baffled and uncertain of his options.

Leaning down from his desk, Lord Mansfield tendered a benevolent smile.

'You are free to go, James Sommersett,' he said gently. 'You are a free man.'

'Thank'e kindly, sir,' said Sommersett, with visible incredulity. His deep frown said it all.

Profoundly affected by Sommersett's bewilderment, Jonas looked through a watery haze.

Suddenly, cheering and clapping accompanied by jeers and taunts erupted in the courtroom.

Heartened by the many congratulations, Sommersett managed a dazed smile.

Sighting his scowling antagonist, Jonas smiled with satisfaction.

'Methinks Matthew Fleming looks rather ashen,' he said with pretended concern.

'Unprincipled men are oft revitalised by a setback, Jonas,' warned Mistress Beecham. 'Mark my words, Matthew Fleming will be out to settle scores with someone.'

'Even if Fleming persists with plantation slavery with a renewed vigour,' said Jonas, 'this anti-slavery campaign, though fledgling at present, spells tribulations for his trade.'

A stentorian voice barked, 'Clear the courtroom!'

In between barristers and Granville Sharp's agents, Sommersett was steered towards the entrance. Pandemonium broke out. Uttering oaths and curses, pro-slavery advocates jostled the departing victors. Abolitionists raised a defensive passage to the porch.

'Clear the courtroom!'

The chamber rapidly emptied.

Mingling with high-spirited members of the League on the cobbles outside Westminster Hall, Jonas was tearful. With the word 'discharged' still pounding in his head, he grew truly overjoyed.

'Not once did you doubt Sommersett would win, dear wife,' he said.

'The superior instincts of a woman, dear husband,' said Faith flippantly.

'I second that,' said Rose.

'Aside from all that,' said Grace Puddlewick, 'we should remember that a consequence from Sommersett's victory is the fresh momentum it gives our cause.'

''Tis said about fifteen thousand slaves in England could be freed this instant,' said Elijah Drinkwater. 'Reckoned at one hundred and fifty pounds apiece, slave-owners are justly set to lose a mighty sum. I suspect the loss of slave price for slave-owners and the unemployment of freed slaves was what might have taxed and slowed Mansfield.'

'Methinks after this judgment,' said Jeremiah Puddlewick, 'many slave-owners could well baulk at paying wages and might instead throw their slaves onto the streets. I wonder if some owners will turn employer, bear the loss and retain the services of their erstwhile slaves as paid employees.'

'Is that honesty or optimism you espouse, Mister Puddlewick?' asked Rose Greenwood.

'Hope, Mistress Greenwood,' said Grace Puddlewick, laughing. 'My dear husband brims with it.'

''Tis thoughtful my better half draws attention to my only flaw,' guffawed Jeremiah Puddlewick.

'On this famous occasion,' said Mistress Beecham heartily, 'it calls for a celebration by the League at Pilgrims. Oh, that Thomas Beecham was here to witness this day.'

'Celebrations would be most appropriate, Mistress Beecham,' said Grace Puddlewick eagerly. 'Were Thomas Beecham here with us, God rest his dear soul, he would be glad to hear the chatter and laughter of such an occasion in his home.'

'Hundreds of black and white supporters are making merry with Sommersett in the nearby Lamb and Flag public house,' said Mister Miracle. 'And blow me down, they are said to be even charging admission.'

'Then we shall eagerly pay to cross the threshold,' said Elijah Drinkwater, laughing with gusto. 'But we shall stay only for the toast.'

'Afterwards,' said Mistress Beecham happily, 'we shall all repair to Pilgrims where a feast awaits us. This is a very special day.'

''Twill prove to be a defining moment in England's Atlantic slave trade, Mistress Beecham,' said Rose Greenwood. 'And 'tis a day the likes of that weasel Matthew Fleming believed would never come to pass.'

Discreetly tugging Jonas's sleeve and then glancing warily around, the Second Mate spoke in a hushed voice. 'Solomon Festus and his henchmen have been sighted, Mister Guinea. He was seen slinking into yonder tavern with Messrs Fleming and Co.'

Turning to his wife, Jonas caught the anxiety in her eyes.

'Despite Fleming's slaving forays,' he whispered reassuringly, 'this trade will in due course be abolished. I shall just have to stay out of his way until then.'

'How long do you think that will be?' she asked scathingly.

Cautioned by her mocking tone, he faltered.

What can I say? How can I tell her I have not an inkling of the date for abolition? Who does?

Following a prickly pause, he was curt. 'As long as it takes.'

He was unconvincing and he knew it.

'That is all very well, Jonas,' she said petulantly. 'So long as you know that 'as long as it takes' may well be for the rest of your days and mine.'

Perturbed by the reality in her retort, he nonetheless raised a worrying matter.

'Not once this day have I set eyes on Henry Jackson?'

'Nor I.'

'Unlike Henry not to attend Sommersett's hearing.'

'You fear for Henry, don't you?'

'Of late,' he said, taking her hands affectionately, 'slave-hunters have been alarmingly evident. Because of his work in hiding runaways, Henry could have long been a marked man. I have walked the dark narrow streets and alleyways of Limehouse. Aye, I fear for Henry. In the next day or two, I will take a carriage to his cottage.'

A Sapphic Enlightenment

Pilgrims
Friday
26 June 1772
19.00 hrs

Behind floor-length crewelwork curtains, the withdrawing room was candlelit hushed and tranquil.

Youthful in a cream chemise gown with turquoise sash, Faith belied her forty-nine years. Pouring Taylor's Port into two Georgian glasses, she carried them across the chamber.

A gadding coquette even at fifty-two, the pert-nosed Rose Greenwood sat poised on the Chippendale sofa. Seemingly composed in her grey silk gown, her furrowed brow said otherwise.

'This should help even out any ruffles,' said Faith gently, passing her friend a glass.

Downing a mouthful, Rose gulped and closed her eyes.

'In view of what I am about to tell you, that tipple was compulsory,' she said. 'I said I would tell you at the King's Bench what changed my outlook on the plantations.'

'What with all the kerfuffle at the King's Bench,' said Faith, taking a generous swig of port, 'it was not possible for us to have a private word.'

'Let me have that word with you now,' said Rose, taking another large swig. 'Where shall I begin? Do you recall those long sultry Pertiguan sunsets?'

'I do.'

'How perfectly arousing they were?'

Blushing and giggling behind her hand, Faith said, 'Indeed I do.'

Dropping her head despondently, Rose heaved a long telling sigh.

'Tis out of character, thought Faith, frowning. Troubled by her friend's abrupt change of manner, she edged closer.

'We have nigh on been lifelong confidantes, Rose,' she said quietly, taking her friend's hand. 'We share myriads of secrets, which always puts us under oath. Accordingly, I will share this confidence with no one.'

Raising her eyes, Rose's tears dripped onto her gown.

'I really don't know how to say this to you, Faith,' she said awkwardly. 'Especially after how I scolded you about your slave lover who led the uprising. Pray frown not on what I am about to tell you, dear sister. After the uprising I too had an affair of the heart — with a woman. Mother and father never found out — thank God. I have told none other.'

Flabbergasted by the disclosure, Faith's mouth fell open.

'You... you... had... bodily...relations... with... a woman?' she asked.

The quake coursing through her was palpable. Not once had she ever considered that Rose possessed womanly inclinations. Incredulity was swiftly succeeded by a hankering to know more.

'In my creation I was not made to love or be loved by men,' said Rose assertively. 'That is why I never took up with any of the unattached bucks on the island. Manliness does not thrill me so, whereas my lover's touch was heavenly.'

'How did she end up in your cot?'

'Recovering from the revels of the previous night,' said Rose, 'I was sprawled in a planter's chair drinking French brandy and reading. In a slightly sozzled state through that sweaty afternoon, I sat eyeing a lissom being sashaying before me across the verandah, back and forth, back and forth. Beneath sparkling moon-drops, my inhibitions crumpled. We shared a decanter. By the end of that sultry evening, we had succumbed and eagerly she came to my cot. To cut a long story short, I was smitten by my house slave, Ruth.'

'Mother of God, Rose!' she exclaimed. 'What made you choose a lover so close to home? You know the complications I had with mine.'

Closing her eyes briefly, Rose opened them with a misty other-worldly look.

'Jet-black and flawlessly proportioned, a selfless lover and staunch companion,' she said dreamily. 'I had her freed whereupon I had her tutored. Two enthralling years we spent together. We basked in pastimes during our days and for our nights we were cocooned in my cot. You might think that when I was her owner, I had simply taken advantage of the powerless and readily available. There you would be wrong. Once freed and sans slavery, we grew with like tastes. Granted, Ruth could be a little wary, but she was a woman of veritable substance and she made me feel like no man could. And trust me, Faith, the feeling was well-reciprocated.'

'What with my chequered history, Rose,' laughed Faith, 'I could not possibly judge you. Pray continue.'

'One night Ruth disappeared,' said Rose, sniffling into the handkerchief and sipping port. 'Her broken bloodied body was discovered under the straw in the stables. I was shaken and wracked with indescribable grief. Ruth was lawfully free, yet she had been stripped naked, shackled and flogged to death by a spurned overseer who fled the plantation.'

'Did you trace the monster?' she asked, horrified.

'Nay,' said Rose, heaving a sigh and shaking her head, 'and it would not have brought her back. Besides, enough blood had been shed. Her murder had bared the ungodliness of my life. How had I believed that our civilisation was superior? 'Might is White' and 'White is Right'. Slave ships of the Middle Passage waved that flag like a cudgel. Slave markets guaranteed limitless stock, the plantation's turned profits and the Navy protected the trade. Besides, the trafficking was endorsed by a good number of churchmen who as well turned a profit from it.'

'I know not how I ever stooped so low as to tolerate the plantation regime and said not anything,' said Faith, shaking her head with chagrin.

'Terror is oft assisted by the silence of bystanders,' said Rose ruefully. 'I, like you, remained silent. Moreover, I never questioned the principles behind our dominance. Ruth's murder converted me. Shame forged a deep loathing of the trade. At a substantial financial loss, but a considerable profit in peace of mind, I sold my plantation and freed my slaves overnight. To help them establish themselves, I gave each twenty pounds. I felt somewhat better for doing so. It had been my expressed desire to bring Ruth back to England, to live in London and Rye. Of course we would have been incredibly discreet.'

'Rose,' said Faith softly, clasping her friend's hands. 'You and I are so alike. Having done not anything to alleviate the horrors meted out on slaves, we lived off the profits from their labours. If truth be told, Rose, it was only when we had lost our lovers did we finally recover our moral senses. Despite having been rooted in a dubious existence on the plantations, we have sworn with the League to bring an end to the slave regime. Or else history might smear all English men and women with the taint of slavery.'

Refilling her glass, Rose held a wounded look. 'I feel cheated,' she said.

Knocking back a mouthful of port, Faith wiped her lips and dabbed her eyes.

'You know I bear a deep wound inflicted while on the Tamarind Trees Plantation,' she said mournfully. 'Day in, day out, I still pray for my child; sold by my stepfather on the night of his birth to a plantation on another island all those years go. I still crave to know what has befallen my son. He was twenty years of age on the fourteenth of June. Jonas knows all of it. My love for him and our children mollifies the pain I feel for my loss.'

'I have not ever forgiven your stepfather for his action in the Auction House,' said Rose. 'I have not so much as looked at the monster since before I departed. However, Faith, I cannot in truth ask you to keep secrets from your husband. But given the communal aversion to my Sapphic tastes, I would prefer if you did not share with anyone the confidence I have shared with you.'

'There are proclivities of a wife a husband need not know,' said Faith quietly. 'This little heart-to-heart is one of them. Surely you cannot be the only woman averse to masculine charms?'

Slumping back into the sofa, Rose heaved a long drawn-out sigh.

'I feel quite exhausted by my admission and our reminiscences,' she said, fanning her flushed cheeks. 'Nay I am not alone, dear sister. I find comfort with one of two others, a teacher spinster and the other a married woman. A group of us regularly meet at my house in Rye. Do you think I will ever find another like Ruth?'

'You will find another,' said Faith, swaying from the effects of liquor.

This Cloud Will Soon Pass By

Sunday
28 June 1772
16.00 hrs

It had been an agreeable sunlit day thus far.

The chandlery's black lacquered carriage rumbled along the pitted, cobblestoned Highway. Churchgoers and street sellers abounded on both sides of the wide thoroughfare. Jabbing excitedly out of the window at the passing sights, Solomon and Olivia squabbled and teased. Passing a fatherly eye over his playful offspring, Jonas smiled benignly at Faith and Mistress Beecham. Having attended a service at Wesley's Chapel in City Road on the occasion of John Wesley's birthday, they arrived back at Pilgrims for dinner.

Savoury odours wafted along the hallway.

'Roasted lamb,' cried Solomon, rubbing his stomach. 'I am so hungry.'

'And roast parsnips,' said Olivia eagerly.

Bending down and lovingly caressing her children's faces, Faith said, 'We are all hungry. And I want you to eat all your sprouts, Solomon.'

'Yes Mama,' he said reluctantly.

'Oh my,' said Mistress Beecham. 'I just love the reassuring aroma of cook's roast potatoes dipped in goose fat coming from the kitchen.'

No sooner had the late repast begun than there was frantic pounding on the front door.

Frowning at his wife and Mistress Beecham, Jonas rose anxiously to his feet.

Suddenly, his seven year-old daughter dashed out of the chamber and just as swiftly returned.

'Three mans at the door, Papa,' said Olivia. 'Mistress Honeypenny see them.'

'Wait here, children,' he said, leaving the chamber.

Tom, Jack and Breathless, friends of Henry Jackson, stood panting heavily on the front steps.

Startled by their obvious distress, he beckoned them into the hallway.

'Where is Henry?' he asked.

'Yer' gotta come quick, Mister Guinea,' said Breathless. ''Enry bin snatched by Solomon Festus.'

Gasping with shock, Jonas blinked repeatedly. Vulnerability fractured his composure as beads of sweat ran down his temples. I have lived in fear of this moment, he thought. His heart pounded, so much so, he could barely utter a word. Finally, he sputtered, 'When?'

''Bout midday,' said Breathless. 'Three white men grab 'im in Narrow Street.'

'Do you know where they took him?'

''E were flung in a carriage. We followed 'em ter a ship called *Mary Louise*.'

'Where is she berthed?'

'She be a two-masted flyer, moored in Rotherhithe, an' she sails this night.'

'Then we have no time to waste. First I must speak with my wife and fetch my coat. My family are eating supper. Wait for me.'

'We wait 'ere fer yer, Mister Guinea.'

Struggling to keep control of his rattled senses, he staggered back into the dining room. Masking his fears with a strained smile, he spoke to his children.

'A dear friend needs my help,' he said. 'I must go with those men.'

Beckoning his wife and Mistress Beecham to the withdrawing room, he was candid.

'Solomon Festus has Henry Jackson,' he said, anxiously mopping his brow. 'He has been caged on the *Mary Louise*, a barque moored at Old Salt Quay in Rotherhithe. She is set to sail this night.'

Slumping onto the oak corner chair, Faith crossed herself.

'Mother of God!' she gasped. 'Festus could have snatched you, Jonas!'

Putting her hands to her temples, a dazed Mistress Beecham sank into a chair.

'Kidnapped?' she asked, scowling, 'and despite Lord Mansfield's judgment?'

'Regardless of the change in the law,' said Jonas, 'slave-hunters abound in numbers on the heels of Mansfield's judgment. 'Tis clear His Lordship did not consider enforcement of his judgment.'

'Typical,' spat Mistress Beecham.

'We will need a Judge's Order to stop the *Mary Louise* sailing,' said Faith, pulling the sleeve of his jerkin. 'We need a sympathetic lawyer.'

'Luckily we know a lawyer,' said Jonas.

'Who?' asked Mistress Beecham, frowning.

'Aaron Drinkwater!' replied Jonas. 'And 'tis fortunate he lives below Redriff Marsh in the village of Rotherhithe — right next door to Judge Whitlock, who I am told is the maverick of the Bench. I daresay they dwell nigh on a stone's throw from the *Mary Louise*.'

'I seem to recall Aaron Drinkwater berating the League for accepting your sailing with the *Redemption*,' said Mistress Beecham. 'On receiving a look from his disconcerted pater, the poor man visibly paled and instantly reversed his opinion. Though he has a fairly complex relationship with courage, methinks he will be eager to atone for that earlier mishap.'

'Aaron Drinkwater will no doubt be ready to make up for that inconvenient hiccup,' said Faith. 'Go see him, Jonas. Whatever our opinion of the man, he means well and his knowledge of the Bench is said to be second to none.'

'You should know,' said Jonas, 'that Drinkwater as well possesses a dizzying intelligence on London's slave-hunters. All the same, we must keep this abduction from the children. They are too young to experience such horror.'

Frowning at first, Faith gave him a wan smile.

'Mister Foggerty is at present in the chandlery preparing orders for the morrow,' she said. 'Better take him with you for protection. Come safely home with good tidings, my dearest. For now I will tell the children you have gone to help a friend. Though methinks before long and without frightening them, we must make them aware of the dangers on London's streets.'

'You rebuke me rightly, Faith,' relented Jonas. 'I cannot go on shielding them from everything. Let us tell them about Henry when I return. I pray we reach him in time.'

'Tread with great care in the alleyways, my son,' said Mistress Beecham softly. 'Given Henry's misfortune, I could not bear to lose you in a likewise fashion. You should know my aging heart is not what it used to be. With a stroke of luck, this cloud will soon pass by.'

'Methinks not,' said Jonas quietly.

Donning a frock coat, he boarded the chandlery's carriage with Tom, Jack, Breathless and Mister Foggerty. Tensing his jaw, he gazed out of the window.

In the hands of the chandlery's flashman, the hushed vehicle sped westerly through Sunday streets. Shortly, the carriage was clattering along Jamaica Road into Bermondsey. At a quarter past five, it turned into Old Paradise Street and juddered to a halt outside Hollyhocks, Drinkwater's double-fronted Georgian pile.

Closely tailed to the front door by Foggerty, Jonas knocked.

Moments later, he was in the withdrawing room relating Henry's abduction to Aaron Drinkwater. Wordlessly extracting a rolled scroll from a drawer, the lawyer threw on a black silk frock coat.

'I have in my hand a readied summons,' he said. 'All a judge has to do is to fill in the name of the vessel and sign it. Accompany me next door to Mariner's Lodge to see Judge Whitlock. Though the man has been known to drop the odd gaffe, I know him to be greatly perturbed by the depravities of the slave trade. Moreover, he is quite partial to cocking a snook at the powers that be — on almost every issue.

'Then let us be gone, Mister Drinkwater,' said Jonas, itching to depart. 'Many, many thanks for your speedy response.'

Arriving at Mariner's Lodge, a sedate Georgian townhouse, Drinkwater knocked while Jonas looked gloomily around the neighbourhood.

A diminutive, elderly, twinkle-eyed housekeeper opened the door.

''Pon my soul, Treadwell, you are looking delightfully frisky this day,' said Drinkwater cheerily. 'Which lucky cad has your favour then? Is Judge Whitlock at home?'

'Why, Mister Drinkwater, my ears wait on your proposal,' replied the housekeeper, tittering behind her hand and then shakily curtseying. 'A good day to you, sirs. I know the Judge will see you, Mister Drinkwater. Follow me to the library, gentlemen.'

Stepping into the musty, book-stuffed sanctuary, Jonas was reassured by the appearance of the judicial bigwig. Bulbous-nosed and claret-faced, Judge Whitlock was a kindly-faced man with a spongy handshake.

Methinks his soft hands have lifted not anything heavier than books or a gavel, thought Jonas, smiling.

''Tis good to put a face to the one Drinkwater has been holding forth about, Mister Guinea,' said the Judge, inhaling a pinch of snuff from the back of his hand. 'You may not know that I attended Oxford University with Thomas Beecham. Having imbibed our way through countless tutorials, we wobbled a route to our Law Degree. It could be reasonably argued that we gained qualifications by intoxication. Mighty fine grog it was, as well.'

'I was not aware of that, your honour,' said Jonas, laughing courteously. 'I am mightily charmed to make your acquaintance, sir.'

'But I am most intrigued to be meeting the first black to head an English company.'

'I do not know if I am the first, your honour.'

'You're the first I have heard of, Mister Guinea,' replied the Judge, smiling broadly. 'You will have to accept that challenging burden. Against you, all others will be judged. By all I have heard of the profits of your chandlery, you set a fine example. Now Drinkwater, why do I have the honour of your presence?'

Listening to the account of Henry's kidnapping with a deepening scowl, the Judge reacted with a grim smile. Without ado and with a scholarly flourish, he signed the prepared summons. Aaron Drinkwater was in possession of an injunction prohibiting the departure of the *Mary Louise*.

'I pray the *Mary Louise* has not already sailed,' said Jonas feverishly. 'Otherwise, Henry will have been shackled to the 'tween deck to begin his passage into slavery.'

'If she has sailed,' said Drinkwater hotly, 'I swear not ever to stop trying to get Henry back, however long it takes.'

By this lawyer's passion, thought Jonas, I know he will keep his word.

'What now, gentlemen?' asked the Judge, inhaling a pinch of snuff.

'The *Mary Louise* is moored at Old Salt Quay on the western edge of Redriff Marsh, your honour,' replied Drinkwater. 'We must be away, sir, for she sails this night.'

'Be gone this instant,' said the Judge warmly. 'Pray call on me under healthier circumstances, Mister Guinea. Drinkwater will arrange it.'

'My wholehearted gratitude for the summons, your honour,' said Jonas, delivering a crisp bow. 'I bid you farewell, sir, and I look forward to meeting you again on another occasion.'

Glancing at the cherry-wood grandfather clock in the hall, Jonas clenched his teeth. It was six-thirty. Pursing his lips, he walked hurriedly from Mariner's Lodge, followed by the lawyer.

Unsettled by the trepidation in the carriage, he gave a weak smile and looked out on to the streets. Every yard nearer to the *Mary Louise* heightened his anxiety, whilst the lawyer's features were discernibly draining of colour. A little after seven o'clock he sighted Redriff Marsh. In what felt like minutes the vehicle stopped by Old Salt Quay, a groaning tar-timbered structure bordered by tall tufted marsh grasses. His shoes met the cobbles and he scanned the desolate locality. Except for a gaff-rigged Dutch barge, two fishing boats and their crews, the dock was empty. If the *Mary Louise* had been there, an empty berth said she had sailed.

Wracked with grief, tears tumbled freely down his cheeks. Falling backwards against the carriage, he wept openly.

'I failed you, Henry,' he cried. 'I swear we will find you, my friend. We will bring you home.'

Striding briskly away to talk to the fishermen, a shaken Drinkwater hastily returned.

'*Mary Louise?*' Jonas asked.

Pointing at a vessel under foresails downstream of the jetty, Drink-water said crossly, 'She is yonder rounding Limehouse Reach. Fisher-men said she sailed with the tide. We are too late, Mister Guinea, but we shall not give up.'

'We must go to Limehouse to give Henry's wife the terrible tid-ings,' said Jonas, grief-stricken.

'I shall accompany you,' said Drinkwater. 'I share your consterna-tion and your heartache, my friend. A most terrible event has taken place this day.'

'I daren't 'ave you snatched as well, Mister Guinea,' said Foggerty doggedly. 'I will stick close an' follow you to Limehouse as well.'

'We go wi' ye, Mister Guinea,' said Breathless. 'Mistress Lorna bin a good friend of we fer a good long time.'

It was eight-thirty. Conveying six tight-lipped low-spirited occupants, the carriage rumbled through the darkening environs of Narrow Street. Mesmerised by the candlelit blackened dwellings, Jonas sat pondering bygone times with Henry.

Looking anxiously around the carriage, he asked, 'How do we tell Henry's children they may not ever see their father again? How do we tell Mistress Jackson she may have to journey on with a life alone?'

'We tell 'er 'cos she mus' 'ear it from 'is friends, Mister Guinea,' growled Breathless.

The carriage halted outside Henry's cottage. Foggerty remained in his seat.

Shadowed by his companions, Jonas crossed the dusty cobbles to the front door. Pausing to muster his nerves, he knocked.

The door groaned slowly open.

'Why 'tis you, Mister Guinea,' said Mistress Jackson cheerily. 'Henry be not 'ere, but he be not long. Won't you step inside for some broth while you await 'im, sir?'

Stepping into the mildewed hallway, Jonas grasped both her hands.

'I-I-I regret I-I ca-carry terrible ti-tidings, Mistress Jackson,' he stammered.

'Why yer got water in yer eyes, Mister Guinea,' said Mistress Jack-son, frowning. 'What terrible tidings, sir?'

'Henry has been kidnapped!'

Venting a blood-curdling screech, Mistress Jackson crumpled like a rag doll. Assisted by the lawyer, Jonas lifted her from the floor and carried her into her small bedchamber.

Responding to the sudden turn of events, Breathless, Tom and Jack promptly shepherded her children into the parlour.

Lying on her back and opening her eyes, Mistress Jackson turned her face into the bolster and began to sob.

'Where ...is... my... Henry?'

'Henry has been abducted by Solomon Festus, the slave-hunter,' said Drinkwater, gently clasping her hands. 'He is on a vessel bound for the Indies as we speak. I am a lawyer, Mistress Jackson. I swear to leave no stone unturned to get him back.'

'Twill be easier said than done, thought Jonas grimly. I have not the heart to tell her the *Mary Louise* passed by in sight and hailing distance of her cottage, with Henry shackled in her hold.

Sending the children to their frantic mother, five men gathered in the parlour for a whispered conference.

'I say we start a fund to support Henry's family,' said Jonas. 'I will contribute five pounds here and now.'

'I as well,' said Drinkwater, readily extracting his purse.

'We got two pounds, a few shillings an' a few pennies, Mister Guinea,' said Breathless. 'We live nearby. We care an' share what we 'ave wi' Mistress Jackson. Henry was our good friend.'

Bequeathing the ten pounds to Mistress Jackson with the promise of more, Jonas bade farewell to the lawyer, who hailed a separate carriage. With Foggerty, he took the melancholic journey back to Pilgrims through darkened hamlets. Now and again flashbacks of happy days with Henry materialised in frightening visions. From the comforts and plenty of Pilgrims, he ploughed into a brutal depiction of a slave plantation. Propelled into a cane field by the sting of the lash, Henry started to swing a machete into the cane. Sweating profusely, Jonas was jolted out of his reverie.

'As long as I live, Mister Foggerty,' he fumed, mopping his brow, 'I vow not ever to give up trying to get Henry back.'

'No godly soul can abide men sellin' 'umans like cattle, Mister Guinea,' said Foggerty, shuddering. 'Ye can well count on me to 'elp yer free Mister Jackson.'

'Thank you kindly, Mister Foggerty,' he said. 'Gladly I accept your help. All we have to ascertain is to which island Henry has been taken and to which plantation he has been sold.'

'I'll 'ave a word wi' mates in the docks,' said Foggerty, 'as to which island the *Mary Louise* 'as sailed.'

'Then, Mister Foggerty,' said Jonas with resolve, 'we shall start our quest in the docks.'

Ignatius Sancho

Pilgrims
Wednesday
5 October 1774
14.30 hrs

Plane trees rustled wildly, shedding the burned autumn harvest. Cotton-ball grey clouds scudded across pale blue skies. Shafts of sunlight stabbed the leaf-ridden Highway as handcarts and carriages trundled to and fro. In the wake of an icy wind, fallen leaves accumulated in doorways along the thoroughfare.

Stationed on the cobbles in front of Pilgrims, a scruffy-hatted street trader loudly hawked bundles of firewood from a cart. Screeching to a halt, a mud-spattered covered black landau stopped behind the street trader.

Attired in a moss-green frock coat, Jonas alighted. Francis Barber followed, smartly-dressed in a dark blue coat with high-standing collar. Jokingly sticking his fingers in his ears at the volume of the trader, Jonas bounded up the steps to be greeted by Tuppence Honeypenny.

'Mistress Guinea is in the withdrawing room with Mistress Beecham, Mister Guinea,' she said, beaming. 'A grand fire burns in the hearth. Your company brings a glad eye to a body, Mister Barber.'

'I see you're in robust health, Mistress Honeypenny,' said Barber, grinning broadly.

Strolling into the warm chamber followed by Barber, Jonas made for the bow-fronted corner cabinet and the decanter of Madeira.

'A good day to you all,' said Jonas cheerfully, passing Barber a glass of Madeira. 'And 'tis a good dry day for voting. 'Tis said that a rainless day positively affects voter turnout and thus the result of a General Election.'

'I won't say you look in the pink, Francis,' Mistress Beecham chuckled, sipping a cup of Darjeeling, 'but I know you get the gist.'

'Indeed I do, Mistress Beecham,' said Barber with a mischievous smile, 'yet inside me, I do believe I am in the pink.'

Everyone laughed.

'And I do have to say,' said Mistress Beecham, 'that I am not sure the outcome of this General Election will make any difference to the present fraudulent affairs of state.'

''Tis good you are here on Election Day, Francis,' said Faith from the Chippendale sofa. 'Come, Francis, take the weight off your feet. Have you an opinion on the election?'

''Tis a pleasure to be here,' said Barber, smiling and settling in the wingback armchair. 'To answer your question, Mistress Guinea, 'tis a great misfortune we have not the vote.'

'My word,' exclaimed Mistress Beecham, looking up from a newssheet, ''tis predicted the Tories will win the General Election with a large majority. And that obsequious Lord North is expected to continue as Prime Minister. Apart from his success four years ago in the Falklands Crisis, this bungling politician, if it comes to a fight, will most probably lose the American colonies.'

'Since abolition of slavery was not in any manifesto or on his lips,' said Jonas scornfully, 'I cannot say I am joyful at the prospect of North's government.'

Sitting down on the Queen Anne wingchair, he continued, 'Francis and I have just quaffed a glass with the first black man qualified to partake in an election...'

'At last a miracle,' said Faith.

'Ignatius Sancho,' replied Jonas, 'and this very morning he cast his first ballot in the Westminster constituency. Ye shall meet him on the morrow when he visits the chandlery.'

'Oh my,' said Mistress Beecham happily. 'What is Mister Sancho's trade?'

'Sancho is unusual for a greengrocer,' said Francis Barber admiringly. 'Why, he has written much on the horrors of England's trade in slaves. He even holds discourse with men like Thomas Gainsborough and David Garrick, whom I have as well had the pleasure to meet at Doctor Johnson's.'

Rolling his eyes affectionately at Barber's proud description, Jonas grinned.

'My goodness,' said Faith, raising her eyebrows, clearly impressed. 'What shall I wear to meet one who walks with giants? What is he like?'

'He's eight feet tall and not of this world,' jested Jonas. 'His eyes are on stalks and he has puffball mushroom ears.'

Covering her mouth with her hand, Mistress Beecham sniggered. Sitting further back in his seat, Barber laughed softly.

'I am serious, Jonas,' said Faith adamantly. 'What does the fellow look like?'

'Medium height, pleasing features and an elegant bearing,' he said. 'His black scratch-bob wig gives him a somewhat refined look. In spite of his gout, he's coming to inspect our churchwarden clay pipes with the view to buying some for his shop.'

'I see you're won over, Jonas,' said Mistress Beecham.

'I liked Mister Sancho immensely,' said Jonas, 'and he is an easy fellow to befriend.'

'I first met Sancho at Doctor Johnson's,' said Barber. ''Twas then I heard him speak powerfully on the iniquities of the slave trade. In addition, he writes petitions in the form of letters to Members of Parliament, men of letters and men of influence. Extraordinarily, he receives replies.'

'Pray tell me more about Ignatius Sancho,' said Mistress Beecham.

'Of the little he knows and has told me of his early years,' said Barber, 'Sancho said he was born on a slave ship bound for the island of Grenada. At two years of age he was brought to England and given to three sisters who lived in Greenwich. Through good fortune or fate, he eventually obtained a position as valet to the Duke of Montagu.'

'My word,' exclaimed Mistress Beecham, sitting bolt upright and pushing aside her cup of tea. 'To be in the service of the Duke of Montagu, Mister Sancho must be punctilious. And you say he writes?'

'As well as fathering six children,' said Barber, 'he taught himself to read, write and compose music. In the past, he wrote to Reverend Laurence Sterne, author of *Tristram Shandy*, asking him to use his influence in the lobby for abolition. Ever since then the two men have been in regular correspondence.'

'Mister Sancho does indeed sound eccentric,' said Faith.

'Retiring from the Duke's service because of his gout and bequeathed a legacy by the Duchess of Montagu,' said Barber, 'he opened a greengrocers in Charles Street with his wife, Anne. Sandwiched between Downing Street and the Houses of Parliament, he sells rum, sugar and Trinidad tobacco.'

'Rum, sugar and tobacco,' reiterated Faith, frowning.

'Aye,' said Barber quizzically.

'Is that not slave produce?'

'I daresay it is,' said Barber almost inaudibly and looking uncomfortable.

'Prominent men dwell in his neighbourhood,' said Jonas, distracting his listeners from Barber's obvious discomfort. 'Apparently Ignatius Sancho's shop regularly turns into a meeting place for the likes of the portrait painter, Richard Cosway; the sculptor, Joseph Nollekens; the painter, John Hamilton Mortimer and the reformer, Charles James Fox.'

'Oh my,' said Mistress Beecham, widening her eyes. 'Ignatius Sancho converses with some very clever men. I am very much looking forward to meeting this phenomenon on the morrow.'

''Twill be a pleasure to encounter such an extraordinary character,' said Faith. 'But I ask again, should an abolition campaigner be selling slave produce?'

'A pertinent question,' said Jonas, pausing thoughtfully. 'But I can only think that it is due to a lack of trading connections. In truth, black traders are excluded by the wholesale markets. Therefore, they are restricted to the commodities they can acquire for their shops. In such circumstances, slave produce is most likely the best they can hope for.'

'I see,' said Faith, relenting.

'I am eager to know,' mused Mistress Beecham, 'about the markets that do admit black traders.'

'I as well,' said Jonas. 'So I shall make enquiries for the League.'

'I wonder if anyone can satisfy a long-held curiosity?' asked Faith, leisurely examining the sparkles in her glass, and then looking enquiringly around the chamber.

'If possible,' said Jonas, frowning.

'I will try,' said Barber, putting down his glass.

'Then tell me this,' said Faith boldly. 'What is so general about a General Election in which no one in this chamber can vote?'

'An interesting question warrants an answer,' said Barber, creasing his brow.

'Men won't give women the vote,' said Mistress Beecham crossly, 'though I cannot fathom why. 'Tis believed that those who have the power to change the status quo, who as well have the vote, seem to find women a threat.'

Smirking at Mistress Beecham's scornful aside, Faith sipped Madeira.

'Barber and I,' said Jonas evenly, 'do not have the vote because we are not independent householders.'

Nodding his agreement, Barber remained silent and noticeably irritated.

'We are family, Jonas,' said Faith. 'Though at present, I might add, a voteless one.'

'Aye,' said Jonas, clearly uncertain why she had mentioned the marital fact.

''Tis settled then,' she said crisply.

'What's settled?' he asked, frowning.

'We are married and have brought two beloved children into this world,' she replied. 'Therefore, we shall add your name to the title deeds of Greensleeves and ye shall have a vote. Pardon me for not thinking of such before now.'

'There is not anything to pardon, dear wife,' he said. 'I thank you heartily for doing such. And I know ye will agree with me if I vote for the political party that advocates abolition.'

'How right you are, dear husband,' said Faith, giggling.

'What if the first abolitionist prospective candidate to stand for Parliament were in the Deptford constituency?' asked Mistress Beecham. 'Were that to come to pass as it appears more likely, then we shall add your name to the title deeds of Pilgrims.'

'I thank you, Mistress Beecham,' said Jonas joyfully. 'I am right-handed, so I would give my left arm for the right to vote.'

'I ask you all,' said Barber, with a mocking laugh. 'In these covetous times, where might we find such a rare breed as an anti-slavery politician?'

'One will be along to stake his claim,' said Mistress Beecham firmly, 'even if only to make his name.'

Hurricane

Ocean Bay
Pertigua
26 August 1781
Noon

On the wooded clifftop overlooking Ocean Bay, Asabi, the Captain of Freetown, embraced her son. Stepping back and casting her eyes over him, she smiled.

Round-faced, tall and wiry, she adored his noble bearing in his tattered black breeches and jerkin. From the instant he learned his father took his life awaiting execution by the English, something of the night entered the youth. Subsequently, his kindly, lucid eyes turned inscrutable. Despite swathing his dark feelings in nuggets of jest, a threatening tempest dogged his footsteps.

'Twenty-nine years an' so like your father,' she said lovingly.

'I feel him in me, Ma,' said Abi. Then, looking pensively into the distance he spoke with mettle in his eyes, 'I will finish what you plan wi' him.'

Smiling affectionately, she shaded her eyes from the glare and stared out to sea. A warm, clear and airless day was crowned by a boundless indigo sky. In the far distance, the horizon was darkly menacing. Like a phoenix arising from shimmering waters, the towering guano-encrusted Three Apostles sparkled like saintly beacons in the noonday sun. Squawking incessantly in the bright clement airs, black-headed gulls ringed the craggy granite pillars. Dolphins cavorted across the bows of outward-bound vessels. Then, she spotted her objective — the after effects of the slow nervous fever that had greatly afflicted the island.

A battered gaff-rigged fishing boat dropped anchor half a mile from the granite stacks and a quarter mile from a smartly-dressed, moored man-o-war. Despite the distance across the mirrored waters from the anchored vessels, the monotonous invocations of the shipboard clerics were carried on the breeze. She saw forty-two naked slaves dumped overboard following perfunctory prayers on the fishing boat. A short while later from the man-o-war, the haunting resonance of a bugle and a stirring drumbeat sounded. Ceremoniously, smartly-outfitted seamen gently slipped ten stitched shrouds into the waters.

'Dead blacks on fishing boat, dead whites on warship,' she retorted, shuddering angrily.

'Far apart in life is black and white an' far apart in death,' said Abi dolefully. 'All look the same to monsters o' the deep.'

Warmed by the honeyed lilt of his island accent, she gazed affectionately at him. His was softer than the timbre of her African tongue, which despite the years away from Ake, she had never lost.

More than thirty years on the island — over a year on a slave plantation and the remainder as a runaway — she was now fifty-two years of age and her hair was streaked with grey. No longer could she dash about as nimbly as when she arrived. Even now, she still suffered painful spasms along the lengthy weals caused by the whippings from slave drivers on the coast of Guinea. As well, she experienced intermittent twinges from leg injuries picked up in skirmishes during the uprising. Both wounds now hindered her movement. She was not the hellcat she used to be.

Truelove, her lover, had lately succumbed to the slow nervous fever. Twenty years had passed since Tomba had sailed home to Guinea on the *Redemption*. Twenty free but challenging years had passed during which Freetown's fortifications and a string of scout locations had been tried and tested; her son had a wife and three children; Freetown's school had flourished; and twenty more runaways had found their way from the plantations to the stronghold. They still had occasional skirmishes with the Mongoose Gang. Markedly, however, Freetown's militia had repelled a Redcoat assault with orders for her capture.

Leading Freetown's militia from time to time, she raided planta-tions remote from the capital for food and ammunition. Once, to foster terror in Jamestown's white populace, she dispatched a midnight raid into a plantation on the outskirts. Causing panic was her objective. The ploy succeeded. For the next three months, all adult white males, excepting the gentry, were obliged to take turns in the armed patrols of Jamestown.

Narrowing her eyes at the woebegone funerary task force, she muttered aloud, 'Do they mask a sneak attack wi' this burial?'

'As he bury his dead?' asked Abi, frowning.

Pulling him around to face her, she was adamant.

'Forget not, Abi,' she said. 'The English got big hunger. They not get rich and powerful 'cos they bin asleep. They got greedy an' then they make plan. They sail to another's land an' sow chaos. Wide awake wi' plenty o' muskets, they get rich.'

From between a tall cluster of purple bougainvillea, a lookout suddenly stepped out.

'Redcoats an' Mongoose Gang bin shootin' up Lake Disappointment,' said Joseph, heavily panting and pointing behind him. 'Them kill lookout then them go.'

Closing her eyes and shaking her head, she asked, 'Who dead?'

'Samson.'

Staggering backwards with her head in her hands, she keened. 'Aiiii, an' so young.'

Born in Freetown, at eighteen years the strapping Samson had never been a slave, unlike his parents. Having escaped from the China Lights Plantation twenty years before, they were her close friends. Now she would have to carry the sad news to his family in a hamlet a quarter-mile from Freetown.

For the most part, freedom in the mountains, swamps and grottos of northern Pertigua had been rewarding. Over two thousand runaways lived in camps strewn in the dense foliage not far from the headquarters encampment, the stronghold cavern of Freetown. All the outlying sites possessed varying degrees of order and disorder.

Freetown's structured grotto sheltered ninety-three adults and twenty-two children, most of whom had been taught to read and write. Lookouts spent a week's duty sited around Lake Disappointment. In relative safety, the runaway militia roamed over a challenging, luxuriant terrain and kept the atmosphere inhospitable for Redcoats.

Her abduction from the village of Ake on the coast of Guinea was an omnipresent wound, as was her life cruelly stolen from her kind and enslaved by a sugar plantation.

So long ago an' all in one life, she thought, blinking back tears.

Above all, the inhabitants of Freetown had to maintain a constant watch for Redcoat and Mongoose Gang patrols. At the same time, they tended camouflaged farms holding goats and pigs and large patches of beans, greens, tomatoes, sweet potatoes and hot peppers.

'Freedom 'as a price,' she sighed.

A westerly gusted across the clifftop.

Putting his hand on her shoulder, her son broke her daydream.

'Devil in that wind an' hell not far behind, Ma,' said Abi.

Blue skies turned grey.

Suddenly, a powerful wind made her struggle for breath. The bushes flailed westerly along the cliff top. Palm trees arched in skeletal contortions. Huge raindrops flattened the undergrowth and muddied the parched soil. Trickling through her flimsy cotton garb, water soaked her skin.

Turning to the lookout, she yelled above the wind, 'You see Redcoats go?'

'Me see them go,' said Joseph.

Leaning into the powerful airstream, she peered down the rain-lashed shore.

Storm petrels were winging into cliff-face crevices. Huge waves churned the shoreline. In the strong foaming backwash, uprooted trees jostled with mangroves being dragged out to sea. Sixty feet below her, a barque had foundered on the shores of Ocean Bay. Moreover, the vessel was now being lashed by the incoming waves into the mangroves.

Soaked to the skin, she wiped her sopping face and looked up through the driving rain.

Far away and high over the sea, storm clouds twisted into a menacing whirlpool. Spiralling inwards, blowing, sinking and rising, the phenomenon was moving slowly along the northern coast.

'A big storm is on the way, Ma,' said Abi, wiping his face. 'I see plenty o' water in them clouds. We mus' get back to Grace and the chillen.'

'That one-eyed monster is no storm,' she said, striding ahead. 'Back to the cave quickly an' warn everyone, grab clothes an' food. Eye o' this monster wi' scuff down the coast. Freetown get flooded an' Jamestown get drowned.'

By the time they reached the citadel, the tempest was howling. Flying spray hampered visibility and waves lashed the cavern entrance. Leaning into a powerful wall of briny air, her sodden clothes clung to her. In the thunderous roar that filled the interior, it seemed as if demons had been unleashed.

The air was filled with shouts and screams. Children had been moved safely onto a basalt shelf by the rear entry of the cave. Adults worked frantically to shift possessions and rations from the shacks to higher ground.

From the mouth of the rain-lashed cavern, she heard a jarring rumble over the reef from the ghostly murk out at sea. Sighting the wave she most feared careering towards the cliff face, she shuddered and pushed her son and the lookout.

'To high ground at the back of the cave!' she screamed.

Leaping onto the high wide ledge across the back of the cavern, she huddled with other residents. Spellbound, she watched the crest of the towering roller, gleaming with froth and thirty feet higher than others, crash down over the threshold of the cave entrance. Foaming seawater surged through the grotto and flooded numerous shacks. While the powerful backwash carried off a number of them, the one-eyed monster threatened to wash away the other habitats. Unable to differentiate family or friend in the muted light, she remained immobile for the night.

Again and again, she saw waves strike the grotto and relentlessly seethe through the cave a few yards shy of the ledge. Watching helplessly, many saw their few possessions washed away on the wake of successive waves. During the stormy sopping dark hours, she was not fearful of attack.

'Runaways not got a lot to lose,' said Abi glumly.

'Jamestown got much more to lose,' she said acidly. 'Think o' all them fancy houses wi' fancy decoration, roads carrying sugar, warehouses full o' sugar, hard cash, gold an' secret treasures — all under water. They suffer so much damage, Fleming an' Redcoats be too busy to trouble us. We hear soon 'bout Jamestown from the scouts.'

By the early hours, the hurricane winds had fallen to a gentle breeze. A weary silence echoed through the cavern. Dawn promised a crystal clear day.

Hearkening to rising voices, Asabi joined others off the ledge.

'Me lost Justice,' wailed his lover. 'Me man bin wash away.'

'I take 'ead-count wi' Joseph, Ma,' said Abi.

The children were all accounted for. Two men had drowned. Having taken refuge further along the same ledge, Abi's wife and all three children were safe.

'Food washed away,' said Abi. 'We get plenty o' fish after such a big storm. We need food. Let we go fishing, Ma.'

Shinning down the ladder from the cavern onto the apron of sand below, Asabi caught sight of a splintered notice board blown from Jamestown. Pinned to the panel was a poster from the Weekly Pertiguan Times, which she read aloud:

'10 August 1781. Run away from the Tamarind Trees Plantation, a brawny Eboe man named Ishmael, marked TT on his left shoulder, of a pole black complexion and bit of his wide nose cut off; speaks pretty good English and used to conceal himself about Jamestown. Whoever takes him up and gives notice to Benjamin Bateman agent of Tamarind Trees Plantation, so as he may be had, shall be rewarded with twenty shillings over and above mile money.

'Run away from Captain William Paget a yellow Negro wench, named Ebony, marked W P upon her back. Whoever brings the said Negro to her master shall be well rewarded, and whoever entertains her be it at their peril.'

'Pig shit!' she spat, contemptuously flinging aside the notice board. 'Jamestown be chaos after this hurricane. Slaves wi' be forced to clean it up.'

'Them talk of Ishmael like goods,' said Abi angrily. 'How do he get a bit cut off his nose?'

'A slave is property an' owned like a chair,' she scowled, 'like Tamarind Trees owned by Frederick Bradshaw. Your father an' me escape from his plantation. You were not sold like cattle an' hunted like wild animal wi' dogs. You was born free, Abi. Thank Papa Goodwill you do not know how to be a slave.'

From the admiring stare blazing from his eyes, his gratitude was evident.

Smiling affectionately, she embraced him.

''Cos o' you an' my father I not been a slave, Ma,' said Abi, beaming. 'You bore me a free spirit. Thank you an' Papa Goodwill. What 'bout Ishmael's nose?'

'Ishmael sabotage sugar mill an' stop sugar making for two weeks,' she said. 'For that he got a notch cut slowly from his nose. His nose bleeds for weeks. When it stop bleeding, he wake up. So frit to get cut again, he fired a barn, steal two muskets an' run away.'

Abi winced.

'You talk to Ishmael since he arrive?' she asked. 'Tho he be cruelly hurt, the man's got fresh legs an' he bin' dancing an' laughing anywhere he go. You should. In few days, Abi, come wi' me to Samson's kinfolk. Now storm done, we get good fishing. Come my son, let we go an' fish.'

'We eat good wi' Grace an' children this night,' said Abi, laughing.

Some days later, Asabi and Abi halted a short distance from a cluster of fan-shaped palms screening a handful of shacks situated few hundred yards south of Freetown. Samson's father stepped out from the bushes. Accompanied by two wild-eyed characters with muskets, Doctor Sam raised his hand.

'Wait, Asabi,' he said, chuckling, 'we got killer ants cleanin' shacks.'

'Killer ants?' said Abi, eyes wide with surprise.

Disregarding her son's amazement, Asabi leaned against a tree.

'Take long?' she asked casually.

'Them soon go,' said Doctor Sam.

'I bring you sad words my friend,' she said solemnly, pulling him aside.

His face clouding over, Doctor Sam spoke fearfully. 'Why you so sad, Asabi?'

'Samson bin' shot by Redcoats at Lake Disappointment.'

'Me God!' cried Doctor Sam, staggering backwards and turning a sickening grey. ''E badly 'urt? 'E dead?'

'Samson give his life for runaways,' she said gently. 'We bring him to you in few days. Together we bury him with love an' respect.'

Lowering pained eyes to the ground, Doctor Sam said mournfully, ''Is mother an' me weep for 'im this night, Asabi. An' 'e get blessing of Papa Goodwill. Samson be loved all 'is eighteen free years. That be a lifetime more than we 'ad on them plantations.'

'We grieve in the open an' get surprised by Redcoat patrols,' said Asabi, guardedly scanning the stumpy undergrowth. 'Death and grieving is strangers for us, 'cos we have not ever been given time to grieve. When England's men robbed our freedom, we cried out an' cried out an' then cried inside. We're all done wi' crying. We will weep for Samson this night, Doctor Sam. An' we got no time to stan' out here off-guard talking 'bout it.'

Sensing she had been overly hard on a heartbroken father, she turned to Abi and changed the subject.

'You not know of Doctor Sam's agreement wi' killer ants then?' she asked.

'Killer ants mek contrak to clear huts?' asked Abi sceptically. 'What come next? Soon you tell me ants can cook.'

'Keep Redcoats near an' keep killer ants nearer, Abi,' said Doctor Sam, wiping tears from his eyes.

'Killer ants?' reiterated Abi incredulously.

'Them come from Guinea long ago wi' slave ships,' explained Doctor Sam. 'We find nest close by an' mek peace wi' no words. Same we do in my village in Guinea.'

'How ants know when to come?'

'Time comes to rid shacks of nasties, we drop food 'ere,' said Doctor Sam, pointing at a neatly hewn rut across the track. 'We lay food trail through five shacks and back to 'ere. That be the signal an' area we want clean. Ant scouts come. Ant workers an' soldiers follow. Wi' huge cutting jaws, them mash up every livin' thing in them path.

Poisonous snakes, spiders, scorpions an' mosquitoes get eaten. Them will even kill an' eat a man to the bone. We—'

'What you do?'

'We wait 'ere an' stay out o' their way,' replied Doctor Sam. 'In the night, we watch where we tread. As quick as they come they go. Not a livin' thing be left alive in the huts. Not like Pertigua's white men, killer ants keep their word. We not get slow nervous disease 'ere 'cos o' the ants.'

Narrowing his eyes with respect for Doctor Sam, Abi nodded his head with admiration.

Asabi smiled.

'Master everything 'bout this island, Abi,' she said.

'Even the ants?' he joked.

'Specially ants 'cos they act like English,' she said dogmatically. 'They both attack wi' force an' cunning. No matter what you do, Abi, you mus' keep Jamestown away from Freetown. When I is gone, runaways say they will make you, the son of Kayode, Captain of Freetown. That is why you must be as one with anything that moves.'

'You teach me well, Captain,' he said lovingly. 'I learn even from ants. On clifftop under stars this night, we mus' roast pig with Grace and our chillen.'

'Me belly howling, boy,' she said, then turned to Doctor Sam. 'Ants go 'fore long. An' when it's safe to cry, we fetch Samson to bury an' we cry wi' you, my friend.'

Old Friends and Traitors

Freetown
Sunday
31 August 1783
07.00 hrs

Woken by the 'gleep gleep' calls of whistling toads secreted under piles of coconut husks, Asabi opened her eyes. Shafts of warm sunlight burst through gaps in the shuttered window of her shack. For a short time she lay on her back staring up into the banana-leaf roof.

'Still I ache for Truelove beside me,' she sighed. 'My son be born free. We is all still free. Thank God for Freetown.'

Yawning and stretching, she rose and donned a clean threadbare jerkin and breeches. A chilling feeling settled inside her. Shrugging off the dark sensation, she pushed open the shutters.

Waiting for her to rise, her three grandchildren stood up from her son's bordering shack and chorused, 'Look what we 'ave for you, Gran'ma!'

Stepping out onto her verandah, she laughed and beckoned them.

Wearing coarse calico dungarees, the trio brought a banana-leaf basket of mangoes, bananas, papaya, rose apples and her favourite beverage, a gourd of sarsaparilla. Even with the comforting arrival of her grandchildren, she nevertheless felt anxious. A black-browed albatross veering into the wind cast a shadow on her spirits. Frowning, she turned from one side of the soaring cavern to the other, scanning the surroundings.

The heat was rising. Morning shadows rippled on the sunlit limestone walls of the grotto. Olive-throated parakeets shrieked and fluttered in the fruiting shrubbery at the entrance. High above, the cackle of laughing gulls echoed around the roof. A cooling gust filled the interior. The tide was out.

Wisps of smoke from cooking fires carried the aroma of pork and red snapper on the light wind. The wit, chatter and camaraderie of departing hunters bode well. Bantering, laughter and the spats of the day were well underway. All appeared normal, yet she still felt uneasy.

Sunlight was pouring steadily through the cave entrance. Her grandchildren had gone to a nearby shack to play. Sitting down on the edge of her verandah, she was joined by Abi and Grace, bringing gossip from the plantations.

Suddenly, sidling out from between the shacks, Asabi saw Hezekiah. Falling silent, she nodded perfunctorily with a lukewarm smile.

Thickset, of medium height and a dark yellowish complexion, Hezekiah returned a tepid grin. With a skinny surly companion, he walked by towards the entrance of the cave.

With Hezekiah out of earshot, she sighed.

'Hezekiah say he be a carpenter by trade,' whispered Abi. 'When he break out o' the plantation he claim he carry off two sets o' tools. In one year I not seen his tools an' I not seen him carpenter anything in Freetown. He were seen three days ago idling on white ground by China Lights Great House. I say he be Fleming's eyes an' ears.'

'Hezekiah got a forked tongue,' said Asabi irritably. 'When last I met in secret wi' our go-between, Hezekiah was spotted idling around behind my shack.'

Whistling typically out of tune, Shadow turned up with his sinewy frame clad in his trademark stained baggy pirate slops, sleeveless jerkin and Monmouth cap. Beside him wearing yellowed breeches stood a bare-chested Dogbite, a sawyer by trade. Shadow was so-styled owing to his uncanny ability for passing undetected in and out of Jamestown, whereas Dogbite was so-called because the mongrel that bit him died soon afterwards.

'Sarsaparilla, my friends,' she said, beaming.

'We got ter talk, Asabi,' said Shadow, taking a long, gulping swig. 'Me think Redcoats plannin' ter storm Freetown.'

'Me feel—' began Dogbite.

'What you feel, Dogbite?' she snapped mockingly. 'First time me heard you mumble in days. Me thought you dead.'

Guffawing loudly, Dogbite slapped the ground. 'Me feel—'

'Asabi,' a voice yelled.

Anxiously, she turned.

Ben, the go-between, was waving from the cave entrance.

Squinting, she beckoned him.

Around thirty years of age and of regular build, the dark brown courier's smooth looks had been marred by slight pitting in his cheeks from the smallpox and a deep gash from an overseer's musket butt across the bridge of his nose. But his sincerity and the kindliness of his person more than made up for his disfiguring scars. So certain was she of his allegiance, she had relied on him as her eyes and ears long before Truelove's passing. Thus, he acted as Freetown's principal go-between with Alexander Fairfax.

'Sit your backside down, my friend,' she said. 'Let sarsaparilla from a tankard made by our potter cool you down, man.'

'Mister Fairfax give me a message, Asabi,' said Ben, sitting down with a broad smile. 'Ship called *Pilgrim* be here in fourteen days ter take twelve runaways to Guinea. He say that bastard Fleming know 'bout the *Pilgrim*. An' he say Fleming setting up attack 'gainst Freetown.'

'That what me come to tell you, Asabi,' said Shadow, grinning smugly.

'When he say Fleming attack?' asked Asabi.

''Bout seven days,' replied Ben, 'wi' Redcoats, planters, overseers and Mongoose Gang.'

'Redcoats in seven days,' she snapped, clenching her jaw and shaking resolve. '*Pilgrim* anchor in fourteen. I see Fleming's cunning. He plan to stop *Pilgrim* sailing with runaways.'

'Them got all heads up one backside,' said Abi tartly. 'A big attack on Freetown be a very bad plan. We stop them every time an' we stop them again. We set traps them won't forget.'

'We give them a fight so hard Redcoats won't rush back,' Asabi fumed. 'If they capture Freetown, they will lash us back to the cane fields. I be Captain of Freetown. I say it time we settle this area wi' good houses, schoolroom, meeting place, shebeen an' temple for Papa Goodwill. Can we do all that by hiding forever in the mountains?

The morrow belongs to our children. Time has come for we to start a well-ordered village an' grow a town. To get all that we mus' force the English to sign a truce. I read big revelations in white man's Bible. For defence o' Freetown we need a big revelation from we — one so big Fleming will be 'fraid to tread in these mountains or anywhere near Freetown. An' we got time to make plan. So after this fight, Freetown will be free.'

'We do what them do,' growled Dogbite, 'an' we do it 'fore them do it.'

Plainly befuddled by his companion's logic, Shadow grinned and scratched his head.

From nowhere, Hezekiah emerged from between nearby shacks holding a string of fish.

Scowling at Hezekiah's stealthy appearance, Asabi was seized by sudden misgiving.

'That man be informer,' she said beneath her breath.

Flourishing his catch in the air and laughing, Hezekiah disappeared with his friend up through the rear exit of the cave.

Leaning guardedly towards his listeners, Ben scratched his head and whispered, 'We see Hezekiah go to fish an' walk in front o' we, yet he come back wi' fish an' walk from behind we. What he up to? How much you think he hear?'

'Not sure,' said Asabi, scowling thoughtfully. 'Don't think much.'

Conspiratorially craning forward, Abi lowered his voice. 'Way me sees it there be jus' three ways into Freetown. On mountain track above Lake Disappointment, we set a death trap. Narrow track wi' rock face one side, big drop on other. It tek only a few o' we to stop an army. Lookouts blow *abeng* horn when Redcoats sighted. At Snake Pass where track narrow an' bend back on itself, we roll flaming grass drums onto track, 'fore an' after troop o' leadin' Redcoats. Trackside bushes so dry them easily burst into flame. Them bushes burn an' smoke fiercely. From track ahead o' Redcoats an' track behind them, we pour musket fire at trapped Redcoats. Dead surprises do the rest.'

Heartened by her son's hard-nosed strategy, she grinned admiringly at him. Jus' like his father, she thought.

'We do it,' she said quietly. 'Gather chiefs o' big runaway settlements, Abi. We mus' all meet this night.'

Clapping his hands and nodding affirmatively, Ben frowned. 'Who sail to Guinea on the *Pilgrim*, Asabi?'

'Them who be not long in Pertigua more likely to still recognise kinfolk in Guinea,' replied Asabi unequivocally. 'Freetown Council agrees them who sail wi' the *Pilgrim* be them who be on the island shortest time. Least it help kinfolk who been grieving an' not grown cold back home.'

'Why you not go home, Asabi?'

'I am Captain of Freetown,' she said softly, raising her tearful eyes skywards with an ache in her voice. 'Abi was born on this island. His father Kayode buried on this island. Truelove buried on this island. Over thirty years I been on this island, Ben. Now I find I been gone from Guinea too too long to go back. I confess I been gone too long to start again.'

Moved by her pained confession, Ben gently grasped her arm.

'Me got blood friends in Freetown,' he said solemnly. 'Me been 'ere so long, blood friends turn into family. Passage to Guinea too risky for me bones. Thank we an' Papa Goodwill we got 'nough muskets to keep we free. Mister Fairfax ask what more we want.'

'Abi be right 'bout track to Lake Disappointment,' said Shadow doggedly. 'We mus' block the two other ways into Freetown. East an' west along cliff top tracks leadin' to Freetown, we set devil traps wi' some serious ambush. Me see it like this. To rattle backsides night 'fore Redcoats attack, we attack while them is still gathering. Works better if we know when Redcoat is coming.'

Lowering her eyes thoughtfully, Asabi gave her heartfelt opinion.

'Surprise attacks waste our strength,' she said, turning down Shadow's suggestion. 'We defend the three tracks into Freetown. This fight we mus' win. Mister Fairfax be another matter. He white an' he been a loyal friend. For gone twenty years, this shipping agent act go-between for runaways' boun' for Guinea on five ships: the *Redemption*, *Sarah Ann*, *Homeward Bound*, *Moonlit Waters* and now the *Pilgrim*. For all that time, the man take risks for we his friends. He be now past sixty. Even if Mister Fairfax get older, we know he wi' not fail us. We make sure *Pilgrim* sail wi' twelve runaways. That be how Freetown say thanks to Mister Fairfax an' his League.'

Pausing for a meditative swig of sarsaparilla, she continued dispassionately. 'Shadow take you into Jamestown jus' after sunset, Ben. Ask Mister Fairfax if he can give timely warning o' Redcoat raid. While you gone, Freetown prepare a dangerous barricade. Hurry back. Come an' see Redcoats march into firestorm.'

The sun had reached its zenith over a halcyon day. In, out, and around the cavern, black-headed gulls coasted acrobatically on the skittish breeze. Smoke was still rising from cooking fires. Following the protracted exchange regarding the fortification of Freetown, a proposal was readied for the meeting that night. On his way to meet Alexander Fairfax after nightfall, Ben set out for Jamestown with Shadow and Dogbite.

For the time being, she flopped on the verandah with her son and his wife Grace, sorting rice and black-eyed beans, eating dried fish and mangoes, swigging rum and sarsaparilla. She told them of her plan to outsmart the boasters on the Freetown Council that night. Admired as the woman of the late famed Captain Sodeke, who with her had planned and led the island's most successful uprising, her position as Captain of Freetown was secure.

'If it's true Fleming know 'bout the *Pilgrim*,' she said hotly, 'the devil will hurl every musket he got to mash us up. Then, for the next seven days, the planters and overseers wait in the shadows wi' the Mongoose Gang for the *Pilgrim*. You know we be no match for tested Redcoats on open ground. We mus' stop them in the mountains an' on cliff top 'fore they get anywhere near Freetown.'

'Fleming wi' not set foot in Freetown!' snapped Grace, waving a machete above her head. 'He not get his hands on my family. Me chop off his knees.'

'Ter hack off his knees right,' said Abi mischievously, 'we need dry grass, fire an' lots o' poisonous snakes. Me talk to snake hunter, Cuffy. Colleking deadly snakes be like manna to the man. Me got a sudden passion for snakes.'

Frowning quizzically at her son, she spoke softly, 'Keep this plan from Hezekiah. The man bin' heard crying his want for a woman. Tell him we planning a jump-up to welcome women who freshly run away. We hold it on night of Redcoat raid. Put eyes on him.'

Naked Elements of the Weak

Whistling ducks were winging westwards. Passing cane fields on the sparsely inhabited outskirts of Jamestown, Matthew Fleming's carriage joined other carriages and wagons rumbling the half mile towards the heart of the metropolis. Staggering about the dusty road, rum-sozzled singing seamen slowed traffic.

Turning through the main gates of Fort James off the lively thoroughfare, Matthew Fleming's carriage trundled to a standstill outside Saint Catherine's Chapel. In the precincts of the garrison, it was sticky and sultry, with tension in the air. Stepping anxiously onto the parade ground, he wiped his brow and smoothed the creases of his blue cotton frock coat.

Pressed vociferously by the claret-faced sergeant-major at double-time across the parade ground, all ranks half-heartedly fell-in with muskets and fixed bayonets before officers. In the stark silence that followed, the kitchen door clanged open. A tousled youth stepped out and lobbed leftovers into a corner of the quad. At once, snapping and snarling service mastiffs fought over the scraps. Bellowed orders restarted the proceedings.

Shaking his head contemptuously, Matthew surveyed his surroundings.

Set upon a lofty crag at the eastern entrance to Jamestown, the fortress was sited fittingly close to Drake House, the island's seat of government. Of a square construction with bastions on all corners, the fort was surrounded by an outer retrenchment. Designed espe-

cially for this stone-built outpost was the George III coat of arms in
coade stone. Boasting a large airy kitchen, the fortified establishment
comprised barracks housing four hundred and fifty men, a drill hall,
officers, sergeants and corporals' mess, storehouse and a powder magazine next to the chapel.

Following the pre-action military prayer service, combative red-
coated officers and frock-coated plantation owners began reconciling
strategies in the chapel for the assault on the runaway stronghold.

Turning to the fort commandant, Matthew Fleming pulled out a
monogrammed handkerchief and smiled.

'Such frightful humidity, Sir Thomas,' he said, mopping his face,
'is akin to inhaling steam while neck-deep in water. Makes thee hanker for the coolness of the dales does it not?'

'Set against the spell cast by these idyllic climes,' said Sir Thomas
Plombley in a soft cultured Yorkshire accent, 'even the delight of the
dales could equal this paradise. And the captivating sunlight kissing
my noggin makes me lively. It reminds me of a long-gone harmony
on the plantations when we had flamboyant sunsets with punch. Call
them echoes of yesteryear, Mister Fleming. In those rumbustious
unregulated times, runaways kept running, not continually popping
back to make tedious unfriendly house calls.'

'You shall have that peace after the looming action, Sir Thomas,'
said Matthew emphatically. 'Of that I wager.'

Falling-in behind the podgy new Governor, Sir Preston Osborne,
he heaved a weary sigh. Down the pillared nave and through the west
tower entrance, he stepped onto the dusty parade ground.

A forceful expression of an expanding empire, Fort James had been
built by his grandfather, Sir William Fleming, in 1625 'to guard against
sudden surprise'. To contend with the current menace of runaway
raids, it was due to Matthew's persistence that plantation owners had
forced the previous Governor to use the island's exchequer to finance
the reinforcement of the fort.

Sniffing imperiously, Matthew scrutinised England's newest envoy
solicitously.

Taking the regimental salute with the commandant of the Pertiguan
Regiment, Governor Osborne stood sweating in the afternoon sun,

puffed-up, bewigged and frock-coated with a purple sash of office. Lackadaisically eyeing the ranks of marching soldiers, his nostrils twitched with disdain.

Noticing that Percival Sedgwick, a planter from Troublesome Creek on Little Pertigua, had joined him, Matthew rolled his eyes. Addressing the former rival for his wife's hand, he spoke quietly behind his own.

'Methinks this Governor is purely a well-connected podgy peacock, Percival,' he said scornfully. 'Provided he concurs with the Cartel's way of doing business on this island, he will derive great benefit from his well-appointed colonial sanctuary in the sun.'

'I'm told that your podgy peacock, as you put it, has the ear of the Prime Minister, Matthew,' said Percival Sedgwick in a sniffy strangled accent. 'Despite his fifty years, Osborne remains an unadulterated serial seducer. Some say he owns a frightening turn of face and is not one to be trifled with. 'Tis said by others that he's simply a tactless Lancastrian Protestant. Have you, perchance, laid eyes on Lady Penelope Osborne? Bereft of cleavage she is, poor woman. Her haggard countenance and skeletal frame suggests she has for long been suffering his fornicating shenanigans. The man has yet to make a start with the fillies of Jamestown.'

'Not if he desires tranquil days,' said Matthew, laughing. 'On a nugget of an island, Percival, "tis rash to turn the one who one must trust and knows one's secrets into a scorned adversary. Burdened with vexation from the certain reprisals from Lady Osborne and her trusty womenfolk, he would most certainly lose much of that paunch on unremitting tenterhooks.'

'He imperils his office,' said Percival Sedgwick, shaking his head.

'Nay, Percival, he merely imperils his peace of mind. Governorship is a reward usually for surreptitious services rendered. After appointment, a blind eye is turned to the esteemed individual's accumulating out of sight of His Majesty's Government. To amass capital on Pertigua, Osborne needs only his self-indulgent faculties. But first, he will have to think of England and turn his wife into a striking sweet-tempered gracious spouse — if he knows what's good for him. And then he will have to get his fat little mitts grubby in partnership with the West Indies Sugar Cartel — and like it. Shan't he?'

'I daresay he shall,' sniggered Percival Sedgwick. 'And if His Manicured Excellency does figure out what's good for him, I expect him to accept and endorse this island's idiosyncratic customs.'

A bout of bellowed orders concluded the regimental parade. Dismissed troops slung muskets and grumbled off the parade ground. Stewards materialised with trays of rum punch for officers.

Convened with the Governor, Percival Sedgwick and the commandant, Matthew was affable.

'Do you deem your musketeers fit for our impending manoeuvres, Sir Thomas? They looked a mite sluggish and crestfallen to me.'

Goaded by the gibe at his troops, the commandant retorted, 'I'll have you know, Mister Fleming, many of my men saw action in the surrender and destruction of the weapons depot on the Dutch island of Saint Eustatius. You should be aware that about half of all American Revolutionary military supplies are acquired through that island. And the trade between that island and the United States was the primary cause for the fourth Anglo-Dutch War which, as we speak, is still ongoing.

'I admit some of my musketeers appear battle-weary. But make no mistake, Mister Fleming: all are battle-hardened and readied for the fight. Freetown will be in our hands within days.'

'Make certain it is, Sir Thomas,' said Percival Sedgwick firmly. 'Runaways have long been a plague on our plantations. In the past two years they have been particularly vexatious and 'tis high time we did something about it. Put an end to their terror attacks and you will earn the plaudits from indebted plantation owners.'

'And your loyal planters will want more than a mere example made of this so-called Captain of Freetown,' warned Matthew. 'Give the planters something that will stiffen their fortitude, Governor. I believe the vixen to be the female embodiment of Jonas Guinea on our shores.'

'Mister Fleming,' said the Governor authoritatively, 'I am told that over a good few years, many fine men have died trying to arrest this woman. If we cannot take the witch this time, the Prime Minister himself has instructed me to sign a treaty with the rebels. Then we shall just have to like it, shan't we? So you never did lay your hands on Jonas Guinea?'

This Governor seems too well-acquainted with my private crusade, thought Matthew.

'As long as that blackguard breathes, Governor, I shall persist,' he said.

'Methinks you have borne bad blood against Guinea for quite some time, Mister Fleming,' said the Governor impassively. 'In a few days we await the *Pilgrim*, dispatched by his League to purloin our runaways. On the morrow, I trust your antagonism towards Guinea will not hamper a clear head against Freetown. Not anything worse than the impediment of bad blood before a battle, Mister Fleming.'

'On several occasions Jonas Guinea and his confounded League have pirated our slaves,' said Matthew heatedly. 'The *Pilgrim* will be another such attempt. As a result, he has cost our plantations thousands of pounds in lost chattels, sugar production and profits. Had your slaves been looted, Governor, would you not feel and do likewise? I gave my father a pledge to put that right. Bad blood undrawn consumes, Governor.'

Surprised by the trenchant response, the Governor chuckled.

'Pray remember me to your good father, Mister Fleming,' he said. 'I trust he is in hearty shape. As the colony's principal plantation owner, I trust his profits are robust and hope he is at ease with your mother on Turtle Island. On a day like this, sir, does Jamestown not look magnificent?'

'Methinks Jamestown's harbour justifies the praise we have all heard,' said Matthew thoughtfully. 'You may not know that my father is worsening, Governor. The man is in his eighties and quite bedridden. He has not walked the gardens for quite some time. Doctor Clutterbuck tells me he has only months. My wife and mother are beside his cot. Before that untimely event comes to pass, it would gladden the old man greatly to hear of Freetown's downfall.'

'I believe your revered pater was responsible for much of what we see,' said the Governor, sweeping his arm in an arc covering the lush topography. 'To further Pertigua's sugar trade with England, he constructed the most delightful and well-located waterfront in the Indies, which has given a profitable legacy to all. I am saddened to learn that he is in such infirmity. I pray he pulls through. 'Tis clear to me, sir — we can hasten his recovery by taking Freetown.'

Basking in the reflected respect for his father, Matthew gazed down on the horseshoe-shaped harbour on the Sabbath.

Suitably mesmerised, he made a painstaking reconnaissance of the picturesque stone waterfront with its sheltered anchorage. Church-going carriages and open-topped landaus were rattling back and forth along the re-formed Promenade Road. Absent was the muddy tidemark from the flooding two years previously. Repaired and repainted warehouses marched smartly along the length of the restructured dock. The lemon-yellow Customs House and the rebuilt orange-painted Savannah Tavern sparkled in the sunshine. Buyers and slaves were filing in and out of the lately enlarged Auction House. Multicoloured houses and taverns nestled side by side on both sides of the curved road. Colourfully clad planters wandered the dockside confabbing with friends, merchants, overseers and tally clerks, whilst their flamboyant wives and companions sat in carriages or promenaded along the waterfront. Stevedores directed slaves loading and unloading the five barques in port. A sixth barque was careened on the hard of the renovated Careenage having her bottom scrubbed. Fishing boats and skiffs speckled the unruffled waters at low water.

''Tis a truly arresting moment, Governor, but for the imminent hostilities with the runaways,' he said, gritting his teeth.

'In many ways the storm would appear to have fashioned a renaissance for Jamestown, gentlemen,' said the Governor. 'Between Jacob Leverton, the architect sent from London, and Pertigua's slaves, 'tis said the harbour has been rebuilt stronger than before the tempest. I am truly astounded by the result. Now gentlemen, let us turn our attentions to the surrender of Freetown.'

Conscientiously clicking his heels, Sir Thomas Plombley was plain-spoken.

'This instant, gentlemen,' he said imperiously, 'we can call on five hundred infantry and one hundred and thirty overseers as well as the Mongoose Gang, split into three squads. I am dispatching a squad along the high mountain pass to Lake Disappointment and the others along the two clifftop tracks to Freetown. We shall then have the run-away militia between us. Having not had the benefit of instruction in military tactics, I am convinced they will not anticipate simultaneous offensives on all three fronts. I expect to take the Captain of Free-town. Hence, we avoid our previous error when we attacked on one front and were beaten off.'

'If we're going to fight to win, Sir Thomas,' said the Governor forebodingly, 'we run the risk of losing. So I trust you are certain that your strategy is watertight.'

'I-I-I am very co-confident, G-Governor,' said the commandant.

Matthew frowned. That was the first occasion he had noticed the commandant's stutter.

'I might add, Governor,' said Matthew, 'that although I whole-heartedly support Sir Thomas's strategy, methinks this skirmish will not be a straightforward business. Ravenous runaways bristling with muskets will put up a bitter fight to maintain their freedom. In con-trast, our sedentary overfed musketeers may lack as much incentive to shoot as straight as the enemy. But whatever you do, Sir Thomas, do not underestimate the aptitude of this virago and purported Captain of Freetown.'

Jabbing his finger at a group of poker-faced black men wearing tricorne hats at the side of the parade ground, the Governor asked, 'Who are they, Sir Thomas?'

'The Mongoose Gang, Governor,' replied the commandant. 'Per-tigua's waged official trackers. They enforce laws regarding runaways. Free blacks like them have no taste for slaves any more than we. Thanks to their expeditious efforts, we apprehend most runaways be-fore they get anywhere near Freetown. And being of blood with the runaways, they are put to use countering runaway tactics with our field commanders.'

'See the mulatto with the dark yellow complexion, Governor?' asked Matthew.

'Which one?' asked the Governor grumpily, taking a perfunctory glance. 'Niggers all look alike to me.'

'The mulatto in the scruffy osnaburg jacket and moth-eaten hat?'

'Aye,' frowned the Governor. 'What about him?'

'That man is exceedingly cunning and plausible. While slaving in the docks, he regularly passed himself off as a freeman to go carousing in the taverns. He has just reported to me from Hezekiah, one of my slaves whose escape I arranged from my China Lights plantation. In return for his manumission, chattel house and plot of land in his name, Hezekiah agreed to run away to Freetown to act as my mole.'

'A blooded strategy, if I might say, Mister Fleming,' said Sir Thomas, grinning. 'May I ask how you firstly inveigled the nigger's connivance?'

'Hezekiah succumbed to two naked elements rampant in the weak.'

'And what might those be?'

'Greed and betrayal.'

'Veritably succinct I'd say, Mister Fleming,' said the Governor dryly.

'Greed and betrayal is Hezekiah's way of life, gentlemen,' said Matthew unequivocally. 'He betrayed to the mulatto that on the night of the morrow, Freetown plans festivities at which the Captain herself will be present. So five days ago, I covertly arranged the theft of four barrels of rum for their carousing — with any luck into a state of intoxication. It should at any rate dull their fighting prowess, particularly when musketeers rattle their drunken bacchanal with volleys of blistering shot.'

'Valuable intelligence and a foresighted ploy, Mister Fleming,' said Sir Thomas approvingly.

'I am eager to see the stronghold that has for so long kept an English militia at bay,' said the Governor. 'Doubtless you have been there, Sir Thomas?'

'N-Nay, I have not,' said Sir Thomas, clearly discomfited. 'N-no one who has has ever r-returned to d-describe its design.'

'Can we take it then, Sir Thomas,' asked Percival Sedgwick snippily, 'that after so many years the army has little understanding of these runaways, except whereabouts they are vaguely located?'

'They employ hit-and-run tactics, Mister Sedgwick,' said Sir Thomas defensively. ''Tis an unconventional mode of warfare deuce difficult to pin down. What's more, the acres of swamp in which they hide shudder with dangerous snakes and poisonous arrows.'

'We know where this self-styled Captain will be, Sir Thomas,' said the Governor crisply. 'We know where the runaways are. We know who will be victorious. And I am confident you will prosecute this action against the runaways with the expected fervour of an English officer. And I might add with some certainty, Westminster will not look kindly on any loss of seasoned troops to a wanton pack of runaways.'

'What will be will be, Governor,' said the commandant tersely, devoid of a stutter.

'This night, Mister Fleming,' said the Governor, 'you will of course reside with us at Drake House. On the morrow we can proceed on horseback to the hostilities after an excellent midday repast.'

'Why thank you kindly, Governor,' he said, smiling and giving a crisp bow. 'I plan to return with glad tidings to Turtle Island following the fall of Freetown.'

'What with the delightful company of you all,' said the Governor, rubbing his podgy hands together, 'a splendid supper shall be had this night. Whilst downing rum, Madeira and whatever else with a few good hands of quadrille, we shall be regaled by the string quartet I had dispatched from London to fill my official residence with the works of George Frideric Handel and Johann Sebastian Bach. You can be most certain that we shall furnish you with a diverting gathering this evening. As we speak, Lady Penelope entertains a government official, his wife and friends, and Squire Horatio Cholmondeley, a plantation owner with a thousand slaves on the island of Jamaica. 'Tis good company before the fight.'

Reckoning on Mount James

Lake Disappointment
9 September 1783
10.00 hrs

Rivulets of sweat ran down Asabi's face. Wiping her brow, she scanned the area.

At the site of the former Freetown on the sweltering forested swamp-island of Lake Disappointment, her brigade had dug-in some distance behind its abandoned shacks. Bounded on three sides by a range of mountains, the bordering valley echoed with the commotion from versicoloured parrots. Whistling, squawking and squabbling, the hook-billed marauders searched the fruiting shrubs on the rugged north face of Pertigua's highest peak, Mount James. If not for the birds, the surrounding terrain remained uncannily hushed.

Two hundred men and women with muskets lay concealed in the lofty cordgrass. Her trusty mastiffs, Hunter and Arrow, lay panting close by. Brothers from an abandoned injured mastiff bitch she had rescued close to Bamboo Bay, she had then reared them from birth.

Parting the cobwebs between the swaying grass stems, she reconnoitred the face of the mountain.

Flanked by Shadow and Dogbite, her keyed-up sweaty musketeers were strung along the southern shores of the swamp-island and in crevices on the mountainside. Having kept the womanising informer Hezekiah preoccupied in the preparations for a gathering to welcome women freshly run away, she had then tricked him into accompanying the brigade to Lake Disappointment. Thus, she afforded Hezekiah no time to slope off to meet up with his white contacts from Jamestown.

Set half a mile from the northern foot of Mount James, the forested isle was surrounded by crystal clear waters, mangroves and mudflats, successively chased by acres of reed and sedge beds, scrub and stretches of forest and grasslands, rocky outcrops and ridges. By way of well-constructed defences, they sowed camouflaged trails and fake paths that led to booby traps and quicksand. An outsider unfamiliar with the wild terrain and straying off the track would likely die from hunger or suffocate in a bog.

Taking a good toke from a yellow clay pipe, she passed it to the nearest musketeer and gave a broad smile. Nervous laughter rippled through the cordgrass. Sweating out the dead time before commencement of hostilities, a trail of precious memories drifted through her mind.

Raising watery eyes, she muttered beneath her breath as if uttering a prayer. 'Kayode, Truelove an' Faith, I could have made not anything of me but for you. Abi be with me for this fight. We mus' win to stay free.'

Blinking back tears, she trained her recently appropriated telescope at Mount James. Peering halfway up the rock face, she scanned along an elongated outcrop supporting a partly wooded track. Locating her son's two ambush posts, she saw men secreted in bushy trackside crevices forty yards apart.

'Abi's lookouts will blow the *abeng*,' she said.

'When Redcoats bin seen,' added Shadow.

Having helped them elude, frustrate and hold the planters and Redcoats at bay for decades, the illustrious *abeng* cow horn was again the instrument to galvanise them into this action.

Suddenly, from the eastern end of the valley, a lone *abeng* horn wailed.

'Redcoats bin seen on the track,' said Shadow breathlessly.

Just then, she heard the two *abeng* horns half a mile away, sited along the clifftop some distance from Freetown, signalling the sighting of the advancing enemy.

'Them attack back an' front at same time,' said Shadow. 'This 'ouse be right ready ter sen' hot musket balls. I sen' a scout ter see what goin' down by Freetown.'

'If only the white men be ready to settle this fight wi' words,' she said, shaking her head dolefully. 'If only they can give us back what we have lost. They will not talk 'cos they come only to take back their property. No man will ever lay violent hands on me again.'

She thought about the other two brigades of the runaway militia — four hundred men and women — tensed up and sited along the clifftop overlooking Ocean Bay, and her own third brigade on the forested slopes of Mount James and in the cordgrass of Lake Disappointment.

Spotting movement on the mountain track through the telescope, she held her breath.

Yards from the first ambush post, an endless red file of foot soldiers were snaking up the track. The first twenty had barely cleared the first ambush post when two man-sized blazing grass drums, propelled from a crevice, thudded into the procession. Two soldiers were sent flailing into the abyss to their deaths. Parched trackside foliage burst into a fierce blaze. Fanned by the wind, the inferno cut off the following soldiers. Almost at once from the second ambush post further ahead, two more flaming drums rolled onto the track obstructing the way ahead. Sighting the perpetrators shinning down readied ropes, she turned and smiled at Shadow and Dogbite.

'Our men got away,' she gloated. 'Soldiers have been cut off from their comrades. Abi's plan work an' now he finish 'em off. Now we teach the Governor an' Fleming, we fight an' we all die or we all be free. We will not go back to be slaves.'

Across a deep gorge, from the wooded section of the track ahead where the track snaked roughly back on itself, Abi's concealed musketeers fired at the fire-trapped soldiers. In the subsequent short bloody exchange of fire, twenty Redcoats lay dead on the track. Disbelief at such an unimaginable disaster was palpable among the remaining soldiers watching helplessly. She heard a gaggle of screamed orders. Bugles blared. Frantic soldiers spun around and started shuffling back down the track. Bent on getting off the mountain track, a few lost their footing and plummeted to their deaths. Impulsively, her musketeers began firing at the withdrawing soldiers.

'Stop shooting,' she shouted. 'They be out of musket shot. An' they be back. We sleep here this night. English not give up so easily. I tell you they be back in daylight an' bring plenty o' muskets. Keep

Redcoats fighting in the mountains an' swamps an' we win. They like to fight on flat open ground. Since it takes Redcoats too long to turn their heads, we hit and run 'fore they do. Come, Shadow, we plan for what Redcoats do next.'

During the ensuing chatter between the tensed waiting fighters she stood alone, gazing through the tall grasses at the mountain while gripped by an uncanny silence in a miasma of dark fears. Shaking off her many uncertainties, she sat with Shadow and Dogbite through the afternoon with an eye on retreating Redcoats until they were well out of sight.

Applause suddenly rippled through the cordgrass. The ovation was growing gradually closer and louder.

Frowning, she turned to ascertain the cause of the cheers. She smiled.

Led by her son, grime-streaked musketeers responsible for the demise of many Redcoats strode into the garrison and slumped on the ground. In the jubilant aftermath of taking first blood from a chancy action, euphoria breezed through the camp.

Stretching out her hand, she laughed.

'Come son, come sit by me,' she said. 'Come tell me what happen up on the track. You leave lookouts up there?'

'Fret not, Ma,' said Abi, sitting close to her and breathing heavily, 'I leave lookouts in mountain hides to watch for Redcoats. Up on mountain when Redcoats get close, all go wrong. Grass drum fires go out. I sweat a river on the spot. Redcoats walk past, so close me can smell their sweat. Real quiet like, we get down an' blow 'til we get drum blazing an' push it on track. We come down to eat an' sleep.'

'You all got guts, Abi,' she said, smiling. 'Fight for freedom bin' very bloody. Be bloodier on the morrow. We eat an' sleep.'

'Mango not a lot for a fight,' said Shadow, chuckling. 'Suckling pig better for we.'

'No fires after dark,' she said firmly. 'We stay cold an' eat cold. Fire show up this place like a star in the dark. Pass it on.'

Shortly after sunset, the rasping wheeze and fast clicking trills of the ashy-faced owls could be heard. Widespread belief whispering up from the plantations that owls were witches increased the unease in the hyper-vigilant camp.

Just then, Shadow's scout arrived back from Freetown.

'Redcoats attacking Freetown 'long clifftop 'ave lost many many men,' said the scout, shaking his head while heavily panting. 'Redcoats back off an' mek camp in Bamboo Bay. Freetown 'ave nine dead an' four wi' bad wounds.'

Disturbed by the number of Freetown's dead, she broke away from the group. Tears filled her eyes. Trailed by her son, she walked gloomily towards her former shack where she had loved his father.

'Papa here wi' us this night, Ma,' said Abi quietly, putting his arm tenderly around her shoulders. 'His spirit gives me strength for the fight.'

'We mus' force Redcoats to make peace,' she said with quiet resolve. 'They lost many soldiers this day. They wi' lose many more on the morrow.'

Bamboo Bay

9 September 1783
23.45 hrs

It was warm, moonlit and nearing midnight. Sporadic gusts whipped from the south. Only the timbre of waves lapping the sands breached the ominous echoing hush. Dismounting in angry silence from his reconnoitre of the isolated Bamboo Bay, Matthew Fleming paused on the edge of the military encampment and wiped his brow. Holding the reins of his panting steed, he scanned the curved bay bordered by the giant bambusa clumping bamboo.

The half moon was waxing. The quiescent sea and the camp, the foreshore and foothills were bathed in a soft translucent light. Sudden flurries down the strandline and the fixed dune zone sent the spiky-leaved marram grasses rustling against a blue-black sky. Sentries had been stationed the length of the foreshore. The night watch had begun.

''Tis a shameful day,' he muttered. 'Who would have thought it would come to this?'

Appraising the camp from the water's edge, he fortified himself with swigs of his favoured Glenturret whisky from a silver hip flask.

Following the day's hostilities, the acrid stench of Faversham powder hung in the air. Startled by explosions during the conflict, seabirds were now unsettlingly absent. Billeted in dozens of wedge tents, the Pertiguan Regiment were bivouacked in rows along powdery white sands. Nearby lay a stockpile of provisions for a regiment on the march, abutting a stack of tin kettles, hatchets, bell tents, drum cases, powder bags, water flasks, haversacks and knapsacks.

Hitching his horse to the regiment's long rail, he walked up the shore to a large gable-end marquee situated on the crest.

A sentry pulled aside the entry flap. Smoothing his frock coat, he stepped into the convened summit. He nodded in turn at the Governor, Sir Preston Osborne, the commandant, Sir Thomas Plombley, uniformed officers of the regiment and the frock-coated Percival Sedgwick. Filling a glass from the flagon of rum on the table, he took a sip. Taking the chair next to the planter, he sat back and assessed the ring of severe expressions and glazed eyes.

Bring in the coffins, he thought.

Oil lamps burned brightly inside the campaign headquarters. Furnishing the spartan interior were four canvas cots, two wooden trunks and the regimental colours stuck in the ground. The stench of sweat was surpassed only by the stench of despair. Between the two central pillars of the tent, the ashen-faced men responsible for the day's disastrous events sat around a map-covered trestle table looking in consternation at the Governor, resplendent in his formal dress coat.

The Governor got the post-mortem underway.

'Sir Thomas,' he said bullishly, his gold-faced lapels glinting in the flickering light, 'His Majesty's Government demands a complete breakdown on what has occurred here this day.'

Startled out of his stupor, Sir Thomas replied, 'First we must torch Freetown, Governor, and then a comprehensive breakdown shall be provided forthwith. Including, I might add, the names of all those party to the planning.'

Noticing the Governor squirm at the commandant's sideswipe, Matthew took sides.

'As the representatives of the West Indies Sugar Cartel,' said Matthew pompously, 'Mister Sedgwick and I as well need to understand just how a mob of bungling sambos bested trained white musketeers.'

'Niggers won't stand and fight,' snarled Sir Thomas, reddening defensively. 'They hit and run. And they hold to no established battlefield tactics.'

'Excuses if I might say, Sir Thomas,' said Matthew, glowering and sitting upright in his seat. 'Englishmen are lying dead all over the place and you say 'tis because the niggers won't stand still? Piffle, sir.'

'A mere three tracks into Freetown you said,' added the Governor quizzically.

'My officers did not expect all three tracks to be alive with snares and musketeers shooting from concealed positions,' said Sir Thomas. 'They did not anticipate niggers to be working as one. And they did not imagine them to be so readied. We expected a disorganised rabble and found an army.'

'More excuses, Sir Thomas,' said Percival Sedgwick scornfully. 'From where you say the niggers have sited themselves, they could well hold off your regiment in perpetuity. Mayhaps your troops will next time display a more appropriate strategy and come better prepared.'

'The regiment was well-prepared and the strategy was sound,' said the commandant. 'An offensive on all three tracks simultaneously should have given us the element of surprise.'

'*Should* have given you the element of surprise, Sir Thomas,' said Percival Sedgwick derisively, 'is not the same as giving you the element of surprise.'

'Sir Thomas,' said the Governor accusingly, 'why do I have the distinct feeling that your men were expected? Moreover, you clearly took no precautions for such a turnabout.'

'After all that has been said and done here, Sir Thomas,' said Matthew, 'and in spite of your well-laid plans to surprise the runaways, your men were obstructed on all three tracks. I don't suppose that was a coincidence.'

'"Twas bloody maddening to see comrades caught off guard and slaughtered,' said a beetroot-faced Major. 'Niggers are ruthless.'

Sniffing a pinch of snuff off the back of his hand into his left nostril, the Governor asked, 'How many have we lost, Sir Thomas?'

'I am awaiting the surgeon's account, Governor,' responded the commandant.

The Governor took another pinch of snuff.

'And you never even sighted Freetown or her villainous captain,' he said, as if lost in thought.

'Seems to me, Sir Thomas,' said Percival Sedgwick condescendingly, 'you used the wrong tactics. You fought the wrong battle and did not win the day. Were you a runaway, would you stand and fight an army with infinitely superior weaponry and expertise? Or would you strike that army with an uncommon action?'

'Forgive me, Mister Sedgwick,' said the commandant cuttingly. 'Had I been advised of your illustrious expertise in military strategy, I would naturally have sought your invaluable advice aforehand.'

Turning scarlet at the scathing censure, Percival Sedgwick fell silent and looked away.

'Sir Thomas Plombley,' said the Governor frostily. 'I made it clear to you that His Majesty's Government would not tolerate unacceptable losses. In a colony as small as Pertigua, any loss is offensive. In the space of a day you have lost an unknown number of Englishmen to a horde of cold-blooded felons.'

'I-I-I should remind you, Governor Osborne,' said the commandant hotly, 'that you and I devised this little operation together. At all planning meetings you were present, sir. My officers will confirm such before any Board of Inquiry. I suggest that while we are all licking our wounds, we put an end to these scapegoating shenanigans. In the meantime, while you cobble together an appropriate report for London, my regiment will prosecute the morrow's action with improved fervour.'

'I as well suggest we belay laying blame and start considering our next course of action,' said Matthew adamantly. 'The fact is we cannot have niggers going around casually murdering their white masters on a slave island lest it become an epidemic.'

'How came you by this command, Sir Thomas?' asked Percival Sedgwick with undisguised disdain.

Turning his face away from the commandant, Matthew smiled.

Just then, a chisel-jawed, blonde-haired character materialised beside the commandant. Despite the heat, the man wore a blood-spattered woollen justaucorps coat reaching to the knees with stockings and buckled shoes. It was the regimental surgeon. Passing a folded piece of paper to the commandant, he was crisp.

'Casualty figures, Sir Thomas.'

Scouring the paper, the commandant scowled and thrust it at the Governor.

'Good God, Sir Thomas!' exclaimed the Governor, glaring at the commandant. 'Twenty-six dead and twelve wounded. In the space of hours, twenty alone were lost on the mountain track. These losses cannot be easily explained away. I'll be a laughing stock in London.'

'London should be the least of your worries, Governor,' said Matthew mellifluously. 'It could not have been foreseen that these niggers would have the nous to set ambushes along all three tracks. Furthermore, such sharp-shooting musketry at those Redcoats trapped on the mountain track could not have been anticipated. The runaways were undoubtedly waiting for us, Governor. I smell a rat and he's close to home. I wager that someone with abolitionist sympathies on our side has clued-up someone on theirs. But who?'

'It matters not who, Mister Fleming,' said Sir Thomas gruffly. 'We can leave that to the Board of Inquiry. My regiment will re-engage the runaways on the morrow. This time we shall destroy their hit-and-run campaign and force them into a conventional fight.'

'Ye shall not re-engage the runaways on the morrow, Sir Thomas,' said the Governor sharply. 'I shall not permit it. I am under government orders to settle this matter post-haste. England has lost many good men over countless years trying to quell these particular runaways. The cost in English blood and lost sugar production has been far too high. The niggers in these mountains cannot affect sugar production, especially if we have a pact with them. I believe the time has arrived for a settlement — nay indeed a treaty.'

'A treaty!' exclaimed Percival Sedgwick, clearly horrified.

'Yes, Mister Sedgwick, a treaty,' said the Governor emphatically. 'But first, Sir Thomas, we shall unnerve the runaways by doing not anything. For the next three days your men shall remain in their tents while we let the niggers stew. An officer, two privates and Mister Fleming shall accompany us on the Wednesday to form a party of truce. You and I, Sir Thomas, shall lead the delegation to sign the peace treaty on open ground. Gentlemen, let me be clear. I shall brook no interference in this matter.'

Speechlessness befell the marquee as uncomfortable looks darted around the table.

Sitting upright with vigour, Percival Sedgwick disgorged his ire.

'Are my ears deceiving me, Governor Osborne? Do you, an Englishman, truly intend to make a truce with niggers? That sends a suspiciously spineless signal does it not? Why not gift them the Great Houses and the plantations as well?'

'Are you baffled by the sudden change of tack by politicians, Sedg-wick?' inquired Matthew mischievously.

'I have long suspected,' said the Governor, peering intently around the assembled faces, 'that they who deem black men fit only to be slaves are not best placed to be of assistance when compelled to ne-gotiate with them. Dirty tasks need dirty hands. To that end, Mister Sedgwick, 'twould be better for you not to partake in what comes next, for we shall be up to our armpits.'

Tossing his head scornfully, Percival Sedgwick said angrily, 'By its very nature, Governor, slave-ownership means a master cannot ever slacken reins. Following this little debacle, if word gets out that free niggers are wandering around in the mountains, hunting, fishing and copulating, it will tempt slaves to run away. You make a grievous mistake, Governor. In these islands, sir, white men do not go about making deals with niggers.'

Silence again struck the occupants in the marquee.

Sedgwick recognises not the political winds of change, thought Matthew.

'To my mind,' said the Governor, fastidiously examining his nails, 'fanaticism is the last bastion of scoundrels who habitually, I might add, seem not to find common cause with common sense. Coherent actions are what is required here, gentlemen. The PM desires I speedily resolve this matter. The loss in English blood to quell these runaways is utterly unacceptable. Not another Englishman shall be sacrificed in the futile pursuit of these confounded niggers.

'I have drafted a conflict truce comprising eight articles. I want you all to read it and agree it by the morning. After approved amendments, we shall sit down with the runaways to sign it. Then, gentlemen, we shall have peace on Pertigua. Of course, Mister Sedgwick, I understand if you feel you cannot bring yourself to endorse these articles. Methinks if you did indeed find the wherewithal to support these articles, it would prove somewhat healthier for a number of your, shall we say, doubtful holdings and activities.'

Coughing, spluttering and purple-faced at the gubernatorial browbeating, Percival Sedgwick composed himself with discomfited effort.

'F-F-Far be it for me to hamper government policy, Governor Osborne,' he said, breaking out in a sweat and speedily capitulating. 'Of course I shall sign. You have my word on it.'

'I am so relieved our strategy finds accommodation with you, Mister Sedgwick,' said the Governor courteously. 'I knew you would not let your somewhat hasty aversion to the treaty jeopardise your fortune by impeding the progress of the new order.'

Hurriedly mopping his brow, Percival Sedgwick heaved a soft sigh of relief and took large swigs of brandy from a silver hip flask.

For three days, a standoff reigned between the runaways and the Redcoats. No Redcoats were reported on the mountain track, in the valley surrounding Lake Disappointment or along the cliff top near Freetown. Despite the duration of the strenuous watch during which there were the customary internecine clashes, Freetown's musketeers remained steadfastly at their posts. Sometime during the third night, Hezekiah disappeared.

'We have not time to track down an informer,' she scowled. 'We know where he go.'

Frowning and scratching his head, Dogbite asked, 'Where?'

'To look for his white masters,' she said. 'Hezekiah knows not what we plan. So he be no use to them.'

Averse to informers vanishing from under her nose, Hezekiah's disappearing haunted her.

Treaty

Lake Disappointment
12 September 1783
11.00 hrs

Following a light shower, the day dawned with a red-orange sky. With the increasing light, the temperature began to soar. A coast eagle wheeled and soared majestically on the updrafts above the deserted valley. Smouldering bushes speckled the sunlit battleground from the fires of the past days' hostilities.

In sweat-stained jerkin and breeches, Asabi sat in the cordgrass with her mastiffs lying alongside.

'Been three days now,' she muttered. 'Where is these Redcoats?'

Unexpectedly rising and taking a few steps forwards, the mastiffs stopped and growled.

'Look,' said Abi, pointing at Mount James.

Musketeers scrambled to take a look at what had drawn Abi's attention. Standing up, Asabi raised her telescope.

Carrying a white flag about half a mile away, several white men on horseback were approaching from the end of the mountain track.

'Them give up?' said Shadow uncertainly.

'Redcoats not ever give up,' she said with a drawn-out sigh. 'They come to tell us to surrender or we die. They don't come to make peace.'

The sun was nearing its zenith.

With sweat trickling down the nape of her neck, she stepped up onto a small hummock.

For what felt an age, she watched the sluggish progress of the approaching delegation across the valley floor. In due course, the deputation came to a halt ten yards away in the cordgrass. With eyes locked on her coterie, the white men warily dismounted. All at once, that weight called hate reared its head between black and white, so much so it was almost visible.

Stepping down from the hummock biting her bottom lip, Asabi's heartbeat accelerated.

Drawing warily closer, they halted a few yards from her. The party included a fresh-faced young officer, a bemedalled crimson-faced officer and a man in a tanned frock coat.

A stiff, tubby, side-burned character in a fancy dress coat addressed them.

'You are looking at the Governor of Pertigua, Sir Preston Osborne,' he said superciliously. 'The gentlemen with me represent the interests of the government of England and the plantations on the Crown Colony of Pertigua. Who speaks for you?'

Jabbing a thumb at herself from where she stood, Asabi spoke with barely concealed hostility.

'I be Asabi, Captain of Freetown, an' I speak for all runaways,' she said coldly, her nostrils flaring. 'If you come here to tell we to give up, you waste your ride down the mountain. We wi' not surrender to cut cane, Gov'nor Osborne. Slavery be all 'bout sugar an' white people got big hunger for sugar. If you love sugar so much, break yer own backs cutting yer own cane. Runaways wi' stay in Freetown an' we wi' fight till we die.'

Startled by her scarcely disguised animosity, Matthew looked anxiously around.

What manner of name is Asabi, he thought. These runaways have no end of muskets. Striking as this woman is, she is no fool. By his pompous approach, I doubt if this Governor knows that she is the woman of the notorious Captain Sodeke, who with her connivance led the uprising. If not, I pray he is at least aware we deal with a cold-hearted character. I will tread with great care.

'They call me Mister Fleming,' he said in his best peace-making voice. 'We come not to talk of dying or to ask for your surrender, Captain Asabi. We come here for just the opposite. In the first instance, the Governor asks only that you listen to his proposal. And secondly, you will agree that between us, hundreds have lost their lives over many, many years?'

Nodding suspiciously with narrowed eyes, she stayed silent.

Caught by a sudden gust, the grasses rustled and fractured the tense brief hush.

'Is it not time we put a stop to this carnage?' asked Matthew fervently. 'Do you not want to live without fear of discovery and attack? What the Governor offers is an agreement between our peoples to guarantee that peace.'

'Agreement!' she exclaimed, looking askance at Abi and Shadow and then back at the Governor. 'Agreement 'tween we?'

'Aye, an agreement with a peace treaty,' said the Governor, as if his offer to runaways were a routine event. 'Peace, Captain Asabi. Peace for all time. What say you?'

'What trap is this?' she asked, scornfully narrowing her eyes at the Governor. 'Peace? Two times now your Redcoats come in force to kill us or take us back as slaves. Is that what you call peace? Your Redcoats fail then an' will fail again. What kind o' peace you offer now? What trap you set?'

'No trap,' said the commandant crisply, 'merely a wise course in the circumstances. As things stand, we could go on fighting and dying until the sun drops from the sky. What the Governor proposes is an end to the dying, a farewell to muskets between us. That way we do away with the needless slaughter.'

'You stand wi' the people of Freetown, Gov'nor,' she said proudly. 'We be not so foolish to give up 'cos a white man say so. If you speak truly, then tell me more 'bout your peace.'

'Can you read, Captain Asabi?'

'Not 'cos you helped, Gov'nor,' she answered curtly. 'I read an' write well.'

The Governor pulled a scrolled document out of a silk sausage bag. 'I have set out eight articles in this paper to secure the peace. We shall give you time to read it and talk it over among yourselves. At midday on the morrow, we shall return here when we shall hopefully reach a settlement. Then the war will be over.'

Holding his eye unwaveringly, she raised her hand.

'Be not so quick, Gov'nor,' she said. 'If there be no tricks buried in your paper an' you keep your word to leave us in peace, then an' only then, Mister Gov'nor, the war wi' be over.'

Before mounting his horse, Matthew looked intently at her.

'Captain Asabi,' he said, 'I was wondering if you know a runaway called Hezekiah.'

'I do not, Mister Fleming,' she said, straight-faced. 'You forget where you put your slaves?'

'You are a formidable opponent, Captain Asabi,' said Matthew. 'Grudgingly, you have my respect. After the morrow I trust we shall both look forwards to the peace.'

'We have peace, Mister Fleming,' she said loudly as his mount plodded away, 'if your Gov'nor be not verberlating from both sides of 'is mouth.'

Given her incredulity at the turn of events, the historic occasion scrambled her thoughts. Hearing huge sighs of relief from her son, Shadow and Dogbite, she had her answer ready for the morrow.

Returning to the encamped runaways, she waved the treaty document triumphantly in the air and then shouted details of the truce to her dumbstruck listeners. Throughout the sultry afternoon, while taking sips of rum, she kept watch on the delegation as it trotted away across the valley and disappeared up the mountain track.

Putting her arm around her son's shoulders, she said, 'Send word to Scroggs, Abi. You find him along clifftop by Freetown. Tell him he sorely needed to hear white man's treaty.'

'I go forward and find him, Ma,' said Abi, striding away.

'You not trust Scroggs, Asabi,' said Dogbite categorically.

'You notice?'

'What 'e do?'

'Not bad enough he a runaway on a slave island,' she scowled, 'the man's a bigot 'gainst women. Yet he call 'is woman 'is Queen. What that 'bout? He truly 'ate that a woman be Captain o' Freetown.'

Deepening Scroggs's antagonism was the fact that Freetown was also the acknowledged headquarters of the runaways. And being the woman of the legendary Captain Sodeke and co-leader of Pertigua's largest uprising bestowed on her the legitimacy of Captain in the eyes of the runaway majority.

'Women good for pum-pum and mekin' baby an' be Queen,' Scroggs had said.

'Him get a good kicking if he put one eye on me woman,' growled Shadow.

'Women on Freetown Council get Scroggs angry,' she said, 'so he take he an' 'is followers out of Freetown to live by Ocean Bay. He forget women fight an' die jus' as hard as men in the uprising. Now he get 'is Ocean Bay posse to defend Freetown 'gainst the Redcoats. For once he did right. When he get here he likely be drunk, so give him only sarsaparilla to keep he awake.'

Leaving her contingent in position at Lake Disappointment, she started back for Freetown with her son, Shadow and Dogbite. Their rejuvenation was palpable. Despite her soaring spirits at the prospect of freedom in the mountains, she felt mournful.

'For long long years we been fighting whitey,' she said, shaking her head, 'yet this first time I shake a white hand an' he 'ave an open smile.'

'You think 'im white all over, Asabi?' asked Dogbite, straight-faced.

'Them no colour below them clothes,' growled Shadow.

Recollecting the rapes by her owner, Frederick Bradshaw, while a house slave in the Great House of the Tamarind Trees plantation, she snapped, 'Them white.'

'What happen if we settle wi' Governor, Ma?' enquired Abi. 'When you think Redcoats gone for good?'

'If we put our mark to this treaty, Abi,' she said, 'we will be free from nightfall on the morrow. On this soil we will build houses for our families an' a school for our chillen. We will raise Freetown on the plateau above the cave an' live with no fear of attack. We mus' not ever forget dead friends who not witness this laying down of arms.'

'I wi' not forget, Ma,' said Abi firmly.

Pomegranate reds from the dying sun flooded Freetown's cave entrance. The evening was warm and clear. Contained in the cavern for safety during hostilities, the squeals of children echoed around. Space was cleared around a welcoming fire. Two wooden flagons of sarsaparilla and a dozen halves of coconut husks were set on the ground.

Swigging from a bottle of rum, Shadow passed it around.

'Wi' rum,' he guffawed, 'drink to freedom, my friends, 'fore Scroggs show 'is face.'

Before long, Scroggs appeared from the back of the cave. Wearing stained clothes and carrying a musket, he stopped beside the fire with a disagreeable-looking companion.

From the mysterious Kongo country and of medium height, Scroggs was stout with smooth black skin and round-faced. Comprehensively illiterate, he spoke little English and bad French. A mason by trade, she knew him to be about forty years of age and a very great drunkard. Despite the brewing evidence in his glazed eyes, he was surprisingly sober.

'We mash 'em Redcoats up good, Asabi,' said Scroggs, with a broad gap-toothed grin. 'Me bring Benjamin ter 'ear this treaty.'

'They offer a treaty cos we fight to a standstill,' she said, smiling. 'They can't force us from here. An' we can't leave Freetown. They can't win. We can't win. Drink sarsaparilla. You know we all.'

'Me say whitey frit,' said Scroggs. 'He know he not beat we.'

'An' we not ever beat him,' she countered. 'Come, sit man.'

Settling cross-legged around the fire, a warm breeze wafted through the grotto.

To lessen Scroggs's patent unease parleying with a woman, she smiled and asked, 'You eat, man?'

'Lemme 'ear this 'ere treaty woman,' said Scroggs with brusque impatience.

'Cool your mouth wi' sarsaparilla, man,' she snapped.

Unfurling the scrolled treaty, she began to read:

'That all hostilities shall cease on both sides forever.

That the said Captain Asabi, the rest of her Captains, Adherents and Men and Women, shall be for ever hereafter in a perfect State of Freedom and Liberty.

That they shall enjoy and possess for themselves and Posterity for ever, all the Lands situate and lying between Bamboo Bay to Mount James to the Deception Bay peninsula, to the amount of two thousand acres.

That they shall have Liberty to plant the said Lands with Coffee, Ginger, Tobacco and Cotton, and breed Cattle, Hogs, Goats, or any other stock and dispose of the Produce or Increase of the said Commodities to the Inhabitants of this Island. Provided always, that when they bring the said Commodities to Market, they shall apply first to the Custos, or any other Magistrate of the respective Parishes where they expose their Goods to Sale, for Licence to vend the same.

That in case this island be invaded by any foreign Enemy, the said Captain Asabi, and her Successors herein and after named, or to be appointed, shall then, upon Notice given, immediately repair to any place the Governor for the time being shall appoint, in order to repel the said Invaders with her or their utmost Force; and to submit to the Orders of the Commander in Chief on that Occasion.

That if any White Man shall do any Manner of Injury to Captain Asabi, her Successors, or any of her People, they shall apply to any commanding Officer or Magistrate in the Neighbourhood for Justice; and in case Captain Asabi, or any of her People, shall do any Injury to any White Person, she shall submit herself or deliver up such Offenders to Justice.

That if any Negroes shall hereafter run away from their Masters or Owners on the Plantations, and fall into Captain Asabi's Hands, they shall immediately be sent back to the Chief Magistrate of the next Parish where they are taken; and those that bring them are to be satisfied for their trouble, as Legislature shall appoint.

That a White Resident to be nominated by His Excellency, or the Commander in Chief for the time being, shall constantly live and reside near Captain Asabi and her Successors, in order to maintain a friendly Correspondence with the Inhabitants of this Island.'

'Freetown can live wi' that,' said Asabi crisply, looking around at her son, Shadow and Dogbite, who all nodded.

Passing Scroggs the scroll she knew he could not decipher, she looked away.

'If you agree, then I put my sign on this document.'

Pretending to read the paper, Scroggs speedily passed it back to her and grunted, 'Me 'gree.'

'You sure you agree with everything?'

'Aye,' he said, narrowing his eyes with suspicion.

'We will not support number seven,' she said unequivocally. 'Free-town will not ever give runaways back to plantations to be slaves.'

'Yo' say that to this white man Resident?' asked Scroggs belligerently.

'We help this Resident build a cosy dwelling in Bamboo Bay,' she said, with a roguish twinkle in her eyes. 'The Resident then be far 'nough away from us. To talk to we, the Resident will 'ave to climb halfway up a mountain an' take a long walk to get to Freetown. He not be doing that a lot in the hot sun. When he reach here tired out, we give him strong rum an' a woman to show him around. After his chat wi' her, the Resident will not know where he be. An' he not ever recognise a runaway among we.'

Abi grinned at Dogbite, who chuckled.

'If runaway gits ter Ocean Bay,' snarled Scroggs, 'we sen' 'em back ter whitey. That keep we be safe in Ocean Bay.'

'That make you one selfish son of a bitch, Scroggs,' she said force-fully. 'Go set up your village in Ocean Bay wi' your own rules. How you be so wicked to send a soul back to plantation? We will sign an' keep to this treaty, but for the bit that says we agree to give runaways back.'

'We do tings differen' in Ocean Bay,' growled Scroggs arrogantly. 'Woman knows 'er place, an' that be under.'

Though the encounter had been unpleasant, a decision had been made. Freetown and Ocean Bay would be separately led by Asabi and Scroggs respectively. Agreeing to meet her from time to time to settle common crises, he and his friend strode out of Freetown. As they melted into the darkness, she noted the haughty airs in the man from the Kongo.

Next day at midday, as agreed, the five horsebacked peace delegation arrived with a pine-topped scissor-legged folding table. In the cordgrass of Lake Disappointment, the table was erected under a tall heavily-leafed jacaranda tree, encircled by the runaways. In the shade of its spreading branches on the seventeenth day of September, 1783, at two o'clock on a sunny afternoon, the treaty was duly endorsed. On behalf of Freetown's runaways and the Pertiguan Government, it was signed by Captain Asabi and Governor Osborne respectively. The historic deed was witnessed by Matthew Fleming and Shadow, who signed with his birth name, Femi.

Excited shouting erupted from the cordgrass.

'We free! We free!' cried the assembled runaways.

'Now our fight is ended, Mister Fleming,' said Asabi, grim-faced.

I wonder if she awaits the *Pilgrim*, thought Matthew. She gives not anything away. No matter. This treaty will not curb my intent to apprehend the vessel.

Shaking his hand, Asabi scrutinised the brown-eyed white face with its carefully manicured sideburns. This man got cold cold eyes, she thought, an' he be one cruel man. We mus' tread wi' care when we go to meet the *Pilgrim*.

'I trust time will heal the hostility you own, Captain Asabi,' said Matthew with hesitant magnanimity.

'Time heals much, Mister Fleming,' she said tersely, 'if yer people give it time.'

'You have that time from this instant, Captain Asabi. The Redcoats shall not be back.'

'Give a message to Frederick Bradshaw, Mister Fleming.'

'Aye?'

'Tell the man Captain Asabi say to keep his backside away from Freetown.'

Shaken by the spleen spewed at his fellow planter, Matthew calmly replied, 'I will pass on your message, Captain Asabi, though I doubt Mister Bradshaw will be ever be risking his neck around these parts.'

This treaty got a nasty taste, she thought, an' we mus' swallow it.

In an inhospitable rocky corner of a slave island, as thousands of slaves languished in brutal subjection on its plantations, the runaways of Freetown won freedom inside two thousand acres.

Reflecting her compromised circumstances with a deep scowl, she quietly asked, 'What kind o' freedom Freetown got when black people stay slaves on plantations, Mister Fleming?'

'Slaves shall remain the property of their owners and will go on cutting cane, Captain Asabi,' Sir Thomas interjected brusquely. 'Plantation slaves figure in no part of this treaty. You can be most certain that shall remain so.'

Incensed by his wounding response, she fumed, 'Freetown swallows a sour freedom, Gov'nor.'

Blithely ignoring her statement, the Governor turned to depart.

''Tis an appropriate moment for us to take our leave of you, Captain Asabi,' he said. 'I bid thee a good farewell and good fortune, even if I do find these circumstances to be somewhat bizarre. We shall not need to be bothering thee again. In three days the Resident will arrive with a small party to help him get established in Bamboo Bay, as you suggest. He will be here only to aid communication between us. Not anything more.'

'Not anything more' pounded in her ears. An age of terror was over and before her lay fresh horizons.

With a marked air of fulfilment, the peace delegation mounted their horses and trotted off across the sunlit valley leaving their table behind.

A blood-red sphere sat above the horizon.

Feeling bruised and brutalised, she tottered alone to her old shack clutching the treaty document. Dropping to her knees, she stared hard at the vellum scroll for a long long while. Suddenly letting out a long harrowing groan, teardrops rolled from her eyes. Constantly being on the alert, hiding, fighting and dying were all at an end. An unthinkable euphoria tore through her. A tremor rippled down her backbone.

'Kayode an' Truelove not here to witness this day,' she said, noisily exhaling.

Stifling an anguished cry, she collapsed sobbing onto the dirt floor.

Entering the shack, Abi dropped to his knees. Gently cupping her face in his hands, he spoke softly.

'You sad, Ma?'

'A famous day for Freetown, my son,' she said.

'Bin a great day, Ma.'

'Your father not here,' she said.

Pausing thoughtfully, Abi tenderly stroked her face.

'Captain Kayode Sodeke was a good good man, Ma,' he said proudly. 'Like you and my father, I too hope to be Captain of Freetown.'

Wiping her eyes and sitting upright, she gave him a loving smile and then gazed through the doorway into the distance.

'Your father an' me was young when we break from Tamarind Trees plantation,' she said, sighing softly. 'Freedom's years in Freetown 'ave been breathtaking. We got so many plans an' dreams 'fore the uprising. He act like nothing was beyond him. All was possible. An' he did it wi' such gladness. I loved yer father deeply, Abi. An' I tell you this: a woman gives her heart to a man just once in her life. An' she give it only to the one who is her *kadara* – destiny. Your father was my *kadara*. We make the uprising to free the slaves an' seize the island. Now all we got is a free bit o' it. Slavery still bleeds across the plantations.'

''Papa an' you were slaves, Ma,' said Abi admiringly. ''Cos you break out together, I was born free. I know not how to be a slave. The bit of the island we got mean my chillen will go to school every day and learn about the big world. I will keep alive the Yoruba in them. Aye Ma, bit of the island we won means no one in Freetown will ever be a slave.'

'In spite of the treaty, Abi,' she said, 'Freetown will give shelter to runaways.'

Gently raising her chin with a cupped hand, Abi looked at her and frowned. 'I hear you, Ma. Will this Resident not know when he find new face in Freetown?'

'The Resident not know, Abi,' she said assertively. 'In white eyes one black face look like 'nother. Something tells me we got to change the time an' place to meet the *Pilgrim*. Tell only Shadow an' Dogbite. Apart from them sailing to Guinea, let the rest think we meeting the *Pilgrim* in Deception Bay. Don't fret Abi; whitey will break something in the treaty, an he hope we don't fin' out.'

'How can man 'oo been a slave sen' 'nother back to slave-owner?' Abi asked indignantly.

'Yer mean Scroggs?'

Abi nodded.

'Don't mind Scroggs, my son,' she said dryly. 'He deceives only himself. Black like we is not a promise. Keep your eyes on plants an' animals an' learn.'

With the ink barely dry on the treaty document, she had resolved that Freetown could not honour Article Seven in the contract.

The sweet smell of frangipani wafted on the warm evening airs.

The *Pilgrim*

Near Ocean Bay
24 September 1783
01.00 hrs

Stars speckled the dark heavens. Low-flying silhouetted gulls cried raucously on course for the Three Apostles. A sliver of moonlight splashed across the eastern end of Ocean Bay, glistening on the water like a pallid strip of silver.

A mile across the Bay, off the primary promontory of the unevenly serrated western shoreline, the blackness of the sea enveloped passing vessels. Without lights a quarter-mile off the headland, a square-rigged three-masted barque, the *Pilgrim*, swung silently at anchor on an outgoing tide.

Peering to the north-west, Asabi anxiously made out the lanterns of several distant vessels bobbing up and down in a moderate sea. The prevailing offshore breeze augured good sailing conditions. Earlier in the afternoon, HMS *Invincible* had sailed ominously by on her easterly patrol across Ocean Bay but was not expected back till the morning. With a treaty in force, Jamestown's land forces were banned from entering the self-governing district of Freetown. Instead, His Majesty's Navy and slave-owner's privateers sporadically patrolled Freetown's fragment of coastline.

So many informers about, she thought. Good we change the site for the *Pilgrim* this night. The *Invincible* will not be sure where to lie in wait for us.

Off the foot of the limestone cliffs, lengthening waves and whitecaps threw up whits of spray. Poignant whispered farewells were whipped away by the moderate breeze. Twelve tensed men and women were bowing surreptitiously out of a nightmare. Shoved off in two jolly boats sent out from the anchored barque, the returnees and four oarsmen soon melted into the darkness, homeward bound to the coast of Guinea.

Waving a heart-breaking farewell from the shadows, she turned and ambled away in tears. Closely followed by Abi, Shadow and Dogbite, she wobbled her way betwixt the boulders dotted about the sands. She was heading for the moonless corner of Ocean Bay where they would ascend the sloping recessed rock ledge to the clifftop.

'Haaaa,' cried Abi gleefully. 'Gov'nor not find out we change time an' place to meet the *Pilgrim*.'

'An' if this Governor asks us, Abi,' she said, looking around her companions, 'nobody 'round here seen a *Pilgrim*. Wi' no proof we seen her, Gov'nor can do not anything. An' Scroggs know not anything o' the *Pilgrim*.'

'Scroggs so drunk, days an' nights look same to he,' said Dogbite with a high-pitched laugh.

'When *Pilgrim*'s lantern be on the horizon,' she said, 'we go back to Freetown to drink to a safe blessed journey.'

A few hours later from under the manchineel tree on the clifftop, she sighted the *Pilgrim*'s stern lantern dipping below the horizon.

Noisily exhaling, she said with determinedly, 'We mus' till this land an' build a fine town. An' we got to get books an' fin' a good teacher. We got a long rocky way ahead, my friends. An' we free to build a strong Freetown or sit in a prison o' rum an' idling like in Ocean Bay.'

'Now me know we set to build Freetown proper,' growled Shadow, grinning.

Outside the eastern-most boundary of Freetown's land holding, moonlight cast a pale glow across the clifftop of Ocean Bay.

Seething quietly in the shadows, Matthew Fleming pulled out his gold pocket watch. Running his fingers along the pierced repoussé decoration, he noted the time: four o'clock. Biting his lip with chagrin, he cast a final look down along the desolate shore of Deception Bay.

Sullenly turning to the weather-beaten commandant, he said, 'Methinks we won't be sighting the *Pilgrim* this night, Sir Thomas. Mayhaps the bird has flown or was not ever here.'

'You didn't hear from your man Hezekiah then, Mister Fleming?'

'Fearing for his life,' replied Matthew, 'Hezekiah did not dare return to Freetown after the treaty was signed. And the informer who took his place clearly gave me erroneous intelligence about the *Pilgrim*'s whereabouts this night. From the moment that treaty was signed, Sir Thomas, we needed a fresh network of informers.'

'You were not alone in that error, Mister Fleming,' said the commandant sympathetically. 'I as well received matching intelligence from my agents and informers. I agree with you. With a treaty in force, we certainly need to develop fresh procedures regarding the free niggers of Freetown and the safekeeping of the plantation slaves. Ye planters must devise an unassailable barrier that deters slaves running away. 'Twould prove darned difficult trying to distinguish a runaway from among Freetown's free niggers.'

'I hear what you say, Sir Thomas,' Matthew concurred. 'You speak much-needed fundamentals. Will you accompany me on the night of the morrow when I address the members of the old guard of the West Indies Sugar Cartel?'

'Delighted, Mister Fleming,' said the commandant. 'But how can I be of service to thee?'

'While sugar yields fluctuate, Sir Thomas,' said Matthew, lowering his voice, 'certain rich men have their heads wedged between breasts and buttocks stuck aloft in a somewhat mind-numbing attempt to deny change. I ask you to help me rouse these diehards and end the Cartel's penchant for floundering in perpetual antidotes.'

'Forestalling is easier to swallow than medicine, Mister Fleming.'

'I am heartened by your words, Sir Thomas. Mayhaps you might even consider unveiling your 'unassailable barrier' to help prevent slaves becoming runaways. Coupled with your apt criticism of the disorganised plantation regime and your reputation for corrective strategies, I am certain we can outfox the Cartel's reactionaries and stamp out their inflexible mind-sets.'

'I am confident, Mister Fleming,' said the commandant, 'that any proposition I make will wither the flow of runaways from the planta-tions to a mere trickle inside a year. On the question of the slaves, the plantations ought to band together under a united strategy. That will put us in a position to control utterly any movement of any slave on or off all plantations.'

Mounting waiting mares, Matthew set off with the commandant:

'Let us away, Mister Fleming. The officers and men can fall-in behind us on our way to Jamestown. Were you expecting anyone special on the *Pilgrim*?'

'Like who?'

'Jonas Guinea, for instance?'

'I was hoping to seize the *Pilgrim*, Sir Thomas,' chuckled Matthew. 'But if I were awaiting Jonas Guinea, we'd have fetched overseers and twice as many soldiers with us this night. To take the principals of this League is a prize the Cartel has long sought. I sail to London soon to meet my brokers. Mayhaps there I shall again cross swords with that jumped-up Guinea.'

Missing Years

On twenty-ninth day of June, Iceland's Skaptar volcano erupted, killing approximately nine thousand people. In the first week of July, the fall-out arrived over London as a cloud of dust and sulphur particles. The metropolitan air turned brown. Casting a rust-coloured light on the ground at midday, the sun looked as bare as a clouded moon. Combining with the first snowfall of the year, brown snow descended on the metropolis. And like the houses in the surrounding boroughs, Pilgrims shivered under what looked like a cinnamon blanket.

Entering the withdrawing room and laughingly waving a letter in the air, Jonas said, 'I have just received the most delightful tidings.'

'Who is the author of such a glad report?' asked Faith.

'Aaron Drinkwater.'

'By the fever about you, Jonas, I can tell it is something of note,' said Mistress Beecham. 'Pray tell.'

Unfolding the missive without ado, he began to read:

'Hollyhocks
Old Paradise Street
Village of Rotherhithe
9 November 1783

Dear Jonas,

I have this day received joyous tidings from Alexander Fairfax. He has at last located Henry Jackson, who is presently owned by Jethro Wittard of Tall Trees Plantation, Pertigua. Fairfax has spoken to this fractious gentleman numerous times and at great length. Wittard is finally willing to part with Henry for no less than two hundred and fifty pounds – an extremely extortionate sum I might add. As agreed with your good self, I had instructed Fairfax to make the purchase on our behalf and that he would be reimbursed by us. Fairfax wrote that he could not think of a more tragic tale than Henry's. So much so, he has donated fifty pounds towards his liberation. It is down to you and me to refund the remaining two hundred pounds. I trust this will meet with your approval—'

'I shall as well contribute, Jonas,' Mistress Beecham said, interrupting his reading. 'Pray, read on.'

'This auspicious occasion causes me to reflect that in the search for our dear friend,' read Jonas, 'my correspondence with Mister Fairfax has spanned many years. To summarise: Fairfax tracked Henry down to the Auction House on his arrival in Pertigua. He was sold to the Five Bells Plantation, Pertigua. Over the intervening years Henry was again sold to three different plantations on two different islands, before being finally purchased by Jethro Wittard of the Tall Trees Plantation.

I am now delighted to inform you that Henry is homeward bound on the barque *Marie Gabrielle*. She is expected to dock at Old Salt Quay in Rotherhithe on the twenty-second of this month. It would give me undeniable pleasure to accompany you to meet the *Marie Gabrielle*. I very much look forward to meeting the culmination of eleven years of effort. I am rapt with such joy to know that we have returned Henry once again to the bosom of his loving family and his friends.

Your loyal friend,
Aaron Drinkwater.'

Dropping the letter to his side, Jonas gazed out of the window and heaved a long sigh.

A prolonged stupefied silence ensued in the chamber.

Turning around, he saw two fuzzy figures wiping their eyes and smiling. That was when he realised he was looking at them through tears.

'I feel mortified I could do not anything more to free Henry,' said Faith. 'But I am truly beside myself with happiness at his return. For the odds against such an eventuality must be exceptionally high.'

''Tis remarkable,' he said. 'You did all you could, dear Faith. Merely finding Henry among the islands and plantations took Drinkwater ten years, and another year to negotiate the price for his purchase. You began Henry's retrieval with your letter to Alexander Fairfax asking for his assistance.'

'We must give Henry and his family a splendid homecoming here at Pilgrims,' said Mistress Beecham. 'And then we shall carriage them back to Limehouse.'

'Methinks in view of Henry's contemptible sufferings,' said Jonas thoughtfully, 'the least his friends can do is to find him a position either in our chandlery or close by in Deptford.'

'I heartily concur, Jonas,' said Mistress Beecham. 'Henry and Mistress Lorna must suffer no more.'

'I shall write to Francis Barber at once,' said Jonas. 'I know he will want to accompany us to welcome Henry back.'

'Mister Foggerty also played a part, Jonas,' said Faith. 'He will want to meet Henry as well.'

On the twenty-second of November at around ten o'clock on a dank overcast morning, a cloaked reception party of four sat in a carriage in the snows of Rotherhithe by Old Salt Quay.

A little after, at eleven o'clock, the quay was enlivened by men running to docking stations.

'Ship ahoy!' shouted a cockney voice.

Peering out of the carriage, Jonas smiled.

''Tis the *Marie Gabrielle*!' he exclaimed, stepping onto the quay.

'You are right, Mister Guinea,' said Foggerty, laughing.

Captured as a prize from the French during one of England's many wars, a scruffy three-masted barque of about one hundred feet was nearing her mooring. A monkey's fist flew from the docking vessel, after which the hawser was hauled in until she was securely tied up.

When the gangplank slammed onto the snow-laden dock, activity erupted around the battened hatches. Excise men, tally clerks and stevedores swarmed aboard the ship.

'To be plucked from a London highway and awaken in a cane field must have just about destroyed him,' said Drinkwater, scowling. 'What part of the man have the overseers not destroyed? D'you realise his sons are now twenty-one and twenty-three years of age and eleven lost years with their father?'

'It confirms that even a simple walk on the streets for a black can descend into a nightmare,' said Barber indignantly. 'And with vested interest, the investing connections of the slave-owners, known as Members of Parliament, refuse to legislate against the slave-hunters. 'Tis reliably reported that many of them employ the services of the slave-hunters.'

'I did 'ear that Members o' that Commons got slaves in the Indies,' said Foggerty.

'I believe that to be entirely accurate, Mister Foggerty,' said Jonas.

'Sugar finances industrial invention and has made rich men richer,' said Drinkwater, 'while the dynamic backbone of their business — the seamen, overseers and the unwitting millworkers — are remunerated with the measly crumbs falling from rich tables.'

Searching through the bodies discharging the *Marie Gabrielle*'s cargo onto the quayside, Jonas caught sight of his friend.

Swathed in an outsized green boat cloak and carrying a pitifully small bundle, a withered figure stumbled off the gangplank and stood quivering on the quayside.

Shocked by his friend's appearance, Jonas faltered. Tears welled into his eyes.

Eleven heartbreaking years had passed by. It was indeed Henry. Sallow folds of skin hung where his chubby cheeks had been. Gone was the spirited demeanour of an activist. Darting eyes alive with fright, he was half-crouched, cadaverous and burdened with torment. Henry now possessed a deeply wounded soul.

Seeing Barber, Drinkwater and Foggerty staring aghast, Jonas smiled and opened his arms.

''Tis me, Henry,' he said.

Shambling awkwardly through the snow, Henry halted a step away and stared blankly ahead. Then, his eyes flickered and narrowed. Memory seemed to widen them. Tears rolled down his shriven cheeks. A feeble wispy voice squeaked, 'Is that you Jonas?'

'It is I, Henry.'

'Is that really you, Jonas?'

'It is really I, Henry.'

Clutching Jonas's arm with a sudden vigour, Henry wailed.

'They lashed me and lashed me, Jonas. I could not reach you. I could not escape. What has befallen my beloved Lorna and my sons?'

'We have not ever stopped looking for you, my dearest friend,' said Jonas, embracing him. 'You may remember Mister Drinkwater, who corresponded through the years with Alexander Fairfax, and Francis Barber who with Mister Foggerty and myself, kept inquiries about you progressing through the years. Mistress Lorna and your sons are in good health and are very excited to see you. I have missed you so much, Henry. We are gathered here this day to see justice done and to welcome you home.'

Suddenly, putting his hands over his face, a fifty-one year-old man stood before them and bawled like a baby with such profundity it was affecting. He felt there was a fever in the man's cry and it was burning him up inside. The man he had known as Henry was in attendance. Only just. In truth, Henry was all but a derelict.

Wiping his eyes, Foggerty cleared his throat.

Taking the lawyer's hands and looking directly at him, Henry spoke with a frail voice:

'I thank thee, Mister Drinkwater. Mister Fairfax impressed on me the persistence of your correspondence through my terrible lost years. From the bottom of my heart, dear sir, I thank thee.'

'I did not know what terrible events can happen to black citizens on the streets of London,' said Drinkwater, still holding Henry's hands. 'I did not know that your people walk with such trepidation every time they venture out. But what I now know is not the England I know and that saddens me. It tells me I do not know my country.

Regardless of how others might feel, Mister Jackson, I want you to know that this Englishman is unbelievably gladdened we have you free and back home.'

Unexpectedly embracing Henry with vigour, Drinkwater stepped back wiping his eyes.

Smiling admiringly at the camaraderie, Jonas pondered. Besides Drinkwater's unstinting efforts for over a decade for a black other, that singular embrace transformed him from being not just a well-intentioned Jewish Englishman in his membership of the League, but a cherished and dependable friend.

Aside from Henry's occasional bewildered silences, the journey to Pilgrims was pleasurably peppered with his questions about his wife and sons and what had happened during his long absence. The carriage was nearing Deptford Dockyard when they learned how Henry had been abducted by the slave-hunter, Solomon Festus. Envious of Henry's connections and standing in the impoverished village of Limehouse, his detailed movements and whereabouts had been betrayed by a rival member of his abolitionist faction.

'But the betrayer is black like you, Mister Jackson!' exclaimed Drinkwater, clearly horrified.

'You should be aware, Mister Drinkwater,' said Barber, raising his brows without emotion, 'that backstabbing is a human affair. It possesses no colour.'

'Jealousy 'as a sinister way of breaking friendships, Mister Drinkwater,' said Foggerty. 'Roun' me neighbour'ood, I see friends dobbing on friends ter the excise men. An' they is all white.'

'An accident is hard luck,' scowled Jonas. 'Betrayal is somewhat premeditated and disturbing.'

Given such treachery, he thought, Henry possesses a noticeable lack of interest to get even.

'You seem without vengeance, Henry,' he said. 'Yet a traitor sent you into slavery and robbed you of your wife and family.'

Leaning back with a long-drawn sigh, Henry said, 'Praying on the plantation, I vowed that if ever I was free, I would not waste my freedom on revenge. I knew then, as now, it would not give me back the stolen years. For the good of humankind, slavery must be abolished.

I hate no one. I will not ever look back. If ever I do, it won't be with hate. I look instead to the morrow with hope.'

'Mistress Lorna, your sons and your friends will nurture you back to rude health, Henry,' said Jonas. 'Tom, Jack and Breathless have fetched them to meet you at Pilgrims.'

For the first time since disembarking from the *Marie Gabrielle*, Henry gave a broad smile. 'My family can then begin rebuking a trustful old man for his long absence.'

So far as Henry was concerned, his quiet droll witticism concluded a cataclysmic episode. The carriage was rocked by laughter as it came to a halt outside Pilgrims.

Solomon Guinea

'A good morning to you, Mistress Guinea,' said the clergyman, lifting his hat.

'A good morning to you, Reverend Baskett,' said Faith with a broad smile. 'I thank you for calling and ye can be certain we shall all be at service on the morrow.'

From the top step, she exhaled and surveyed the neighbourhood.

A cloudless blue sky extolled a bright sunny day and fresh morning airs sparkled good cheer. She took a deep breath. Swallows twittering in the plane trees above the traffic on the Highway augured harmony. Despite her usual qualms about the wellbeing of her family, all seemed well.

Closing the front door and looking closely into the oval walnut mirror in the hall, she smoothed her features and patted her cheeks.

The soft translucent skin that once flattered her features was shrinking onto her bones. Time had taken its toll. The fruitless search for her baby sold into slavery somewhere in the Caribbean wrought a fierce teary scowl. The years had also been rewarding. In her sixty-first year, on her son's twenty-first birthday, she was stirred with gratitude for the memory of her years with his father. On her horizon lay the ripening of her years, watching her offspring flower while nursing Mistress Beecham. Smoothing the rumples in her striped green and white silk taffeta gown, she smiled and exhaled.

Preceded by a fresh-faced maidservant, a bleary-eyed, mobcapped, white-haired Tuppence Honeypenny shuffled into the hallway with a maidservant.

'Mistress Beecham was right poorly the past night, Mistress Guinea,' she said croakily. 'Tossing and turning she was, and twice in her slumber she cried out for the late master. Her breathing was difficult. Shall I send for the doctor while she is with you in the withdrawing room?'

'Nurse told me you have been up much of the past night, Mistress Honeypenny,' said Faith affectionately. 'I shall myself send for the doctor. Methinks you should spend this day resting in your cot.'

'I thank you muchly, Mistress Guinea,' said the housekeeper. 'These old legs ain't what they used to be.'

Watching the housekeeper hobble towards the stairs, Faith heaved a long ponderous sigh.

Tuppence Honeypenny had entered service at Pilgrims at barely twenty years of age, she thought. At sixty-eight, she has slipped into the winter of her years. Dear loyal companion, I harbour a dread we might one night find that during your slumber your esteemed days had come to an end.

Instructing the maidservant, she said, 'Fetch your shawl, Polly. Make haste to Doctor Fosbery's chirurgery. Tell him Mistress Beecham did not sleep at all well the past night and will be in much need of a visit and a soporific for this night.'

'Ter be sure, Mistress Guinea,' said the maidservant, 'I wi' give the good Doctor yer message.'

Entering the withdrawing room, she sat on the opposite side of the Chippendale sofa from her daughter with her son in-between. Her husband occupied a wing chair close by.

Having insisted on being present to give her grandson his birthday gift, the nigh-on bedridden Mistress Beecham had been assisted onto the daybed near the sofa. There she lay, breathing laboriously under a knitted woollen blanket with a mobcap over her silvery white hair.

The crow's feet and lines that ran from Mistress Beecham's nose to her receding lips have grown deeper with the passage of time, thought Faith. Since last winter's passing of her cherished confidante, Reverend Whitehouse, still clutching his Bilston Battersea Truth enamel snuff box, she has gradually declined.

Exhibiting the hallmarks of a nonagenarian, Mistress Beecham had walked at a snail's pace with the aid of another and her cane, she was given to flatulence and oftimes spat when she spoke, had poor eyesight and was hard of hearing. As well, she had not had a good night.

Having become a silent partner in Thomas Beecham, Chandlers, Faith's time was taken by Solomon and Olivia's education, the chandlery and two houses, Pilgrims and Greensleeves. To assist her and the Pilgrims' household in the nursing of Mistress Beecham, she had called on Mistress Trowbridge in the nearby Poppleton Street. A former seamstress, Mistress Trowbridge conducted a highly regarded business from her home supplying nurses for the sick-nursing of 'those in the autumn years'. Faith duly hired one nurse and a relief to provide round-the-clock care between them.

Staring benignly at her children, she smiled.

She adored her clear-skinned beige-brown offspring; her son with his brown eyes and curly hair, and her statuesque daughter with her spiralling flaxen hair and blue eyes. Looking at them with a mother's eye, she felt only love and could not see colour. Then, as was the family's birthday tradition, she turned to her husband to address their children.

Blinking back tears and clearing his throat, Jonas spoke with fatherly affection:

'I had hoped but could not envision, dear wife, that the naughty and noisy gurgling babies we brought into this world all that time ago would grow to be the clever, striking adults who sit with us this day. On this anniversary of your birth, Solomon, I say to you: hold close not to the shore but pull for the horizon, for you have your whole life ahead of you. I thank you, my children, for bringing so much happiness and hope into the life of an old man in these troubled times.'

'You speak for us both, dear husband,' said Faith blissfully. 'And I, your mother, cannot thank you enough for so beautifully combining your parent's colours, cultures and customs.'

'I thank thee heartily, sir, and thee as well, mother,' said Solomon, beaming at his parents. 'When I see the impediments for we of colour in London Town, I cannot but be thankful for giving us such a beneficial introduction into good society. I pray we may one day contribute sufficiently to justify your constant efforts to our constant good.'

As well, thought Faith smiling affectionately, I love the words, the turn of phrase and thoughtfulness of our studious offspring.

Opening his presents, Solomon received a volume of *Robinson Crusoe* and a pristine signed copy of *A Dictionary of the English Language* by Samuel Johnson from his father; a silver pair case pocket watch made by John Fullam of London, with the initials SG engraved on the back, from his mother; a walnut-handled nib pen and inkwell from his sister; a gentleman's walking cane with a Malacca shaft from his adoptive grandmother, Mistress Beecham; a copy of *A Modest Proposal* from Francis Barber and a brass compass from Parson Merriweather. Knowing of Solomon's love for flowers, the maidservants had filled a basket with raspberry-coloured hollyhocks and blackish-purple lavender surrounding his sweet-scented favourite, blue night-scented stocks.

'Night-scented stocks are heavenly,' said Olivia, 'though I might say that dainty blue for a man might raise an eyebrow or two, Solomon.'

Making a face and laughing at his sister, Solomon was light-hearted.

'Where on my face does it say I was going to wear pink stocks in the street, dear sister?'

'We shall have goose this night for dinner, Solomon,' said Faith, smiling.

'I love roast goose!' Olivia exclaimed.

'As do I,' whispered Mistress Beecham from the daybed.

'And ye shall have goose, Mistress Beecham,' said Faith, delighted by her participation. 'Cook is preparing the feast as we speak.'

Beaming around the chamber with glistening eyes, Solomon quietly responded, 'What can I say but to thank you all for such splendid gifts?'

'After you have read *Robinson Crusoe*,' said Jonas, in a pretended effort to keep his inching smile away, 'you can start by enlightening us with your observations.'

'What observations in particular, dear husband?'

'I should like to know what contentious positions he deduces the author knowingly or unknowingly wrote about his man, Friday.'

'The same can be said of *A Modest Proposal*, Jonas,' said Mistress Beecham.

'That is so,' Jonas grinned. 'Mayhaps, Solomon, we could as well have a view of the work of Jonathan Swift?'

'I shall study the books with alacrity, sir,' said Solomon, 'and shall heartily give thee my opinion on what I deduce.'

Casting loving looks over her family, Faith said, 'On Solomon's twenty-first, we shall celebrate with a cup of hot chocolate. Chocolate for you as well, Mistress Beecham?'

Coughing into her handkerchief, Mistress Beecham nodded weakly.

'Chocolate,' they said, in unison.

Pouring a readied jug of the beverage into five cups, Faith passed them around.

'To Solomon,' said Jonas, raising his cup.

'Solomon,' they chorused, raising their cups.

'What would you most like to do on this fine day, my son?' asked Jonas.

'To meet Olaudah Equiano,' said Solomon unequivocally.

'Why he?' asked Olivia.

'I was moved by his letter to the *Public Advertiser* on the very existence of slavery, and I want to hear more of the politics from his viewpoint. You, sir, have spoken much and well of him. I believe in what Mister Equiano has said about the abolition of the institution of slavery itself and not merely ridding England's colonies of slaves. I would very much like to meet him. Would it be possible to meet him this day, sir?'

'Before your birthday dinner this night, young man, put on your best frock coat,' said Jonas. 'We shall take a carriage to Tottenham Street in the West End of London. I have arranged to meet Francis Barber at the house of his friend, Olaudah Equiano himself.'

Solomon's mouth fell open. Recovering himself, he gasped, 'A thousand thanks for fulfilling an aspiration of mine, sir. To have the chance to thank Mister Barber for his book leaves me speechless.'

'Scholarly men from whom you will learn much, Solomon,' said Jonas.

'An excellent occasion for Solomon to meet Mister Equiano, dear husband,' said Faith lovingly. 'I will arrange for two men from the chandlery to accompany you.'

'Such good sense, dear wife,' he said, smiling thankfully. 'I shall carry my sword cane.'

'And I shall carry my new cane,' said Solomon proudly.

'Listen, Olivia,' said Faith, 'while our menfolk are away gallivanting and seeing the sights of London Town, we can go to a meeting of the Deptford Female Anti-Slavery Society. I say 'tis an apt moment for you to join and contribute to the campaign for abolition. Anti-slavery societies are beginning to spring up in a few towns and cities. And a significant percentage of those populating the societies are working women. I think you agree that on this shameful issue women must play a part.'

Clearly surprised, Olivia said, 'I will be delighted to go with you, mother! I am eager to attend a protest gathering and learn about the composing of petitions and—'

'Will all that not interrupt your studies, Olivia?' asked Jonas, winking at his wife.

'Studies to what end, sir?' asked Olivia. 'Women cannot go to University or enter a profession and women of colour, doubly so.'

'Men of colour as well cannot attend University,' protested Solomon.

'Instead of University and a profession, sir,' said Olivia, 'I believe 'tis the duty and obligation of thinking women who have appreciated the brutality being committed on the slave plantations to enjoin a campaign to bring slavery to an end. Good society cannot prevent women campaigning; which there or thereabouts, puts women in the same fight and on the same side as Mister Equiano, Solomon.'

Making a face at his sister, Solomon laughed.

We have raised a somewhat feisty daughter, thought Faith.

Catching the eye of her grinning husband, she smiled.

'You will find it instructive in more ways than one, Olivia,' said Mistress Beecham, wearily and slowly. 'Working women, poor women and a few wives of doctors and lawyers. You will witness the luck of some and the misfortune of others. Yet all have found common cause in the campaign for abolition. I would step out with thee lass, but alas it would take us a week to get there. Methinks you want to get there in the foreseeable moment.'

The chamber resounded with laughter.

'Methinks we should go and change our clothes, sister,' said Solomon, making for the door.

Suddenly, a panting maidservant appeared.

'Doctor Fosbery wi' be 'ere within the hour, Mistress Guinea,' said Polly.

'I thank you, Polly. Have a tonic for your efforts. Turning to her husband, she asked, 'Are you absolutely certain our children cannot attend University? Not even Solomon?'

'I have made exhaustive enquiries,' said Jonas with resignation. 'The Universities will not admit blacks as students. Our children will not be allowed to matriculate to any University. Long and hard have I pondered on this should such a situation arise. We must speak of this on the morrow. 'Tis time we do so. And 'tis time to board our carriage.'

Keeping her feelings to herself, she bade farewell to her menfolk and closed the front door.

Stepping into the withdrawing room, she collapsed in tears into a wing chair.

'Life can sometimes be so cruel to womenkind and peoples of a different hue, Olivia,' she sighed. 'I hope it will not always be so. 'Tis fortuitous we have good friends. I believe your generation will experience a slightly easier time than mine. Thank God.'

'I pray that is so, mother,' said Olivia, dabbing at her mother's cheeks. 'But even I do not believe I will live to see fairness between black and white or men and women.'

'That you won't,' snapped Mistress Beecham.

There was a knock at the door. The doctor had arrived.

Pass the Baton

Tottenham Street
Saturday
19 June 1784
13.00 hrs

It was a hot bright afternoon beneath an azure sky. On the border of the newly built suburb of Fitzrovia, Jonas's carriage arrived at the wide cobbled Tottenham Court Road. The parish reeked of wealth and indigence.

Fashion-plated couples strolled affably from shop to shop. A row of clockmakers, jewellers, perfumers, upholsterers and cabinetmakers was interspersed by the signboards of carpenters and victuallers. Drunks leaned groggily against buildings and plane trees. Butchers in striped aprons shouted meat prices from shop fronts. Loitering around for handouts, raggedy urchins frolicked in horseplay. In the doorways of some houses, comely streetwalkers flirted with podgy clients. Inside an excavated hole bounded by a mound of earth, smudge-faced plumbers sweated over repairs to a fractured lead pipe. Frock-coated gentlemen with sword canes ambled insouciantly by.

'Stand clear!' yelled the driver at passers-by.

In the farrago of speeding traffic, a red hansom cab collided with a careering green landau. Somewhat disorientated, richly-dressed occupants reeled furiously onto the cobbles spitting threats and curses at one another. Begrimed labourers wearing neckerchiefs, grubby waistcoats and breeches stood jeering from the roadside.

'Ain't yer got bloody eyes!' yelled a cockney voice.

'Ye coulda killed a body.'

'Dandy dimwits!' yelled another.

Mocking laughter riddled the bystanders.

Catching the eye of the elder of his two cockney minders, Jonas grinned.

'Fitzrovia appears a fiery-tongued parish, Mister Sawyer,' he said.

'Gets 'ot in the shadows roun' these parts, Mister Guinea,' said the minder, guffawing.

'On occasions, Mister Sawyer,' said Solomon, smiling, 'methinks good fortune and adversity make for awkward bedfellows.'

Methinks I have paid not enough attention to my son's awareness of the disparities in society, thought Jonas, smiling to himself.

Clattering past shops, houses and taverns, the cries of the street sellers sporadically invaded the carriage. Before long, the driver turned into Tottenham Street and pulled up at the near end. Beyond a row of plane trees stood a tired, brick-built, temple-fronted terrace of houses with sloping Welsh slate roofs hidden behind stone parapets.

'Which is Mister Equiano's dwelling, sir?' asked Solomon eagerly.

'Number thirty-seven,' said Jonas, stepping out of the carriage and pointing. 'Methinks that one with the blue door.'

Leaning into the carriage, he briefed the minders.

'We may be a while, Mister Sawyer,' he said.

''Tis a kind warm day wi' plenty o' buxom milkmaids ter gawk at, Mister Guinea,' said the minder, ogling the womanly foot traffic. 'Besides, Smythe an' me see a penny pieman on corner o' street.'

Grinning at the minder's wanton mindset, Jonas said, 'Bide the time with a pie or two, Mister Sawyer, and I shall reimburse thee.'

'Thank ye kindly, Mister Guinea,' said the minder. 'An' being yer son's twenty-first, we be right 'appy ter linger 'owever long.'

Briefly eyeing his son's blue wool broadcloth frock coat, breeches and black shoes with silver buckles, Jonas strode proudly to the blue door. Lifting the knocker, he brought it down twice.

In linen shirtsleeves, embroidered silk waistcoat and dark breeches, Francis Barber appeared at the door. Warmly embracing him and his son, his friend was buoyant.

'Your presence has been sorely missed, Jonas. Welcome to the lodgings of Olaudah Equiano, Solomon.'

'"Tis good to see you again, Francis,' said Jonas. 'How fares Mistress Elizabeth? You received our invitation to supper Wednesday next?'

'Elizabeth is in fine fettle, Jonas,' said Barber. 'She thanks you both for your kind invitation. Pray tell Mistress Faith that Elizabeth is most eager to speak with her. The good Doctor has even granted me time off for your supper. And he wishes to be kept informed of your next visit.'

'I am eager to call on the good Doctor again,' said Jonas. 'Also, so thankful to you for your part in his release from the plantations, Henry Jackson is keen to renew your acquaintance.'

'Of course, Jonas,' said Barber chuckling, 'though I trust Henry has not received yet another compulsory Pertiguan summons?'

Rolling his eyes and shaking his head, Jonas smiled.

'Nay, Francis, he has not. Thank God.'

'Henry Jackson owns a confoundingly flabbergasting fortitude, Jonas,' said Barber with admiration. 'I would not have relished such an enforced return to Jamaica, nor would I have been as forgiving as he. Given such generosity of spirit, Henry should be canonised.'

'Methinks,' said Jonas thoughtfully, 'that Henry decided he could only move forwards by not keeping hold of that burdensome load called hate.'

'Forgiveness does seem somewhat less onerous,' said Barber. 'Just goes to show the godliness of the man. Come with me, gentlemen.'

Off a short passageway, Jonas entered a simply-furnished, medium-sized parlour-cum-kitchen. Before him stood the man he had heard and read so much about.

Setting a kettle onto the cast-iron hob grate filling the chimney opening, a manicured Olaudah Equiano turned around and gave a crisp bow.

Awash with admiration, Jonas smiled.

About forty years of age with dark brown skin and of medium height, Equiano's sharp eyes conveyed tenacity. Wearing a jet-black tail wig, high-collar frock coat, white silk cravat, ruffled dress shirt, embroidered waistcoat and silk knee breeches, he had an elegant charisma. And there was an assertive air about him.

Having bought his freedom, Jonas pondered, this erstwhile slave became a seafarer, merchant, explorer, writer and now abolitionist. He is undoubtedly a man of conviction.

What is more, Jonas knew Equiano was well-connected and greatly regarded by England's leading abolitionists. And he suspected resentment lay not far behind from some on the heels of the newly acclaimed.

'Welcome to Tottenham Street, Jonas Guinea,' said Equiano with outstretched hand, 'and by his fine looks I take it this is your son, Solomon?'

'Olaudah Equiano,' said Jonas, shaking hands, ''tis a pleasure to shake your hand. And ye are right, Solomon is indeed my son.'

'Welcome to my lowly abode, Solomon,' said Equiano, shaking his hand. Lowering his voice, he said, 'I trust you will pardon my boldness, Jonas. Francis said ye were one of a syndicate that executed a daring expedition aboard a merchantman curiously called the *Redemption*.'

'That is so,' said Jonas, grinning bashfully. 'And I mind not that Francis chose to entrust the intelligence with thee.'

'Francis's inspiriting tidings captivated my spirits,' said Equiano. 'Thou, sir, have my admiration for an extraordinary achievement. In view of your penchant for innovative strategies, I am certain 'twould be useful to exchange ideas with thee. For instance, I would be glad to hear your thoughts on the *Zong* massacre. Moreover, how can it best be exploited by the campaigners for abolition?'

Warmed by Equiano's African and English elocution, which Jonas had affectionately dubbed 'brogue of the middle passage', he answered with the sagely voice of an elder.

'Olaudah, I would gladly share my thoughts and feelings about what was not anything less than mass murder. First let me pay tribute to your letter in the *Morning Chronicle*, particularly the part about the abridged rights free people of colour possess in England. You uttered the complaint of all black citizens.'

'Regrettably, gentlemen,' said Equiano thoughtfully, 'negro liberties in England have yet to engage the interest of the educated or knowledge of the populace and thus affect the votes of the politicians. In time, I suspect those very liberties might someday seize this nation in some dispute.'

'What do you think might happen, Olaudah?' asked Barber.

'At the time negro liberties in England grow to be a burning issue,' said Equiano reflectively, 'I predict the populace will be spectators to a froth-ridden political altercation resulting in half-hearted change, much like now. But this godforsaken slave trade presses—'

'Profits prevent abolition so the trade persists without let,' said Jonas tersely.

'Thus any campaign must leave slave-owners in no doubt that abolition is axiomatic,' said Equiano. 'The worst effects of this trade may yet ripple through time and rear up in a catastrophic disturbance on African societies of the morrow. I have only the evidence of my experience that it may, for instance, give rise to conflict in those lands for generations. I say that, together with our white supporters, we must intensify the campaign with boycotts, more petitions, more conversation and more speeches to hasten abolition.'

''Tis imperative then,' said Jonas, 'that the campaign find a politician who has backbone enough to table an Abolition Bill before the House of Commons. That Member must be able to cite instances of the protest and rallies by the populace confirming the demand for abolition.'

'Were the good doctor not ailing,' said Barber, 'I know he would be of assistance for such action.'

'Having long been a supporter of abolition, Francis,' said Equiano, 'I know Doctor Johnson would willingly assist with his counsel if he could. Pray extend my warm regards to him. I will seek the help of my friend Ottobah Cugoano, a free man and erudite. Methinks given his analytical disposition, Ottobah is essential.'

'The good doctor received an article written by Ottobah Cugoano this very morning,' said Barber, 'but which I have yet to read.'

'Isn't his name also John Stuart?' interjected Solomon politely.

'Indeed it is, Solomon,' said Equiano indulgently. 'To avoid being sold back into slavery after his manumission, Ottobah had himself baptised John Stuart. Unlike Ottobah, but like most others, my owner forced a slave name on me. He named me Gustavus Vassa. I have shared flagons of ale with Ottobah over the questions of England's slave trade. And I will not ever forget the night he told me that his sole abiding memory was his slave price: a gun, a piece of cloth and some lead.'

'Good God!' Solomon exclaimed, 'Mister Cugoano was traded for rubbish.'

'At present,' continued Equiano, 'Ottobah makes copious notes for a work about the slave trade. He has sought my assistance for the endeavour. I have of course accepted. 'Tis entitled: *Thoughts and Sentiments on the Evil and Wicked Traffic of the Commerce of the Human Species.'*

''Tis a somewhat germane designation in these dangerous times,' said Jonas, nodding approvingly.

'Gentlemen,' said Equiano, in a voice to concentrate minds, 'if we intend putting our heads together on the atrocity of the *Zong*, 'tis imperative you all soon make Cugoano's acquaintance. I shall arrange it.'

''Tis a puzzling serendipity,' said Jonas, lightly massaging his left temple. 'Torn from cultures interrupted by slavery, we Africans stand here this day far from our native land. 'Tis said God works in mysterious ways. And I have yet to understand why.'

'I was born in Deptford of loving mixed parentage, Mister Equiano,' said Solomon, frowning. 'To which country would you say I belong?'

'Your mother is white, your father is black and your skin is brown,' said Equiano with warm sincerity. 'That merely makes you a human being like everyone else. The ancestry of your parents makes you no less English or African. However, in England it is essential for them with darker skin to expend irksome moments avoiding those who suffer a crisis with any colour that is not white. Then again, I have found many in the populace who suffer no such predicament. Regardless of what anybody says, you can be as African or as English as you choose, Solomon. Ye are a child of both.'

Narrowing his eyes at the response, Solomon then beamed and the look in his eyes was admiring.

Moved by Equiano's inspiritment of his son, Jonas's eyes wandered cordially around the room.

Sunlight streamed through a box-sash window exposing the bare pinewood boards and grey-painted pine-panelled walls. A quarter-sawn oak clock adorned a bare wall. Four rickety ladderback chairs sat around an oak gateleg table with a cracked top. A pair of fruitwood holders with beeswax candles stood on the table beside a copy of John Wesley's *Arminian Magazine*, issues of *Lloyd's List* and the *London Review*. A small oak slant-front writing desk occupied a corner close to a Glastonbury chair. On the adjacent wall, a rough-hewn oak shelf was occupied by numerous tomes and a bible box. True to a spirit with the sea in his marrow, a bow-front stick barometer was secured to a wall away from sunlight.

'I have been so charged by your company, gentlemen, I have forgotten my manners,' said Equiano, picking up a bottle and pulling out the Glastonbury chair. 'Pray forgive me, please be seated. By chance, I have been donated a case of Jackiron rum by a patron. I put a few aside for the occasion of your visit.

''Tis been some time since I tasted Jackiron,' said Jonas.

Sitting down and savouring the fiery rum, he was briefly lost in thought until he heard his son's eager tones.

'I was captivated by your article in the *Public Advertiser*, Mister Equiano.'

'Any aspect in particular may I ask?' asked Equiano, raising his eyebrows and smiling.

Winking playfully at Jonas, Barber smiled and turned to watch.

'I can answer that, sir,' said Solomon with youthful enthusiasm. 'My eye was seized by your argument that England's free people of colour, in addition to the usual tribulations, as well risk wayside abduction and enslavement. I am of like mind, sir.'

'You are observant and clearly troubled about the wellbeing of black citizens, young man,' said Equiano. 'I trust you to carry on the struggle we have started. Although we live in times of great change, I expect the rights we speak of to take more than a generation.'

'However long, sir,' said Solomon intrepidly, 'we will carry on the fight for the abolition of the slave trade as well as identical rights for black people in England. My sister, sir, feels likewise.'

'Then, Solomon,' said Equiano, 'you should hear the tale of the slave ship *Zong* from one who obtained it first hand from an involved party. Hearken to the gall it takes to avoid responsibility by claiming insurance for the massacre of slaves. This is what abolitionists are up against and—'

A willowy street seller slid past the window with a head-borne basket of red fruit.

'Ripe strawberries sweet and tender!' she cried.

Blinking at the distraction, Equiano took a sip of rum and turned his chair.

'My friends,' he said quietly, as if divulging confidential intelligence. 'The *Zong* massacre was a deed of such cold-bloodedness, it rendered me speechless.'

'I am keen to hear about such an event,' said Barber.

'In March 1783,' continued Equiano, 'I brought to the attention of the anti-slavery campaigner, Granville Sharp, the case of the slave ship, *Zong*. Owned by the Gregson Shipping Company out of Liverpool, she was a square stern ship of one hundred and ten tons burthen. According to experienced slave ship masters, a vessel of her size would, as a rule, carry around one hundred and ninety-three slaves...'

'A ridiculous number for such a small vessel,' said Jonas.

'Whereas the *Zong* shipped a cargo of four hundred and forty-two slaves,' said Equiano.

'A suicidal consignment!' exclaimed Solomon.

'Down to incompetence and navigational errors,' continued Equiano, 'she strayed into the Doldrums and soon ran short of drinking water...'

'Bumbling oafs,' said Barber, rolling his eyes scornfully.

'On the orders of her master, Captain Robert Stubbs,' said Equiano, 'one hundred and forty-two slaves were flung overboard.'

'Good God!' cried Solomon, gulping down a mouthful of rum.

'I had heard about the *Zong* but few specifics,' said Barber, scowling. 'But listening to the account of one who has been closer to the events brings home the horror they must have suffered watching the ship sail away.'

''Tis an atrocity that shall not be easily forgotten,' said Jonas, slapping the table crossly.

'With unashamed impudence,' said Equiano, 'the Gregson Company claimed the insurance for the loss of the slaves. Thomas Gilbert, the insurance underwriter, disputed the claim. A court in Jamaica found for the Gregson Company. Nevertheless, on appeal with new evidence at the King's Bench in Westminster Hall, Lord Mansfield, the self-same who freed James Sommersett, overturned that judgement and ruled in favour of the insurers. And despite Granville Sharp's attempts to have the ship's owners and crew prosecuted for murder, he has been thus far unsuccessful.'

''Tis mass murder!' cried Solomon. 'And as expected, the murderers have gotten away with it.'

'I hope that account of the *Zong* assists your appreciation of the depths to which the slave-owners will sink, Solomon,' said Equiano. 'In the face of growing opposition from their own horrified countrymen, these ministers of destruction are dismissive of challenge and will stop at not anything. I trust that confirms what ye have hitherto ascertained about the murky waters the anti-slavery campaign has entered?'

'It does indeed, sir,' said Solomon, shifting uneasily in his chair. 'And drowning slaves off the *Zong* has razed any illusions I may have mistakenly contemplated.'

Grinning at his son, Jonas said nothing.

'Given the blatancy of the *Zong* massacre, gentlemen,' said Equiano, looking at each face in turn, 'ye must be in no doubt we embark on a monumental undertaking to give this hateful trade a fitting funeral.'

'And I shall be a pall-bearer,' said Solomon heartily. 'Pray hear me out, Mister Equiano.'

'By all means,' said Equiano, sitting back in his chair.

'I have notions about what else is needed in this campaign for abolition but cannot be certain,' said Solomon. 'For I do not know what acts the opposition might be prepared to carry out in their dying throes. This buffeted hide I wear with pride is a political issue. I accept that. But it has as well endowed me with the painful experience of a black. So ye see, sir, I feel I am duly tempered for the task.'

Steeped in pride by his son's justification, Jonas turned his eyes to the window and into the street.

'Tis a pity your mother is not here to hear your words this day, he thought.

'I am told that 'tis your twenty-first birthday, Solomon?' said Equiano.

'That is so, sir.'

'Do you know that among us here this day, Solomon,' said Equiano, smiling, 'you are the only man who has not ever been a slave? I say thanks be to God for that. Methinks we can as well be grateful to your mother and father for that. However, I want to thank you for your presence here this day, for you are a testament to the persistent survival of the African. Then tell me young man, how does it feel to be black and free from birth?'

'I was raised a free man in an age of slavery, sir,' said Solomon, smiling. 'Wearied of the 'good humoured' contempt for people of my skin, I appreciate that I have been honed by apprehension. Walking past slaves in the docks makes me feel like a member of some exclusive club. If truth be told, I am racked with guilt and outrage. Aye, I feel guilt, because while I am free, that man with my skin is not. Outrage because he merely breathes at the abrasive behest of his master, his mortal God. Despite all that, sir, for this campaign I harness the fortitude and prudence of your generation alongside the callow vigour of my own.'

'Well said, my young friend,' said Equiano.

Nodding at the eloquence of his offspring, Jonas smiled.

'A greater truth I have yet to hear,' said Barber, chuckling and sipping rum.

'Sometimes it takes colour or creed to make a good man do bad things, gentlemen,' said Jonas raising his glass. 'Let us hope that England's forthcoming white generations will find a productive accommodation with her black generations where ours have thus far failed, and I might add, through no fault of ours.'

'Aye,' they cried, guffawing and clinking glasses.

'Regrettably due to the immensity of the trade,' said Equiano, 'we shall be compelled to entrust this struggle to our children. Consequently, the task for my generation is to teach and motivate the young, and them their children. That will ensure the slave trade will not ever be repeated. Enslavement or conquest will only be successful if a past subjugation is forgotten.'

Scowling deeply, Solomon said, 'Not ever before have I heard anything as heartless as the *Zong* massacre. Though the master of the *Zong* lost his claim at the King's Bench, he ultimately won, for not he nor any member of his crew received punishment. But for England's vexed problems with colour, I would settle for being called to the Bar. As a member of the legal profession I would not rest till justice had been done.'

Filled with regard for his son's grasp of events and aspiration, Jonas winked at Barber, who smiled. Turning away, he appraised the young man in a new light.

I was not aware that Solomon had grown so militant, he thought. Right before me in Pilgrims, my boy has matured and is well-equipped to prosecute and hold his own argument.

'Plantation beatings for free people of colour have been replaced by the prejudicial behaviour of some in England itself,' said Equiano. 'It could be reasonably argued that people of colour are merely fugitives in this life. I ask ye, my friends, can fugitives anywhere ever feel truly secure? But will the dissimilarity of the fugitive come to unsettle some of England's communities? Mayhaps the fugitive reminds the settled that all things change. Confidence will be sorely needed on both sides.'

'Black citizens can be abducted off any street at any given moment,' said Jonas angrily. 'How can they ever feel secure enough to assemble that confidence? Especially since most are poor and none have found a means to rise above the position of secretary?'

'I know not of any,' said Barber dryly. 'In truth, my friends, we are exiles in a foreign land. By all accounts, service is the lot of the immigrant. Given our education, have we not proved that we are able to do more than just be in service? I am certain all that will change with persistence and time.'

Thrusting forwards with the passion of his age, Solomon protested, 'Is the *Zong* massacre not sufficiently brazen for someone to do something?'

'Few people know as yet, Solomon,' replied Equiano calmly. 'Though the massacre took place in November 1781, the first and only newspaper account of it appeared in March 1783. As a result, our campaign has the task of disseminating the account of this repugnant deed. We must spread word of this massacre as far and wide as possible.'

'You asked how the *Zong* might be exploited by the campaign for abolition, Olaudah,' said Jonas. 'Methinks for the public campaign and any prospective prosecutions, 'tis imperative to begin gathering the testimony of slaves and former slaves as well as the evidence of the methods used for working slaves to death cutting cane and for crushing plantation revolts. Moreover, the *Zong* should be used as a *cause célèbre* and rallying cry for abolitionists. She can stand as a symbol of the evil that typifies the lives of slaves.'

'Indubitably, Jonas,' said Barber. 'What more say ye?'

'Our petitions,' said Jonas readily, 'should draw attention to the ungodly pestilential conditions in which slaves are kept by some men from an allegedly God-fearing nation. By using words and diagrams on leaflets, we will draw attention to the *Zong* massacre and the terrors of the Middle Passage.'

''Tis imperative to emphasise that no man from the *Zong* has ever been charged with murder,' said Barber forcefully.

The sun's rays were weakening and the shadows growing longer with the afternoon. Four jarring chimes pealed from the wall clock. Momentarily, all that was evident was the sound of sipping and the clatter of chairs and the shuffle of legs.

'For the benefit of an admirer embarking on a somewhat tricky voyage, sir,' said Solomon deferentially, 'would it be impertinent to request an anecdote or two from bygone times?'

Giving an infectious grin that narrowed his eyes, Equiano said, 'I like your candour, Solomon. 'Tis heartening to meet a fellow traveller.'

Refilling all glasses, Equiano took a sip, sat back and began to speak, 'I am Igbo from the village of Essaka on the coast of Guinea. I was enslaved as a young boy and sold ten times before I could buy my freedom for forty pounds. Of all the memories of those harrowing years, the most abiding is the iron muzzle bridle. 'Tis a device strapped around the mouth to keep slaves silent, leaving them barely able to eat. It was fixed for sometimes several days.'

Catching his son's pained expression, Jonas said nothing.

'During my first days as a slave I held bizarre notions,' said Equiano, scoffing. 'Like the eyes of portraits followed me wherever I went in the house. And that any clock would inform my master about what I did in his absence.'

The parlour exploded with laughter. Glasses clinked. Chairs screeched on the boards.

'It gets much worse, gentlemen,' he continued. 'One night, I wearied of the punishments my blackness wrought on my being. My skin was to blame. Can ye believe that out of desperation I sought to change my appearance? In an attempt to whiten my skin, I scrubbed it with soap and water over and over and over again.'

Jolting the table in his surprise, Solomon upset a nearly-drained glass.

Paying no heed to the table-top mishap, Equiano continued:

'Over twenty years, I saw Georgia, Turkey, Martinique, Montserrat, Grenada and France. In 1773, I sailed as a deckhand aboard the HMS *Racehorse* on Lord Mulgrave's expedition to find a passage to India across the North Pole. Mulgrave found not a route, but I gained much comfort reading many of the scriptures. And as well, I learned a great deal about the world, its humans, their fears and their frailties.'

'Through the course of your eventful life, sir,' asked Solomon breathlessly, 'what sustained your spirits?'

'At times in my life,' said Equiano quietly, 'I had truly considered self-destruction. Christianity saved me. Now I see the invisible hand of God in every episode in my life. Every generation learns from the last, but not all pull in the same direction. Thus, fellow-traveller Solomon, it behoves me to pass on to thee a baton with which ye as well will forge ahead with the quest for abolition. I am certain you will use it.'

Visibly affected by his hero's championing, Solomon beamed.

'For well over a century we and countless others have slaved in the cane fields, my friends,' said Barber. 'Given the gathering momentum of this campaign, I sense change about us. And I foresee within twenty to thirty years this trade will be brought to an end. At that time, in order to bring about a comprehensive healing for their age and the one after that, our descendants here and on the coast of Guinea will have to question and resolve this slave saga to disentangle themselves from it. 'Twill not be easily accomplished.'

'There is much in what you say, Francis,' said Jonas. 'History's lessons tell us that abominable events beget inevitable responsibilities. Acknowledging responsibility for the protocols of the slave trade and the inevitable subsequent demand for reparations will not be straightforward or painless for the African kingdoms or for England. But what we do with the abolition campaign we do for them of the morrow, in the hope they take a different path.'

'I accept the baton and will play my part in the campaign, Mister Equiano,' said Solomon. 'While those of our skin sweat in servitude on slave ships, on plantations and in England, our people will continue to languish in the shadows of bondage. So I intend not to stand idly about.'

Grinning broadly, Jonas spoke with the rapturous tones of an admiring parent, 'Methinks you came of age this day, my son.'

'I thank you, sir,' said Solomon. 'I did not anticipate such conversation on this anniversary.'

The hubbub on Tottenham Street suddenly entered the parlour. Traders were haggling right outside the window. Carriages were dropping and picking up fares. A chatty family traipsed by as they peered nosily through the window.

Pensively setting down his glass, Barber said, 'We need more and better connections between black and white peoples.'

'Right now methinks we have three,' said Equiano quietly. 'Do we not already share the blood of offspring between black and white? Solomon stands as an excellent testament. Do we not enjoy friendships between black and white? And can you not see that the mutual contribution to the campaign for abolition is a third such bridge? In the fullness of time, others will arise.'

'In the meantime,' said Jonas, 'we are obliged to endure provocative newspaper articles like the one authored by Phillip Thicknesse. Sometime in '78, he penned an invective that ended with the portrayal:

'In every town, nay in almost every village are to be seen a little race of mulattoes, mischievous as monkeys and infinitely more dangerous.'

'In some quarters that opinion has not changed,' said Barber with a derisive chuckle. 'Thanks to providence much of the populace do not to subscribe to such vitriol. We ought to counter such articles in print. Let us ask our white friends to help us identify cooperative newspaper editors.'

'Aye,' said Equiano heartily. 'Methinks 'tis as well time to discredit misconceptions about African people. Slave-owners continue to propagate the inferiority of the African. And it would seem that elements of the clergy in their pulpits preach that slavery has divine sanction. I pray to know which God told them that.'

Responding to the laughter, Equiano topped up the glasses. 'We must inform the citizenry that we Africans hail from many cultures,' he said with quiet vehemence. 'We talk in many tongues steeped in ancient traditions from ancient civilisations. We are not mules, our brains are not black and we don't eat worms.'

Scornful laughter shook the parlour.

''Tis said that history is about the way we remember,' said Barber, wiping his eyes. 'So my friends let us do our lawful damnedest to make certain we leave something that not anyone will forget.'

Glancing at the clock, Jonas stood up.

'Fret not, Francis,' he said, 'we shall leave evidence of the part we played. Alas I fear we must break up our gathering, my friends. The family await our return for Solomon's birthday dinner.'

'Without further ado be gone, young man,' said Equiano, rising to his feet with affection in his manner. 'Laughter and a full belly gives a body vigour for the fight.'

Standing up brimming with the regard of an admirer, Solomon said, 'Having given thought to the sentiments I have been honoured to hear in your parlour, Mister Equiano, I will try to live up to the example you all have set.'

'How fares thee, Solomon?' asked Barber, standing up and changing the subject. 'What studies do you pursue?'

'Many thanks for my volume of *A Modest Proposal*, sir,' said Solomon. 'Given by your hands, sir, I shall always treasure it.'

'I thought you would take much from Mister Swift's narrative,' said Barber. 'And I would be interested in your opinion of his work. Call on Gough Square to give me your thoughts.'

'I would be delighted to visit Gough Square, sir,' said Solomon.

'Indeed you must,' said Barber, like an affectionate relative.

'As for my studies, sir,' said Solomon with irritation in his voice. 'They will not lead to any qualification. I shall not be allowed to matriculate to University. Thanks to the good offices of father I am instead gainfully apprenticed to Thomas Beecham, Chandlers. I am presently clerking in the stores.'

A brief silence ensued.

Narrowing his eyes with affection for his offspring, Jonas smiled.

Taking a sip, Equiano put down his glass and spoke impassively, 'You are not the first who could not matriculate to University, Solomon. University is considered above the station of poor whites, women and blacks. We are in good company. A fundamental change for your dark-skinned status will be required, which I believe is a long way off. When the likes of us are finally accepted as part of the English body politic, we will then be able to enjoy all the rights our new station entitles us to. One of which will be matriculating to University. For that to take place, 'twill require a radical change in the posture of the powers that be. That breed of change, Solomon, comes not easy to old cultures.'

'I had set my heart on a career at the Bar,' said Solomon.

'When the way is barred to your objective, Solomon, you take another path,' said Equiano quietly. 'A good education was the first precious step you took. Having a waged occupation apprenticed to a reputed company is the second. You are a fortunate young man. Even with my erudition, I still can only find work as a house servant and sometimes as a valet. I am making notes from my research for a book which I trust will provide me with the necessary funds. I will enlighten you all about my work when next we meet.'

'I look forward to our next meeting, Mister Equiano,' said Solomon.

'And so we shall, Solomon,' said Equiano. 'We shall exchange letters. Pray visit again soon.'

Twilight was upon them. Lamplighters were trudging past the window. The wall clock said a few minutes past seven.

Taking leave of Equiano and Barber, Jonas entered the carriage on Tottenham Street and sat down beside his son.

'I thank you for your patience, Mister Sawyer,' he said, smiling. 'And I trust you have had enough to eat and drink. You shall be recompensed as agreed.'

'We stuffed our bellies an' gawked at the buxom ladies hereabouts, Mister Guinea,' said the minder with a snigger. 'I 'ope you had a right hearty occasion.'

'We most certainly did, Mister Sawyer,' said Jonas. 'That we did.'

Signalling the driver to set off, he settled back to ponder over the day's events.

Over many years, Barber, Equiano and I forgot our African languages from lack of use, he thought. Despite that loss, we remain Africans. We as well have in common the sea, the slave plantations, divine intervention, manumission and a good income. Barber, a former slave, is now secretary to Doctor Johnson; Equiano a former slave, blazes a reputation as a writer; while I, a former slave, am a family man and partner in a successful company. As well, my son has gained a mentor of good reputation and I a like-minded friend.

'All things considered, young man,' he said, laughing and putting an arm around his son, ''tis been a grand day at the office.'

'Aye, sir, that it has, sir,' said Solomon, beaming.

Twilight yielded a velvety moonlit evening. The bells of the baroque parish church of Saint Paul pealed half-past eight.

Clattering to Deptford the carriage was soon rumbling along the Highway. Earthly shadows faded into the dark corners of the street. Odours of horse dung and sewage wafted through the warm airs. Hatted costermongers were yet hawking fruit and vegetables from oil-lamped barrows. Hindering traffic on a street corner, a circle of ballad singers stood under a lamppost lustily crooning David Garrick's *Heart of Oak*. On both sides of the thoroughfare, sailors and merrymaking locals spilled onto the road. Some were toasting muffins over braziers. Others gathered near lanterned stalls selling hot pies and chestnuts.

Sighting Pilgrims silhouetted against the night sky through the plane trees, Jonas heaved a happy sigh.

Rattling to a standstill outside Pilgrims, the carriage pulled up behind a hooded lanterned yellow cabriolet drawn by a restive mare.

An eerie disquieting hush shrouded Pilgrims. Candlelight and oil light glowed from virtually every window and the front door stood wide open. In the hallway under the candelabra, he could see the housekeeper, the cook and a maidservant in huddled chatter.

His wife suddenly emerged on the top step frantically waving a handkerchief.

Seized by foreboding, he sprang out of the carriage followed by his son. Bounding up the steps, he embraced his fretting spouse.

'What is wrong, my dearest?' he asked. 'Have we suffered house-breakers?'

'Thank God you are home, Jonas,' she said, dabbing her eyes. 'I have been frantic with worry. We have not attended the Anti-Slavery Society. When we were leaving the house the nurse called us back. Mistress Beecham was experiencing difficulty with her breath—'

'Good God!' he exclaimed, staggering backwards.

'I sent for Doctor Fosbery,' she said hastily. 'Though her breathing eased, it was fitful. A little after four o'clock she was seized by sweats and a crippling chest pain. I fear she is failing, Jonas. The doctor is with her now in her bedchamber. I have sent for Reverend Baskett—'

'I must go to her,' he said, turning away impatiently.

'She asks for you constantly,' she said. 'Come let us hasten to her, dearest, for I fear she may not have long.'

Closely followed by his sobbing wife and children, he mounted the stairs apprehensively. Memories rushed wildly through his head. Drawing near her bedchamber, his throat dried. Dabbing his eyes with a handkerchief, his gut feeling said Mistress Beecham was failing.

'God forbid,' he exclaimed quietly, almost to himself.

Leaving his family in the doorway, he stepped inside.

At odds with the expected sepulchral conditions for a failing Quaker, the chamber was awash with light. Brass pulpit candlesticks with lighted candles stood on either side of the oak four-poster. Candles sprouted along the Georgian side tables, on the flap of a tall rococo walnut bureau bookcase and on the writing desk. Fresh stands of hollyhocks and roses graced the four corners of the chamber. The bright composition bore all the hallmarks of her hand. It was as if she intended to leave the stage as she had lived by discharging vigour before her flame was quenched.

Rising from the panelled-back oak settle, the nurse discreetly left the chamber.

Picking up his black leather bag, the frock-coated physician was succinct.

'Mistress Beecham has suffered a heart seizure,' he whispered. 'I have tapped and listened closely to her chest. Her heart grows weaker. She breathes very shallow now. I fear she has not long, Mister Guinea. I have prescribed Sydenham's Laudanum to relieve her pain, to be taken whenever the need arises. I fear I can do not anything more for her. We can only pray she pulls through. She is in God's hands now. She has been asking for you. I shall wait in the withdrawing room.'

Apart from his family outside the open door, he was alone. Until now, he had refused to contemplate or imagine life without her. But the tidings he had feared had at last been uttered by his wife and now the doctor.

Gazing down on her supine figure, his head churned and his lips quivered.

Her wizened features peeked from under a mobcap. Propped up by bolsters, she lay night-shirted under cream woollen bedclothes and appeared to be in deep slumber.

Taking her frail, furrowed hand, he sat down on the bed.

Slowly opening wrinkled eyes, she smiled and gave his hand a feeble squeeze. With laboured faltering breath, she said:

'You are my beloved son, Jonas... I have not long... with you. Though... we be not... of the same skin... we have been a loving family. Our kinship... was made not... by the consent of... men... but from God-given senses... deep within you... and I. Our bond dwells... in a realm affected not by the governance... and bigotry of mortals. Our kinship grew... above and... beyond the understanding... and...imaginations...of others. You... are truly...my blood. You are beyond hue my beloved son...'

'What will I do without you?' he asked.

Giving him no answer, her chin sank into the bedclothes for anxious moments. Then raising her head, she took a long rasping breath.

'We had…a splendid journey… you… and I,' she said, discharging a gravelly chuckle. 'I could not…have wished for…a more…loving…companion. As well my love is for Faith. Pray… keep up… the…search for…her…son…'

Teardrops trickled down his cheeks. At death's door, true to her selfless brand, the one who had dotingly mothered him from the age of twelve asked after another.

Swallowing the lump in his gullet, he said, "Pon my soul, Mother, I shall not ever quit the search. Kinship binds me to right that wrong for Faith. But how can I ever repay you for the sanctuary, food, education, home and love you have given me? You have the love of an eternally grateful son. And I say you have been a loving mother. Freed from a slave island, I was blessed to have found a home with you and Mister Beecham. I—'

'Come…come closer…Jonas…hearken to me,' she rasped. 'The… books… are…in order. I… happily…bequeath Pilgrims… the Chandlery… and my shares…to you… with provision…for Cousin Mildred…the League…the Deptford…Almshouse… the Methodist… Christ Church… Mission…'

'Your light shines ever brightly, Mistress Beecham,' he said, sniffling and wiping his eyes. 'I shall carry out your wishes precisely. But I know you will improve—'

'Nay…nay…Jonas…my…time…draws… nigh. I…can hear… him…'

Her frail voice petered out. Her eyelids closed. Abruptly taking a long phlegm-ridden breath, she said, 'Draw…the curtains…so…I… may…see…the day.'

Pulling back the heavy woollen fabric onto the moonlit Highway, he turned and gulped down the blockage in his parched throat.

"Tis a…glorious…day…my son,' she said faintly.

'Aye that it is, Mother,' he said.

Her eyes opened wider. Her breath came now in ragged, low gasps. Stupefied by her moribund state, he held his breath.

For what felt an aeon, an eerie hush settled on Pilgrims.

Staring vacantly into the distance, her voice cracked the stillness of the chamber.

'Thomas…he…comes,' she hissed.

Giggling girlishly she stretched out a frail arm. He reached to take her hand, but before he made contact, her earthly limb flopped down onto the covers and stayed quite still. On a warm night under a strawberry moon, eyes that once sparkled with vitality assumed a blank pellucid stare.

Spurred by innate Yoruba traditions, he stood up and said, 'An *Onile*, a Spirit of the Earth, has passed away!'

Solemnly and softly he kissed both her cheeks. A daunting ghostly silence filled his ears.

Stepping into the chamber, his sobbing wife and children collapsed around the bed. Apprehension and sorrow overwhelmed him. Tremblingly kneeling down with his elbows on the bed, he put his hands together and prayed. Then, he sat on the side of the bed sobbing. At that moment he felt his wife's arm around his shoulders.

'Alice Beecham truly loved and treasured you, my love,' she said, wiping her eyes. 'After the doctor has departed, let us take the carriage to the Christ Church Mission and light candles for a magnificent soul with a life well spent.'

Wiping his eyes on his sleeve he spoke quietly to his wife.

'Aye we shall light candles,' he said. 'With Olivia, Solomon and Mistress Honeypenny we shall mourn the passing of a great lady.'

Thomas Beecham, Chandlers

Monday
19 July 1784
13.00 hrs

Above the chandlery in the office next to the rope-loft, downcast greetings were exchanged. Chaired by the company secretary, Aaron Drinkwater, an Extraordinary Meeting of the shareholders of Thomas Beecham, Chandlers fell into sombre session. After fulsomely lamenting the death of Mistress Beecham, the members toasted 'a feisty pioneer and a noble friend'. The sole item on the agenda was the confirmation of Jonas Guinea as sole proprietor with Faith Guinea as silent partner. Given his inherited seventy-five per cent shareholding, the outcome was never in doubt. Nevertheless, a ballot was required by law.

Aaron Drinkwater tapped his gavel on the table to draw attention. 'Ladies and gentlemen, consistent with statutory obligations we are obliged to take a vote on this motion.'

A unanimous show of hands approved the proposal.

The soft clink of glasses and a subdued toast with sherry was all that marked another momentous event in Jonas's life.

Under the cloud of Mistress Beecham's passing, he and his wife had been confirmed sole partners of Thomas Beecham, Chandlers. On their behalf, he thanked Jeremiah and Grace Puddlewick, Reverend Augustus Baskett, Parson Merriweather, Captain Miracle, Captain Battersby and his son, Robert — all of whom were also members of the League.

'Ladies and gentlemen,' said Aaron Drinkwater with a smile. 'I believe the partners wish to inaugurate their management of the company with an innovative proposal.'

Leaning forwards, Jonas addressed the shareholders solemnly.

'Although the chandlery depends on foot traffic,' he said, 'our revenues have nevertheless remained steady. To improve the order book, we plan to gain fresh orders by fetching our tackle out to anchored ships in the guise of salesmen carrying samples. We shall start by engaging three good men from the chandlery and seek replacements from among experienced chandlers. We judge that three such outfitted salesmen, selling and promoting our goods on the vessels, should significantly increase our trade and our profits.'

'We will steal a march on Jeffersons of Poplar,' said Captain Battersby approvingly.

'A novel initiative, Mister Guinea,' said Aaron Drinkwater.

'Why from the chandlery, Mister Guinea?' asked Jeremiah Puddlewick.

'Our men are familiar with our merchandise and know how they are assembled. In this first instance, we believe that our experienced men are best placed to effect good sales.'

'A progressive project, Mister Guinea,' said Grace Puddlewick, smiling. 'I am keen to learn what other changes for the chandlery you have in mind.'

'I daresay this is not the occasion to have that conversation, Mistress Puddlewick,' said Jonas courteously, 'but we thought that 'tis proper to table such a change at the earliest opportunity. I ask shareholders to be patient. The partners shall table the results at our next meeting.'

Making eye contact, Reverend Baskett gave a cold watery smile.

Methinks this priest harbours something bleak inside, thought Jonas.

Given the partnership had been properly recorded, the meeting was ended. One by one, the members bade farewell and walked quietly to their carriages.

Ambling thoughtfully to the withdrawing room, Faith opened the oak corner cupboard. Heaving a long weary sigh, Jonas slumped on the Chippendale sofa. Uncorking a bottle of Chateau Chauvin St

Emilion reserved for very special occasions, she dispensed the cherry-red wine into two glasses. Beaming at him, she sat opposite on the wing chair and solemnly lifted her glass.

'I give you a toast, my darling,' she said buoyantly. 'A toast to a magnificent life lived and the soul of Mistress Beecham who will forever live in our thoughts. And I give you a toast to our partnership.'

'To Mistress Beecham,' he declared, raising his glass. 'She who cannot be forgotten is not ever truly departed. A robust partnership will be a testament to her affection and to her memory.'

'I second that, Jonas,' she said, 'but what now?'

'What now?' he asked, puckering his brow. 'Why, we have a thriving business to reorganise and a campaign to sustain.'

'Ownership and shareholdings of the chandlery have been settled. What does the morrow hold for our family?'

'Solomon is apprenticed to the chandlery,' he said. 'Olivia is keen to do likewise. We both know she is eager to train in the workings and management of the company from the storeroom upwards. And when we are gone, we shall leave the company to our children...'

'I knew that would be so,' she said.

'Then,' he said, 'we can be certain that whatever happens with the inclination by some to confuse England's black citizens with plantation slaves, our children will always have work.'

'Methinks you're entitled to know, my dearest husband,' she said, tossing an engaging smile, 'that with your dutiful consideration for the business of the chandlery, the activities of the League and the campaign for abolition, life in our household does go on.'

'And what does that mean?' he snapped.

'You may not have noticed, for example,' she teased, 'that our son has of late, been taking tea with and writing poetry for a certain young lady.'

'You are right, my dear,' he said apologetically. 'I have been far too embroiled in financial matters to have noticed. I did not know. But why do you tell me all this now?'

'Solomon is old enough to marry,' she said seriously. 'They make a good match. He has not asked for her hand and would not until he has asked you for your blessing. So while you are considering your offspring's prospective occupations, you might as well put that in your paternal estimates.'

He grinned. 'Is Olivia seeing anyone?'

'Not as yet.'

'Who is she who has stolen Solomon's heart?'

'Sienna Baskett, the only child of our shareholder, Reverend Augustus Baskett,' she said. 'Nearly nineteen, she's a comely young thing and quite smitten with Solomon, who I must say is love-struck. You will be delighted by his choice.'

Pausing momentarily at the thought of his son's choice, he smiled and asked, 'Does Reverend Baskett approve? Has he said anything?'

'His wife approves,' she said. 'Baskett has mouthed a great deal and not all of it digestible. This alleged clergyman rejected Solomon in no uncertain terms. He said, "Methinks your acquaintance with my daughter is indecent. I will not have my daughter bedded by a nigger."'

'A man of the cloth actually said that?' Jonas asked, aghast. A cold fury welled inside him.

Likewise, a tight knot twisted in Faith's gut at the recollection. Envisioning men like the cleric poisoning others with the notion that carnal relations with black people watered down white blood, she sat up sharply.

'Our children,' she said vehemently, 'are an excellent repudiation of Baskett's bigotry.'

'In truth, for our children in matters of the heart,' he said ruefully, 'colour may at times still be an obstruction. We live in small-minded times.'

'How dare Baskett spew that over our son,' she snarled, swallowing a mouthful of wine. 'His vulgarity startled and angered Solomon, who has vowed not to give up. Baskett is the very same saintly cleric who supped with us on untold occasions. Not once did he ever let slip so much as an inkling of what he truly harboured and has lately revealed. The Devil himself could not have been more accomplished in the dark arts of duplicity.'

'Baskett secretes intolerance in his hallowed vestments,' he said. 'He has not the spunk of Reverend Whitehouse, who regrettably bequeathed him shares in the chandlery.'

'Nor does he share the worldliness of his wife,' she added. 'I have many times taken tea with her. Prudence Baskett appears a humble doting mother, but she is in truth a firebrand masquerading as a vicar's wife. Her liking of Solomon is plain to see. And she is adamant that her daughter must follow her heart provided her admirer's prospects are good. She accepts Solomon's prospects are good. Methinks you and Reverend Baskett had better meet soon to sort it out.'

'Now I understand that look Baskett flung in my direction,' he said, almost to himself. Smiling at her, he said, 'I will speak to Solomon. Then, I will write to the cleric and propose a meeting. Mayhaps we shall learn how he squares his membership of the clergy and the League and the campaign for abolition with his expressed revulsion of black skin. I am keen to hear how he thinks God would judge him betraying his Christian principles.'

Falling back into the sofa giggling, she suddenly sat up with scheming in her eyes.

'Could we not spend a week in Kent?' she asked, with a guileful accent in her voice. 'We have not visited Greensleeves for over a month. Invite the Reverend and Mistress Baskett for a few days in the countryside. You can observe Baskett out of his proverbial sanctimonious surroundings, so to speak. The opportunist in him will accept your invitation because he is like an outsider itching to be favoured the dining table and withdrawing room. Given the willing connivance of his wife and daughter, women may well bring about a more constructive outlook in the man. Not forgetting Parson Merriweather, whose worldly-wise experience will make an ideal foil for Baskett's narrow-mindedness. During our absence from Pilgrims as before, we shall leave the chandlery in the safe hands of our general manager, Mister Wilkins, assisted by Olivia and Solomon.'

'I shall dispatch an invitation to Baskett right away,' he grinned, 'on the pretext of a discourse on the scriptures for the League's forthcoming petitions.'

Clapham

Holy Trinity Church
Common land of Clapham
Sunday
5 September 1784
14.00 hrs

The sun was a hospitable golden orb dispensing heat through the afternoon. Under blue skies, cloudy mare's tails streaked to the horizon. On the wild common land of the rural village of Clapham, leaves had started to turn with the last vestiges of summer.

Holy Trinity Church stood near the northern edge of the sizeable triangular area of drained common land held for the parishes of Battersea and Clapham. Rebuilt in 1775, the house of worship was a brick structure with a nave, chancel and south chapel. Three segmental-headed windows lighted the chancel to the east, with a large semi-circular window to the south.

Mopping his brow, Aaron Drinkwater sighed contentedly at the working men and women crowding the meadow around the Church.

'We could not have asked for better conditions, Jonas,' he said, smiling broadly.

'Methinks this climate encouraged many more to attend, Aaron,' said Jonas, laughing softly.

A stone's throw away, dotted around the Long Pond under the spreading oaks, children played and picnicked with their families on the wavy-hair grasses. Sporting umbrellas, courting couples ambled through the melick grasslands and over the sweet vernal-grasses of the meadows. Between giant clumps of blackberry bushes on cleared scrubland, spirited youths scampered about in boisterous games of football. Steadying head-borne wicker baskets, piemen and shapely orange-sellers trudged about.

On a rutted track across the common, Jonas spotted a column of crabby-faced men on horses laden with bulging panniers. He lowered his voice and grinned.

'Tea smugglers.'

'In broad daylight!' exclaimed Aaron Drinkwater, smiling. 'Cheeky bastards. And no doubt with the connivance of a few Customs and Excise officers. You do know this common is the route for smugglers making for Stockwell village? 'Tis the heart of London's black market in tea.'

'I truly did not know that, Aaron,' said Jonas honestly. 'How did an upright citizen like you come by such underworld intelligence?'

'Connections, Jonas,' said Drinkwater, winking and chuckling mischievously. 'You might recall I am a lawyer.'

Grinning at the response, Jonas surveyed the animated locality.

Beneath spreading horse chestnut trees on the crowded northern meadow surrounding the Church, an open meeting airing the protests of the anti-slavery lobby had just ended. The rambunctious event had been staged by the League Against the Importation of Negroes from the Coast of Guinea. Noted for being the putative meeting place of the Clapham Saints, a group of social reformers and philanthropists with abolitionist tendencies, the hallowed precincts of the Anglican Church was deemed most suitable.

Beside his son by the southern corner of the spiritual sanctuary, Jonas waited with members of the League, watching the dispersing crowd. Through the drooping fronds of the willow dangling over the nearby Cock Pond, he saw a lacquered yellow landau veer from Rookery Road into Clapham North Side and screech to a halt. Stepping airily onto the cobbles, two men with canes mustered. Then, they walked purposefully across the meadow in their direction.

Suddenly, the lawyer seized his arm.

''Tis Matthew Fleming!' exclaimed Aaron Drinkwater.

With a disparaging groan, Jonas closed his eyes momentarily.

'An unforeseen participant,' he said. 'What skulduggery is he up to?'

'Mayhaps he hastens here to atone for his sins,' said Solomon sarcastically. 'Whatever he peddles he can peddle it elsewhere.'

'By the looks of Fleming and his confederates,' chuckled the shipowner, Jeremiah Puddlewick, 'they have not come to invite us to tea.'

Appraising the approaching frock-coated figure, Jonas thought the erstwhile coxcomb had been fleeced by his forty-nine years. Once clear brown eyes were now lustred with disdain. Round-faced and bulbous-nosed, his sweptback chestnut hair and clipped sideburns were greying. Heartless deeds had turned a formerly unexceptional individual into an unreconstructed tyrant.

'Stay close to me, Solomon,' said Jonas in an undertone. 'Take your first close look at the face of inhumanity from one who believes colour makes a body inferior. Watch closely, listen, and learn.'

'I shall, sir,' said Solomon nervously.

Halting a couple of yards away, Fleming dipped his head with chilly civility.

'Good afternoon, gentlemen,' he said courteously. Nodding amiably at his silk-coated friend, he said, 'Sir Nicholas Pollock and I represent the West Indies Sugar Cartel. We think your League's campaign slates our trade with undeserved condemnation. I was told of your action on this common late this morning. Post-haste, we came to attend your meeting to challenge the myths about the slave trade. Bearing in mind your irksome campaign, gentlemen, we believe that 'tis high time we all laid our cards on the table.'

Suddenly, the shouts of the footballers pervaded the setting. Rising imperceptibly, a barrier of tension slipped in between them.

Aware of the sinews tightening in his neck, Jonas mustered a supercilious smile.

'In view of the fact you own slaves, Mister Fleming,' he said, 'just how were you intending to persuade an abolitionist audience?'

Edgily scratching his cheek, Solomon grinned nervously.

Raising his cane with angry eyes, Sir Nicholas Pollock's lips curled.

'It may come as news to your kind, Mister Guinea,' he said contemptuously, 'but slavery is legal in the colonies. Do your supporters know the abolition they seek will put many of them out of work? They are entitled to hear the facts. But I see we came too late.'

'Tut tut,' admonished Aaron Drinkwater. 'Lateness has oft lost fortunes, Sir Nicholas. Mayhaps the slave trade will meet with a similar
fate. You might like to know that our supporters attend as a matter of
Christian conscience, not employment. I'm told that in some quarters conscience is considered to be a somewhat obstructive inconven-
ience — gets in the way I believe.'

Smirking at the comment, Solomon put a hand bashfully over his
mouth.

Flabbergasted by the reply and turning purple, Sir Nicholas spluttered unintelligibly.

Plainly irked by the affronted demeanour of his companion, Fleming's face reddened, his eyes grew cold and hard and he spoke with
barely concealed animosity.

'We like not your disposition, Mister Drinkwater, nor do we wish
to remain in the presence of you gentlemen a moment longer than we
need. So I will come to the point. Your League's interfering conduct
threatens England's trade. Were you to succeed, you would give
England's competitors a march on her. We will protect that lawful
trade and defend our lawful profits. Your League's meddling will not
be countenanced. Call an immediate halt to your campaign. Stop
stealing our slaves and we will overlook what has already transpired.
In no uncertain terms, be aware you face the weight of London's
financiers.'

'You procrastinate, Mister Fleming,' chuckled Jeremiah Puddlewick.
'Don't make me laugh. Were your profits in such good health, you
would not come prancing here to have words with abolitionists. We
have no fear of your bankers. Moreover, we know of no effort to steal
your captives by any member of our League or any other. Were that
to come to my ears, I would naturally applaud. And—'

Interrupting the shipowner, Jonas addressed his antagonist coldly.

'Methinks you have sighted the inauspicious signs for your trade,
Mister Fleming. Abolition is clearly not a fantasy as you have claimed,
or you would not be fretting. England wakens and the enemy you
fear appears on the distant horizon. The slave trade is under threat
and your plantations will ultimately go under. Confronted by a mere
whisper of change, you resort to threats?'

Visibly bristling at the retort, Fleming growled, 'Set not foot on Pertigua in any capacity, Jonas Guinea, or I will take thee myself.'

Stepping backwards with fright, Solomon's mouth fell open.

'Despite my many responsibilities, Matthew Fleming,' said Jonas nonchalantly, 'I will try to remember to fit your forewarning into my crowded schedule.'

'I like not the thrust of your attitude nor anything about you, Jonas Guinea,' said Fleming combatively. 'The fact that you cleave to a station above that of your kind gives cause for concern. But to parade your luck by aping the white man with all manner of pretentious affectations I find troubling, nay indeed, I find frightening. Methinks your kind is an enemy within. Mark my words, gentlemen, the morrow will prove me right.'

'Having no wish to ape the likes of early man, Matthew Fleming,' said Jonas assertively, 'my liking for that brutish breed has not ever been under consideration. Methinks, therefore, that should suffice about my feelings for you. Though I suspect that in the climates of the morrow our peoples might well become friends. For now, the plantations stand in the way.'

'Sugar plantations are lawful,' said Fleming sharply.

Guinea has a fresh poise about his person, he thought. I daresay being sole proprietor of a profitable chandlery has a tad to do with it. A nigger with resources and attitude…

'Slave plantations are as well beneficially located in remote locations,' said Jeremiah Puddlewick. 'Consequently, Mister Fleming, they operate away from prying eyes in near secrecy. Moreover, if the rations and spiritual guidance you say plantations provide were as you say, why then do they arouse such antagonism? Surely if the conditions were not cruel, you would not be averse to inspection. We cannot ever subscribe to the buying and selling of human beings, to hide them away on plantations without remuneration. That is called an atrocity, Mister Fleming.'

'We are humane and have not anything to hide, Mister Puddlewick,' said Sir Nicholas. 'Unacquainted eyes could not read the specialised manoeuvres on a plantation. Our slaves are regularly fed and watered—'

'Sounds like cattle to my ears, Sir Nicholas,' said Jonas. 'And I suppose they roam the cane fields purely for the exercise?'

'Cane-cutters cut cane,' said Sir Nicholas sharply. 'What else do you think they do? From the plantations, England receives vast shipments of sugar. In turn, the slaves obtain good lodgings, good food, fine apparel and Christian teachings—'

'None of which can be verified, as well you know, Sir Nicholas,' said Aaron Drinkwater.

'You can take the word of an Englishman, Mister Drinkwater.'

'I am a practising lawyer, Sir Nicholas,' he retorted. 'You ask me to trust the word of them with vested interests?'

'And why such obscurity?' asked Jonas.

'We have no need for obscurity, Mister Guinea,' said Fleming. 'It may have escaped the attention of your kind that the sugar plantations are over there and not over here. The obscurity you refer to is called the Atlantic Ocean.'

'Why drag them across the Atlantic?' asked Jeremiah Puddlewick.

'Africans are a vulnerable species and need protection, Mister Puddlewick,' said Sir Nicholas. 'They originate from lands where there is no administration to speak of. In fact, indolence is routine. They openly exhibit themselves in lewd conduct and eat all manner of obnoxious fare. Oftimes they eat each other. Being raised on indolence, they have to be cajoled to work—'

Angered within by the knight's fallacious portrayal of Africans, Jonas cut him short.

'Cajoled is simply a euphemism for torture, Sir Nicholas,' he said derisively. 'And you say they work happily without monetary recompense as well? Why so?'

'Transportation, lodgings, provisions and clothing cost money, Mister Guinea,' said Fleming. 'They must be funded somehow.'

'It has oft been said that excesses happen behind closed doors, Mister Fleming,' said Jonas. 'As well 'tis said that unobserved unchecked systems generally give way to unbridled power. Methinks that the slave regime has long ago slipped into that abyss. What say you?'

Stung by the question, Fleming reddened.

'I say the slave brand you bear does not ever fade, Mister Guinea,' he said with scathing sarcasm. 'Fine tailoring changes not anything.'

Jolted by what he heard, Solomon's eyes held unease. I must ask father about his slave brand, he thought.

'I am certain you would agree, Mister Fleming,' said Jonas, nodding at his son, 'that despite the blaze of breeding in some, empty-headedness flares regrettably like a beacon.'

'Given the benefits of an English education, your black friend is the exception, Mister Drinkwater,' said Sir Nicholas, diverting attention from his companion's exasperation. 'Unlike your kinsmen, Mister Guinea, you clearly have the wits to retain information and can, I am reliably informed, perform tasks other than that of manual labour. You are a rare breed indeed. And you are lucky. I trust you will use your God-given gift wisely, but with sufficient wisdom not to meddle in the business of white men.'

Bristling at the brazen warning, Jonas winked calmly at his son and replied impassively, 'For myself, Sir Nicholas, I would have termed meddling to be that which is being illicitly conducted by English men along the coast of Guinea as we speak. Do they not act as if that African territory was a mere annexe of England? Moreover, they brutally depopulate that land. Then they forcibly sweat Africans in the cane fields without monetary recompense. That is not doing business, as you like to put it, Sir Thomas, 'tis a violent mugging. You dub me a rare breed. A backhanded compliment if ever I heard one. I just happen to have been fortunate to have met with a factor called opportunity.'

Muttering beneath his breath and barely keeping himself in check, the knight's narrowed eyes were cold and hard.

'Cartels like yours have used every means at their disposal to frustrate and stifle the campaign for abolition,' said Jeremiah Puddlewick. 'You will fail not only because we grow in numbers, but because your moral philosophy is bereft of common sense and compassion. Making profit off free labour has no place among civilised peoples, Mister Fleming. Have you no sense of wrongdoing?'

'Our civilisation is superior, Mister Puddlewick,' said Fleming confidently, 'and the industrious commerce of the white man has furnished the backward blacks with a more productive existence. We save them from themselves, lest they would be openly fornicating or dispatching one another. We have provided them with shelter, education and a profusion of new skills and trades, and furthermore, we have as well brought them closer to God. I see it as our Christian duty. I cannot comprehend your objection.'

'We are supported by the King, Law and Church,' added Sir Nicholas hastily. 'What more do we need? Is it not reasonable that blacks compensate with their labour for our many disbursements on their behalf? What can be so wrong with that?'

'Then, Sir Nicholas,' said Aaron Drinkwater, 'you clearly have not so much as what can be termed a rapport with a Christian conscience. The price you ask Africans to pay for uncertain disbursements is cruelly onerous, Sir Nicholas. Do you not see that 'tis not possible to consolidate extremes? You will not give up your slaving. We cannot give up our campaign. I see that no good would come from a continued exchange with you. I bid you good day, sir.'

'A good day to you, sir,' replied Fleming gruffly. 'Let us away, Sir Thomas. Methinks better company can be found at Bootle's.'

'One moment, Mister Fleming,' said Jonas, taking a forward step. 'Aye?'

'It can be difficult in the metropolis for black citizens, Mister Fleming. I thought you might like to know that I take exceptional precautions when on the streets.'

'Why tell me? What do you fear?'

'Abduction, Mister Fleming,' said Jonas curtly. 'I'm told there are slave-owners who even stoop to using slave-hunters to kidnap off the streets of London. You would not resort to such unchristian tactics would you, Mister Fleming? 'Tis said it saves slave-owners the tedium of fetching Africans from the coast of Guinea. Such an attempt was made on my person. It failed miserably, of course. I believe the thugs retreated with bloody noses and a good drubbing.'

Turning beetroot while stifling his quivering belligerence, Fleming shook his head.

'Now now, Mister Guinea,' he said condescendingly. 'You really must try to temper your unproven suspicions. It could give a body a problem.'

'Slave-owners sit at the root of England's forthcoming problems, Mister Fleming,' said Jonas. 'For knowingly or unknowingly,
slave-owners will bequeath England's peoples with the responsibility
for their deeds.'

Turning to his companions, Jonas smiled imperiously. 'Methinks
'tis time to take the carriage back to Pilgrims, Aaron. We have a big
conference to prepare for.'

'Aye we do, Jonas,' said Aaron Drinkwater, giving him an amiable
slap on the back.

''Twas an excellent assemblage, Jonas,' said Jeremiah Puddlewick
heartily.

'Aye Jeremiah,' said Jonas, 'that it was. From this open meeting we
have gained countless more supporters. Come Solomon, this night
we shall have that talk about primeval man and the shortcomings of
their age.'

Plainly bewildered by the amity and ease between the white and
black men of the League, Fleming remained silent with fury in his
eyes.

Producing a greatly watered down smile, the knight of the realm
spoke with conciliation in his voice.

''Tis disappointing we could not have attained an understanding,
gentlemen,' said Sir Nicholas.

'You do not understand, Sir Nicholas,' said Drinkwater unequivocally, 'for 'tis you who cannot read the warning signs.'

Adjustment

Greensleeves
Saturday
11 September 1784
12.30 hrs

A warm sun sparkled high in a cloudless sky. All around, the land yawned in a tapestry of autumnal splendour divided by hedgerows. In the distance, Jonas heard the clamour from the hunt dogs. House martins darted in and out from under the eaves. Everywhere, the drone of insects filled the air. All seemed as it should be.

Inhaling deeply as he stood on the carriage drive, he looked anxiously at his wife. In the offing lay an unedifying dispute with Reverend Baskett.

It had been a bright morning — so bright he could hardly believe summer had come and gone. The trees and flora were changing hues — leaf greens to ochres, garnets and russets. Some leaves had begun to fall. He knew that rain would not be far away.

''Tis a fine day for the Baskett's visit,' he said.

''Tis fortunate you have talked with his daughter before now,' said Faith.

'Mistress Sienna flaunts such piercing green eyes,' he said, grinning. 'Solomon chooses a feisty one and is going to have his hands full. She is an engaging young woman who knows her own mind. Bit like her father, I'd say.'

'Seems her father does not understand or appreciate his mettlesome daughter,' she said.

'Baskett is so distracted by Solomon's colour, he sees not the man,' he said scathingly. 'A guaranteed error whoever it is. I cannot believe that a purported clergyman and member of the League could be blinded by such discrimination.'

'To my mind, Baskett is utterly possessed by what his neighbours think,' she said. 'He strikes me as a small-minded, frightened functionary who is frantic to be thought well of. On the other hand, his wife cares not a fig for what anyone thinks.'

''Tis not going to be easy to change a mind steeped in doctrinal self-righteousness.'

'No one told you it was, Jonas.' she said resolutely. 'Now whatever you do, my dear, you must not show irritability—'

'I'll have you know,' he said, ''twas not me who said of Baskett and I quote, The Devil himself could not have been more accomplished in the dark arts of duplicity, unquote. It suggests to me you already possess attitude enough that might be inadvertently displayed.'

Momentarily looking anxiously at him, a truce suddenly suffused her eyes.

'Touché!' she said.

'I promise to act the epitome of reason, my dear, for Solomon and Sienna's morrows depend on our talks,' he said seriously. 'Do you suppose Baskett's opposition is founded on intolerance or sober conviction?'

'Ignorance,' she said without hesitation. 'Not once has Baskett ever tried to hold a consequential exchange with Solomon. Methinks he baulks out of fear. Yet, I feel optimistic about the outcome of the visit. Sienna desires this match, her mother desires it and I desire it. The poor man knows not the grit of strong-willed women.'

'Let us endeavour to drag a fossil into the eighteenth century,' he said, grinning.

Inside the house, the hallway clock struck one o'clock.

Shuffling across the carriage drive, the sexagenarian housekeeper wheezed, 'I 'ear a carriage, Mistress Guinea.'

''Tis Reverend Baskett and his wife, Mistress Bracegirdle,' said Faith. 'We are ready to greet them.'

Rumbling onto the carriage drive, the vehicle rolled to a halt and disgorged its passengers. They were a provincial pair, originally from Halesworth, Suffolk, a place not noted for seeing a black face.

Jonas appraised their guests.

Resembling an immovable oak of medium height, Reverend Augustus Baskett was portly, bulbous-nosed and dimple-chinned. His wife, Prudence, smiled fulsomely at them. She was appealing, middle-aged and matronly with steely green eyes and russet brown hair flecked with grey.

She looks as if a lie would wilt on approach, thought Jonas, smiling.

Following hearty introductions, Jonas invited them into the house.

Gently restraining Faith to let the men walk ahead, Mistress Baskett's smile dissolved into fret. Lowering her voice, she hissed, 'I must have words with you at once, Mistress Guinea!'

'Why, what is the matter, Mistress Baskett?'

'I have tussled long and hard as to how to say this.'

'Pray tell me?'

'And as if matters are not complicated enough,' said Mistress Baskett. 'What were they thinking? More to the point, what did they think would come of it?'

'Come of what, Mistress Baskett?'

'Lately, the pair have been meeting at the house of a close friend by Saint Alfege Church, Greenwich. I thought not anything of it until I saw the signs. Sienna is with child, Mistress Guinea. Solomon is the father.'

Shaken by a force that rattled her senses, Faith knew at once the tidings spelt confrontation or compromise with Reverend Baskett.

'Are you sure about this?'

'I most certainly am.'

'Knowing Sienna, Mistress Baskett,' said Faith, 'I cannot imagine it could be anyone else but Solomon.'

'I agree.'

'Does Reverend Baskett know?'

'God's servant wouldn't recognise new life until a howling newborn was plonked right down in front of him,' said Mistress Baskett. 'If he knew about Sienna's present condition, the man would turn apoplectic.'

'Then, Solomon and Sienna must be married as soon as possible,' said Faith, 'but not in such haste as to turn heads. Before anyone is the wiser it will be over. Married only slightly ahead of schedule I'd say.'

''Twould send cruel tongues a-wagging if they did not wed,' said Mistress Baskett, looking much relieved. 'Anywise, 'tis what our children want and as well they do so with our blessing. Reverend Baskett shall not hear of it until after they are wed.'

'Say not anything to anyone, Mistress Baskett,' said Faith. 'We will speak privately after luncheon. The men are set to have words about the matter. I daresay my husband will pour something on troubled waters. Come, Mistress Baskett, let us tuck into roasted pulled and devilled pheasants with a buttery-cream sauce. We shall scheme better after that.'

Entering the dining room they found the men listening to the sozzled octogenarian house resident, Parson Merriweather, citing a passage for the League's forthcoming petitions:

'Brethren, be not wise in your own conceit. To no man render evil for evil, but provide good things not only in the sight of God, but also in the sight of all men. Romans. Chapter Twelve and—'

'My word, Augustus,' cried Mistress Baskett, interrupting the discourse, 'such a fine table is indeed a most hearty welcome.'

''Tis good to receive you both at Greensleeves,' said Jonas.

'I am delighted you accepted our invitation, Reverend Baskett,' said Faith. 'Of course you know Parson Merriweather.'

'We were charmed to receive your invitation, Mistress Guinea,' said Reverend Baskett. ''Tis a splendid chance to explore ideas for our petitions. Good to keep your company again, Parson.'

Following grace intoned by Parson Merriweather, the meal was eaten with much banter and laughter. Deferring to Baskett's repute for a robust red tipple and Faith's determination to make an impression, she brought out bottles of Chateau Monbrison Margaux for the repast.

Sure enough, Reverend Baskett exclaimed, 'Excellent, Mistress Guinea! 'Tis good on the nose and sharp like bright cranberries.'

'Pray give your cook our thanks for such a moist pheasant, Mistress Guinea,' said Mistress Baskett. ''Twas a grand spread indeed.'

'During your visit with us,' said Jonas, 'we can take the carriage to the chalybeate spring in Tunbridge Wells.'

'We would very much enjoy such a diversion, Mister Guinea,' said Mistress Baskett. 'And we did so look forward to visiting Greensleeves. Before now, I have had the pleasure of becoming acquainted with your son. A most charming young man and I must say—'

Leaning tipsily forwards clutching a glass, Parson Merriweather garbled, 'I hear young Sholomon ish taken with the fair Mishtress Shienna. A truly good match, I have to shay.'

An icy chill exploded into the luncheon. Eyes darted frantically about.

Without blinking, Reverend Baskett held a bleak deadpan stare.

'Blabbermouth,' muttered Faith beneath her breath, rolling her eyes.

With a glance at his disconcerted wife, Jonas coughed to divert the discomfiture in the chamber. Calmly looking around, he decided he would be forthright.

'I'm told our offspring have interests in common, Reverend Baskett,' he said. 'Have you heard of such?'

'Aye,' said Reverend Baskett grudgingly.

'What say you?'

'I am agin' it, Mister Guinea.'

Catching Mistress Baskett's eye, Faith smiled.

'Why so, Reverend Baskett?' asked Jonas quietly, dragging up a winning smile. 'Are we not all friends here? Can you not share your objection with us?'

Visibly squirming, Reverend Baskett exhaled noisily and set down his glass. Flushed faced he stared at the table and then slowly raised his head.

'Let me be candid with you all,' he said. 'I want not anything mixed for Sienna.'

Stifled gasps filled the room.

Putting her hand over her mouth, Mistress Baskett glowered at her spouse.

Shaking his head without a word, Parson Merriweather topped up his glass.

'You mean…African…with English?' asked Jonas, barely conceal-
ing his astonishment.

'I see like with like for my daughter.'

'Even if our daughter cares only for Solomon and gives not a fig
about like with like?' asked Mistress Baskett quietly.

'I am her father, I have to guide her.'

Sobering up, Parson Merriweather leaned forwards.

'Even if you take the wrong path, Augustus?' he asked. 'We have
all made mistakes.'

'What does that mean?' snapped Reverend Baskett defensively. 'I
act in her best interests.'

'Mayhaps we should let her make her own mistakes and not our
mistakes, my dear,' said Mistress Baskett. ''Tis possible Sienna knows
more about what's in her best interests than we. Don't you think?
Have you spoken with her?'

Caught unawares by the unruffled rationale of his wife, Baskett
stayed with a steady and slightly chafing gaze. But the set of his jaw
etched a tale of uncertainty.

'Mixed marriage is not against the laws of God, Augustus,' said
Jonas calmly.

'Nay, but when it comes to my daughter I find the mixing of blood
contentious,' said Reverend Baskett. 'I have to be honest.'

'I have known you for a good few years, Augustus,' said Parson
Merriweather, taking a swig of wine. 'I did not know you held such
opinion—'

Interrupting the Parson, the furrowed-browed Reverend Baskett
spoke apologetically.

'Neither did I, Parson Merriweather, until I heard about my
daughter's fondness for Solomon. Speaking to your son I fear I was
somewhat brusque, Mister Guinea.'

Indicating he had heard, Jonas glanced at his mutely vexed wife
and sat back with ruffled composure.

'We are men of God and not given to idle chatter, Augustus,' said
Parson Merriweather. ''Tis in any case your daughter and not you
who wishes to consort with Solomon. Surely then only they will bear
the effects of any mistake, if indeed it is one? What difference would

their relationship make to anyone else? I say we should all support the match.'

'It would make a difference to me, Parson Merriweather,' said Reverend Baskett with quiet discomfort. 'I have always tried to live up to the moral principles of my ministry, yet I feel this has found me wanting. I confess 'tis when my kin is concerned that I shy from the realness of mixed unions. Does that make me unchristian? I am uncertain; nay I do not relish kin of a different colour. What will he be? English or what? Christian or what?'

'Fiddlesticks!' snapped Mistress Basket. 'It not only makes you unchristian, Augustus, it makes you uncharitable. You are sufficiently acquainted with Solomon and have many times conversed with his sister, Olivia. Do either of them appear confused or strike you as not knowing who they are? They are English, Augustus, only brown. Or mayhaps you can point me a Statute that states that the English can only be white. If you are born in England, you are English. That is the law, Augustus. I shudder to think if it were any other way.'

Watching Reverend Baskett listening to remonstrations from his wife, Jonas saw him flinch with every question she posed.

'How do you square such contrary opinion with your membership of the League?'

'Offspring from such union will be shunned,' retorted Reverend Baskett.

'Everyone is shunned by somebody at some time, Augustus,' countered Mistress Baskett. 'Like everyone else, a brown Englishman will naturally make his way in society to find companions as best he can.'

'We might be shunned,' protested Reverend Baskett.

'I beg your pardon, Augustus,' said Mistress Baskett quietly, 'but I thought we were discussing the match between Solomon and our only child. Saying how we might be shunned sounds not like it.'

'We do have to consider the effects on the entire family,' argued Reverend Baskett.

'Effects that will be principally felt by Sienna herself,' said Mistress Baskett. 'Above all, Augustus, what her aunts and uncles, those I have spoken with, are considering is how best they can support the couple, not about how the match affects them. We all believe Solomon to be an upright young man with good prospects. I am her mother and I believe Sienna will be happy with Solomon. Be generous, Augustus. Sienna is our only child.'

At those last words, Jonas saw the corners of Reverend Baskett's lips twitch. Eyes that had been glazed with resistance, blinked, not one or twice but thrice. Promising stirrings looked afoot. Drained by the exchange over a sensitive personal issue, Reverend Baskett bit his lower lip and his head lolled thoughtfully to one side.

No doubt he is considering the disagreeable consequences of his opposition, thought Jonas. He heard the trace of resignation in Reverend Baskett's soft sigh.

Setting down his glass quietly, Reverend Baskett gave his wife a chastened look.

''Twill take some getting used to, my dear,' he said in quietly conciliatory tones. 'I shall ponder on all your good counsels and ask for divine guidance in my prayers. Let us speak of it again on the morrow.'

'You will of course take communion with us in the morning, Reverend and Mistress Baskett?' asked Faith.

'Aye that we shall,' said Mistress Baskett. 'Is the church far?'

'St Mary's Church is in the nearby village of Speldhurst,' said Faith. 'We shall take a carriage. The vicar delivers most thought-provoking sermons.'

'In the light of our deliberations,' said Reverend Baskett, 'I believe taking communion would be most appropriate.'

Under a cloudless sky, the warm September day wore the smudge of autumn. Grassland, hedgerows, shrubbery and rough-barked oak trees displayed shifting hues of green. The few yellowing leaves that had fallen said that autumn was underway.

Following the service at St Mary's Church, they filed chattily into the dining room in Sunday-best gowns and frock coats.

'For luncheon, cook has prepared a fine roast beef,' announced Faith enthusiastically. 'And I have a Chateau Balestard La Tonnelle St Emilion. Methinks you might be partial to this silky fruity offering, Reverend Baskett.'

'I did not know you were quite the connoisseur,' said Reverend Baskett, raising his eyebrows. Chortling as if he had been given an imperceptible fillip, his bulbous nose poked into the glass and then he took the draught of an aficionado. ''Pon my soul, Mistress Guinea, I have to say a bodied vintage to follow an excellent service.'

Cook and two maidservants entered the chamber bearing platters. After dishing out the victuals and filling the glasses, they departed.

'St Mary's is a charming sanctuary in a comfortable parish,' said Parson Merriweather, taking several sips of wine and forking a sliver of beef. 'That complacent vicar gave a surprisingly inspiring sermon.'

'Love thy neighbour was the vicar's mantra,' said Faith dismissively. 'In itself 'tis not conversational, but as a matter of interest, did anyone hear mention of the colour of that neighbour?'

'The vicar did as well say all men are equal before God,' said Mistress Baskett with a touch of sarcasm. 'One could be forgiven for thinking that 'equal before God' includes not women or people of colour. Though it's not for me to say, Augustus, it would appear that there are some who are more equal than others.'

Reluctant to butt into a family squabble, Jonas grinned at his wife and said nothing.

'We live in rather unequal times, Prudence,' said Reverend Baskett in ecclesiastical tones. 'That is why I am troubled by our daughter's choice.'

'A strong loving Christian family will support mixed-blood offspring,' said Mistress Baskett with dogged conviction. 'They will, after all, be of our blood.'

'Any offspring from our children will need much support, my dear,' said Reverend Baskett in a mildly warning voice. 'In all conscience, Prudence, I cannot risk the happiness and morrows of my only child and family on my opposition.'

'Mayhaps not all our family will be kindly at first, my dear,' said Mistress Baskett testily, 'but then they will just have to get used to it, won't they? What say you, Mistress Guinea?'

'Given the convoluted attitudes some folks have towards mixed-blood children,' Faith soothed, 'Reverend Baskett is right to be concerned.'

Raising his eyebrows as if he had been thrown a lifeline, Reverend Baskett sipped wine and sat back.

'You see eye to eye with me then, Mistress Guinea?' he asked.

'Aye I do, Reverend Baskett,' said Faith, 'on condition that you bear in mind who are as well some of the culprits for such bigoted attitudes. There are countless white men who bed African women forcibly and then proceed to spurn their mixed-blood offspring. Moreover, let us not overlook that though generally accepted by black, offspring of white and free blacks are oftimes shunned by the Africans themselves. It takes a great deal longer to change attitudes, Reverend Baskett, than ever to change the law.'

His eyebrows arching at the detachment of his wife, Jonas heaved a hushed sigh. Her fervour is seldom wide of the mark, he thought.

'On both sides,' said Faith, 'it can be testing for mixed-blood children. And 'tis very challenging for anyone abhorred. Whereas any offspring from Solomon and Sienna will be born into a mostly loving family and be well-provided for—'

'Aye they would,' interjected Mistress Baskett.

'I believe if they are given the opportunity of their white counterparts,' said Faith, 'mixed-blood children who are cherished and educated can make similar contribution. While there is slavery, prejudice will continue to flourish—'

'Unquestionably,' said Reverend Baskett, gently thumping the table.

'Evidently,' said Parson Merriweather, topping up his glass.

'Following the abolition of slavery,' continued Faith, 'prejudice borne from slavery will last for countless generations to come. In the first place, England should not ever have dabbled in the immoral realm of buying and selling human beings. It is up to people like us to put right the wrongs of some of our countrymen. But then you know that is what bedrocks the League's mission.'

'I am still of the same conviction, Mistress Guinea,' said Reverend Baskett, as if his allegiance to the anti-slavery cause was being queried. 'We must speak of this again, Mistress Guinea. And I suspect you are of the same mind as your wife, Mister Guinea?'

'I am an African, Reverend Baskett,' said Jonas, as if surprised by the question. 'My colour is a political issue, so you might understand why I have a vested interest. Moreover, I do share the views of my wife. And I share the opinion of Olaudah Equiano on this very matter. We blame it on England's first slave traders who deemed that peoples not civilised in their likeness must be primitive—'

Reverend Baskett hurriedly raised his hand to interject. 'I am an admirer of the writings of Mister Equiano. I'm told he has as well written much on the subject of intolerance.'

'Only the week last past we had dialogue on the subject of prejudice,' said Jonas.

'What about prejudice?' asked Reverend Baskett.

'Has it always been with us?' asked Jonas, looking around. 'Surely prejudice is not inborn in the intellectual and communal virtues that typify humankind? We know that the agitators propagate prejudice like an exacting type of subjugation. It could be thought that prejudice against any minority is founded on the belief that a distinctive feature, such as colour, makes them lesser than their subjugators. Devalued by colour, 'tis easier to enslave those deemed thus inferior.'

'Prejudice is clearly fashioned by man,' said Mistress Baskett, nodding enthusiastically.

'Can you not see, Reverend Baskett,' said Faith, 'that prejudice is more likely the result of slavery, not the instigator of it? Have we not all seen how bigotry is perpetuated by some in order to maintain some chancy pecking order? Brown and black start at the bottom. We live in strange times, sir. As we speak, England's slave trade is simultaneously lawful and immoral?'

Scratching his chin, Reverend Baskett scrutinised the faces of his listeners as he took a generous swig of wine.

'Over this match of late,' he said solemnly, 'I have suffered an inconsiderate seizure regarding bloodline. I have listened to your counsels, my friends. And you all deserve to share my thoughts regarding your well-meant urgings.'

'Pray do, Augustus,' said Mistress Baskett sincerely, 'we must reconcile our differences over this match.'

Giving her an affectionate smile, he spoke with quiet calm. 'All the way to Greensleeves I struggled with my inner voice. Seen from my point of view, a mixed-match was unthinkable—'

'Was unthinkable,' reiterated Mistress Baskett.

'I am coming to that, my dear,' said Reverend Baskett firmly. 'Mistress Baskett's support of the match, your many good counsels and a pointed sermon has given me thought for much reflection. As well, I was struck by a verse in Psalms: For thou, O God, hast proved us: thou hast tried us, as silver is tried.'

''Tis a most appropriate quotation, Augustus,' said Parson Merriweather tipsily, topping up his glass. 'One time or another, we are all put to the test. When I gave benedictions over departing slaves on the coast of Guinea, I categorically failed God's test. Still now on the coast of Guinea, the attendance of a man of the cloth furnishes slave-owners with spiritual justification for their wicked activities. I was young and foolish, selfish and mired—'

'What do you mean by mired, Parson?' asked Mistress Baskett.

'As a blinkered seminarian I was awash with ambition, ma'am,' replied Parson Merriweather shamefully. 'Blinded by prejudice, I saw not the people. I saw not even the inhumanity in plantation slavery because the Africans were deemed sub-human. By us, I might add. It was my Damascus moment. Since that cruel errant ministry, not a day passes without my being afflicted by pangs of conscience. You could say my membership of the League is a cardinal part of my redemption.'

Glancing at his wife, Jonas noticed her watery eyes.

'Do we ever know when we will have to face an examination sent by God?' asked Reverend Baskett. 'Would we recognise a test when it shows its face? I have even asked myself if this mixed-match was my ordeal.'

'It might be, Augustus,' said Mistress Baskett quietly.

'I have this day arrived on the other side of an affecting quandary,' said Reverend Baskett. 'I accept that fear of the unknown played a part, my friends. I cannot in truth tell you why. I may sometimes seem a somewhat self-opinionated spirit, but I am in truth not that certain. I have worried that an unforeseen biology may still rear its head. I am still not entirely at ease with this mixed-match, but without it I suspect my discomfort would be far the greater. Come the day of Judgement I want to be able to face my God and tell Him I did right.'

Momentarily, the soothing hush that entered the chamber was overwhelming. Polite coughs and throat-clearing, sips of wine and the clink of glasses were all that could be heard.

Jonas's thoughts heaved with incredulity as to what had just occurred. Catching a furtive nod between Mistress Baskett and his wife, Jonas pondered its consequences. Something about Mistress Baskett gives me more confidence in England's morrows, he thought.

Realising what she had been wanting over the past months had finally been attained, Mistress Baskett relaxed.

''Tis difficult enough for any match,' she said. 'What chance would their match have with bellyache from her parents? I as well have a little concern as with any other. But who are we to tell anyone who they should or shouldn't love. Telling Sienna who to choose would be your choice, my dearest. It might even be thought as tantamount to bullying. And you are not a bully, Augustus. I can vouch for that. You have the love of a doting daughter and you have chosen not to jeopardise that. I thank God you are the man I married.'

Abashed by the fulsome praise from his wife, Reverend Baskett began fidgeting with his William Kipling pocket watch. Raising his flushed features, he gave all a demure smile.

'Ultimately,' said Parson Merriweather, blithely refilling his glass, 'any complications in the match cannot be laid at your door. But with your pivotal support I am confident the match stands as good a chance as any other.'

'When would be a good moment to get together, Mistress Baskett?' asked Faith, giving her a sisterly smile.

'I should say this upcoming week would be timely, Mistress Guinea,' replied Mistress Baskett, chortling and raising her glass.

Narrowing his eyes at the women, Jonas smiled and pondered.

Given the knowing looks between them it would seem a pact has already been sealed, he thought. Solomon will be soon a married man.

Olaudah Equiano

Freemasons' Hall
Great Queen Street
London
Sunday
20 August 1786
16.00 hrs

Alighting from the carriage with his son on Great Queen Street, Jonas pushed his way through the crowded Freemasons' Tavern to the back door. Crossing a small flower garden, they arrived at the Freemasons' sanctum of Sandby's Hall.

Entering what resembled a mahogany-panelled Roman Doric temple embellished with Masonic symbols, he looked around and smiled. The huge chamber was agog with conversation. A throng of mostly frock-coated white men and their spruce wives mingled with a good number of frock-coated mixed-blood and black men with their wives. It looked a typical gathering of the League.

Attending members of the League sat on a row of chairs on a raised platform. Chatting among themselves were Jeremiah and Grace Puddlewick, Reverend and Mistress Baskett, Parson Merriweather, and Captain Battersby and his son, Robert. Captain Miracle and Aaron Drinkwater were bent over the platform's edge passing down manacles, mouth irons, thumbscrews and other objects of suffering. At the harrowing reality of the instruments of slave torture, horrified gasps reverberated around the cavernous chamber.

Giving his friends a polite bow, Jonas turned back to continue his search.

'Mister Equiano is by the pillar over there,' said Solomon above the hub-bub, nodding at two men of slim build. 'Mister Equiano beckons us, sir.'

'Equiano's message to meet him here was intriguing,' said Jonas, pushing forwards. 'Let us join him.'

Olaudah Equiano had a winning aura about him. In a smart brown frock coat, his head was held high and a broad grin dominated his good looks. Moreover, the sparkle in his eyes gave the impression he had agreeable tidings to dispense. In austere contrast, his cadaverous companion wore a sagging frock coat on his frail frame. A sallow look owned his black face and a thin scar ran down his right cheek.

''Tis good to see you, Jonas, and you too Solomon,' said Equiano. Turning to his companion, he said, 'Meet my good friend, Joshua Dobson. We first met when we were cutting cane in the Indies. He is lately manumitted and justifiably still devastated by his plantation experience. Joshua is still finding his feet. I know you will give him a welcome befitting a returned brother.'

From a submissive demeanour, Joshua Dobson cracked a warm toothless smile.

'Good ter see yer, sah,' he said.

''Tis my great joy to meet you, Mister Dobson,' said Jonas, giving him a broad smile and a trade card. 'This is my son, Solomon. When you are sorted, please come and meet the rest of my family and dine with us. Pray count on us as a friend.'

'Me thank you, sah,' said Joshua Dobson, with wounded misty eyes. 'Me bin gone long time. Me need frens.'

'I was intrigued by your note, Olaudah,' said Jonas.

'Let us talk after Drinkwater's announcement, Jonas,' said Equiano, 'I think you'll be interested in what I have to say.

'My friends,' cried Aaron Drinkwater. 'Welcome to a gathering of the League Against the Importation of Negroes from the Coast of Guinea—'

From the back of the chamber a grouchy voice yelled, 'What 'ave Sambos got ter do wi' me?'

'I'll tell you what they have to do with you,' said Aaron Drinkwater with gilded disdain. 'If your trade depends on slaves or sugar in any way, my friend, which is nearly everything, I advise you to find another business, for you will not ever receive a more shameful duplicitous shilling off the back of human suffering. And you ask what they have to do with you? I see—'

'Well said!' shouted several voices amid rowdy applause.

'I see we have an Orang Utan philosopher in our midst,' he continued. 'Otherwise, irritant permitting, we are here to congregate with others of like mind…'

Applause and laughter assailed the chamber.

'My friends,' said Aaron Drinkwater, raising his arms, 'you are each welcome to step up onto this platform to make any related announcements to our gathering. If not, we are here to intermingle to exchange strategies and notions for petitions to the Commons. And forget not to acquaint all of any changes in the movements of slave-hunters and slave vessels…'

Raising his voice in sepulchral tones, he continued:

'We intend to make demands of the government to abolish the slave trade. To help our cause we will need witnesses to give evidence to Parliament about the said trade. Any of you who have witnessed or partaken in the trade and rejected it will be needed to give testimony to what they have seen. Any seamen among you who have witnessed at close hand the cruelties we speak of, step forward and be prepared to give witness as to what you have seen. We are here to campaign for the end of the slave trade. And we're not going to achieve that by sitting on our hands.'

At once, the chatter rose in volume.

'I want to have a few words with your father, Solomon,' said Equiano. Gesturing towards his friend, he added, 'Mister Dodson will keep your company.'

Leaving Solomon in conversation, Equiano steered Jonas to the back of the chamber.

'I am well underway with my book, Jonas.'

'Have you a title?'

'*The Interesting Narrative of the Life of Olaudah Equiano or Gustavus Vassa, the African.*'

'In these fraudulent times, Olaudah,' said Jonas, 'an honest title is truly refreshing. I like it very much. Bearing in mind that honesty is a phenomenon perplexing to much of the press, your title should seize their attention. Have you yet found a publisher?'

Cocking his head with remarkable equanimity, Equiano quietly said:

''Tis nigh impossible, Jonas, to find a publisher who will publish a work from a black hand. I will have to publish and distribute it myself.'

'That takes courage, Olaudah,' said Jonas. 'I will help you distribute your book. I as well will subscribe.'

'Thank you gladly, my friend. I knew I could depend on you.'

'How long before you finish your manuscript?'

'About two to three years. I have thankfully gained a number of eminent subscribers who have advanced payment. I continue to look for more. I will show you my list of subscribers when we next meet.'

'After you have acquainted your readers with the atrocities being perpetrated on slaves, Olaudah,' said Jonas, 'your words may well inform a generation. Readers cannot say they did not know. Moreover, a clear statement from one such as you will give an inspiring stimulus to the campaign for abolition. My friend, I know you will inscribe an account in a language that will be understood by those of conscience and men of influence. Methinks written with your vitality, Olaudah, the pragmatic experience of a former slave could well unite people of conscience against the trade.'

Suddenly, a dumpy character climbed onto the platform.

'Wallace Breedlove of Holborn,' he said. 'And right glad am I to be with you. Be aware slave-hunters have this morning arrived in the vicinity of Cheapside! Be attentive, for the slave-hunters loiter near Ye Olde Cheshire Cheese. Now I give you Mistress Fiammetta Watts of Clerkenwell, who is here to tell you about a most upsetting incident she witnessed.'

Middle-aged with silver flecked hair, the kindly-looking Fiammetta Watts wore the black garb of an upright governess. Stepping eagerly forward, her manner was astir with indignation.

'Early this morn,' she said in a tutored accent, 'I did see slave-hunters set upon a black gentleman out walking with a white gentlewoman. Separating him from what I then learned was his wife, the hunters began to drag the poor man away. Were it not for the quick thinking of bystanders, who fought off the slave-hunters, the poor man would be well on his way to a plantation. Can you imagine the heartbreak his wife and our sister would have endured?'

Howls of 'shame' followed her account.

Turning back to Jonas, Equiano asked, 'Heard about the Committee for the Relief of the Black Poor?'

'Nay, I have not.'

'In response to the numbers of penniless black men walking the streets of London, the Committee was established by a group of philanthropists. No doubt guided by the influence of Granville Sharp, the Committee has invited me to partake in their Sierra Leone Resettlement Project.'

'To do what?' said Jonas, raising his eyebrows. 'It heartens me that you are finally writing your book, Olaudah. For the account of the slave will at long last be aired. But are you not risking much on the stamina of an amalgam of philanthropists to successfully establish such a settlement in far-off Sierra Leone? Ultimately, good intentions may not be enough. And is not this Committee merely transporting poverty out of sight? What is the assignment?'

'I'm told I will be the Commissary of Provisions and Stores for the Black Poor in Sierra Leone,' said Equiano unemotionally. 'In three months, with a naval escort of the *Nautilus*, the vessels *Belisarius*, *Vernon* and the *Atlantic* will sail for Sierra Leone with more than seven hundred blacks as colonists aboard. Sailing with them will be white craftsmen and their families along with eighty white wives of black men.'

'The quizzical might say that this expedition is somewhat expedient,' said Jonas with a trace of scepticism in his voice. 'But given your many accomplishments I can see why they seek to have you in their employ. Exactly what are you being asked to do? Am I addressing the first black citizen to be selected for a government appointment? I am impressed.'

'My task will be to work with others to help resettle London's black poor in Sierra Leone. The Committee are calling the location Province of Freedom. I take for granted any government post for a black is most likely equivocal. However, I shall gain new insights and invaluable experience. Otherwise, it might be construed that we have not equal mental faculties with whites and thus unable to take responsibility for anything more than cutting cane. I judge 'tis not easy being first in anything.'

Giving Equiano a knowing smile, Jonas said, 'The settlers may well challenge the name Province of Freedom, Olaudah. Will they be given any recompense for the encouraged transfer? Will you be the only black involved? Will you be salaried? Have you any doubts?'

'The committee have vouched to pay twelve pounds to each embarking settler. I will have a salary, which I have yet to learn. Methinks I'm the only black involved, aye. But my foremost doubt is the fleet superintendent, Joseph Irwin...'

'You certainly choose your bigwigs to cross swords with. But why him?'

'Mayhaps because methinks the man's a fraudster,' said Equiano, tapping his nose. 'Which for the time being I shall keep from his ears.'

'I would. Who will you have to deal with on the coast of Guinea?'

'Two kings and a few chiefs.'

'Why them?'

'Obtain their cooperation for our resettlement in their region and quieten any fears about the Committee's intentions.'

'Brood not over the query of others,' said Jonas, 'but a sceptic might argue that an auxiliary was being dispatched to Sierra Leone to soothe ruffled feathers.'

'A pessimistic view but true,' said Equiano, smiling. 'Although 'tis a rare moment when my black hide warrants recognition, expedient though that recognition might prove to be. I have no illusions as to what I can achieve in this venture, Jonas. But can you see any pitfalls? What are your thoughts? Should I take it?'

'Methinks 'twould be prudent to take the post, Olaudah. Who can it offend your attempting to settle brutalised souls in stable surroundings? Besides, think of the experience you will acquire. But be aware, 'twill not be long before someone will be so aggrieved and constricted to be sat down as equals with a black man. Then, he will seek your downfall. This fleet superintendent, Joseph Irwin, may well prove to be yours. If the venture runs into difficulties, you might be an ideal scapegoat. The weakest link and all that. But then I am an incurable cynic.'

Stepping backwards, Equiano guffawed.

'I shall keep your counsel in my thoughts, Jonas. I as well wanted you to consider a proposition.'

'Aye?'

'Ottobah Cugoano and I believe that we Africans living in London should do something more in the fight against slavery. We must band together to speak with one voice. In the coming morrows it must be said that we black people, as a body, fought against slavery as well, lest it might be accidently forgotten—'

'I have ached to hear of such an objective,' sighed Jonas. 'I will hear more.'

'We intend to form a group called the Sons of Africa,' said Equiano. 'This cooperative will persistently write petitions to Parliament to abolish slavery. We will send letters to magazines and newspapers and make speeches far and wide to the citizenry. Our members will be sons of Africa by descent or by birth. Will you join us, Jonas?'

'As you know I am fully occupied managing the chandlery, which has shareholders and is still growing. I have oft wept in hope for such a collective. I would want to give productive time to the Sons of Africa. Let me speak to Faith to see how we can make it possible. Can I give you my answer when next we meet, Olaudah?'

'I know you are as resolute as I to abolish slavery, Jonas,' said Equiano. 'And I as well know that if you can join us you will. I most certainly do not want any reduction in the number of the few black men in business in London town. I will wait for your answer and if you cannot I will fully understand. 'Twill make no difference to our good friendship. Let us return to the proceedings at hand.'

Rejoining Solomon and Joshua Dobson, Equiano said, 'How fares Mistress Sienna and your daughter, Solomon? How old is Emma now?'

'Mistress Sienna is in good spirits, sir. Emma is one year old and gives us much joy.'

'How swiftly time has travelled,' said Equiano, smiling. 'I was hoping you would assist me with collating my research notes.'

'Gladly sir,' said Solomon with the eagerness of devotee. 'Would Saturday next be soon enough?'

'Saturday it is,' said Equiano. 'We shall best them yet.'

'Aye, sir,' said Solomon, with a smile stretching from ear to ear.

Kadara

Pilgrims
Wednesday
27 August 1786
15.00hrs

Gazing thoughtfully at the rowdy Highway from the ground floor office, Jonas sighed.

'I have seen much despair in my life,' he muttered to himself. 'And by the grace of God, I have known much happiness. In truth, I have encountered much that good and bad can muster. Hope? Despite the seemingly unstoppable march of the slave plantation, I have hope. Why? I cannot say. I feel I am still scrabbling through the murk for the light. But there is no dark without light. With a good loving wife who still aches for her auctioned son, we have raised two wonderful children and a healthy granddaughter. Given the evident poverty of many, we fortuitously eat good food under a fine roof. We have undoubtedly been blessed.'

Vacating the ground floor office, he ambled pensively across the hall to join his wife in the withdrawing room. Strong sunlight blazed into the lucent chamber. Glancing through the open windows, he heartened to the virescent hues of the trees, grass and shrubbery through the garden. The evocative scent of honeysuckle wafted into his nostrils. A snug familiarity enveloped him.

'I have just read a Newgate Prison report on one William Blenkinsop,' said Faith. 'He's charged with *feloniously stealing out of the stable of Reverend John Henderson about one bushel of Oats.*'

'What prison term did he fetch for his efforts?'

'He is to be hanged outside Newgate!'

'Good God! Hanged for stealing a bushel?! What would he get for stealing a few grains?'

'The foul diet rich Judges dish out to poor men without counsel,' she said, scornfully shaking her head, 'is sufficient to make a poor man believe he stands a hair's breadth from slavery.'

'The poor may well deem themselves slaves,' he said. 'On the word of the most recent *Gazette*, Admiral Arthur Phillip has been ordered to assemble a fleet of eleven vessels off Portsmouth. Under orders, he will in about a year set sail with over seven hundred convicted men and women bound for Australia. An unbiased observer might think the Admiral's prisoners were white slaves.'

'Hardship seems to help the poor side with the slaves,' she said.

'Have you seen Olivia?'

'She's entertaining friends and a certain freckled admirer in the dining room.'

He beamed.

'I'm told his father is an eminent lawyer,' he said with an approving tone of voice.

'What if his pater were a tradesman?'

'Well…,' he said uncomfortably. 'I-I m-mean…'

'Holy Mary Mother of God!' she exclaimed, crossing herself and chortling. 'Why, Jonas Guinea, I do believe I detect a vestige of social prejudice. 'Tis curiously the trait you have often accused me of. And 'tis induced no doubt by the want of a good match for Olivia. Fret not, my dear, your secret is safe with me. Though I shall keep it from Reverend Baskett, who you might recall exhibited comparable anxieties to your own about his daughter. Except his old saw was about colour, yours appears to be about status.'

Tongue-tied by her opinion, he rendered an uncomfortable smile and stayed tight-lipped.

'Who was that at the front door earlier?'

He was thankful for the change of subject. 'Captain Pickersgill,' he said. 'Newly appointed master of the *Redemption* who lives close by. He'd agreed to deliver Fairfax's dispatch to our address.'

'Alexander Fairfax?'

'Aye.'

'I have not heard from him in quite a while.'

'This letter has only my name on it, my dearest,' he laughed. 'By the time he last wrote to me, Fairfax had already showed his mettle securing Henry Jackson's release. What a heartful man. What a glorious afternoon. Shall we have some Madeira and read his letter?'

Raucous laughter, squeals and giggles suddenly burst out of the dining room. Gurgling and shrieking from the upstairs nursery combined with the rumpus downstairs. One-year-old Emma was learning to walk. Euphoric parental noises followed the toddler's lumbering steps. Solomon and Sienna had their hands full.

'On second thoughts,' he said, winking, 'shall we read his letter in the garden?'

'I shall fetch the Madeira,' she said, chuckling her way out of the room.

Stepping through the French windows, he wiped his brow in the heat of the sunny afternoon. Heady scent from the rose beds wafted along the topmost garden step. Stretching and inhaling deeply, he revelled in the stock of Damask roses as he pondered on the past years.

Returning with a decanter of Madeira, she filled two glasses. Betwixt the hollyhocks, she settled on the limestone bench.

Alighting beside her, he said, 'Odd how even in the unlikeliest moments, Matthew Fleming appears like an unspent phantom. Though now he troubles me not as much, I remain on my guard. I have many cherished thoughts about Mistress Beecham, without whom I could not have accomplished any of this. I think about our venture with the *Redemption*, as well as about Tomba and the returnees to the coast of Guinea. It was on a day like today that in memory of the late Thomas Beecham the great lady renamed the house Pilgrims.'

'I oft reflect on Zachariah and how he sheltered me throughout the uprising,' she mused, staring glassy-eyed into the distance. 'What has the man done with his re-established life in Guinea? Compared to him, though raised with airs and graces, Matthew Fleming is merely a crude street-fighter togged up in posh dress. Power over others is all the man craves. Still, we'd best stay on our guard where he is concerned. I married you for good or bad.'

From Fairfax's elegant wax-sealed correspondence he extracted another.

'This is for you, my dear.'

Accepting the letter and looking momentarily at it, she handed the letter back to him. Tears filled her eyes. She muttered, 'You-you read it for me, Jonas.'

'I shall, but I'll read Fairfax's first.

Alexander Fairfax Esq.
Shipping Agent
Off Promenade Road
Pertigua
6 May 1786

My dear Jonas,

I pray this letter finds you both in rude health.

A recent correspondence from Aaron Drinkwater prompted me to pen a few words to you. I had always intended to congratulate you on your marriage to Mistress Faith and regret not having done so before now. I so do now, my dear friend.

Only this morn I reflected on our first encounter in my office in Pertigua. Above all I offer belated apologies for my inquisition of you regarding Mistress Faith on that occasion. Despite your insecure position you behaved with much decorum. I admired you risking a return to the island on which you had been enslaved, aware you could be seized and sold. Moreover, I now appreciate the dread you so ably disguised as you stood in my office. It all happened so long ago, but utterly insufficient for time and tide to slight our memory of that exhilarating episode.

Given good society's furore over a mixed match, it did not occur to me then that you and Mistress Faith might have been so disposed. But getting to know you on the island and after much soul-searching, I recognised the possibility. Nay, I was not aggrieved; I found myself delighted for you both, my friend. And I am told you have two fine children. May God bless thee, thy union and thy family.

Possessing a perplexing courage I do not possess, I believe you and Mistress Faith are the running dogs of the morrow. On the other hand,

I am an unreformed dilettante. I was and am an arid old shipping agent, partial to his comforts and rooted in antiquated habits.

Despite our ethnic difference, I believe you and I are upright dissenters. Bonded by our membership of the League, we are devoted to the campaign for abolition. It was you who taught me that my world is bigger than my country. Gladly I thank you for that. My memory of you brings a warm glow to these aging bones.

Pray give my warmest felicitations to Mistress Faith. I will call on you both when I return to London. I enclose a letter to Mistress Faith from Asabi, Captain of Freetown and formerly known as Florence in Tamarind Trees Great House.

Yours affectionately,

Alexander Fairfax.

Post scriptum: No doubt you would be mortified to hear that warehouses on Jamestown's waterfront belonging to Matthew Fleming were latterly razed to the ground. I wonder who could have been so malevolent. Although I did learn that the undeniably worthy perpetrator was one of Fleming's own slaves who promptly absconded no doubt to Freetown.'

Chuckling softly at Fleming's comeuppance, Jonas turned and heaved a long wearisome sigh.

'Fairfax's correspondence explains a great deal,' he said. 'So many lives have been destroyed.'

Opening the second letter, with paper bearing pot watermarks most likely furnished by Fairfax, he sat down and read aloud the lightly tutored script.

'Freetown
2 May 1786

Missy Faith
I write you many times for years. I got no way to get letter to you. Past day I meet fren of Mister Fairfax. He say he sen me letter to you.

It be thirty year past we meet in Kayode shack to say bye to you. Make haste, men and woman of Guinea. And may God go with you. They wos your last words you say to we. You help man you love flee wi nother woman. I tink it hard for you to do what you do. Strong voices tell you it can be no other way. I tank you from my heart for help we escape.

I pray you shine appy in England. Mister Fairfax say you get marry to Jonas Guinea. And he say you got two chillen. I know your mix be smart and look good. I learn much from hate I carry on plantation. I is still Captain of Freetown. We got some born from rape by white men, so we got mix blood mong we. Them is our people. And them be strong and teach we that mixed blood not mean them got mix-up heads.

Pray tank Jonas Guinea for come wi *Redemption*. Tell him I one of three who get cut off by Redcoats in mangroves when we make for *Redemption*. Now I bin long on dis island than I ever was in mother country on coast of Guinea. I stay on dis island for ever. My tears cut a river when I tink of what I mite ave done wi my life if I not ever bin slave.

I ave son wi Kayode. His name be Abisogun and he now be pass thirty. He got a woman and I got three granchillen. It be three years since we sign treaty of Freetown wi Governor Osborne. Runaways free and live in place call Freetown by swamp of mountain. We build a town wi school and store and gathering ouse. I is so appy to be free. Yet I still urt bad from slavin on plantation. I still boil wi anger I lose Kayode. I still rage bout my kidnap from Ake. In sad times, my love for Kayode bends me out of it and I feel appy. I love freedom so deep I hold poison only for Frederick Bradshaw.

I need you to know Kayode not suffer long when he in prison. He eat bean that bring swift easy dark. You and me love Kayode. I tink we each love difren part of same man.

Slavers off *Pelican* shallowed my roots and steal my morrows. Strange it be white and black in London and off *Redemption* who come to save we. It tell me that like black, they be two kind of white. I know one day white like you will numbar more dan them who do not anything bout slavery. Den slavery be no more, or dis joy we got be stain wi sorrow wi no end. Not good. I so appy I got good frend in England town.

I got hope. I got more Missy Faith. I got life wi' hope.

Asabi.'

Powerfully affected by Asabi's words, Jonas gulped down the lump lodged in his gullet. Dropping the letters, he raised watery eyes at his wife and took her hands. Sorrow belaboured her looks. Teardrops glistened haltingly down her cheeks. Putting his arm tenderly around her shoulder, she fell against him sobbing into his chest.

'T-that h-hateful s-step f-father s-sold m-my s-son,' she stammered. 'My-my child i-is a s-slave! Where for God's sake is he? How fares he? Is he yet alive? Soon after he took his first breath he was cruelly wronged. All the footsteps he has trod through his fragile life have been fraught with injustice. I am certain of that. Just as I am certain that I will not ever forgive Frederick Bradshaw for enslaving my flesh and blood. Forsooth, I could take not even a glance at Pertigua, for it harbours such harrowing visions and memories I find hard to banish. Yet, having spent the best part of her life on it, Asabi will remain there for she now has slighter instincts for her motherland on the coast of Guinea. Ahhhh, my love,' she sighed. Shaking her head despondently, she continued, 'This ghastly business has begot such a horrendous outcome.'

'Undoubtedly,' he said softly, drawing her closer. 'And although hardly significant at present, the accursed trade shows some signs of flagging. We will carry on agitating for the death throes of it. 'Til then, we must hold onto hope. We might even—'

'Yet,' she softly retorted, quizzically looking up at him, 'England's slave regimes charge on relentlessly leaving their prisoners without hope. And 'tis exquisitely certain that a man without hope can be a very dangerous man. This is what becomes of imperiously unsettling the ways of others. We have been brutalised and diminished by a superlative feat of legalised bondage. And as well in keeping with the philosophy of this duplicitous trade, falsehoods will probably be employed to describe all our yesteryears, which may yet even cloud our morrows. Lest England's descendants fear we did not anything, we need to leave clear testimony of our fight for abolition. But until abolition, my love, we will just have to hold on to hope then, won't we?'

Nodding at her statement, he smiled thoughtfully while pouring Madeira.

Deep raspy squawks from mallards fractured the following hush. Feathery woodsmoke wafted along warm airs. Hovering skylarks whistled their sparkling song across the garden.

Clinking glasses, they toasted a good day.

'We have yet to find your son,' he said quietly. 'Although I feel he is as much my son as yours. As God is my witness, I will not ever give up our search. Such is the effect of the woeful complexities shadowing a barbaric trade. Supposedly enlightened men trafficking humans for rich owners whose backsides never even leave their cushioned seats. As a result, countless families have and are yet being rent asunder. Like everyone else involved, we'll just have to keeping picking up the pieces of many shattered lives…'

'With shattered dreams,' she muttered almost beneath her breath.

'Fret not, my dear. We'll leave evidence of the campaign against slavery in the petitions, speeches and in books like the one Equiano is writing. I daresay his shall not be the only tome. But pending abolition as you say, my dear, we shall just have to hold on to hope then, shan't we?'

Stroking his neck lovingly, she laughed with an assurance born of contentment.

Pondering on how their lives had been shaped by the years, he remembered a host of ordeals as they sought brighter morrows. She was now a charismatic sixty-three years and he a tested fifty-nine. Slavery will be abolished one day, but will we live to see it?

Inseparable from that cherished night in Greensleeves, vital decisions, chilling incidents, extraordinary encounters and joyful reunions had bonded their trust.

Love holds no colour for us, he thought. Wedlock has proved belonging in such perfect clarity I feel the ensuing years have been truly inspirational.

Quiescent beside the hollyhocks on the limestone bench, they watched the moon rising from beyond distant rooftops. By and by, 'neath a starry black August sky he put his arm around her. Resting her head against his shoulder, they pottered through the garden with the letters and re-entered their frolicsome candlelit home called Pilgrims.

Acknowledgements

Above all, to my dear friend and editor, Dr Jill Sudbury, an assiduous structuralist whose passion for precision contributed greatly to the telling and cadence of this tale; to my beloved son, Segun, who kept up my spirits; to my long-term collaborator and illustrator, Claire Lawrence, who over many years has patiently and skilfully fleshed-out my chronicle into the map of Pertigua; to Ajero forest Juju man, 'Sunshine' Oguntoye; to my proofreader, Dr Kayleigh-Jane Moore; to historian, Dr Foluso Balogun; to my long-standing friend and supporter, Chris J O'Dell; to David Elliot of Quartet Books; to Tony Mills, upon whom I foisted philosophical ideas during our numerous discussions, along with Sidney Payne; to historical re-enactors Paul Lawrence and Jim Eames, whose knowledge and skills furthered my understanding of eighteenth-century cannons, especially Jim's poems, *Ode to the Heroes* and *Blessed Memories*; to my readers, Peter Beecham, Sola Agbede, Sonora Baskett and Michelle Diaz; the staff of the British Library's Map Room; to Sheila Harman of Pilgrims; to the Leighton-Trew family; to Graham Knapp of GK Autos, Oxford for keeping my car on the road in such good condition for my numerous research trips; and to Josh Bryson, typesetter, and Gareth Hobbs, designer, for their assistance exceeding my expectations.

And most importantly, special gratitude to Dr Zoe Maria Jane Astroulakis, Consultant Cardiologist, and her team at St Georges Hospital, Tooting, who saved my life, as well as to the caring and compassionate nurses and domestics of Belgrave Ward. *Adupe* — thank you.

Remi Kapo
London
September 2017

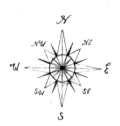

Map illustration © Claire Lawrence.